Dennis

THE TEMPTATION OF JEREMY

A novel of sexual temptation, human frailty, courage, love and forgiveness. Set in Puritan England in the years 1644 to 1654 against a background of civil war, political upheaval, witch-hunts, and the rigid moral code and hypocrisy of the period.

Contains some explicit passages.

ALBION BOOKS

To Maggie

Dennis Younger
author

Published 1998 by Albion Books
1 Providence Street, King's Lynn, Norfolk PE30 5ET

British Library C.I.P.
Younger, Dennis
The Temptation of Jeremy
I. Title
823.9'14[F]

ISBN Number 0 9531810 0 6

Except for the following historical characters; Matthew
Hopkins, John Stearne, Oliver Cromwell, John Bradshaw; all
characters in this book who speak are imaginary and do not
relate to any real person living or dead. The village/town of
Brentham does not exist and should not be confused with
Brantham. For the purposes of this story the author has
removed the village/town of Lavenham and an area to the
south from the map and put in its place the imaginary
village/town of Brentham and the imaginary Stourland
estate. As far as the author is aware there never was a
Stourland estate or a Marquess of Stourland.

Printed by Beaufort Press, Glencaple, Dumfries DG1 4RD

To Pearl and Janet

I dedicate this my first novel to my late dear wife Pearl who was with me when I made the plot and encouaraged me in its beginning, and to my good friend Janet who encouraged me in its completion.

AUTHOR'S ACKNOWLEDGEMENTS

To the writer of fiction set in any period other than the one in which we live there falls the task of painstaking research, for although the story and most of its characters may be fictional, the background and historical events against which it is set must be accurate.

Due to sad personal circumstances, this novel, with only two chapters written, lay untouched for many months. When I picked the task up again, I was pleasantly surprised at the helpfulness with research of people previously unknown to me.

I acknowledge gratefully the ready willingness of the following to answer my questions and supply information on some less well known historical matters. Mr David Griffith of Newmarket Local History Society and Sealed Knot; Dr John Sutton, Cambridge; Mr Gerald Curry of Bury St Edmunds U3A History Group; Ms Rhona Martin, an author; the staffs of the Suffolk Record Office, Bury St Edmunds, and the Suffolk Library, Bury St Edmunds.

I will also mention the following excellent books of reference from my own bookshelves which were by my side almost the whole time I wrote:– *Oliver Cromwell* by John Buchan published 1934; *The English Civil War Day By Day* by Wilfrid Emberton published 1995.

CHAPTER 1

Jeremy took a short cut across Pearson pastures to his home. Walking in the late afternoon sun, he did not at first see Eve seated on the grass in the shade of a tall hedge surrounding the Pearson homestead. The girl rose to greet him, her golden hair falling to her shoulders as she removed her linen cap. Advancing towards him with a smile and a greeting she proffered her hand, but he was too gauche to take it. She stood close. Her femininity overwhelmed him. They talked–or she talked–he could only stammer clipped replies. He excused himself that he needed to get home.

He regretted his nervousness. This was not how it had been in his dreams and fantasies. He turned to go back, but she had gone.

Jeremy's mother greeted him with a kiss on arrival at the Goodway farmhouse. A mother's kiss for a boy. He had dreamed of a lover's kiss from the girl. But that would only be if he was a man. This afternoon had proved he was not yet a man.

His father was still in the fields, but the horses had been stabled. He took one to go back to the forge for his baggage, crossing the Pearson pastures again in the forlorn hope that Eve would be there. She was not, and he reflected again in misery on his lost opportunity.

His thoughts turned to the earlier happenings of the day, and the tiresome journey on the stage wagon.

He had been glad at the sight of a few hedges, for this meant they were near home. The better off in the south-west Suffolk village of Brentham had started to enclose their nearer ploughlands and parks, creating an oasis among the areas of unmarked fields beyond. On the horizon, remote from the rutted and stony tracks which men called roads, lingered remnants of primeval forest, the home of the vagabond, for not all were prosperous in this Suffolk of 1644.

Brentham was a large village with a population of over two thousand. Regarded by many as a town, it had a market square and a small market, though most preferred to take their produce to larger towns a few miles away. A more important centre of local activity was the green, for here was the presbytery, the church, the forge. And here stood, until it was banned, the maypole. Here still stood the instruments of punishment; the whipping post, the stocks and the pillory. Also here was the pond used increasingly of late for the swimming of witches, which some regarded as justice, others as sport, and others as cruel injustice. Grown prosperous on the woollen trade which had peaked more than a century before, Brentham had now started to go into decline.

Although tired of the wagoner's chatter of declining trade and a war that was not going well, he had been glad of the man's invitation to sit beside him for the journey. The juddering of the lumbering stage wagon had made him conscious of the torment of his rising manhood on this hot July day. His fantasies were of Eve who was beyond him socially, and his pleasure to pretend that he was coming home to her. For he was seventeen, and the young are permitted such fantasies.

The wagon came to a halt outside the forge. It was the collection and delivery point for goods coming to and leaving the village. Jeremy alighted and the wagoner handed down his baggage.

Samuel Bloom, the blacksmith, on seeing the wagon, broke away from an already thinning crowd round the pond across the village green. He was a short and muscular man of swarthy complexion.

'Whass afoot?' asked the wagon driver.

'The widder Potter,' replied the smith in broad Suffolk dialect. 'She was denounced a witch, so she's been swum, on the orders of that man Hopkins. Him wot they call the witchfinder general. The poor old biddy was harmless enough. She drowned of course, so now that hypocrite Dowdy is pratin' how her soul has gone to Heaven 'cos she was innocent. Of course, if she hadn't drowned, they'd hev pronounced her guilty and hung her.'

'But yer do believe in witches, surely, Samuel Bloom?' asked the wagoner.

'I ain't pronouncin' on nothin' today even though I often do, an' got the marks on my back to show for it. Thass too hot, an' the sight of that there ole post fair make my back itch.' He nodded in the direction of the whipping post on the village green, which he had made acquaintance with a couple of times in his life, due to his lack of obsequiousness to those in authority. 'Come on, let's get this stuff off and under cover, in case a storm come up arter all this heat.'

Jeremy had listened to this conversation with interest. All over England a belief in witchcraft, born in the mists of pre-history, still lingered. Witch hunting, backed by the force of a medieval law still in force, waxed rampant in East Anglia and neighbouring counties, spearheaded by a zealot, Matthew Hopkins, the witchfinder general, son of a Suffolk clergyman; the minister for Great Wenham.

✱✱✱

With wheels crunching the rugged track, the lumbering, squeaking stage wagon went on its way. Samuel Bloom noticed Jeremy at last.

'Jeremy lad. Forgot yer was there in all the excitement about widder Potter an' getting the stuff off the wagon. Nice to see yer.'

The blacksmith was a close friend of Jeremy's parents, tenant farmer Silas Goodway and his wife Mary. He liked Jeremy and had long looked on him as a possible future husband for his daughter Bessie.

'I'd heard yer was comin' home, but was sad to hear your father was hevin' to take yer away from Cambridge 'cos he couldn't afford it no more. I know he allus wanted yer to hev a fine education an' become a lawyer.'

Jeremy assured him that he didn't mind, although he was bitterly disappointed at having to leave Cambridge. The decline in the wool trade and other economic ramifications of the terrible times were so reducing his father's circumstances that he could no longer afford to support his ambitions for his son.

'I s'pose,' went on Samuel, 'yer was waitin' to ask me to put your bags in the shed until yer can come back with a hoss to fetch 'em. No need for that. Bring 'em over to the cottage. The wife and Bessie would like to see yer.'

Although he was just five feet eight tall, Jeremy had to duck to enter the low doorway of the cottage. Mrs Bloom and Bessie looked as if they had been crying. Bessie blushed on seeing him. He noticed a soft swelling of her bosom that was not there the last time he had seen her. She was now fifteen and starting to blossom into womanhood.

'I expect they been weepin' about poor widder Potter. Is that right wife?' asked Samuel.

'Thass so cruel, so cruel,' said the plump and homely Mrs Bloom with a sniff. 'Master Jeremy. Nice to see yer agin. Can yer drink a tankard of ale afore yer walk home? I don't doubt it was a long hot journey on the wagon.'

'Thank you Mrs Bloom. That's most kind,' replied Jeremy.

Bessie left the room to fetch the ale at her mother's command, blushing as she returned and handed it to the young man.

They sat awhile talking about the difficult times, because it was a time of strife. For approaching two years Englishman had killed Englishman. On one side an autocratic King believing in his divine right to tax and rule without Parliament, supported by the power of the Anglican Church. On the other, a Parliament of landed gentlemen and merchants anxious to protect their property and money and assert their right to rule, supported by a rising tide of non-conformity.

'I hear Squire Pearson has put a word in for yer to be the new clerk to the committee of parish brethren,' said the blacksmith.

'Yes, he wrote and told me,' replied Jeremy.

'Well, thass somethin' to use your education for anyway. Though I wouldn't fancy workin' for ole Dowdy myself.'

'But surely the Reverend Jones . . .' Jeremy began.

'Pah!' expostulated Samuel. 'A weak man. Sail afore the wind, thass Jones. Dowdy's the one that'll be givin' yer orders, mark my words. Trouble is, Squire Pearson's too nice. His word should be law in this parish.'

Jeremy changed the subject by asking after their son,

3

twenty-five-year-old Joseph.

'We only seen him once since he joined the army,' said Mrs Bloom. 'That was a couple of months since. Then he was full of new ideas from friends his got in with. "Levellers" or somethin' they call the selves. That quite worry me.'

'Pah, woman!' put in Samuel. 'There ain't nothin' wrong with them ideas, if they ever come to anything of course.'

Jeremy finished his ale and took his leave. His mind turned to the conversation that had just taken place about the times and the fearsome Mr Dowdy–a product of those times.

* * *

No battle during England's bitter civil war was destined to be fought on the soil of Suffolk, for here was the heart of Parliamentary territory, secured early in the struggle by one who was later to become famous, or otherwise, depending on viewpoint. Although a Puritan, Oliver Cromwell was an Independent and in favour of freedom of worship provided it did not seek to bring back the power of the Anglican Church to rule men's lives.

Not everyone among the multitude of sects encompassed by the description, "Puritan," shared this opinion. On the back of strife rode intolerance. In many Parliamentary areas Puritan extremism was on the increase. To these men it was not a struggle between autocracy and potential democracy, but a war against sin. Every human weakness or pleasure was to them sin. Convinced of their own rectitude in the sight of God, they despised those of more moderate opinion and those who, calling themselves by the new title of "Leveller," saw the struggle as one for the rights of the common man, through a futuristic dream of universal suffrage.

The parish committee of Brentham consisted of elders of the congregation. They represented the "brethren," a term applied to members of the congregation, men or women, of known Puritan beliefs. Prominent on that committee, and seeing himself as a beacon of righteousness, was Obadiah Dowdy, the very epitome of hypocrisy and self-esteem. At that time, fifty-nine years of age and a master tailor, of sober dress and woeful countenance. A bigot who sought to rule in his own sphere.

Of course, Obadiah should not have been able to rule, for there were several before him in the natural pecking order. Pastor Jones for instance. He had been an Anglican clergyman before the war. But perceiving the way things were going in those troubled times and, although also a magistrate, being a rather weak character anxious above all to protect his living, he chose to dissemble and sail before the wind.

Then there was the village aristocrat, the Marquess of Stourland, an aged bachelor in the Manor House. But he was not really eligible, having only recently inherited from his deceased brother, an avowed Royalist who had lost his only son. He also lost local influence at the same time. The new Marquess had often declared his neutrality, but was distrusted as a secret Royalist. The Manor House was known locally as Brentham Manor, which was a misnomer since it stood outside the parish boundary. Only a small part of Brentham fell within part of the vast Stourland estate which stretched many miles to the south.

Then, in the Grange, towards the northern boundary, there was Nathaniel Pearson, a magistrate, regarded as the village Squire in the absence of the Marquess, since next to the Manor he owned the most land in the district. Indeed, as far as Brentham itself was concerned, apart from the common and some freehold properties, three-quarters of the land was Pearson property. Nathaniel Pearson's ancestors had founded Brentham.

Squire Pearson was a Puritan of the more moderate sort. A most amiable and jolly man, whose pleasant disposition often led him to defer to the opinions of those of lesser social standing. A member of the county committee, the overall governing body of Suffolk under Parliament, he was the object of envy by the self-righteous Obadiah Dowdy. As Obadiah saw it, only Nathaniel Pearson stood between him and the exercise of unlimited power in the parish, which was his right as the most godly. His right and his duty to lead the people out of the morass of sin into which their weaker souls were dragging them.

✳ ✳ ✳

When Jeremy arrived back at the forge with the horse, Bessie was outside. She blushed again and bobbed a half-curtsy. He noticed once more the just perceptible swell of her virgin bosom. Here was the girl–the other was a woman. Perhaps he was destined to wait for the girl. His courage had deserted him with the woman.

Samuel came out of the cottage with his baggage. 'There's been a message from Reverend Jones. You gotter meet him an' Mister Dowdy tomorrow morning' at 9 o'clock over there, about the work yer been offered.'

Jeremy thanked the blacksmith for the message, and hefted his bags on to the horse. He found the courage to flash a smile at Bessie, who blushed before she turned and fled.

When he arrived back home, his father, lean and gaunt from a lifetime of toil, was in from the fields and his mother had prepared a large meal. Over supper there was much talk once more about the times.

There was little rest for Jeremy that night. The heat, the torment of his missed opportunity with Eve, and apprehension about his interview in the morning, combined to rob him of sleep.

✳ ✳ ✳

The next day, after his interview, Jeremy toiled the whole day around the farm helping his parents until the evening meal. In a way he wished that he could stay and work on the land. Afterwards he felt the need to be alone.

He was not looking forward to his employment. The interview with the Reverend Jones and Obadiah Dowdy, with its exhortations against idleness and impure thoughts, and doom laden talk about the wages of sin, had been very discouraging. He did not understand the ranting by Dowdy about impure

5

thoughts. How could one control what came into the mind?

Tomorrow he must by necessity start work, but this evening he would walk and reflect in the fading light. Back in Cambridge some of the older scholars had scoffed at his strict upbringing and inexperience, regaling him with tales of adventures, real or imaginary, in whorehouses and with tavern wenches. But that had been before the clamp down on morals they assured him, with sighs and clicking tongues. So much he must needs miss.

The Goodway's farm was next to Pearson land, for Silas Goodway was a tenant of theirs. In fact the only tenant. The Pearson's farmed all the rest of their substantial holding themselves. This had been easily accomplished in times of peace with two sons to help manage. Unhappily, since the troubles they had been a house divided. The youngest son, against the wishes of the household and the trend of the area, had rushed off to join the Royalist cause when the war started, and thrown his life away in a senseless duel against one of his own comrades following a tavern brawl. Later the elder son, John, had answered the Parliament's call and was now a serving officer.

Jeremy paused a while as he approached the driveway to the Grange, his thoughts straying again to Eve, the nineteen-year-old daughter of the family. He had found the chance meeting with her the previous day both pleasant and disturbing. That she was a beauty there was no doubt, with eyes that seemed to have a misty look and prominent moist lips which were always slightly parted. But she was beyond him surely. Higher on the social scale and two years his senior. Being on private land she had worn her hair loose, discarding the conventional cap, and in the breeze it had brushed his face lightly. She had gently touched his arm in a way some would have thought immodest. Her bosom had risen and fallen tantalizingly as they talked.

The older scholars at Cambridge had taunted him much in his innocence about female bosoms. It behove every lad, they assured him, to strip off his maid before proposing marriage to her. When he had asked the reason for this remarkable advice, they had replied in chorus, 'To find if she has a third nipple of course. How else was a God-fearing Englishman to make sure he did not wed a witch.' For was he not the son of a poor tenant farmer? And as everyone knew, all country people believed in witches. Jeremy would take this ribaldry in good part and hold his own counsel. His father did not believe in witches, but had advised him for his own good health to keep such disbelief to himself.

Jeremy would have liked an excuse to walk up the Pearson's driveway and call at the house on the off chance of catching sight of Eve. But alas he could think of no good reason.

His thoughts were interrupted by the sound of hoof beats in the lane. The rider, Jeremy could see as he approached at a walk, was dressed as a junior officer. The young man nodded in his direction and turned into the driveway. Jeremy walked back home, feeling a pang of jealousy on account of the stranger. Someone as beautiful as Eve would not lack a suitor and doubtless this was he.

✶✶✶

Marcus Kirby was admitted to the Grange as soon as he was announced. The family were at dinner. Eve's heart was set racing when he entered, for she and Marcus shared a love secret.

'Marcus lad!' exclaimed Squire Pearson. 'How nice to see you. Come dine with us. What brings you to these parts?'

'News,' said Marcus.

'Of John?' enquired Mrs Pearson anxiously.

'Don't worry Mistress Pearson. The Captain is well and unhurt. Like as not to be Major ere long they say. But my news is of a great victory. I have been to London with the tidings. I had permission to go back north through East Anglia.'

'Heaven be praised,' cried the Squire. 'Where was this?'

'A few miles from York. Between two villages, Tockwith and Long Marston. The battle was hard and nigh lost. Fairfax's men were in disarray and Sir Thomas himself wounded, when Cromwell came charging with his Ironsides into the enemy's right from the Tockwith end. Twice more, though wounded himself, he wheeled and led them in. The Royalists were in complete rout. Prince Rupert fled the field. Our army now besieges York. The north is lost to the King.'

'Were there many dead?' asked the Squire.

'They say above four thousand. Mostly Royalists.'

'Mercy!' exclaimed Mrs Pearson. 'Let us now pray to God that this will lead to peace.'

'Amen to that,' replied her husband.

Afterwards the men settled down to talk details of the battle. This was of little interest to the women.

'You will stay the night with us, Marcus?' enquired Mrs Pearson. 'The hour grows late.'

'Thank you, Mistress Pearson. That I will and gladly.'

'I'll go and have your room prepared. The one you used last time.'

Eve also excused herself. Marcus flashed her a smile as she left. She blushed in return, for was not "last time" of sweet memory. How she had longed for him to return and claim her. Let the men talk on. It would not all be of battle. Surely he meant to ask her father for her hand in marriage. He had mentioned marriage all those months ago when she became his secretly.

The separation had been cruel. She remembered that first Christmas of the war, in '42, when those of moderate opinion still celebrated the festival. Their friends, the Kirby's had come down from north Norfolk to stay. There had been secret looks between her and Marcus, and secret kisses and whispers. She had quietly drawn back the latch on her bedroom door that night. When the house was asleep he had come quietly to her, and in his arms she had learnt the lesson of love.

7

Disrobing for bed, she relished every one of those sweet memories as she sensuously stroked her body. Forgotten now the terror lest she should have been with child. The opportunity to talk of marriage to parents had not arisen he said. Then she heard that he had gone to the army. She had waited and waited, almost giving up hope. To think that she had only yesterday made to turn to young Jeremy Goodway. But now her Marcus had returned to her. She waited until she heard the household retire. Then waiting some more, she slipped out of bed and quietly loosed the latch to her door. Soon he would come to her again.

CHAPTER 2

It was a long night for Eve as she lay, at first in heated anticipation with tingling breasts and aching thighs, then in the anger and fury of a woman scorned. For he had not visited her as expected, and at length, came the realisation that he would not. For although she waited, listening intently, holding her breath in between her tossing and turning, there had been no tell-tale sounds of creaking floor boards to set her heart beating furiously at the knowledge that her lover was approaching. Her tears mingled into the fitful sleep of early dawn, awakened by the gentle tapping on her door.

In dreamlike imagination her lover was here at last. But why so late?

'Miss Eve, Miss Eve.' The trill voice of Naomi, her maid, brought her to full wakefulness.

'Wait!' she screamed at the girl. For she realised her nakedness. If Marcus had possessed her, she could have trusted Naomi with that secret. But that she had been ready for him and been scorned must never be known. Hastily donning a night shift and going to look out of the window, she called the girl in.

'Just put the water down and go,' she snapped, without turning round, for the girl must not see her tear-stained face. She regretted her tone. Naomi was her friend and confidante, as well as her maid.

In calmer mood after washing and dressing, hope returned. No doubt Marcus had successfully asked her father for her hand in marriage, and would not come to her bed again until they were wed.

She was the last to arrive at the breakfast table. The conversation was in full swing.

'So today you ride up into Norfolk to see your parents?' asked the Squire.

Marcus replied with a rather weak 'Yes.' He seemed somehow ill at ease.

'No doubt you'll be finding a wife ere long,' put in Mrs Pearson. She had often matched Marcus with Eve in her imagination.

'I'm already wed, Mistress Pearson,' said Marcus, the colour rising to his cheeks.

'Wed!' exclaimed the Squire and his lady in unison, offence showing on their faces at not being asked to the ceremony. 'When was this?'

'Several months ago,' replied Marcus in a non-specific manner. 'We have a baby girl now.'

The bile rose in Eve's throat. So that was it; he had been unfaithful. He had come to her bed with a promise of marriage, seduced her and stolen her virginity, then laid with another and got her with child. She could eat no more.

Conversation at the table became stilted.

'I must find a spot in the village to fix a notice about the battle,' said

Marcus at the end of the meal.

'I'll ride with you to the green to post the notice,' offered the Squire, with as much dignity as he could muster. 'Then see you on your way.' Little did he know that this young man had once abused his hospitality and despoiled his daughter.

Eve retreated to her room to give vent to her tears of humiliation and frustration.

∗∗∗

Rebecca Brown woke early from a fitful sleep. She dreaded the waking of Eli, her husband. Heedless of her ailments, he had taken her roughly and she was in pain. She felt for the bruise below her left eye, where he had struck her when she tried to resist. He was a large and muscular man, tanned by the sun and the wind during hours of toil as a labourer on the farm of Squire Pearson. At thirty-two he was at the height of his manhood and scornful of Rebecca. For had they not been wed these ten years and her not conceived, though he had taken her nigh daily.

A tear rolled down her cheek, for she had failed Eli. Every man wanted children. How else could he prove he was a man? She had endured misery in their hovel, with its beaten earth floor, cob walls, and leaking thatch. Scant proof against the bitter east winds that swept East Anglia in winter. She had cried in silent humiliation when he visited himself on a village girl and got her with child. She had felt for him when he groaned at the whipping post as the cat cut his back in punishment for rape. She had tended his wounds. She had ministered to him after they had flogged him again for poaching a rabbit to feed the girl and her bastard.

There was scant food on their table for her, for he had taken from it to feed his mistress. Of the rest, he had eaten most himself, heedless of her needs, despising her weakness and pallor and cough as the consumption wasted her.

She had endured much. When he had beaten her, the widow Potter had given her salves for her cuts and bruises. The widow Potter had given her liquids to help her get pregnant, for she knew about these things, but to no avail. But there would be no widow Potter to give her ointments for the wounds inflicted last night. Widow Potter had died in the pond proving her innocence of witchcraft.

Eli stirred and woke to rampant manhood. He made to seize Rebecca. She leapt from the bed. 'No, Eli,' she pleaded. 'I'm in pain and I'm sick. Can yer not see?'

'Ay. I can see yer. Sick an' ugly.' He rushed over to where she was cringing in a corner, striking her blow after blow. 'Allus sick. Allus sick. Never able to bear children, and when I get child with another they take the skin off my back for it.' He turned from her in disgust and started to dress. She made for the door, went outside, stumbled and fell, sobbing, in the dirt. Her kindly neighbour, Mrs Peters helped her up.

Eli followed her out. Mrs Peters had her arm protectively around Rebecca. 'You're an animal, Eli Brown, beatin' your wife thus,' she called to him, sharply.

'Don't interfere woman. Animal huh! Were I stallion and got mare with foal, they'd give me extra fodder. Were I bull I could beget calves, and they'd praise me. 'Cos I'm a man they flog me an' make me stay with barren wife. I'd be better dead. As like as not she's in league with the devil an' wish me thus.'

'Oh Eli,' sobbed Rebecca. 'How can yer say that. You loved me once. 'Tis God's will. We must accept it or we deserve to die.'

'Pah!' expostulated Eli, turning round and, going to the pitcher of water outside the door, washed himself.

A few neighbours had gathered around at the commotion. He picked up his bag of food from inside and pushed his way through them to go to work. None dared try to stop him, for they feared Eli Brown–he was a man of violence.

✳✳✳

Jeremy arrived at the presbytery for his first day's work. Obadiah Dowdy was there with Reverend Jones. There was little doubt who was really in charge. Dowdy handed Jeremy a sheaf of papers–judgements of the parish court for minor offences.

'You will enter these in the journal in your best hand,' he commanded Jeremy in tones that brooked no argument. He then nodded to Reverend Jones, and the two men left the building.

Jeremy opened the book and picked up his quill. The first entry was about young Dick Stanton, one of Dowdy's apprentices. He was to sit in the stocks for one day from sunrise to sunset. His offence had been to be overheard by Dowdy making a lewd remark to his workfellows about Eve Pearson when she called at his place of business. Jeremy reflected on the harshness of this treatment on one so young.

He was taking the greatest care with his work and had not finished the entries when Dowdy and the pastor returned.

'Leave that for now,' commanded Dowdy, 'and go to the forge and tell Bloom, the blacksmith, to come and see me about repairs in the church. And tell the fellow to be quick, because I want to get to my business.'

Jeremy rose to do as he was bidden, wondering why Dowdy felt the need to see the smith himself. Surely it could have been left to Reverend Jones.

The forge was on the opposite side of the green to the presbytery. Between stood the instruments of punishment. Seated in the stocks, young Dick Stanton, already on his day of unease. Jeremy paused in his progress to offer words of comfort to the lad, a fact that did not escape the attention of Obadiah Dowdy, who was watching from a window.

Samuel Bloom the blacksmith had also seen the incident. 'That was a mighty perilous thing to do lad,' he said as Jeremy greeted him. ''Tis forbidden to offer comfort to those under punishment as yer should know.

Thank God Dowdy wasn't around to see it.'

'The lad is thirsty and asked for water,' said Jeremy, 'and Mister Dowdy is over at the presbytery and wants you to go immediately and see him about work.'

'If Dowdy's still around it'll be too risky to give the lad water. I'll chance it later arter he's gone.' promised the blacksmith.

Samuel went into the forge to put his tools away. Jeremy followed him. He had always been fascinated by the forge, its smell, and its tools.

Particularly fascinating in an evil sort of way were the branding irons. Jeremy picked up two to look at—one to brand a T, the other an M. The blacksmith also served as the village brander, even when humans were to be branded. In accordance with the quaint logic of the times, a convicted murderer who would normally be hanged, could escape the death penalty, if it was his first killing, by reciting word for word a prescribed portion of the scriptures. He would then merely be branded on his thumb with an M prior to lesser penalties of prison or transportation. Likewise, a first-time thief, in recognition of his scriptural recitation, would be branded with the T iron rather than receive the dreaded cat o' nine tails at the whipping post, prior to his transportation.

Jeremy put the irons down and followed the blacksmith out of the forge. Bessie Bloom had come out of the cottage because she had seen him arrive, and was engaged on some needless task at the gate. She bobbed a little curtsy, blushed and murmured a greeting to Jeremy as he made to pass her. He stopped to bow for a moment and, realising she was attracted to him, was surprised to find himself blushing in return. Undoubtedly the girl was pretty in a virginal sort of way. Embarrassed, he turned and hastened to catch up with Samuel.

The encounter with Bessie brought his mind to the more sensual form of Eve, and in the heat of the rising sun he felt his manhood stir. His desire for her was taking over his every waking thought—intruding into his every action.

'You sent for me,' said Samuel gruffly as they entered the presbytery. His words were addressed to the space between Obadiah Dowdy and Reverend Jones. Dowdy he loathed, the pastor he despised as weak.

Dowdy held up his hand to silence him, 'Wait,' he commanded. With his sombre countenance, now white lined with fury, his lank unkempt hair and his hooked nose, he looked a fearsome sight. He turned on Jeremy.

'You stopped to make conversation with the prisoner in the stocks,' he said sharply. 'That is strictly forbidden as you should know. What did you say to him?'

'I--I just offered him words of consolation. S--said I'd pray the day didn't seem too long for him,' stammered Jeremy, now overawed and in fear of the grotesque Dowdy.

'Yonder jackanapes is receiving just punishment for lewd and ungodly words, and for evil and lustful thoughts,' shouted Dowdy. ''Tis his soul you should be praying for, not his bodily comfort. Pray that God in his mercy will accept today's punishment as full atonement for his sinful behaviour. It be far better that he endure a day in the stocks than burn forever in Hell.

'And as for you, Master Jeremy Goodway, the brethren appointed you on the recommendation of Mister Pearson, the so-called Squire. 'Twas not a choice with which I was in whole-hearted agreement. You'd do well to remember what's required of you here. It hasn't escaped my notice that your parents aren't as zealous against evil doers as befits Christian folk.'

Abashed, downcast and loathing Obadiah Dowdy, Jeremy returned to his desk without comment. He was relieved when the three men left the room.

✳✳✳

It was the day for market in Bury St Edmunds. Normally Eve would go with her parents, but today she could not face it. The anguish of her humiliation had been too much. She wanted to be alone–she would feign sickness when the time arrived–but not too much, for on no account must she provoke her mother into staying behind as well.

Mrs Pearson looked out on hearing the clip-clop of the Squire's horse as he returned from seeing Marcus on his way. Although still early, the heat was already starting to shimmer off the cobblestones. She called to Eve.

The girl came down–hair slightly dishevelled.

'Eve!' exclaimed Mrs Pearson. 'Time to go and you not ready. Can't keep your father and the men waiting.'

'No mother,' replied the girl. 'Today I don't want to go. I've a headache. The heat and dust in town will make it worse.'

'You wish me to stay back with you?'

'No, no! It's not too bad, and Naomi will see after me.'

Retreating upstairs to her room and laying down in pretence of rest, she waited to hear her parents and the men depart for market. Desire was upon her in its most uncontrollable form–she hated Marcus for his deception but yearned to have him inside her. She was in a state of high passion.

Satisfied that the market party had left, she went downstairs and out of the house. She would walk around the farm lands, as she had often done of late, getting some gratification for her sensuality by watching muscular labourers at work. This practice had not escaped the notice of Eli Brown, who guessed what her problem was. Often he had schemed in his mind how he could take her. For such a prize he would risk another flogging.

Eve wandered into the stack yard. Today they would be bringing in hay and stacking it. She decided to go to the barn overlooking the yard, because there was a loft with a good view through a small aperture.

Eli was unloading his wagon with his team-mate Amos Peters when he saw her enter the barn. His manhood stirred as he realised this was his opportunity. He said nothing to Amos.

In the barn loft, heat from the previous day still hung around the rafters. From her vantage point Eve could see the two men working stripped to the waist. The lacerations on Eli's back both horrified and fascinated her. Sensuality rose to new heights. Loosening the cord of her bodice, her hand went to her naked breasts as she toyed with the hardened nipples.

'Take the hosses an' wagon back for another load,' said Eli to Amos. 'I hev a small errand for myself off the farm. I'll be here when yer get back.'

'You ain't s'posed to leave the farm during work,' put in Amos.

'Don't argue man, for God's sake. None'll notice if yer don't tell 'em. They'll think I've gone for a grunt or somethin'.'

Amos knew better than to argue with Eli.

Eli made to walk in the opposite direction until Amos had left with the wagon. Then he turned around and walked towards the barn. From her vantage point Eve saw him approach. In heated physical torment and mental turmoil, she knew what was about to happen.

Her heart raced as she heard the creak of the barn door, the shuffle of his feet across the floor, the clump of his boots on the ladder. She watched fascinated as first his head and then his muscular lacerated torso appeared above the loft floor.

'Ha,' cried Eli as he saw her. 'Ready an' waitin' for it with loosened clothes. Been watchin' yer prowlin' around and comin' up here. Guessed what your trouble was.'

He stooped to take off his boots. Then dropping his breeches, he stood naked before her, his manhood in full excitement.

Eve gasped at the sight of him. She had known love from Marcus–but it had been love in darkness–she had never before seen a man. Mesmerised, she stood unable to move as he started towards her. On sudden impulse she picked up a pitchfork standing nearby and, with uncertain gesture, pointed it at the advancing man.

With contempt he knocked the fork aside and out of her hands. He was upon her, fully loosening her bodice and exposing her breasts, ignoring her feeble protests. She felt his strong arms about her as he lifted her off her feet and, raising her clothes at the same time, roughly laid her down in the hay. She made a token struggle but he was in full strength now–there was no stopping him. He said nothing, but with heavy breath and animal grunts entered her. She gasped. At one, ashamed of being taken by so common a man yet taking pleasure in the satisfaction of her craving, she turned her head aside, but he roughly pulled it back. His mouth was upon hers and she was responding. This was better than Marcus had been. Unable any longer to pretend, with gasps and cries, she rose and fell to the movements of his body. Her arms were about him and her fingers tracing the rutted scars on his back as waves of pleasure engulfed her.

With a gasp and a shout he was finished. He lay heavy upon her for a moment. As he rose, Eve, still not fully satisfied herself, started to be overcome by remorse. Tears rolled down her cheeks.

'Whass cryin' for then?' demanded Eli. "Twas what yer wanted. Plain for

14

any man to see.'

He turned and walked towards the ladder, picked up his breeches and donned them. His back was towards Eve. She lay in a state of partial undress, just as he had abandoned her, still weeping.

As he sat down to pull on his boots, he turned again and noticed her. The heaving white bosom as she sobbed, the clothes still pulled up to her waist. He felt his loins stir again with desire. Throwing down the boots he exclaimed, 'Damn me if she don't want more,' and dropping his breeches, flicked his rising phallus with thumb and middle finger. 'An' thass ready to give it.'

He advanced towards her again. With loathing and disgust at what had happened with this common man, Eve jumped to her feet, seizing the pitchfork from the floor and pointed it at him.

'Keep back,' she shouted. 'You'll be flogged for this.'

'Ha! Flogged yer say,' he jeered. 'An' what do yer think they'll do to you? What yer gooner say when ole Dowdy ask what yer was doin' up here with your clothes loosened, when your father was away to market?'

He made to knock the fork aside again, but this time she was more determined and had a tighter grip. So he put his hands round the handle and made to pull it from her. But she hung on as he pulled her along. She tripped and fell towards him. His back hit the sloping rafters as they reached the outer wall, and the fork pierced his naked body below the chest bone. He groaned once and his eyes were opened wide. Blood began to flow where the fork had entered and to trickle from his mouth.

Eve screamed. She walked over to the aperture and screamed again and again. But there was no one out there to hear her. She crept over to look at the man once more. No doubt that he was dead. She would go down and run to the fields to tell them of the accident. She hesitated–would they believe her? And if they did accept it was an accident would she not be punished for fornication? She remembered Eli's jeering words. 'An' what do yer think they'll do to you? What yer gooner say when ole Dowdy ask what yer was doin' up here when your father was away to market.' They wouldn't believe rape.

Time to think–nothing to be gained by panic–her natural cunning took over. There had been much talk in the village of the troubles between Eli and his wife and the punishments he had received. Just walk away. Sooner or later they would find the body and conclude that he had killed himself in despair.

But he wouldn't have stripped naked to do it. Must get the breeches and boots back on to this heavy man. She picked them up and walked over to the corpse. There was blood about. Must not get blood on her own clothes, for she would not be able to explain that.

She went to the opposite side of the loft and stripped off. Advancing naked to the corpse of the man who had so recently possessed her, she felt

15

the first stirring of desire once more.

It was hard work dressing Eli's still warm body in his breeches. Several times she had to stop to rest, to get her breath and let her racing heartbeats subside. She almost gave up. Two or three times she cried in despair, 'I can't; I can't.' But she dared not fail, and out of despair found the strength. With the task at last complete, she collapsed to rest awhile by the body. As her strength returned, the sheer risk of what she was doing and the handling of his loins drove her on to a torment of desire. The boots were easier. She placed his hands back round the pitchfork handle. At length she had finished, but his blood was smeared about her naked flesh. She wiped it off as best she could with a handful of hay before re-dressing.

Time to go now, but she jumped with fright as she heard the barn door open.

'You about here Eli?' called Amos Peters. Eve froze. There was nowhere to hide. If he came up she would be discovered.

But he did not come up. She heard him grumble as he went back out. Back at her vantage point near the aperture, she waited while Amos unloaded his wagon himself. It seemed to take for ever.

After he had finished, she waited impatiently until he left the stack yard. Stealing from the barn, she made her way quickly and quietly back home. She felt dirty. Couldn't ask Naomi to bath her, she might remark on a few remaining blood smears.

Avoiding the front entrance, she entered the property by a wicket gate, set in a side boundary hedge. Further back, at the very end of the grounds, was an arbour behind a screen of trees, with a small lake and summer-house which Squire Pearson had had constructed before the war.

Eve entered the arbour area. She would bathe in the lake to cleanse herself. Her parents would never have approved of that. Stripping off, she laid her clothes out on the warm grass–no one would come here. She bathed and bathed. Taking a large stone she rubbed the remaining blood smears as best she could.

Leaving the water, she lay in the sun on the warm grass to dry. Her mind wandered over events of the last few hours. She remembered that huge man thrusting into her and was overwhelmed with desire. She recalled the face of Marcus and pretended it had been him. Sensuously she stoked her body–felt the hardened nipples with her fingers. Her hand wandered to the moistness between her thighs.

She believed herself to be unseen. But, blinded and deafened by unsatiated lust, she was deluding herself, for she was not unseen.

CHAPTER 3

Obadiah Dowdy had not been in a good mood as he approached Brentham. He did not like Bury St Edmunds, for was it not a place of divided loyalties. True it may be that here they had been early to raise and equip troops for Parliament, but had not the county committee lamely re-instated the notorious malignant schoolmaster, Thomas Stevens, at the protest of pupils, then stood idly by as he defiantly dressed his students in Royalist red. Trade had been bad today, and no information gleaned, so he had left the market early.

Now with Brentham almost in sight, his horse had picked up a stone and gone lame, so he must needs walk. With the nearest smith being Samuel Bloom, nigh two miles away along the stony track, called a road, which first wound its tortuous way around part of Pearson land before descending into the village he sought a short cut.

'Airs and graces of the aristocracy, our self-styled Squire,' he grumbled to himself. 'Enclosing his pastures.'

With contempt he led his horse through the new growth of recently planted hedge and with the parish church now in clear view, started towards it.

The short cut took him close by the mature high yew-tree hedge that surrounded Squire Pearson's domestic property. Being of a prying and meddlesome nature he could not resist the temptation to see if he could look into the private preserve of the man he regarded as an enemy. Finding a place where the hedge was not too thick, he parted the branches quietly until he had a view of the arbour with its small lake.

What he saw made him spring back in disbelief. Falling to his knees and clasping his hands, he raised his eyes to Heaven and chastised the Almighty. 'Have I not been strong in thy service Lord, in pursuit of the ungodly? Why dost thou allow our enemy, the Evil One, to torment me with wicked imagination?'

He looked again. It had not been imagination. His eyes fell once more on the sight of naked Eve engaged in self-gratification. He withdrew again, this time with glee, and made his way to the wicket gate in the side of the property, beyond the arbour area. For now had the Lord been kind to him. He would confront his enemy's daughter in her wickedness, then denounce her to the brethren as a wanton. That would surely be the end for the self-styled Squire Pearson.

But Satan intervened–as he is wont to do with hypocrites. As he reached the wicket gate, poor old Obadiah felt the first stirring in his loins at the memory of what he had seen. He returned to the hedge for another look–and stayed for a long while–until the girl dressed in fact. Now it was too late to catch her.

He returned to his horse and went on his way murmuring repeatedly, 'Get thee behind me Satan. Get thee behind me Satan–for I am a servant of the Lord.'

But Satan would not oblige, and what he had seen stayed very much in the front of Obadiah's mind. He became obsessed with a desire to fornicate with Eve.

***

When Eve's self administrations had at last temporarily put out her fires, worry arose from the cold embers of her earlier craving.

As she dressed, a little voice within her spoke 'What if?' She tried to ignore it as she walked through the garden and into the house. But it would not go away, and in the cool of her room, it spoke to her louder as worry battled with logic.

'What if I was seen entering the barn by someone? Amos Peters for instance. But no, Eli would not have dared come to the barn if Amos had known she was there. A stray thief perhaps, taking advantage of the absence of the market party to steal a chicken? But no, a thief would not risk the whipping post by admitting he had been there. What if I have not been clever enough in making Eli's death look like suicide, and they start to look for a killer? What if an innocent person is accused? Will I then feel strong enough to admit to the rape and accident and risk not being believed, and at the very least suffer public punishment and humiliation as a wanton? What if I am now with child by the low-born Eli–one of my father's labourers? What a disgrace that would be.'

Now in torment, once more her natural cunning took over. Her mind turned to young Jeremy Goodway. She rather liked him, and obviously he was besotted by her. With Marcus out of reach now, and no one else likely, she could do worse. Her father liked him, and would likely accept him as her husband, if somewhat angry at first on believing that he had got her with child.

Eve was not excessively devout, and usually only prayed in church within the sight of her parents. However, on this occasion she fell to her knees in supplication to the Almighty, that she be not pregnant, or if she was that the hot weather would last at least another week.

***

For Jeremy, the end of his first day's employment came as a relief, although he had been glad when Obadiah Dowdy had departed early in the morning. Reverend Jones, although around the presbytery, had not often put in an appearance. Even the open window on this hot day had not eased the heat and stuffiness of the room in which he worked. He had completed his tasks by fairly early in the afternoon and then had only to wait until he was given permission to finish for the day.

For the better part of two hours he had sat day-dreaming and lost in sensuous imagination about Eve. As one erotic scene after another passed

18

through his mind, his loins had stirred and he was deeply conscious of the prominent bulge in his breeches. Clasping his hands, he prayed to the Almighty to give him relief from wicked thoughts. For had he not been brought up to know right from wrong in a Christian home?

Yet in spite of that prayer, my condition doesn't change, he thought. Within two minutes I have carnal thoughts of her again. Could it be that I am already beyond redemption? Could it be that Satan already has me in his power?

Because of the heat, Jeremy had taken his tunic off to work. Hearing Reverend Jones's footfall in the passageway, he snatched the tunic from its hook and laid it across his lap to cover his embarrassment. Having received permission to go, he bid the pastor 'Goodnight' and left, still dangling his tunic before him.

Feeling in need of friendly conversation, Jeremy walked across the green intending to talk with Samuel Bloom. As he passed the stocks, he noticed that young Dick Stanton was either asleep or unconscious from his now near completed ordeal in the sun.

From time immemorial all good English smithies have had a tree outside the premises, and Samuel Bloom's forge at Brentham was no exception. In fact, beside it stood the stump of an earlier tree. Hearing voices from within the smithy, Jeremy sat on this to wait until Samuel should be free, laying his tunic on the ground beside him.

The voices became louder as Samuel and his customer came out of the smithy and into the traverse where the horse stood waiting. 'Cursed stone.' Jeremy recognised the voice–Obadiah Dowdy! Alarmed for no real reason, Jeremy slipped quickly into the cottage garden out of sight.

But sharp as ever, Dowdy, who never missed much, caught a glimpse of him; and the voice of Mrs Bloom as she called, 'Jeremy lad. Come in for a tankard of ale,' could be plainly heard. As he reached the cottage door, Jeremy remembered with dismay that he had left his tunic by the tree stump. Frightened to go back for it while Obadiah Dowdy was around, he hoped it would not be taken by a thief.

But it was–though not by any ordinary thief. While his horse was being attended to by Samuel, Dowdy sauntered over to the tree stump where Jeremy had sat. Nosiness paid off once more. 'What have we here?' he muttered to himself as he picked up the tunic. He could have handed it over to Jeremy, whom he knew to be in the cottage. But his evil instinct told him that some day, somehow, the garment would work for his ends, so he took great care that Samuel Bloom did not see him conceal it in his baggage.

In the cottage, Jeremy slowly drank his ale, looking out of the window from time to time to catch sight of Obadiah Dowdy when he left. Bessie Bloom seemed to want to say something, but blushed and stayed silent each time he looked at her.

Having seen Dowdy go, Jeremy finished his ale, bade Mrs Bloom and

Bessie farewell and left the cottage. Bessie followed him out to the gate. He felt her hand on his arm, and turning was struck by her dark-haired beauty, more so than he had noticed before.

She hardly dared speak what was on her mind, but knew she must if she wanted him.

'Jeremy,' she blushed as she spoke.

'Bessie,' he replied, blushing a little with her, for he sensed what was coming.

'I'm feared yer will think me not modest, but they say yer moon around thinkin' about Miss Eve, Jeremy. Some have noticed.'

'No, Bessie,' he tried to lie convincingly.

'She's not for you Jeremy—she's too old. An' some say there was an officer she wanted.'

'I hadn't heard.' As he uttered these words, a pang of jealousy gnawed his bowels at the memory of the young officer he had seen arrive at the Pearson's the previous evening.

'Father likes yer, Jeremy.'

'He's a good and just man,' Jeremy replied.

'An' mother.'

'I know, Bessie.'

'An' I . . .' Now she was stammering and blushing furiously, and he noticed the gentle swell of her virgin bosom as it rose and fell with her rapid breathing. 'An' I . . .' But she could not finish what she wanted to say.

Right then he could have kissed her, but she turned on her heels and fled into the cottage.

He started to walk home, and for a few brief moments his mind was filled with thoughts of Bessie. Then they were supplanted once more by his obsession with the more voluptuous beauty of the fair-haired Eve.

Until suddenly a window opened into his day-dreaming. His tunic! He retraced his steps to the tree stump; but the garment had long gone. The loss of this tunic was destined to come so near to being his undoing, for a devilish plot had started to take shape in the mind of a truly evil man.

***

From the open door of her hovel, Rebecca Brown noticed Amos Peters return from his day of labour. In fear and love she awaited the return of her Eli.

Further down the row of hovels, Ruth Merton, with hatred in her heart, noticed Rebecca waiting. For ten years she had dreamed of revenge on this insipid creature who had stolen her Eli and lured him into wedlock. But Eli had remained her secret lover. Three of the six children that her husband laboured to rear, believing them to be his own, were Eli's. She had plotted to murder her husband and Rebecca with Eli's help, so she could have him as her own, but though a violent man, Eli was not a natural murderer, and judging her to be mad, had given her up. His back had still been smooth when he left her.

She too had watched in anguish by the whipping post as the lash cut deep and bloody wounds in Eli's back after he had taken the village girl in violence. And this because the weak Rebecca–her enemy–could not satisfy him.

The combination of hatred, jealousy, rejection, murderous plotting, poverty, and rapid child-bearing had combined to change Ruth's appearance and personality. Once a statuesque good-looking woman, she now looked and sounded, harsh and unkind, but because of her height and dominant manner, was able to influence several of the women around her.

As time went on and Eli had still not come home, Rebecca went outside and started to look for him. Mrs Peters, her neighbour, went to her.

'Amos say Eli left the farm a s'mornin' an' never come back.'

The remark was overheard, and news of Eli's apparent defection spread through the row of hovels with the speed of a forest fire. Some pitied Rebecca for her sickness and the beatings she endured from Eli. Some despised her for being unable to hold her man . . . 'No woman whass too weak to bear her man children ain't got no right to him. Stands to reason his gooner go arter somebody else,' they said, in true Suffolk sing and contradiction, with much clicking of tongues.

But the ones who pitied, outnumbered those who despised, so four or five went with Rebecca to the hovel of Eli's mistress in another part of the village, and not finding Eli there, forced the girl to return with them carrying Eli's bastard.

'Now tell us where you're hid Eli Brown, you whore?' the assembled neighbours demanded of the terrified and weeping girl.

'I ain't seen him for nigh on a week,' she sobbed.

"Haps she's a witch an' hev made it so as he can't be seen,' suggested one of the superstitious neighbours, for belief in witchcraft was deep rooted among these simple people.

'But don't forget what Eli said only a s'mornin',' suggested Ruth, pointing in the direction of Rebecca. 'How as she was most likely in league with the Devil.'

'Thass right,' mumbled her cronies, nodding their assent.

✷✷✷

It was a sleepless night for five people. Jeremy–because he was torn between his blossoming affection for Bessie and obsession with Eve–also concern over the cost of replacing his lost tunic. Eve–worried if she was pregnant–also in case she was caught over Eli's death. Rebecca–because of the disappearance of her husband. Ruth–because she sensed that her opportunity for long-awaited revenge on Rebecca was at hand. Obadiah Dowdy–his thoughts swung between lust and remorse for sinful thoughts and glee as he knitted together his evil plot to obtain his ends with the aid of Jeremy's tunic.

✷✷✷

21

In Brentham, the next day started like most others. On the Goodway farm, Silas and Mary both rose early, for on a tenancy as small as theirs it was necessary to labour alongside their workers. Jeremy also rose early from his sleepless night to give his parents such help that he, as a dutiful son, could give before departing for his own employment. He was deeply worried about the loss of his best tunic, and conscious that without money of his own he would have to ask his hard-pressed father to pay the cost of having a new one made.

Obadiah Dowdy, master tailor, was also at his workrooms early to ensure that none of his apprentices or journeymen should be late for the commencement of their work. This attended to, he left to take his own breakfast and noticed across the street, the portly form of Tobias Winscombe, master butcher and fellow member of the parish committee, inspecting his shop front. In his mind Obadiah noted that here was a man who could be easily coerced, for he had often noticed that Tobias could not refrain from staring at beautiful women. He bid his committee colleague an unusually cheerful, 'Good morning.'

On the Pearson farm the day started in the manner of most non-market days. Whilst Mrs Pearson and Eve stayed awhile in their beds, Squire Nathaniel rose early to take his usual morning ride around his lands before breakfast. His labourers had already started.

Amos Peters arrived at the stack-yard with the first load of hay for the day with his new team mate–a young and not very bright lad named Jonas. Amos showed him what to do, and with a crisp, 'Get on with it,' bade him get started.

'Ain't got no fork, Amos,' the lad piped up.

'God help me. What hev I done to deserve you!' exclaimed the older man, raising his eyes to Heaven. 'Why couldn't yer say so afore this? Get over the barn an' look. Should be one or two in there.'

The lad scuttled over to the barn and later emerged shouting, 'There ain't no forks in here, Amos.'

Amos jumped down from the wagon and hurried over to the barn with impatience. 'Hev yer looked proper?' he demanded of young Jonas. 'Hev yer looked up the loft?'

'No, Amos.'

With an impatient sigh and click of the tongue, Amos climbed the ladder. With only his head and shoulders above the floor-level he uttered a gasp and shouted to the lad below, 'Don't come up!'

'Whass the matter, Amos?' Jonas called.

Amos did not answer, but completed his ascent to take a closer look at what he had seen. He descended the ladder as calmly as he could.

'Whass the matter, Amos?' the boy asked again.

Amos grasped him by the shoulders. 'Now, I want yer to run as fast as yer can to the big house with a message for the master–him only. Not nobody else. Not the mistress, not Miss Eve. Not the cook, nor the maids. Understand?'

Jonas nodded.

'If yer tell anybody else the message I'll cut your tongue out.'

Alarmed, and half believing Amos meant it, the boy nodded again.

'Ask the master to come quick. Tell him thass important 'cos Eli Brown is dead in the loft.'

The boy's eyes nearly popped out of his head. He made to run off on his errand. Amos caught him by the arm. 'Whoa there! What am I gooner do to yer if yer tell anybody else afore the master has been here?'

'Y-you're gooner c-cut me tongue out, Amos,' stammered the terrified Jonas.

'Thass right. An' if the master has already left the house, look for him. He'll be about his land somewhere on his hoss.'

The lad scuttled off. Amos stood guard outside the barn.

Nathaniel Pearson had scarce entered the back drive leading from his stables to the lane which connected with the stack-yard when he noticed young Jonas running towards him waving his arms wildly.

The boy was breathless and almost incoherent, but Nathaniel understood the main thrust of the lad's message. He urged his horse into a trot.

For young Jonas, the urge to tell others was overwhelming–but what about his tongue! His fingers went to his mouth to feel this important organ. Had not Amos threatened to cut it out if he told others. What exactly had Amos said. 'Afore the master has been here.' He looked down the driveway. His master was already at the entrance to the stack-yard. In a minute he would arrive at the barn.

Jonas could contain himself no longer. As fast as his legs would carry him, he ran to the fields waving his arms. 'Eli is dead in the barn. Eli Brown is dead in the barn,' he shouted as he galloped around the workers.

The reapers cast down their tools as one man, and made haste to the stack-yard. All except one, who also enjoyed being the bearer of startling news. He ran to the hovels of the labourers for his moment of glory. For Rebecca Brown, it could have been a moment of relief, knowing there would be no more beatings. But she loved Eli, and was in despair. Her neighbour, Mrs Peters, comforted her and walked gently with her to the Pearson stack-yard. Ruth Merton gathered her cronies around her for the same journey.

The tidings spread with the speed of a bush fire and reached the ears of Hermon Stark, the village constable, in his house alongside the village bridewell. A large and broody man, appointed to his position by the justices on the recommendation of the parish and county committees, he took his work seriously. To him fell the task of investigating crime in the parish, and administering punishments, either himself or through his deputy. He also hastened to the Pearson stack-yard.

23

For young Jason, the excitement of giving his news was over. Now alone in the field, and fearful at what he had done, he felt his tongue again. Creeping slowly back to the now crowded stack-yard, he made himself small behind the throng.

Hermon Stark, the village constable, with his deputy pushed his way through and made for the barn. Bidding his assistant to help Amos keep villagers away from the door, he entered and mounted the ladder to join Nathaniel Pearson in the loft and the rigid body of Eli Brown still impaled on the pitchfork that had killed him.

After much discussion they descended, having decided that they could not tell whether Eli had taken his own life, or had been murdered and arranged to look like self destruction. The constable went outside to call Amos in. His deputy whispered in his ear information gleaned from the crowd.

At the sight of Squire Pearson, those who had left their labours, quickly returned to them. The now thinner crowd, mainly of village women, revealed the nervous Jason.

'I di'n't tell nobody afore I told the master, Amos. Don't cut me tongue out, please,' called the frightened lad barely audibly, but nevertheless just loud enough for the keen ears of Hermon Stark, the constable. At a nod from Stark, the deputy grabbed Jason and pushed him into the barn behind the three men.

'I hear,' said Stark, addressing Amos, 'that last evening you told those living near you that Eli Brown deserted his labours yesterday morning and didn't return.'

Amos nodded and grunted his consent.

'Why didn't you tell Mr Pearson when he returned from market?' asked Stark.

'I di'n't want to get Eli into no trouble. It was nigh evenin' an' I hoped he would turn up afore mornin'.'

The constable turned to the shivering Jason and had him explain what he meant by having his tongue cut out.

'And now we hear,' went on Stark, addressing Amos, 'that you threatened this poor boy with violence.'

'An empty threat,' protested Amos, 'to stop him spreading the news.'

'He's not a violent man,' put in Nathaniel Pearson.

'With respect, sir,' said Stark, with due obsequiousness, 'even the meek can turn violent when provoked. 'Twould be better for all if he was locked in the bridewell until a soul can be found that saw Brown leave the farm.'

He led Amos out of the barn and through the waiting women. For Ruth Merton it was the chance she had waited for. She caught the constable's arm.

'What about her?' she cried, pointing at the weeping Rebecca.

Stark halted briefly and looked at Rebecca. 'Too weak,' he said gruffly and made to move on.

Ruth Merton caught his arm again. 'Not by herself. Poor Eli said only yes'day mornin' for all to hear, as how she was in league with the devil to wish him dead. She could hev made him kill his self by witchcraft.'

'Witchcraft hey?' asked Stark, rubbing his chin thoughtfully. 'It'll take more than just you to call her witch for me to do anything.'

'Witch! Witch!' screamed Ruth's cronies at a nod from her.

Even Mrs Peters dropped her protective arm from around Rebecca's shoulders, so relieved that another was suspected as well as her man. In her hour of greatest need, Rebecca was alone.

Stark took Rebecca by the arm to lead her away with Amos. 'It'll need a man knowledgeable in witchcraft to sort this out.'

**

In the Pearson household, Eve heard the news of the finding of Eli's body, and that both Amos Peters and Rebecca Brown had been locked in the bridewell, and that Rebecca would probably have to be questioned by Mathew Hopkins, the dreaded witchfinder general. Her conscience told her that she should speak up, but through fear she kept quiet, taking one more step down the slope to depravity.

CHAPTER 4

In her cage-like cell deep inside Colchester Castle, Rebecca Brown woke suddenly from her doze when the gaoler struck her a blow. 'Master Hopkins has give orders that you ain't gotter sleep. How many times do I hev to say?' the man shouted at her.

Already exhausted by her journey from Brentham the previous day, Rebecca had been kept awake, and was to continue to be kept awake until she confessed the killing of her husband by witchcraft to Matthew Hopkins.

Hopkins had bought the Thorn Inn at Mistley, just across the county boundary in Essex. From this base he plied his evil trade throughout East Anglia usually accompanied by assistants.

He was growing rich, for he charged a fee for each person, usually a woman, who he "proved" to be a witch by obtaining a confession under torture. If a confession was obtained, he would give evidence against the "witch" in the assize court. In the event of a confession not being obtained, the alleged witch would be "swum" in a pond, in a sheet with her thumbs tied to her big toes. If she drowned, she was declared innocent, like the widow Potter. If she survived, she was presumed guilty of witchcraft, because the devil had saved her, and put to death, usually by hanging. Either way, Hopkins achieved a death. His tally of deaths ran into hundreds.

Hopkins had only returned the previous day from a long foray around Suffolk and Norfolk when a messenger arrived at the Thorn Inn from Hermon Stark, requesting that he come urgently to Brentham to examine a prisoner to determine if she had committed murder by witchcraft.

'I returned from Suffolk and Norfolk only yesterday,' said Hopkins. 'Much work awaits me in Essex. The cells in Colchester castle are full to bursting with those denounced as witches. Tell Mr Stark that I cannot come to him for another month, when I make my way to Cambridge. Why the haste?'

'The constable hev another suspect, a man, in the bridewell who had chance enough to do the killin' with his own hands. Only he ain't never done nothin' wrong in his life, so they reckon. So the constable don't want to keep a God-fearin' man locked up if it happen this Brown woman did somehow do it by witchcraft like what some reckon she could hev.'

Matthew Hopkins stroked his beard as he digested this information. The case sounded interesting. Murder by witchcraft. Only a few years gone since they always burnt people for such a crime. Called it heresy. Still the law, but now many judges were just using the rope.

'Tell your master in that case I will question the woman in Colchester. Bid him send her to the castle during the next two days.'

So it was that Rebecca had found herself carried in a juddering farm cart, along a rough stony track called a road, some fourteen miles to the Essex boundary on the River Stour, and another bone-shaking six miles to

Colchester. The journey had taken over seven hours. Her cough troubled her a great deal and she was in pain. With nothing left to live for, she welcomed the prospect of an early death at the end of a rope. She would not resist the questioning.

A young girl shared her cell. She was sobbing with fear at the thought of being questioned by Matthew Hopkins. Rebecca comforted her. Two larger cage-like cells were inside the same room. These were filled with wailing women. There was no light except from the gaoler's lantern. No bedding was provided except a little filthy straw strewn about the floor. There was little or no food, unless friends sent it in. For Rebecca there had been none.

She heard the dreaded step of Matthew Hopkins on the stairway and his rap on the door. The gaoler let him in. His reputation had gone before him–she had expected a giant–an ogre. But this was just a man–not even an evil-looking man. He mumbled something to the gaoler who pointed to her cell. Hopkins walked over and peered in. 'These two,' he commanded the gaoler and turned on his heels.

The gaoler opened the cell door and bade Rebecca and the girl to go with him. In another, lighter room furnished with a table, chair and a few stools, Hopkins sat at the table. The women were made to sit on stools at either corner of the table. Hopkins turned to Rebecca.

'It is said that you killed thy husband, woman. What say you?'

Rebecca bowed her head and murmured, 'Yes.'

Hopkins did not expect so quick a confession, and was rather disappointed. He stood up and walked around to Rebecca.

Taking her hands in his, he put his face close to hers and hissed, ''Tis not sufficient to say thou did it. These hands are too frail. Surely you are in league with the devil through a familiar, one of his imps. What form did the imp take? Was it toad or dog–or perhaps a larger creature for such a stabbing–a man perhaps? Was it the man they took to the bridewell with you–is he your familiar–a servant of the devil?'

Rebecca gasped and cried, 'No!' The gaoler struck her a stinging blow. Hopkins motioned to him to desist. Returning to his seat he turned his attentions to the young girl.

Rebecca was in a panic. She must think up a story that Hopkins would accept. He must not be allowed to claim the life of Amos Peters as well as her own. She racked her brain as she heard the young girl sobbing under questions from Hopkins and blows from the gaoler. Hopkins turned back to her. She hoped that God would forgive the lie she had just thought of.

'The shape of thy familiar, woman. Was it a man?' demanded Hopkins.

'No,' whispered Rebecca, 'A fly–a large fly.'

'A fly!' exclaimed Hopkins, motioning to the gaoler to refrain from striking her. 'How could so small a creature do such a deed?'

'I put the fly in Eli's victuals. It entered him through his mouth an' went to his brain with orders to take his own life.'

27

Matthew Hopkins leaned back in his chair and pondered Rebecca's answer, stroking his beard. It would do. 'By this confession it is to be hoped that God will have mercy on your soul,' and thinking to himself, A fire on this earth would make certain, he continued, 'You will be taken back to Brentham now to await trial.'

Motioning the gaoler to take the women away, and fetch Hermon Stark's messenger, Hopkins took up a quill to write two letters–one to Hermon Stark and the other to Obadiah Dowdy of the Brentham parish brethren. He had met Dowdy only once but regarded him a strict God-fearing man.

The messenger arrived. On reflection, Hopkins decided only to entrust him with the letter for Hermon Stark. The letter for Dowdy he would send secretly by his own messenger.

***

In Brentham, the news soon spread that Rebecca Brown had confessed to killing her husband Eli by witchcraft. The simple folk, and some not so simple, believed it. Mrs Peters was relieved to have her Amos back free once more.

At the Grange, Squire Pearson and his lady were appalled, but did not see what could be done about it. Later in the day the matter was easily dismissed from their minds as a lone horseman arrived, resplendent in the uniform of a major in the Parliamentary army. Scarcely giving him time to dismount, Mrs Pearson rushed out and threw herself into his arms.

'John! Oh John we were so worried about you,' cried his mother. 'That terrible battle.'

'But a great victory,' replied Major John Pearson, as his father, the Squire, joined them. 'Now the tide has turned in our favour. It will be good to walk round the farm again and go once more to market with you tomorrow. Next Monday I must return.'

'So soon!' wailed Mrs Pearson.

John hugged and kissed his mother again.

Eve once more had to wrestle with the forces of good and evil as to whether she should confess to the accidental killing of Eli Brown in order to save Rebecca–then decided against it, salving her conscience by sending in good food to the bridewell for the unfortunate woman. Thus did she take yet another step down the road to depravity. She had another scheme afoot–she must tempt Jeremy into making love. The arrival of her brother was fortuitous. Now there would be scarcely a protest when she asked to be excused attending market on the morrow.

***

In his tailor's premises, Obadiah Dowdy read the letter from Matthew Hopkins with interest. It did not matter much to him what form of punishment eventually fell on Rebecca Brown, but Hopkins was a man it did well to not offend. After all, it was not only women or simple people he had sent to their deaths. But for the moment he would put the matter aside. His

28

loins were astir. Tomorrow was market day again–perhaps she would be bathing and sunning herself once more. Time to get to work on his colleague Tobias Winscombe.

As he stepped out into the street he was in luck, for there was none other than Eve Pearson walking along with her maid Naomi. Outside his shop across the road Tobias stared after them, oblivious to all else. Dowdy crept up behind him.

'Thou art a lusty knave Tobias Winscombe,' he said softly in his ear as he tapped him on the shoulder. 'Committing adultery in public.'

'Adultery!' almost screeched Tobias, his portly form visibly jumping as his mind came back to reality.

'Yes. Have you not read in the scriptures that if a man gazes upon a woman and lusts after her, he has committed adultery with her in his heart?'

'Brother Obadiah,' said Tobias, nervously, 'I was but looking down the street.'

'Tut, Brother Tobias, do not make your sin worse in the sight of God and man by telling falsehoods about it,' intoned the lean and gaunt Dowdy with doleful countenance. 'I have a duty as leader of the brethren to report this conduct.'

The chubby Tobias was downcast. A report to the brethren could mean the disgrace of dismissal from the parish committee, to the detriment of his business. 'But Brother Obadiah, our friendship . . .'

Dowdy raised his hand to stop him. 'Try not to persuade me, Tobias. I will pray for guidance from God on the matter. Now I must bid you "Good Day".'

With that he left a worried Tobias to his thoughts.

✳✳✳

The next day dawned to the early promise of shimmering heat once more.

Obadiah Dowdy decided to trust his most senior journeyman with his market business that day. Trust did not come naturally to Obadiah, but he had other plans afoot.

As Eve had anticipated, no objection was raised this week to her missing the market. Her parent's minds were very much occupied with her brother.

With the market party gone, Eve sent for her maid Naomi. 'I've a secret errand for you. Go to the parish office at the presbytery and speak to young Mr Jeremy Goodway. Bid him come here at 12 noon to see my father. Take good care that you do not run into Mr Dowdy, but he should have left by now.'

'But your father . . .' Naomi started to say.

'Naomi. Do I not treat you well and with great favour?'

'Yes, Miss Eve.'

'And do I not keep your secrets?'

'Yes, Miss Eve.'

'Then pray do my bidding without argument, and keep my secrets.'

With a blush and a curtsy, Naomi turned and went on her errand.

* * *

Jeremy was mystified at the message. Surely the Squire went to market this day every week. He made to question the girl but she had turned on her heels and fled. For some reason he could not explain to himself, he thought it better not to first ask Reverend Jones for permission to go.

Naomi hurried back to Eve. She was breathless, because of hurrying and her nervousness on account of her part in the conspiracy.

'Good,' said Eve. 'I shall now go to the arbour. I don't want to be disturbed. Should anyone ask where I am, say that you think I have gone into the village. Be outside just before noon, and when young Mr Goodway arrives tell him to go to the arbour, but don't follow.'

Naomi blushed and nodded.

Eve walked into the arbour. With more than an hour to wait before Jeremy should arrive she decided to bathe.

* * *

Obadiah Dowdy returned to the place by the yew-tree hedge from where he had spied upon Eve the previous week. He arrived just as she was undressing, and his loins stirred as her perfect naked form was revealed. Sorely tempted as he was to stay, he had more urgent business to attend to, for the time for the further entrapment of Tobias Winscombe had surely arrived, so he hurried to his victim's shop.

Although Obadiah was his colleague among the brethren and nominally his friend. Tobias none the less feared him secretly, and his stomach turned over when he saw him enter the shop.

'I have prayed and thought much about that we spoke of yesterday,' said Obadiah in gravest tones, 'and desire conversation in private.'

Tobias motioned his friend to the back of the premises, but Obadiah raised his hand. ''Tis a fine day. Time can be spared to walk while we talk at length on this serious matter.'

Full of apprehension, Tobias followed him into the street. Obadiah led the way in silence until they left the houses behind and they were on the stony roadway leading north out of Brentham. Soon they arrived at the point where he had entered Pearson land the previous week.

'This is Mr Pearson's private land,' protested Tobias, hesitating.

'Pah!' expostulated Obadiah. 'But a year since, common folk grazed their beasts on it. By what right does our self-styled Squire plant a hedge around it? Come,' he commanded, leading Tobias through. 'After much prayer, my thoughts have guided me into a way where it may be just for me to keep silent about your lust, and how you may expiate your sin. From here we can walk in straight line to the church, where after having talked about it, we may pray.'

'What must I do, brother Obadiah?' enquired the fat Tobias, anxiously.

30

Obadiah Dowdy stopped walking, for he wanted to bring the conversation to a certain point before their path brought them close to where it passed by the yew-tree hedge surrounding the Pearson domestic property. 'You have heard of Matthew Hopkins?'

'The witchfinder general. Ay, everyone has heard of him and fears him,' replied Tobias.

'But he is a Godly man, and powerful to boot,' said Obadiah. 'You would not wish to see me, your friend who keeps your lusty thoughts secret from the brethren, in bad odour and therefore in danger from him?'

'Nay, brother Obadiah. How can I help?'

'You've heard that the woman, Rebecca Brown, now lying in the bridewell, has confessed to Hopkins that she killed her husband by witchcraft?'

'That I have. And it will be our duty in the parish court to commit her for trial to the assizes.'

'Who will probably sentence her to death by hanging, although the law, if strictly observed calls it heresy, which carries the penalty of burning,' replied Obadiah. 'It matters not a jot to me how she meets her death, but I have a letter from Hopkins who feels it will be better for the salvation of her soul, in expiation for so serious a crime, if she perishes by fire at the stake.'

'But the fire is no longer legal . . .' began Tobias.

'If a woman kills her husband by witchcraft it is. A law that is none too strictly enforced in these troubled times,' interrupted Obadiah. 'Some judges, forgetting their sacred duty, even start to question the existence of witches. Matthew Hopkins believes this woman's confession to be unusual. Yet she is so frail that he dared not question her more robustly to obtain a better one.

'However, unofficial burnings still take place around these counties, where the public will demands it.'

'And the witchfinder has a valid point about her salvation,' murmured Tobias. Then out loud, 'What do you expect me to do?'

'You sell meat to the Pearson household I'm sure?'

'Ay. That I do,' replied Tobias.

'And since the devil has you lusting after women as you do, I suspect that you are more than a friend to that plump cook of theirs?'

'But, brother Obadiah . . .' protested Tobias, his chubby cheeks colouring.

'Tut, brother Tobias. Pile not one sin upon another with more falsehoods. This is what I would have you do. Persuade your friend the cook to advise us when our so-called Squire is likely to be away for a day, other than a market day. I will then arrange the Brown woman's parish trial for that day. He will not neglect important business for a simple committal. But as he is a member of the county committee which does Parliament's bidding, he would stop the parish court having her sentenced to burn as being outside its power.'

'Others may object.'

31

'I can over ride them.'

'But I like it not to deceive Mr Pearson. He is a kind gentleman and a valued customer,' protested Tobias.

'You would lose more than his custom if I did my duty and reported your lusting to the brethren,' said Obadiah, with a hint of threat in his voice. 'And why do you ascribe such virtue to him? You've seen how he has now unlawfully enclosed this particular pasture, just like the aristocracy. And again, aping them, he has constructed for himself and his family a private lake and summer-house. Do you have such luxury, for all your toil? Go to yonder yew-tree hedge and look through, to see the truth of my words.' Obadiah smiled inwardly as Tobias waddled over to the hedge, put his head among the foliage, and as expected, stayed much longer than was necessary for a casual look at an arbour. Now indeed would he have him in his power.

Obadiah walked over to the hedge and stood beside his colleague. Tobias was so engrossed that he was not aware of his presence until Obadiah sprang back with pretended disgust and, striking him a stinging blow across his ample posterior, dragged him from the hedge and hissed in his ear. 'Thou art a filthy knave. Now indeed has the devil taken control of your thoughts and actions. Well might I have wondered why you stayed so long to look. I never thought to see such a sight myself. That naked wanton you were feasting your eyes on was none other than Pearson's daughter. My duty is clear. I must report her and you to the brethren.'

With that, Obadiah Dowdy turned away from Tobias Winscombe and strode towards the church. Tobias ran after him as fast as his portly frame would allow, pleading for his indulgence. Near the gate of the church Obadiah decided that his friend had been tormented enough for the moment. He stopped and turned.

''Tis right what you say. Such a commotion would surely cause Pearson to stay in Brentham when we want him out of the way. But I must do the witchfinder's bidding, and we can advise Pearson of his daughter's sinful behaviour privately later. That will stop him from interfering, or blaming us after Rebecca Brown's death. I trust, Tobias Winscombe, that you know what debt of gratitude you owe me for once more withholding news of your lust from the brethren?'

'I do indeed brother Obadiah,' gasped Tobias, his hands clasped as in prayer.

'Then there's another service I require of you, for we shall need a public commotion.'

'Anything you ask, brother Obadiah.'

'There is a woman named Merton. She dwells in the hovels of the labourers, and has some grudge against the Brown woman. As soon as you have discovered the next time Pearson will be away for a day or more, bring her to my home after darkness. I cannot afford to be seen conversing with her. Now let us pray for God's blessing on our endeavours.'

So they knelt together in God's house. The evil hypocrite and the genuinely frightened man.

* * *

Had they stayed awhile longer watching the arbour, the two men would have witnessed an incident of which they could have made much.

Hearing a sound as Obadiah dragged Tobias from the hedge, Eve thought that it must be the sound of Jeremy approaching. So she slipped into the water. It would be more seductive, she felt, to reveal herself to him gradually as she arose glistening wet from the lake. But she had to stay in the water for several minutes, for it was not yet noon.

As Jeremy approached the Grange his heart beats quickened. The message had been to call and see the Squire, but deep down he guessed that Nathaniel Pearson would not be there, for it was market day in Bury St Edmunds. He had dared to hope that it was what it was–a ruse by Eve to see him privately. But in his wildest imagination he had not foreseen the opportunity that was about to be presented to him.

He was intercepted, as arranged, by Naomi as he approached the house.

The girl blushed and curtsied. 'You gotter go to the arbour. Thass at the bottom of the garden, behind the big hedge and trees what go across.'

Jeremy was speechless with excitement. Naomi was Eve's maid. Now he knew it was not the Squire he had called to see. He was numb–he was on air. Expecting to find her seated demurely, he was not prepared.

As he entered the seclusion of the arbour, only Eve's head was visible above the water. Her long golden hair splayed out across the surface. She smiled seductively at him. He noted her pile of clothes on the grass. His thoughts and his loins were in turmoil. He stammered. 'But Miss Eve . . I was not . .'

'Oh be not shy Jeremy,' she cooed at him. 'The weather is hot and the water refreshing. Come and join me.'

He hesitated. 'But your father . . .'

'Father is at market.' Clearly he needs more encouragement she decided. She rose and stood with her feet on the bottom, exposing her breasts, the nipples of which were just above the water line.

He had not seen a woman's naked breasts before, but his mind cast back to the taunting of his fellows at Cambridge. He was tempted, and on impulse took off his tunic and cast it on the ground. Then his Puritan upbringing intervened, and he hesitated. He had a strong erection and was ashamed for her to see him in that condition.

Eve was becoming impatient with him, but was careful not to let it show. She came out of the water, exposing all her nakedness to him. He was full of confusion–he had never seen such a beautiful sight. Water dripped from her long hair and ran in rivulets around every delicious curve. He longed to take her in his arms, but yet lacked the courage.

She held out a hand to him, 'Come let us go to the summer-house.' He

33

was led blindly, his mouth too dry to speak. His Puritan conscience was troubling him again–and fear that he might not do it right.

Now they were in the summer-house he was torn two ways. He needed her badly but panic took over. 'No Eve, this isn't right,' he suddenly blurted out, and turning on his heels, left quickly.

To Eve, the humiliation was unbearable. First Marcus and now Jeremy had spurned her. In the privacy of the arbour she stormed and raged. She picked up Jeremy's tunic and wrung and tore at it in her fury. Then she felt the pain as nature intervened and she looked down at herself. Now she knew with relief that she was not pregnant by Eli Brown.

But she would not lightly forgive Jeremy, much as she liked him. She would not offer herself again until he had proved himself by some manly act.

After dressing, she picked up the crushed and torn tunic, and returning to the house, threw it into the chest of cast-off clothes which the family distributed to the poor from time to time.

As he hurried back to work, Jeremy realised that he had left his tunic, but dared not go back for it. He was worried, and started to despise Eve for offering herself in that fashion. His thoughts turned to Bessie.

He did not notice Obadiah Dowdy walking back to his shop from the church, but Dowdy noticed him, and wondered why he was there, and since he was coming from that direction, if he had been to the Pearson's. He took care that Jeremy did not see him.

CHAPTER 5

Nathaniel Pearson had a touch of annoyance in his voice as he addressed his wife at dinner, two days after Major John Pearson had arrived home.

"Twould be more advantageous if you were to bide here on Monday when John starts his journey back. Cambridge is nigh thirty-five miles away. 'Tis a mite too far for one day if we're to be slowed down with the little cart. I'm only riding so far with him because I've business to transact there. After that I am obliged to go up into Norfolk, for I have business in Norwich, which I could have ridden to directly from Cambridge. Now I shall have to first divert myself to Bury St Edmunds to deliver you into the safe keeping of the market party at the mid-week market. With such hindrance 'tis likely to be the next Sabbath ere I am back here in Brentham.'

Disagreements between the Squire and Mrs Pearson were infrequent, and for that reason all the more interesting to the servants when they did occur. It was not long therefore before Tobias Winscombe was able to inform Obadiah Dowdy that Nathaniel Pearson would be away most all the following week, and most likely his wife and daughter for the first half of the week.

Dowdy could scarce believe his luck that matters should start to flow his way so soon. Only two days after he had coerced his fat friend. It was a pity about the daughter being away though. If he could but spy her misbehaving once more and burst in on her, he would not just be able to stop his enemy, Pearson, making trouble about Rebecca Brown. He would be able to destroy his influence altogether.

A rare smile came to his features. 'You've done well so far, Tobias.' Then returning to his more solemn look. 'Remember what I said. Go now privily to the Merton woman and bid her come to my house in secret this day, Friday, soon after nightfall.'

After Tobias departed, Obadiah Dowdy went straight to the presbytery.

'In your best hand, pen a note to each of the brethren who sits on the parish committee to inform them that the parish court will sit at 10 o'clock on Monday morning,' he commanded Jeremy. 'Put the business of the committal of the Brown woman to the assizes at the top of the list. There are but two other petty matters anyway. When you have written out the notes, bring them to me at my shop for signing. Then you must deliver them.'

***

Ruth Merton had approached Dowdy's house with some apprehension, and as she sat opposite him in the dimly-lit room her fear reached new heights. He sensed that fear and played on it by staring at her for several moments in silence. At length he spoke.

'Some say you are a whore and an adulteress.'

She opened her mouth, but no sound came out.

He continued, 'Some of your children do not come from your husband. I

35

could have you whipped for that.'

She found her voice. 'You can't flog women.'

His tone became more threatening. 'I wield much power in this parish. Don't try to tell me what I can or cannot do. I can have you stripped and marked from shoulders to heels with a good stout cane, and none would dare say me nay–or I could denounce you as a witch. I have the ear of the witchfinder general.'

She was speechless with fear.

'But I care not what happens to you in this life,' he went on, 'for you will certainly go to Hell in the next. But it's rumoured that you hate Rebecca Brown with a great hatred because some of your bastards are the product of her now dead husband.'

Now she began to feel defiant, for he had touched the rawest of spots. 'What of it?' she snarled.

'Take care how you address me,' he warned. 'If you hate her that much, I don't doubt but you would wish her to suffer a more painful death than hanging?'

It was a question–she nodded in silent reply.

'On Monday morning at 10 o'clock, the Brown woman will come before the parish court to confirm the confession she has made, and be committed for trial to the assizes. You will attend the court with several of your friends and set up a commotion by shouting, "Burn the witch".'

She began to feel excited at the prospect.

'Also you will provide some strong men. That fool Stark, the constable, may forget his duty and not want to carry out such a punishment, in which case your men will deal with him and do the burning. We will be excused if there is enough public clamour for it.'

'I'll do my best,' she said.

'You'll succeed. Unless you would rather be denounced as a witch yourself–after you have received a most terrible thrashing.' Dowdy dismissed her with a wave of his hand. 'Now go, whore, and get on with it.'

✻✻✻

On Monday morning, Mrs Pearson awoke early from a fitful sleep in a pool of sweat. Indeed she had lain awake most of the night fretting about the imminent departure back into danger of her beloved son, John.

The physician came quickly when summoned. His limited knowledge did not enable him to recognise his patient's condition as the onset of a repetitive and dangerous illness. ''Tis but over-heated blood brought about by the continuance of the hot weather,' he declared to her anxious husband. 'For a few days she should stay indoors out of the sunshine in a north-facing chamber, then all will be well.'

Eve had looked forward to visiting Cambridge, and imagined that she would still be allowed to go, but her father rebuked her. 'Your duty is to stay with your mother,' he said, somewhat sternly, 'and tomorrow send a messenger with news how she fares to meet me at the Bell Inn in Thetford, where I shall be calling either late on Tuesday or during Wednesday on my way from Cambridge to Norwich.'

Nathaniel, and his son Major John Pearson, then made their farewells and started on their journey.

✳✳✳

Not knowing that it suited Dowdy's evil plotting to pretend not to notice, Jeremy at his desk in the parish office, wondered why he had not been rebuked for coming to work the last few days without a tunic. Having now lost two of the garments, he had no other. He had hoped to catch sight of Eve on Friday when he delivered the court notice to ask her for the one he had left two days earlier. Alas fortune had not been with him, because he had encountered the Squire and could not possibly ask him.

He picked up his papers and walked to the room adjacent to the presbytery that was used as a parish courthouse. He noticed that the room was unusually full, with many labourers' wives, and some men in attendance. There was also a crowd outside. The case of Rebecca Brown had created much interest.

In the absence of Nathaniel Pearson, Obadiah Dowdy assumed presidency of the court. Reverend Jones shirked his responsibility. Dowdy felt in a confident and bouyant mood. Tobias Winscombe had just informed him that the Pearson girl had not after all gone away with her father.

Rebecca was brought in by the constable and his deputy and asked if she still stood by the confession that she had made to the witchfinder general.

She assented in a barely audible whisper.

'Then it only remains for us to commit you for trial at the assizes when you will surely be sentenced to death,' said Dowdy, making a slight nod in the direction of Ruth Merton.

Taking this as her cue, the woman schreeched out at the top of her voice, 'Burn the witch. Hangin's too good for her.'

Her cronies joined in, 'Burn the witch! Burn the witch!'. Other members of the public felt the lust for blood and added their voices to the clamour.

Outside, pandemonium broke out as most of the crowd joined in, demanding a fire. Fights started as a lesser number disagreed. Samuel Bloom was set upon by three men and beaten unconscious.

In the courtroom, Dowdy let the clamour go on while he conferred with his colleagues. Then holding up his hand to silence the public, he addressed Rebecca sententiously, making sure that the commonality would be involved in the guilt of his actions. 'It is clearly the will of the people that you should suffer death by burning here in Brentham. A just and righteous judgement by your peers for so great a crime as yours. A punishment that will exorcise the evil spirit that lives within you, and cleanse your soul to meet your maker. Tomorrow at this time.'

Now fear gripped Rebecca. She screamed and fainted. At his desk,

37

Jeremy felt sick. Hermon Stark, the constable, made to protest, but Dowdy silenced him. Stark could see it was useless to protest here. He helped Rebecca to her feet and led her outside between himself and his deputy. His mind was made up. Get her into the bridewell and he would ride for help.

He led her through the hostile, screaming crowd. His life came to a sudden end, and he did not know from where the fatal blow came. His deputy saw him fall dead to the ground, took fright and fled, only to be set upon and beaten unconscious like Samuel Bloom.

The crowd seized Rebecca and carried her off to the bridewell. She was their prisoner now.

A rider left Brentham heading south for Essex with a message from Obadiah Dowdy.

Dowdy stayed around the presbytery for the rest of the day making sure that Jeremy was kept too busy to get any ideas about leaving Brentham for help.

"Twill be your duty to attend and witness the punishment and write it up in the records in the usual way,' he reminded him.

Jeremy felt sick in his stomach at the prospect.

With having to hang around the presbytery to keep an eye on Jeremy, Obadiah Dowdy found he had time to start another little matter which he had been thinking of for some time. So sure was he that he would soon be able to remove the influence of Nathaniel Pearson, that power-madness was going to his head. He took up quill and penned a short note to the Marquess of Stourland.

Having completed and sealed the missive, Dowdy handed it to Jeremy. 'Take this to the Manor and make sure that you give it to the Marquess of Stourland in person. Tell him you are to wait for a reply. "Tis a request for a meeting between him and leading members of the brethren on an important matter. Make sure that you bring his reply to me before you finish your labours today.'

For the benefit of the coffers of this parish 'tis about time this Royalist, who denies that he is, should volunteer to pay a greater contribution in local taxes until common sense prevails and we are given the power to oblige his kind to do so, thought Dowdy. And 'tis an errand that will take this young fellow a nice long time and keep him from mischief.

Jeremy was glad to get out of Dowdy's way even if it did mean finishing late. It was not until he reached the Manor gate that he realised he had been followed.

Dowdy watched through the gateway down the long drive until he saw Jeremy admitted to the house. Then he walked to his own home, for it would take Jeremy that little bit longer to bring the reply there.

Jeremy was admitted to a large front room by a maid. On hearing that he wanted to see the Marquess, the girl showed surprise and said that she would fetch the goodwife.

His eyes took in the detail of this magnificent room. The top half of the walls above the wainscoting, were covered with wallpaper–a new fashion of the wealthy. He had not seen wallpaper before.

A handsome, buxom woman in her late forties entered the room. Her dress was a little less austere than normal Puritan fashions of the day.

'You're Mr Jeremy Goodway, the maid tells me. And you wish to see the Marquess?' she asked.

'Yes,' said Jeremy with a nod.

'I'm Mrs Francis, the goodwife–Goody Fran the staff know me as. You may address me thus also. The Marquess doesn't usually see callers unless they're of good rank. I can take him your letter.'

'But I've strict instructions to give it into his hand and await an answer,' replied Jeremy.

'Who is the letter from?'

'From Mr Dowdy of the parish brethren.'

'Huh,' snorted the goodwife. 'Why not from Reverend Jones or Mr Pearson? Surely they are in charge before Mr Dowdy? It is they who should be writing to a person of noble rank.'

'Mr Pearson is away at the moment, as he often is, being a member of the county committee. Mr Dowdy oversees much parish business.'

The goodwife clicked her tongue and sighed. 'Ah well, it's an insult, but let me take the letter, and I'll enquire if the Marquess will see you.'

Jeremy was kept waiting a very long time. He took in all the other details. The heavy oak table with a pair of solid brass candlesticks, ornate settle, intricately carved chairs, tallboy, console table, with well displayed silver and brass atefacts. They said most Royalists had smuggled out all their brass and silver to help the King. This man was surely not a Royalist.

At length, a tall gaunt man with silver hair appeared. Jeremy judged him to be at least seventy-five years of age.

'You are Jeremy Goodway, son of a tenant farmer in this parish?' The Marquess spoke in neutral tones. Jeremy was not quite sure if he was being rebuked.

'Yes, m'Lord.'

The Marquess handed Jeremy a sealed letter. 'Here is my reply to Mr Dowdy.' He looked more sternly at Jeremy. 'Does he seek to add another insult to the insult of his letter, that he should send his messenger to me not clad in a tunic?'

Jeremy replied quickly, 'But that is my misfortune, m'Lord. My best tunic was stolen nigh two weeks ago when I left it unattended.'

'Do you not have another?'

Jeremy had to do some quick thinking. He already had enough trouble keeping the loss of his second tunic from his mother.

'Yes m'Lord, but it is torn and in need of repair.' He said a silent prayer asking God to forgive him for telling a lie, little knowing how true his words had been.

The Marquess softened his tone. 'Will you do me a small service?'

Jeremy smiled. 'Most certainly, m'Lord, if I'm able.'

The Marquess handed him another letter. 'This is for Mr Nathaniel Pearson. It's private. Will you make sure he gets it?'

'That I will m'Lord.'

'And take greater care of it that you have done with your tunics!'

The Marquess smiled and with a dismissive wave of his hand indicated that their meeting was over. Jeremy bowed, turned, and walked to the door where the goodwife was waiting.

'Jeremy Goodway.' The Marquess called him back.

'You are the young man who had to break his education in Cambridge because the times lay hard on your parents?'

'That is so, m'Lord.'

The Marquess handed him a small purse.

'There is sufficient in here for a new tunic. Go and order one to be made tomorrow.'

'But, m'Lord,' Jeremy stammered.

'Be off with you.'

Jeremy reflected as he walked up the Manor driveway that he must have made a good impression. And the letter for the Squire would be a good excuse to call at the Grange after he had handed Dowdy his reply from the Marquess, and hopefully ask Eve about the tunic he left. It all helped to lighten the sad events of the day.

***

Eve was in despair. News of what had happened in the village earlier in the day had reached the Pearson household and both she and her mother had wept. Mrs Pearson, who had started to get better, became worse once more and had to take to her bed.

For Eve it had been torment enough that a woman she knew to be innocent had been arrested and had faced the prospect of the assizes where she would almost certainly be sentenced to hang. But that would have been in the future–she had clung to hope that it would not happen. Now, in a few short hours, this poor wretch Rebecca Brown would suffer a terrible death in the fire at the hands of a mob. Too late now to get a message to her father, in the hope he could stop it. If she confessed at this late stage to the accident with Eli what would happen? Lawlessness had broken out, so if she tried to intervene, they could turn on her and put her to the fire with Rebecca. Fear and worry had her in thrall.

'Miss Eve,' said Naomi, entering the room. 'Mr Jeremy Goodway has brought a letter for the master.'

Eve took it from her and noticed with surprise the seal of its aristocratic sender. 'I'll take this and leave in his study for him when he returns.'

For a moment she even thought of appealing to the Marquess to intervene–but no, he had no real power, being a suspected Royalist sympathiser.

The maid interrupted her train of thought. 'Mr Goodway is still at the door an' asked to see yer in private.'

Eve looked at her dishevelled hair and tear-stained face in the mirror. She was still annoyed at Jeremy, but her attitude had softened a little under the pressure of the terrible events of the moment. He probably could not afford to lose a tunic.

She took up a quill and wrote a short note. 'Your tunic was torn. I am having it mended. You may return for it tomorrow afternoon or later.'

Having sealed the note, she handed it to Naomi. 'Tell Mr Goodway that I can't see him now, but give him this note. Then return to see me.'

As soon as Naomi had left the room, Eve hurried out to the discarded-clothes chest. She hoped that the tunic was still there, and was relieved to find that it was.

She was waiting with it in her room when Naomi returned.

'Naomi. This torn and creased tunic was left in the garden by Mr Jeremy Goodway last week. It would be a kindness to mend and press it for him. I could mend it, but it would be mis-understood if I were to be seen doing so. Will you therefore do it privily, out of sight of the other servants and keep in among your things until he calls for it?'

The maid nodded her consent, curtsied, and took the garment, smiling inwardly. Hers was not to ask questions. She did not doubt that her young mistress had been angry with young Mr Goodway about something.

✻✻✻

Rebecca had scarcely slept at all in her tiny bare cell. No one had attempted to speak to her or feed her since she was brought back to the bridewell. She was past fearing death and welcomed it, but was in terror of the pain she would suffer from the fire. Most of the night she had spent in prayer.

Her cough had been more troublesome and on the increase throughout the night. Flecks of blood came from her mouth from time to time. When the men came for her she was almost too weak to stand or walk, so they half led, half dragged her to the stake which had been set up in a sloping field just outside the village. A large and noisy crowd had gathered for the spectacle.

She prayed in silence as they bound her to the stake. Her eyes opened briefly and she saw them put torch to the faggots. The first whiffs of smoke touched her throat and she started to choke. As her diseased lungs burst, a stream of blood jetted from her mouth, and her head sagged in death before the flames reached her. For Rebecca it was over.

The crowd shouted as they saw what they believed to be the evil red spirit exit her mouth and fall on to the faggots to be consumed by the flames.

On higher ground a little way behind the crowd, a smartly dressed man with a goatee beard was seated on a horse. He also saw it, and was well satisfied. With a tug on the reins and a nudge with his knees, he started his

41

ride back to Mistley and the Thorn Inn.

∗∗∗

Jeremy had been obliged to stay to the very end, until the fire was over. Back at his desk in the presbytery, he had written up details of the execution in the journal. It was now early afternoon, and he still felt sick in his stomach at what he had been compelled to witness. Unable to concentrate on other tasks, he decided that he must go home. He cared not whether Obadiah Dowdy or Reverend Jones approved of his going early, he would not ask.

Dowdy's mind had now turned to the strengthening of his position against Nathaniel Pearson. He had been intrigued over the past few days by Jeremy's obvious loss of a second tunic, especially as he had seen him walking from the direction of the Pearson's. In fact, in his mind he had almost reconstructed what had happened six days before–except that his thoughts had taken him further than what had actually taken place.

He saw Jeremy walk away from his work and head along the road leading to his home–and the Pearson's. 'Does fortune smile on me?' he murmured to himself. 'Am I indeed to catch them in the act of fornication, and so get two birds with one stone, Nathaniel Pearson and young Goodway?'

He followed Jeremy at a safe distance until he saw him turn into the Grange driveway, then with elation hurried back to his shop.

∗∗∗

On this occasion Jeremy was not unduly concerned that Eve declined to see him again. Still depressed, his mind was full of the horrors of the morning. With thanks he took his repaired tunic from the hand of the maid and made his way home.

The news that Rebecca Brown was actually dead wrought a great change in Eve. Her parents knew nothing of her exploits. They still believed her to be a virgin girl. She felt the need to tell them all, but could not, for now she had a secret so dreadful that it must remain forever in her breast alone. She had let another die for something she had done, although by accident. This could not be shared with mother, father or Naomi.

She wandered around the garden to be alone with her thoughts. In a state of degradation she wandered into the arbour and gazed at her reflection in the lake. She recalled how two weeks before she had scrubbed the last traces of Eli's blood away in that same water. Maybe she could scrub away her guilt as easily.

Undressing, she entered the water again, and with stone scrubbed and scrubbed to no avail, for degradation is within. Leaving the water, lost in her thoughts she picked up her undershift from the pile of clothes and wandered to the other side of the lake. She looked at the water again. There was but one thing left to do, for she could not live with the burden. Dropping the garment on the bank, she entered the water again and lay on the bottom. But the lake was too shallow for self-destruction, and she was to learn that it is

42

not possible to drown voluntarily.

Frustrated in her attempt, she left the water, and falling to her knees, gathered the undershift to her face and sobbed and sobbed.

∗∗∗

Obadiah Dowdy, having seen Jeremy enter the Pearsons' driveway, arrived back at his shop almost out of breath. Going to a locked cupboard he took out Jeremy's tunic that he had stolen from outside the forge.

'Come with me,' he commanded Tobias Winscombe as soon as he entered his shop across the street.

Tobias meekly did as he was bidden, but due to his excess weight could not keep up with the hurried pace of his leaner colleague. Obadiah turned on him in anger. 'Were you but to tame your gluttony, you would be able to make haste when urgent matters are afoot.'

'Where do we go?' asked Tobias, already out of breath.

'Unless I am much mistaken, to catch the Pearson girl in another act of lewdness, or even fornication. Then indeed would our hand be strong against the so-called Squire should he seek to make trouble when he returns.'

'Fornication!' puffed out Tobias. 'With whom?'

'With our recently appointed clerk, who I don't doubt is the eyes and ears of Nathaniel Pearson into all that I do. But do hurry or we will miss them yet with your slow pace.'

They arrived at the gap in the yew-tree hedge just as Eve left the water the first time. They saw her walk to the other side of the lake, go in and under the water and emerge once more and sit sobbing into her undershift. The loins of both men were astir at the sight.

'It does appear,' hissed Dowdy, 'that due to your slowness, we have missed the lover. She weeps, either because he has possessed her and left, or because he has rejected her. It matters not. We shall have to invent him.'

With that, Dowdy gently pushed the stolen tunic through the gap. 'Come, follow me,' he whispered as he led Tobias to the wicket gate, then into the garden and through the screen of trees into the arbour.

'Harlot! Jezebel!' yelled Dowdy as they rushed in upon the weeping Eve and, grabbing her arms, dragged her to her feet. 'Well might you weep now that you have been caught. Your lover escaped, but we shall find the knave, for he dropped his tunic as he ran.' He motioned to Tobias Winscombe to go pick up the garment.

Tobias brought the tunic over. Eve realised to whom it belonged and did not understand.

'He wasn't here,' she pleaded tearfully.

Dowdy slapped her face. 'You'll both appear before the parish court next week. He'll most certainly taste the lash at the whipping post, and you'll be paraded round the village in public disgrace. I don't doubt that your father will be mightily displeased.'

'What harm have I done that you should make such falsehood against

43

me?' she sobbed.

The handling of the naked girl had stirred Obadiah to a passion in spite of his age, for the devil by now had taken him over. He believed he had the right to do as he chose and for a moment forgot his primary purpose.

He ignored her question. 'But we could forget the whole thing should you consent to submit to both of us here and now. Because I'm sure it will mean naught to you, for you are but a wanton, whatever your upbringing.'

The tears streamed down her face, but what difference did it make so long as no one knew? She was already degraded in her own mind.

So believing his promise she nodded her consent and submitted herself to the unwelcome attentions of Dowdy, who, because of his age and ineptitude, and Eve's loathing of him, did not get the enjoyment from copulation that he expected. He then became angry against himself for yielding to carnal lust, and started slapping her about with his hand. When he had finished doing that, he invited his companion to take his pleasure of her.

But Tobias, in spite of his inclination, could not or would not perform the act. In anger, Dowdy struck him and called him fool.

While the two men quarrelled, Eve quietly donned her undershift and made her escape to the house.

'Now she is away from us, thanks to you,' raged Dowdy. 'It matters not. We have her clothes and the tunic for proof.'

'But you promised her!' exclaimed Tobias.

Dowdy clicked his tongue and looked at his colleague with a sneer. In that moment Tobias Winscombe realised the evil of the man into whose clutches he had fallen, but could think of no way to extricate himself.

So they returned with a party of men to arrest Eve and take her to the bridewell. Then they went to the Goodway's and arrested Jeremy.

CHAPTER 6

Arriving at the Bell Inn, Thetford around mid-morning on Wednesday, Nathaniel Pearson was perplexed. He had expected a message about his wife to be waiting for him, but there was none. A simple explanation might be that she was much improved, and Eve had thought it not necessary to send a message, in spite of his instructions to do so.

After due contemplation he decided to divert himself south to Bury St Edmunds to discover any information the mid-week market party might have about his wife's condition. If nothing was amiss, it would mean he was almost a day late arriving in Norwich, but for the sake of peace of mind he felt obliged to do it.

Arriving at the market place in Bury St Edmunds, he was dismayed to find there was no market party from his farm that day. Some other Brentham traders one might expect to be there were also absent. There was however a trading party with produce from the Manor. Although they knew nothing of Mrs Pearson's illness, they told of the lawlessness in the village, the murder of the constable, Hermon Stark, and the burning of Rebecca Brown.

These tidings caused much concern to Nathaniel, for no doubt that was why no messenger had come to Thetford with news of his wife, and the reason for the absence of several of the Brentham traders from the market. He decided that he must abandon his trip to Norwich and return to Brentham.

Outbreak of lawlessness and the murder of the appointed constable were sufficient reason for a man in his position to ask help from the army. There were at that time about a hundred cavalry of the Ironsides billeted in the town, made up of forty battle-hardened troops engaged on patrol and training duties and the rest recruits being trained under them.

The captain in charge listened sympathetically to Nathaniel's request. 'I can spare you twenty men under a junior officer,' he announced. 'It'll have to be ten of the seasoned men and ten of the recruits. This should be enough to handle a disturbance in a large village such as Brentham. If more should be required, send a messenger.'

'I think it would be better if none of them were Brentham men,' suggested Nathaniel.

'They come from all over the county, so there's but little risk of that,' replied the captain. 'They are in any case well disciplined and won't desert, unlike the militia of the early days. Come, I'll introduce you to the young man that I shall put in charge. His name is Cornet Henry Tripp.'

Tripp and Nathaniel Pearson rode side by side over the ten miles to Brentham. The cornet revealed his age as twenty-five and said that he had been in action many times from the start of the war.

Nathaniel found his conversation interesting, although part of it escaped him, as worry about his wife and the reason for the absence of their own market party returned to the forefront of his mind time and again.

On arrival at Brentham, they stopped first at the his home, the Grange. Bidding Tripp have his men wait outside, he entered the house. All appeared normal, except that the staff seemed disturbed. He mounted the staircase in search of his wife. She greeted him tearfully. 'May the Lord be praised for sending you back to me,' she sobbed.

'I heard rumour of an unlawful burning and the murder of the constable,' he said. 'Is this true?'

'Ay, that it is, it grieves me to say,' she wailed. 'Now there is more trouble, for they have arrested our dear Eve and carried her off to the bridewell.'

'Arrested her!' exclaimed the Squire. 'If Stark is dead, who arrested her, pray–his deputy? And upon what charge?'

'No,' sobbed Mrs Pearson. 'The deputy was grievously beaten by the mob, and with him the blacksmith. I don't know the men that took her. They were a rough lot but were led by that loathsome Mr Dowdy.'

'Dowdy, by God,' hissed Nathaniel. 'Go on wife–what charge?'

Mrs Pearson erupted in a great burst of weeping and threw her arms round her husband's neck. 'So ashamed, I cannot bring myself to say it,' she croaked in almost a whisper.

'But you must, my dear' insisted the Squire.

There was a pause while she dried her eyes and partly composed herself. 'Fornication. Fornication with young Jeremy Goodway,' she finally found the strength to say before the tears started to roll again.

'Fornication; Jeremy; Dowdy!' exclaimed the Squire. 'I doubt not that this is a false charge and a ploy by Dowdy against myself. He takes little care to hide his hatred and envy of me. So now he brings a false charge against our daughter to disgrace me, and the young man I recommended for public employment in the parish. He aims to destroy my influence.'

'I fear the charge may have some substance,' said Mrs Pearson through her tears. 'He claims to have most of the clothes she had taken off. Also Jeremy's tunic. He says he caught them in the act in our summer-house, but that they both escaped, she with only her undershift, Jeremy with his clothes on but he dropped his tunic in the garden. Mr Dowdy claims that Mr Winscombe, the butcher, was with him and will back him up. Also I have closely questioned Naomi, who after first trying to cover up for Eve, finally admitted she had indeed rushed in yesterday in a distressed state clad only in her undershift.'

Nathaniel was struck dumb for some moments while he digested this information and reflected on the seriousness of the situation. Finally regaining his composure, he asked, 'What of other matters? Why do we not have a market party selling produce at Bury St Edmunds market today? Have our people gone with the mob?'

'No!' she cried. 'Only a few. Mostly they have been very protective. Feared for my safety after Eve's arrest and decided it would be best to stay around here. Some of them near the house.'

Nathaniel was glad of that and made up his mind what to do. Giving his wife a comforting kiss on the cheek, he left the house.

'I fear that matters have taken a serious turn,' he said to Cornet Tripp. 'It would be better if you all came with me down into the village, but first I must visit the nearby farm of my tenant. There's been some trouble there.'

The young officer told his men to remount and they followed the Squire to the Goodway farm.

Mary Goodway was relieved to see Nathaniel, although somewhat alarmed that he was in the company of soldiers. She had obviously been crying.

'Oh Mr Pearson, sir. So glad you've come back. Thass been terrible. I'll fetch Silas. He's just around the sheds. Won't go too far from me today.'

'Yes, news of the troubles reached me, so I returned with these men to help restore order if that should be needed. Now my wife tells me that my daughter has been arrested, and I presume that your son has. It's about that matter I wish to talk with you and your husband before I go into the village. Pray hasten to bring him here.'

The woman scurried off and returned a few minutes later with her husband, Silas Goodway.

'Mr Pearson, sir. We was feared as how yer might think ill of us now that our Jeremy hev been arrested on a charge of fornication with your daughter,' said Silas, in apprehensive tones.

'Not of you Silas,' said the Squire. 'But I'd be disappointed in Jeremy were it true. However, I suspect the charge is trumped up by Mr Dowdy to discredit me as the father of Eve, and the one who used his influence to secure your son public employment. Nevertheless, I have to say that things look somewhat black. It appears they have some of my daughter's clothes; also a tunic belonging to Jeremy which they say he dropped in my garden when making his escape.'

'With your leave sir, that can't be,' said Mrs Goodway. 'Jeremy had but two tunics. The first was stolen two weeks ago an' the second we hev here.' She left the room to fetch the tunic Jeremy had brought home the day before. While she had gone, Nathaniel turned to Silas. 'Do you know under what circumstances his first tunic was stolen?'

'He said from outside the forge. It seem he went there to talk with the blacksmiss an' had to wait 'cos Samuel had a customer, so sat down to wait on a tree stump outside an' lay the tunic down. Then he say he changed his mind, an' went to talk with Sam's wife an' daughter instead, an' forgot to pick it up. Then, of all things, if he di'n't go an' forget it 'til he was part way home. Of course, by the time he went back for it, that was gone. I di'n't half tell him off for bein' so careless. We could ill afford a new 'un.'

Nathaniel grunted thoughtfully. 'I don't suppose he happened to say who the customer was with Mr Bloom when he arrived at the forge?'

'Yes. He say that was Mr Dowdy, an' thass why he went to see Mrs Bloom instead. He di'n't want to run into him. You surely don't think he could've took it?'

'Um. I should keep all thoughts like that out of your mind at the moment,' said the Squire. Then turning to Mrs Goodway, who had come in with Jeremy's other tunic and handed over for his inspection, 'Tell me, Mrs Goodway, did Jeremy's first tunic have his name sown in like this one?'

'Oh yes, Mr Pearson, sir,' she said nodding her head as he handed her back the garment.

'That means whoever took it and kept it knew they were stealing,' observed Nathaniel. 'Look. With my influence and these men behind me, I could release Jeremy and Eve by force and stop the charge being heard. But that wouldn't be in the interests of future good order. Far better they stand trial and, if it so pleases God, be found innocent. But there's much I don't like about what's going on. With the constable dead and his deputy struck down, whoever is guarding the bridewell doesn't have a right to do so. I'll try to put the village under military rule for the time being. But first I'll make a private call at the forge.'

He bade them 'Good day,' and returned to the soldiers waiting outside, addressing Cornet Tripp. 'In view of what I've learned, I now think it would be best if we entered the village separately. Our first task will be to arrest whoever is guarding the bridewell. If we go in together, they may be forewarned. I'll go alone first to see the blacksmith. Bide here for one third of an hour, then enter the village as if on a normal patrol. Come to the forge on the pretext of a loose shoe on one of your horses. I will look out for you and guide you to the bridewell.'

Tripp signified his consent, and Nathaniel mounted his horse and started out for the forge. On arrival the smithy was, as he expected, closed. So he went to the cottage and was admitted by a flustered Mrs Bloom. 'You'll be wantin' to see Samuel no doubt, sir? The poor dear hev been most sorely used, but reckon he'll be fit for work tomorrow or the next day.'

On seeing the Squire enter, Samuel made to rise from his chair, but Nathaniel, seeing his bruises and cuts, motioned him to stay. 'Pray remain seated Samuel. You need your rest. I merely called to see how you are and to seek information.'

'I'm farin' well enough now, Mr Pearson, sir, thanks be to God,' said the blacksmith. 'These wounds will fade in time. Maybe I can work the forge again as soon as tomorrow.'

'I wish you well. Now please relate to me the events of Monday.'

Samuel Bloom gave a detailed account as seen from his viewpoint up until the time he had been set upon and beaten up.

48

'Who started the riot?' asked Nathaniel.

'I don't rightly know, sir,' replied Samuel. 'It was like as if the riot outside started on a signal 'cos people were shoutin' "Burn the witch" inside the courthouse. The crowd was quiet afore that"

'You didn't witness the killing of the constable then?'

'No. That was arter I'd been beaten up.'

'Have you heard who guards the bridewell now. Is the deputy constable recovered?'

'No. The wife here heard in the village that he died last night.'

'So,' said Nathaniel, 'now we've two murders and an unlawful burning. And no doubt you've heard that my daughter and young Jeremy Goodway were arrested last evening. Although since both duly appointed law officers were dead, who might have felt he had the power to arrest I have yet to discover.'

'I know nothin' of the matter at first hand sir, bein' situated as I am, but here again the wife did get some rumour in the village.'

'There's just one more thing I will trouble you with,' said Nathaniel. 'Could you cast your mind back a couple of weeks to late on the Wednesday afternoon. I am told that young Jeremy Goodway had a tunic stolen from outside your forge.'

'Thass right. I remember it well. He come back arter he got part way home, and say he'd left his tunic on the grass outside by mistake an' it weren't there no more. It seem he'd called to see me earlier but I had a customer, so he waited a while, then went in to see the wife and Bessie.'

'So I've been told,' said Nathaniel. 'Tell me; who was the customer that was with you when he called first time?'

'Ole Dowdy. His hoss had gone lame with a stone.'

'Anyone else?'

'There weren't nobody else that day arter Mr Dowdy.'

'Did Mr Dowdy leave you at all while you were attending to his beast?'

Samuel thought for a moment. 'Come to think of it, he did. He was in a foul mood when he first come in. About the market bein' bad, an' his hoss. Then he ranted on about you an' how as you'd enclosed your top pasture an' he weren't gooner take no notice of it an' had jus' walked through it, an' all sorts of other nasty things. Then he left the smithy for a few minutes an' when he come back his mood had changed. He was calmer, nicer, insofar as an ole sod like him can be nice. Like he was pleased with his self.'

'I see,' said Nathaniel. 'Well thank you for your help. With the leave of Mrs Bloom and yourself I'll watch by your window for some visitors I'm expecting. As a member of the county committee, I feel it my duty to put the village under military jurisdiction until we get law and order restored.'

After a few minutes Nathaniel saw the soldiers stop outside the forge. He left the cottage to join them, mounted his horse and led them to the bridewell.

Seated outside on a stool was John Merton, husband of Ruth, pistol on lap. Merton was one of Nathaniel's labourers. He blanched at the sight of his employer.

'Who else guards this place?' demanded the Squire.

'The constable,' Merton replied.

'Where is he now?'

'Within.'

'Get him out,' demanded Nathaniel.

Merton tapped three times on the door. After a pause, came the scraping of two bolts being withdrawn. A heavy unkempt man peered out of the partly open door. At a signal from Nathaniel, two soldiers forced it fully open and pulled the man out to stand beside John Merton.

'Brentham is now under military jurisdiction. Who appointed you?' Nathaniel asked them.

'Mr Dowdy,' they both replied.

'Mr Dowdy can't appoint law officers. Only the justices can do that,' said Nathaniel. 'Were you among the party that arrested the prisoners inside?'

The men nodded.

'Then you committed an unlawful act,' said Nathaniel, sternly, 'and are likely to get your backs scratched at the post for your pains.' Then turning to Cornet Tripp he said, 'Arrest them and lock them within.'

The bridewell was a small building consisting of six cells; three on each side of a narrow passage. The first one to the right of the entrance had no door and was used as an office by either the constable or deputy when on duty. Realising that there would now only be one free cell and other arrests might be made, he toyed with the idea of finding Eve and Jeremy better accommodation but still secure. First he went to question his daughter.

After twenty-four hours in her cramped and dirty cell, Eve was depressed, unkempt, and tearful. She fell into her father's arms as soon as he had entered. Under his close questioning, she told all except the rape by Eli Brown and her killing of him, for that was a secret too dreadful to be shared with anyone.

Nathaniel was shocked. 'It does seem to me,' he said, 'although I have little doubt the charge against you is false, that you have brought this trouble upon your own head, and mine, and Jeremy's, by your unseemly behaviour. If I use my influence to stop the charge, you will be held to be at fault, and myself with you as the father of a wanton. If you are found guilty it would scarce be worse. Only by proving you innocent of this charge will matters be improved. I will see what can be done. Meanwhile you must bear the discomfort.'

He next went to talk with Jeremy, who assured him that he had never lain with Eve.

'That I believe, lad,' said Nathaniel. 'And 'tis most gallant of you not to mention that she tempted you to do so in the garden last week. She has already admitted that to me, and how she tore your tunic in a rage because you scorned her, and then had it mended. But it is of the loss of your first tunic I wanted to question you.'

Jeremy related the events surrounding the loss of his first tunic outside the forge.

'That agrees with what I have been told by your parents and the blacksmith. Which means that from last week until yesterday afternoon, you were without a tunic at all. Who else would have noticed that?'

'Mr Dowdy.'

'It wouldn't be in his interests to so admit. Anyone else?'

'Reverend Jones.'

'That may be worth something, but I would rather we had someone more reliable. In any case he'll have to preside.'

'The Marquess of Stourland knew,' said Jeremy.

'The Marquess of Stourland!' exclaimed Nathaniel. 'How so?'

Jeremy gave an account of his visit to the Marquess.

'Then I must try to see him in the morning,' said Nathaniel. 'Hopefully he will come to the trial and speak on your behalf. Now I have much to do and must leave you.'

On leaving the building Nathaniel bade Cornet Tripp to detach as many of his men that he deemed necessary to guard the bridewell night and day. Tripp left six.

The Squire then took Cornet Tripp and his remaining fourteen soldiers to the presbytery. Here he bade him select sufficient men to guard all entrances to the building and the adjacent courthouse night and day and to refuse entrance to Mr Dowdy, Mr Winscombe, and anyone else not having good reason to call, and to make his headquarters there.

Nathaniel waited while Tripp selected nine men for guarding the presbytery and courthouse, then knocked on the door. It was answered by a maid who admitted him along with Cornet Tripp and two soldiers and ushered them into the room where Jeremy used to work.

When Reverend Jones entered, Nathaniel addressed him with unusual crispness. 'Brentham is now under military jurisdiction. It will so remain until lawful order is restored and an investigation into the killing of the constable and his deputy and the unlawful burning of Rebecca Brown can be completed. Now pray show me the papers concerning the charges against my daughter and Jeremy Goodway.'

The pastor laid out the depositions of Dowdy and Winscombe and the book entry relating to the trial date, which Nathaniel was surprised to see was set for the next day.

Dowdy's deposition stated that the accused were caught in the summer-house and made much of the tunic. Tobias Winscombe's was much shorter, and did not mention the summer-house or the tunic. Neither mentioned the rape of Eve by Obadiah Dowdy.

'Whose idea was it that the trial should be at such short notice?' Nathaniel asked.

'Mr Dowdy's.'

'No doubt he sought to have the matter done while he expected me to still be away. It'll have to be changed to next Monday. See to it. And who was to preside at the court, pray?'

'Mr Dowdy himself I suppose,' replied Reverend Jones.

'This is just the trouble. He takes too much upon himself. You're the appointed divine for this parish as well as a magistrate. Except when I do it, it's your duty to preside over the parish court. Yet you seldom even attend it, leaving it mainly to myself. If I'm away, he presumes to lead, but he hasn't been appointed to do so and has no better standing than any other member of the committee. In any event, he cannot sit in judgement as well as be accuser. Neither can Mr Winscombe. Neither can I, being as I am, the father of one of the accused. You must preside and this cornet will be joint-president with you, unless I can find a more senior officer.'

Evening was now approaching, so Nathaniel suggested to Tripp that he attend to his billeting arrangements. For the six men at the bridewell, room could no doubt be found in the constable's house. The presbytery and courthouse together ought to be able to accommodate himself and the remaining fourteen soldiers.

On the way home Nathaniel reflected that with fifteen soldiers assigned to guard duties, only five were left for other emergencies. However the village seemed quiet so he thought he would wait until morning before deciding whether to send for more help. His thoughts then turned to the difference between the statements of Dowdy and Winscombe. Tobias Winscombe he had known for years and regarded as a harmless buffoon, not the sort to get involved in plots–unless of course Dowdy had some imagined hold over him. He decided to call on Tobias Winscombe.

Tobias blanched as he opened his door to find Nathaniel there, but invited him in. He was evasive answering the Squire's questions, especially when the summer-house was mentioned, and when asked if anything else happened.

'I'll leave you with this thought then, Tobias,' said Nathaniel. 'To tell the truth is the right and just thing you must do. However, to bring false charges before a court–even a parish court–is a crime so grave that, if discovered, would earn a fine so large that you are unlikely to be able to pay. Also a painful flogging. I believe the charge to be false, and that witnesses will prove it so. If there is aught then in what you have said or are going to say which is untrue think, while there is yet time to retract, on how deep the cat would sink into your fat flesh.'

With that Nathaniel left. For Tobias, there was to follow five nights with little or no sleep as he fretted and cursed the day he had met Obadiah Dowdy.

Back home Nathaniel went into his study. Mrs Pearson followed for she was anxious for news. He related to her what had transpired. 'There's little doubt that the charge is false,' he said. 'Eve has acted in a most unseemly fashion, so our best defence is to disprove the charge against Jeremy, for I'm certain that Dowdy stole his tunic from outside the forge two weeks ago. The evidence is not as firm as I would like, but we may have the Marquess of Stourland to help us there, which should carry some weight.'

'The Marquess!' exclaimed Mrs Pearson. 'By coincidence there's a letter here from him that was handed in on Monday evening.'

The Squire picked up the letter and as he looked for his paper knife, went on, 'But our best chance of all may be to break down Tobias Winscombe. Something is very wrong there. I saw him–he's nervous and ill at ease. Tomorrow I'll engage a lawyer from outside.'

He opened the letter from the Marquess, read it and exclaimed, 'Now of all things he asks our leave to pay court to Eve and consider him as a suitable husband!'

Mrs Pearson took the letter to read. 'But my dear, he's an old man,' she cried.

'Quite my dear, but after all this scandal she could do worse, although I would much rather there was no scandal and she married young Jeremy Goodway since Marcus has betrayed her. Clearly she's ripe for marriage.'

✳✳✳

The next day was a busy one for Nathaniel. First he sent a messenger up to Bury St Edmunds asking Cornet Tripp's commanding officer, Captain Williams, to favour him by coming to serve as joint-president of the court on Monday, because he felt that an older man would carry more weight with the more bigoted of the brethren that the youthful Tripp.

Next he called upon the Marquess of Stourland. The aristocrat had heard of Eve's arrest and as he entered the room where Nathaniel was waiting said, mistaking the purpose of the Squire's visit, 'Mr Pearson, you have come about my letter no doubt. I fear I must withdraw my interest in your daughter unless her innocence is proven, which I trust you will understand.'

'Indeed I do m'lord,' said Nathaniel, 'but it was not about that I called. It was about the visit to you by young Jeremy Goodway last Monday.'

The Marquess verified all that Jeremy had told Nathaniel, and that on Monday he had no tunic at all.

'Then m'lord I beg your indulgence that you will come to the court on Monday as a witness and say so?'

'That I'll do and gladly,' said the Marquess. 'But what use will it serve?'

'I truly believe that Dowdy stole the lad's tunic to use in this monstrous charge. His purpose is to discredit myself through my daughter, because he sees me as an obstacle in his path to power.'

'Yes,' said the Marquess, 'it does seem that he takes a lot upon himself. I refer to the letter from the parish committee that young Goodway brought.'

What did it contain, m'lord?'

'You mean you don't know!' exclaimed the Marquess. 'I'll fetch it for you. Meanwhile, pray take a glass of wine with me.' He rang for a servant to pour the wine, and left the room to fetch the letter.

As the two men sipped their wine, Nathaniel read Dowdy's letter. 'This is incredible!' he exclaimed. 'There's been no discussion about this in the parish committee. It is entirely Dowdy's idea. The man is totally power drunk.'

The men shook hands and Nathaniel left. He then rode into Sudbury to engage a lawyer.

CHAPTER 7

Brentham was peaceful for the remaining few days before the trial of Eve and Jeremy. Those of the commonalty who had so eagerly engaged in mob rule on Monday and Tuesday were overawed by the sight of the soldiers. Many, knowing they had done wrong, began to fear for the skin on their backs. Two or three feared for their necks, for they carried within them the knowledge that they had killed the constable and his deputy.

Those who were still idle on Wednesday, hoping for more trouble returned to their labours on Thursday.

The brethren who sat on the parish committee, were somewhat concerned, for they realised that what was to take place was not just a simple parish trial for fornication, a commonplace event, but the climax of a power struggle between Obadiah Dowdy and Nathaniel Pearson, the village Squire.

Those of their number who had sat in court in judgement on Rebecca Brown became very apprehensive. Too easily they had accepted Dowdy's persuasion to follow the will of the mob and agree to an unlawful burning. This was a matter that could, if vigourously followed up, lead them to the assizes.

Obadiah Dowdy heard news of the village being placed under military jurisdiction late on Wednesday evening. This came as a surprise to him and was the first inkling he had that things were not all going his way. On Thursday morning he tried to go to the parish office at the presbytery, but was barred by the soldiers on guard. After protesting strongly at this treatment, which he saw as unjust, he was allowed to enter a room in the private quarters of Reverend Jones.

The pastor came through from the office–he was somewhat flustered by events. Dowdy was seething. 'What's this nonsense, barred from entering the parish office?' he asked sourly.

Jones was still in awe of Dowdy, but with a keen eye to his own survival, as ever. 'Mr Pearson claims to be acting on behalf of the county committee, and has placed Brentham under military jurisdiction because there has been a breakdown in law and order, notably in the matter of the death of the constable and his deputy at the hands of a mob.'

'Am I supposed to be responsible for the actions of ruffians?' asked Dowdy.

The pastor thought that Dowdy could well have been responsible, but kept this opinion to himself. 'It's not for that reason you have been barred from entering the parish office,' he said. 'It's because you're one of the accusers in the forthcoming fornication trial, which has now been postponed until Monday. It's held that you cannot be both an accuser and sit in judgement, and therefore cannot serve as president of the court. Neither can you take any part in the trial preparation.'

'Who then is to serve as president, pray? Our so-called Squire, no doubt?' asked Dowdy.

'No. Here again he's ruled himself out from sitting in judgement as a person interested in the outcome, holding it to be unlawful. I myself am to serve as joint-president along with an army officer, because we are under military supervision to ensure that nothing unlawful takes place.' Jones was feeling uncomfortable and wished to bring the conversation to an end. 'Now, I beg you, leave me in peace, for with no clerk, all the preparation and much other labour falls on me. I have a letter here which I have just penned to you, setting out what I have just said. Now, perforce, I must busy myself in finding three brethren willing and qualified to sit in judgement in place of Mr Pearson, yourself, and Tobias Winscombe.'

Dowdy inwardly cursed the pastor as he left. He was well aware that Jones was skilled at protecting his own position, and had just given a masterly display of sitting on the fence. This meant that he was unsure of the outcome. Dowdy started to worry. He decided to call on each of the other brethren who would be sitting on the court.

This however did little to reassure him, and the best he could get even from his most staunch admirer was, 'But surely, brother Obadiah, it's only just that you cannot sit in judgement at the same time as being the accuser. If you know you've attested to the truth then there's naught for you to worry about.'

Clearly, everyone was looking to his own position. Lastly he called on Tobias Winscombe to stiffen his resolve.

'I do declare,' wailed the fat man, 'this matter has me worried. We know that we didn't see them fornicate. It matters not that we believed them to have done so. To be discovered to have given false testimony to the court will bring a terrible fine and maybe even the lash. Ought we not to withdraw the accusation whilst there is yet time?'

'Thou coward!' raged Dowdy. 'To withdraw now would still bring punishment. Smaller punishment, but punishment none the less–and loss of your standing as an elder of the congregation, for no man of worth will call a self-confessed liar friend.'

So Tobias was persuaded to hold on, for he was a weak character who found it easier to agree with the last person who spoke to him. He was in torment.

Nathaniel visited Eve again. She was firm that the incident with Obadiah Dowdy and Tobias Winscombe had been in the open and not in the summer-house. Nathaniel could not see why Dowdy should have embellished his lies with such a detail. It could be his undoing. Of course, there was no way of knowing if Dowdy had looked in there after Eve ran away, but it was worth a try if all else failed. He went again to speak with the lawyer he had engaged.

***

The parish court opened on Monday morning to greater public interest than usual. Some had commented on the fairness of the Squire for leaving his daughter in the bridewell until the trial. Captain Williams had come down to Brentham the previous evening with ten more men, of whom he was prepared to leave six when he returned, which he declared must be the next evening.

The trial began by Reverend Jones, as joint-president with Captain Williams asking Dowdy to speak his accusations. This he did with great glee and venom, generally following his written statement and adding emphasis here and there.

The lawyer engaged by Nathaniel made an intervention to ask Dowdy if he was mistaken by saying that the incident took place in the summer-house. Dowdy knew better than to alter his statement at this stage, but was irritated by the question.

'I've already written and said how I saw the girl in a state of near nakedness enter the summer-house, and the man cast off his tunic and follow her,' he snarled. It was a needless embellishment, he now realised, made out of jealousy and a desire to make the summer-house for ever odious to Nathaniel. He was surprised that his enemy had taken the unusual step of engaging a professional lawyer for a simple parish trial, and this added to his growing uncertainty of his position.

Tobias Winscombe was then asked to speak his accusation, which he did, displaying much nervousness, for he dreaded being asked about the summer-house because he knew that to be untrue, and had not mentioned it in his statement.

He was relieved when the lawyer did not mention the building, but merely intervened to ask if he was sure that he was with Obadiah Dowdy when he first laid hands on Eve. Tobias eagerly affirmed he was.

The wily lawyer knew what he was doing–allowing Tobias to keep an escape route to turn on his colleague and save himself.

Jeremy and Eve were now obliged to answer questions by their accusers who acted for themselves, in the person of Dowdy–Tobias Winscombe did not wish to ask questions. Jeremy denied being in the arbour that day and when challenged by Dowdy that he was seen entering the Pearson driveway shortly before the incident, answered truthfully that he had merely called to collect his tunic which had been mended by Eve's maid.

Eve did not deny that she had been bathing naked in the private lake on three occasions, but believed herself to be unseen. She truthfully denied ever having made love with Jeremy and said firmly that he had not been there that day. An awkward moment came when she had to make some sort of explanation of the circumstances leading to her offer to have Jeremy's tunic mended. She hoped fervently that Dowdy had not seen the earlier incident when she had enticed Jeremy into the arbour. Apparently he had not, for his demeanour showed that he realised he had missed something.

She was in some distress under Dowdy's questioning, but with difficulty refrained from complaining of rape by him at this stage. This was on the advice and insistence of Nathaniel's lawyer, who, with him had agreed plans of action as the case developed. The Squire was in no doubt that if the trial went against Eve and Jeremy, his own influence would be greatly reduced and Dowdy would be unstoppable. Eve, with her reputation already tarnished in the minds of the stricter Puritans, would not be believed on rape in the absence of an impartial witness, unless the charge of fornication was first proved to be false.

Dowdy felt a little disconcerted after questioning Jeremy and Eve. The lawyer's intervention, that he would be bringing forward witnesses about the loss of Jeremy's first tunic, was unexpected and had upset him. He decided to call back Tobias Winscombe for just one question, which he purposely framed in an non-specific manner. 'Did you, at my behest, pick the tunic up from the ground after I had apprehended the jezebel now accused, and bring it to me?'

'Yes indeed brother Obadiah,' replied Tobias. Fear showed on his face and perspiration ran from his brow. He was glad that Dowdy had not asked him which part of the arbour he picked the tunic up from, for the alleged lover had been said to have escaped out the front.

Dowdy indicated that he had finished with him, but Nathaniel's lawyer intervened. The fat man's fear had not escaped his keen eye. Now was the time to start the pressure. 'That was but a brief question your friend put to you. Pray tell us, what part of the arbour did you retrieve the tunic from?'

Tobias hesitated.

'Answer!' said the lawyer, sternly.

'N-Near the back hedge,' stammered Tobias.

'Ah!' exclaimed the lawyer. 'Would that perchance have been near the gap through which you spied on Miss Pearson?'

Tobias glanced fearfully towards Obadiah Dowdy.

'Answer!' shouted the lawyer.

'Yes.'

'Good. Now tell me. When you and your friend entered the Pearson garden to apprehend the girl and her supposed lover, why didn't you go through the gap?'

"Tis not a gap large enough for a man.'

'Not you of course,' said the lawyer, with mock jocularity, 'but what of your friend; he's a thin man?'

'No. Not even him. 'Tis but a place where the branches are thinner and might be bent by a small animal to get in or out.'

'Or a nosy fellow wishing to look in,' commented the lawyer, sarcastically. 'Then from what you say, the supposed lover could not have escaped through there–but of course, your friend has already stated in his deposition that he escaped through the front entrance to the arbour. This means that, since the alleged fornication took place in the summer-house, the lover, in his panic to escape, ran a circuit of the arbour and dropped his tunic by the hedge. Do you know Jeremy Goodway well?'

'Yes,' said Tobias.

'Then you wouldn't have had trouble recognising him as he ran around the arbour in his panic?'

Tobias hesitated

'Answer!' said the lawyer, sharply.

'No,' admitted Tobias.

'You had but little to say in your deposition. Merely that you were there and supported Mr Dowdy in his charges. Since he has stated that he saw Jeremy Goodway, that means, if he has been truthful, that you also saw him, does it not?'

'I thought so,' said Tobias, nervously, unable to think of a better answer.

'Don't lie,' roared the lawyer. 'You either saw him or you didn't–this young man who you've already said you'd recognise as he ran around the arbour. You didn't see him at all, did you, Tobias Winscombe?'

'No. I was concentrating on the girl,' said Tobias, weakly.

'You didn't see him because he wasn't there, Mr Winscombe,' said the lawyer, firmly. 'Did aught else happen before you entered the garden–any small detail?'

'I can think of nothing,' replied Tobias, now in a fearful sweat.

'How was it that you went to the gap that day?' asked the lawyer, less harshly.

'Mr Dowdy came to my shop and bade me hurry. He had seen young Mr Goodway enter the Pearson's front driveway and supposed that an act of fornication would take place between him and Miss Pearson.'

'In other words, he wanted you as a witness?'

'Yes.'

'Why do you suppose he thought an act of fornication was going to take place in the arbour?' asked the lawyer.

'Because we had seen Miss Pearson there in a state of nakedness six days before, when her father was away, and he knew him to be away on that occasion.'

'Was that day, six days before, the first time you, yourself had looked through the gap?' asked the lawyer.

'Yes.'

'Who pointed it out to you?'

'Mr Dowdy.'

'Indeed! For what reason?'

'He bade me go and look at the arbour with its lake and summer-house that Mr Pearson had constructed for the leisure of his family.'

'And this also on a working day,' said the lawyer. 'You were taken from your labours, out of your way, just to trespass on enclosed pasture and spy into Mr Pearson's private arbour. Did this time-consuming journey have any other purpose?'

Tobias did not like that question, and hesitated long in trying to formulate an answer.

The lawyer grew tired of waiting. 'Your silence speaks louder than any answer you might invent, Tobias Winscombe. For the present I've finished with you, but I feel that you haven't been wholly truthful, and I may want to ask you further questions if necessary. Meanwhile I beg you to reflect on the terrible consequences of bringing false accusations and telling falsehoods to a court, not only at the hands of men, but on the day of judgement before God. Did aught else happen just before you went into the garden and arbour that we should know about?'

Tobias was in torment and on the point of saying that he had seen Dowdy push the tunic through the gap, but fear of him if he was not believed and the case was proven, restrained him. He wished fervently that he had not become involved. 'I can think of nothing,' he lied.

'Very well,' said the lawyer, 'but mark this. To fail to remember something important, if discovered, may be considered as great a falsehood as an untruth directly told. Take care to mitigate the peril of your situation while there is yet time.'

The lawyer next called Naomi to give evidence that on the afternoon of the alleged fornication, Jeremy had merely collected his second, repaired, tunic from her hand at the front door and left through the front driveway. 'Miss Eve was too upset 'cos of the burnin' of Rebecca Brown that mornin' to receive visitors,' she explained.

Next he called Silas and Mary Goodway in turn who both confirmed that two weeks before the alleged fornication, Jeremy had reported the theft of his first tunic outside the forge. Also that on the day the charge referred to he had come home early and arrived at a time earlier than the fornication was supposed to have taken place.

Dowdy rose to his feet to disparage the testimony of these three witnesses. 'The personal maidservant of the Pearson girl is bound to try and protect the honour of her young mistress,' he claimed. 'Likewise the parents of the prisoner Goodway are likely to protect the honour of their son.'

The lawyer said in exasperation. 'I declare, this fellow doth seek to discount the testimony of these three witnesses because they are of humble status, preferring to ignore the fact that they are of good character. So now I call someone of noble rank.'

He then put up the Marquess of Stourland, who confirmed that when Jeremy called to see him the day before the alleged fornication he had no tunic at all, and had related how the first one had been stolen outside the forge nigh two weeks before.

When he had finished, Dowdy jumped to his feet. 'Now, it seems, we are expected to take the word of a Royalist. In any case, he only relates what the prisoner Goodway told him. Goodway could have made up the theft story.'

The lawyer next put up the blacksmith, Samuel Bloom.

'When did you know of the loss of Jeremy Goodway's first tunic?'

'Reckon that must hev been less than an hour arter it went missin'.'

'Tell us about it?' asked the lawyer.

Samuel related in detail how Jeremy came back to look for his tunic just as he was leaving off, and how earlier he had been in the cottage with Mrs Bloom and Bessie.

'Who was the customer who was with you while Jeremy Goodway waited at the tree stump?' enquired the lawyer.

'Mr Dowdy.'

'Was he your last customer that afternoon?'

'Yes.'

'Did you suggest any course of action to Jeremy Goodway?'

'Yes. I said he should report it to the constable, Mr Stark.'

'Do you know if he did so?'

'Reckon he did, 'cos Hermon Stark come round to ask me an' the missus about it.'

The lawyer was now finished with Samuel. Once more, Obadiah Dowdy rose to his feet, not to ask questions, but to belittle the blacksmith's evidence..

'Here we have a fellow who has already tasted the lash in his early days for contempt of those in authority. Are we to believe him? In any case the Blooms and the Goodways are friends who will stick together, and yet again I say, the prisoner Goodway could have made up the story of the theft of his tunic.'

The lawyer then indicated that his wished to ask questions of Dowdy himself.

'Obadiah Dowdy. You could have questioned each of my last five witnesses, but chose not to do so, preferring instead to attack the viability of what they said upon one excuse or another. As the last four dealt with the theft of Jeremy Goodway's tunic, I presume that you don't hold this particular matter to be of any account?'

'No,' answered Dowdy. 'I've already said that I consider the whole story of the theft of Goodway's first tunic to be a lie invented by him.'

'When did you first hear that the tunic was believed to have been stolen?'

'Not until today in this court?'

'But I believe it was known to many people in Brentham?' observed the lawyer as a question.

'I'm a busy man in the service of God and this parish, with no time to listen to gossip.'

'Indeed. So you hadn't heard of it?'

'No.'

'Obadiah Dowdy,' said the lawyer, sternly. 'I've already warned your friend, Tobias Winscombe, of the perils of telling falsehoods, and now warn you also. Would it surprise you to learn that our late constable, Mr Stark, was a most meticulous man who wrote all his daily business in a private journal, and in that journal is recorded not only the visit to the blacksmith that Mr Bloom has told us about, but visits to others on the matter, including one to you? The journal is here for you to see.' He pushed the open book towards Dowdy, who was momentarily speechless, for he knew that he had been caught out in a lie.

'Twas but a brief meeting which seemed of little moment and was soon gone from my mind.'

The lawyer brought his open hand down on his desk in exasperation. 'Faith, but this fellow compounds a lie with a feeble excuse.' Then turning to face the joint-presidents said, 'I feel that I have well established the innocence of Jeremy Goodway because he was not there, and pray that you accept this. If you do, then from that flows the obvious; namely that Eve Pearson must also be innocent.'

At this, Dowdy intervened furiously. He realised that his charge against Jeremy was collapsing. That he could survive; but if the case against Eve was lost then he himself would be lost. 'I protest against this argument,' he shouted. 'If it be true that Goodway's tunic was stolen, and I don't accept that it was, it doth but mean that I've mistaken the identity of the lover. My charge against the Pearson girl is sound. She doesn't deny that we came upon her unclothed, and witness that we have all the clothes that she had taken off.'

The panel considered these arguments, and Reverend Jones announced their decision. 'It is accepted that the charge against the prisoner Goodway is not sufficiently proved, and he must be released. However, the charge against Eve Pearson, although weakened by this decision, needs a more robust defence, and her innocence must be more firmly established, and not rest entirely upon the apparent innocence of Jeremy Goodway.'

The lawyer returned to his examination of Dowdy. 'So you now accuse Miss Pearson of fornication with an unknown lover. I will ask you the same question that I asked your friend, Tobias Winscombe. You knew Jeremy Goodway well. Is it likely that you'd have mistaken his identity as he made his alleged wild circuit of the arbour?'

Dowdy could feel the trap closing, and spat out his answer. 'No, it's not likely. It's this court that has discharged Goodway, not me.'

'In your deposition you tell of three occasions when you spied upon Miss Pearson bathing naked. What did you think the first time?'

'That she was a jezebel with such conduct.'

'Didn't you feel that you should have told her father?'

'I considered it.'

'Why didn't you?'

Dowdy was stuck for an answer.

'Perhaps the reason was that you hoped to turn this knowledge to your own advantage at a later date,' said the lawyer. 'Now; on the second occasion that you spied on Miss Pearson, you had Tobias Winscombe with you. You took him purposely?'

'No, we just happened by.'

'Indeed. From where did you come and where were you bound that you should "just happen" to trespass across enclosed land?' asked the lawyer, sarcastically.

'From his shop to the church,' replied Dowdy.

'A pretty detour,' observed the lawyer, drily. 'It would have been nigh four times shorter to go to the church through the main street. Why did you squander so much time?'

'I had much business to talk over with Mr Winscombe.'

'How so, a tailor and a butcher? What is the common business interest?'

'Not our business, but God's.'

'Explain please?' demanded the lawyer.

Dowdy felt himself being cornered, and did not hesitate to let Tobias down. 'I had earlier espied him lusting after women, and wished to talk to him about this sinful practice, especially as he was a member of the committee of the brethren.'

In his seat, Tobias felt very small. He believed all eyes to be on him. All his acquiescence in Dowdy's plotting had been for naught.

The lawyer went on. 'From this answer I believe that you were seeking to coerce Mr Winscombe into being your witness in these false charges. Your real target in all this has been Mr Pearson, has it not? You don't say in your deposition why you felt you had the right to cross private enclosed land, nor why you went out of your way to spy into his private arbour in the first place.'

At this, Dowdy lost his temper and started a tirade against Nathaniel for enclosing his own pastures like the aristocracy and creating an arbour.

The lawyer stood by and let this ill-tempered display continue until it burnt itself out, then continued. 'That pretty speech shows more clearly than any questions I might ask, your utter hatred and jealousy of Mr Nathaniel Pearson. Had you chosen to, you could have told him about his daughter, but you stored this knowledge up until you could find a witness to aid you in making trouble. When Jeremy Goodway carelessly left his tunic outside the forge, I believe you stole it to assist you in this monstrous charge of fornication. What better way to attack the man you hated, but to disgrace his daughter and the young man he had recommended for employment by the parish?,

'A dastardly lie and wild conjecture,' snarled Dowdy.

'I've finished with you for now, but will want to ask you another question or two later,' said the lawyer.

He next put up Nathaniel. 'You've heard Mr Dowdy rail against you at great length for starting the enclosure of your pasture. By what right did you do that?'

'Because it was never common land as such, and has been in our family for hundreds of years. The right of the public to graze their beasts on it was always supposed to be restricted to the lower half next to the church, and against proper payments, an arrangement made many years ago by my forbears. It's because the public have been using the whole of the pasture without permission, and payments are in serious arrears–some for years–that I enclosed it. A fence is under construction to mark the public limit. When that is completed, public grazing will again be permitted against current payments and sound undertakings to pay something off arrears over a period of time.'

'Your daughter has admitted to bathing and sunning herself in a state of nakedness on three occasions during your absence. What do you think of that?'

'I deplore it and have already admonished her, and will do so again, but in fairness to her, I must say that she did it in a private enclosed arbour where no visitors are allowed, or servants, except to maintain it when not in use.'

'So she had every right to presume herself unseen by human eye?'

'Yes.'

'Now. What of the wicket gate?'

'That's further forward than the arbour and for the sole use of our family, since it opens on to private pasture land.'

'So when Mr Dowdy and Mr Winscombe entered that gate they were trespassing on private property?'

'Yes. As they also were when they broke through the newly-planted hedge to gain access to the pasture.'

The lawyer thanked Nathaniel and said he was finished with him. He then addressed the joint-presidents. 'I now wish to finish hearing witnesses by asking an identical question of each of the accusers, starting with Mr Winscombe. It's important that they do not hear one another's answers.'

After some discussion this was agreed, and Captain Williams bade Cornet Tripp to have two soldiers take Dowdy outside and wait with him.

This being effected, Tobias came forward, with sinking heart, to be questioned again. The lawyer gave him a long cold stare. 'Your friend Mr Dowdy didn't forbear to tell of your lusting after women, in spite of your loyalty to him in these monstrous charges,' he said, drily. 'When I asked you earlier if aught happened just before you entered the arbour, you replied that you could think of nothing. I don't hold that to be true, for I believe you were protecting Mr Dowdy. Now you must wonder if it was worth it.

'I'm now going to ask you a question, and later ask Mr Dowdy the same question. Much hangs on whether your answers tally. In his deposition, Mr Dowdy stated that he saw the alleged lovers enter the summer-house and caught them there. In your own deposition you stated that you were with him the whole time. Describe the inside of the summer-house; the colour of its walls; the nature of its furnishings?'

Tobias knew that this was the end; that he must confess and take the consequences. Fear engulfed him. His whole frame trembled and tears welled up in his eyes. With his hands clasped before him as in prayer, he looked towards the joint-presidents. 'This is a question I can't answer, for I was not in the summer-house. Neither was Mr Dowdy. The charges are false and I needs must throw myself on your mercy.'

'Tell all,' invited the lawyer. 'Tell all. Even at this late stage.'

Through his sobs, Tobias told all, including how Dowdy had pushed the tunic through the gap into the arbour just before they entered it, and about the rape of Eve by Dowdy.

When, at length he had finished, Captain Williams told Cornet Tripp to have two soldiers take him outside and wait, and have Dowdy brought back in.

'Just one question, Mr Dowdy,' said the lawyer. 'You stated in your deposition that the alleged lovers entered the summer-house, the girl in a state of nakedness, and that you caught them there. Describe the inside of the summer-house; the colour of its walls; the nature of its furnishings?'

Dowdy knew that he was trapped, but here were no tears, no pleas for mercy. Defiant to the end, he snarled, 'Engaged upon the Lord's work, catching those lost in fornication, am I supposed to notice such trifling details?'

'You can't answer because you were not in the summer-house. That, like the rest of this monstrous charge is untrue. Your associate, Tobias Winscombe, has decided at last to tell the truth about what happened. I'll read you what he said.' He motioned to his clerk, who handed him his notes, and he read aloud the confession that Tobias had made to the court.

While he was reading, Dowdy's face went into contortions as he worked himself up into a rage which exploded as soon as the lawyer had finished; against Tobias, against Nathaniel, against the court, against Eve, and against Jeremy.

At a signal from Captain Williams, one of the soldiers, struck Dowdy across the mouth the stop the tirade.

'I now ask for Eve Pearson to be released,' said the lawyer. This was immediately agreed.

There was then a hurried conference between the joint-presidents and the brethren sitting in judgement, after which Captain Williams bade Cornet Tripp to have Tobias Winscombe brought back in.

On behalf of the court, Reverend Jones then addressed the erstwhile accusers. 'This court will now break until 2.30 o'clock this afternoon. At that time, you, Obadiah Dowdy, will be tried for bringing a false charge and giving false evidence. Also the rape of Eve Pearson, and the theft of a tunic belonging to Jeremy Goodway. You, Tobias Winscombe, will be tried for aiding Obadiah Dowdy in the bringing of a false charge and giving false evidence.'

The time was then shortly after noon. Nathaniel used the break to good effect. Over luncheon with Captain Williams, who was staying swith him, the subject of future good order in Brentham was discussed. 'I feel,' he said, 'that we've no chance of tying Dowdy in directly with the death of the constable. In the matter of the unlawful burning of Rebecca Brown, we could bring a charge, and that would seem just. However, we'd have to charge others among the brethren as well. This would lead to more discord and strife, when what Brentham needs is peace and good order. The unfortunate woman had no kindred in the area. It would be better if the matter were quietly overlooked. What's needed for the good order of the parish is to get rid of Dowdy altogether–to break him and make it impossible for him to live here.'

Captain Williams said that he would argue those points when it came to discussing sentences.

✳✳✳

The court reassembled in the afternoon at the appointed time for the trial of Obadiah Dowdy and Tobias Winscombe. Proceedings were short. The confession that Tobias had made in the morning was read out again. Eve made formal complaint of rape against Dowdy. Jeremy related once more how he had lost his tunic, and identified it. Both men were judged guilty, and the panel retired to consider sentences.

When they returned, it was clear from the faces that one man was not happy. Obadiah Dowdy was still not without friends, albeit now in secret. Reverend Jones pushed the papers in front of Captain Williams, as if he could not bear to read Dowdy's sentence.

'Obadiah Dowdy' said the captain, *'you have been judged guilty of having brought a false charge, and giving false testimony. For this you are sentenced to forfeit all your property and money, save for the clothes you wear and the sum of two pounds. You are also to receive one hundred lashes at the whipping post.'*

There were gasps in the court.

Captain Williams continued. *'For the rape of Miss Eve Pearson of which you have been found guilty, you will receive one hundred lashes at the whipping post. For the theft of a tunic belonging to Jeremy Goodway you will also receive one hundred lashes at the whipping post.'*

Dowdy lost what little colour he had at hearing his fate and at first did not realise that the captain had not finished speaking.

'Your deeds have been so foul that you are also excluded from ever serving on the committee of this parish again, from holding any public office, or carrying on any trade in Brentham. The whipping sentences will be indefinitely suspended if you enter into a voluntary agreement to exile yourself permanently from Brentham. But if you make the agreement and then at any future date come back to Brentham at all, the whipping sentences will be carried out. You have until 9 o'clock tomorrow morning to make your choice. Meanwhile you will be held in the bridewell.'

Captain Williams then pushed the papers back to Reverend Jones for the sentencing of Tobias Winscombe.

'Tobias Winscombe,' said Jones, 'you have been judged guilty of having aided Obadiah Dowdy in bringing a false charge and of giving false testimony. For this you could have been sentenced to forfeit all your property and money and receive one hundred lashes into the bargain. However, we are satisfied that you were not the chief plotter. Therefore, half these punishments would be appropriate–namely half your worth and fifty lashes. You have earned further mitigation by the help you gave the court with your confession. In reward for that we are cutting those sentences in half again, so you will forfeit one quarter of your total worth and receive just twenty-five lashes at the whipping post. You are disbarred from ever serving again on the parish committee or holding public office, but you will be allowed to continue trading. Whipping will be carried out after 9 o'clock tomorrow morning. Meanwhile you will be held in the bridewell.'

***

Tobias in his cell, laid awake worrying about the dreaded cat o' nine tails that he must suffer, and the money he must forfeit, but resolved to work hard to make good his name again.

In his cell, Dowdy raged inwardly. He had no choice but to leave Brentham. Three-hundred lashes would probably kill him if he stayed. In any case, now more or less a pauper and forbidden to trade in the parish, how would he live? He vowed revenge, somehow, sometime, on Jeremy, on the jezebel Eve Pearson, on Nathaniel Pearson, and on that cowardly fool and turncoat Tobias Winscombe. He would never forgive or forget.

CHAPTER 8

In the Pearson household there was a mixture of relief and regret. Relief at having Eve home and regret over her tarnished reputation, for although Dowdy's allegations had been proved false, many thought that she had brought the problems on herself by behaving in an unseemly fashion. There were even some who believed that her admission of naked bathing proved that she was in temperament, little better than a harlot.

Nathaniel had promised the court that he would admonish his daughter and he was going to keep his promise. He had not been in the habit of beating his offspring much when they were young, and his riding crop had not been used for that purpose in many a year. There was some discussion on the morning following the trial, between him and his wife, as to whether it was right for him to beat a daughter as old as nineteen, or whether Mrs Pearson should do it. However, the lady was of too gentle a temperament to undertake such a task, so it was decided that Nathaniel should administer ten strokes while his wife stood by.

Eve was waiting in her room after breakfast the following morning, as commanded by her parents, when she heard their footfalls outside her door. Although she had been pampered the previous evening, following her release, she did not expect to escape without some form of family punishment, and had steeled herself for a possible beating when they entered–her father with riding crop and a letter in his hand.

'I cannot think how long it will take for you, or indeed for any of us, to live this sorry matter down,' he said to her, sternly. 'The only satisfactory thing to emerge is that we have destroyed the charlatan Dowdy. Your own repute is but little better than had you been judged guilty. I've here a letter from the Marquess of Stourland which came while I was away, asking for your hand in marriage. He later said that he wished to withdraw the offer, pending the outcome of the trial. What he thinks now I don't know. Of course, it may well be that one so young as you would not wish to wed so old a man, and I wouldn't force you to do so, but I know not with what decent and well placed young man I'm to pair my daughter, she having a tarnished reputation. So if he asks again, it may be worth your while to consider it–unless of course you want young Jeremy Goodway. That's below your station in life, but he's a likeable lad and I could perhaps advance him. As yet he's too young so it would be in the future, meanwhile I have an unpleasant but necessary duty to perform. Your mother and I have decided that you are to receive ten strokes with this riding crop. Let it be a lesson not to deceive us in future. Will you now bend over.'

Eve did as she was bidden and Nathaniel turned away while his wife lifted her daughter's clothing until there was only one layer protecting her buttocks for the sake of modesty, and told him he could turn back.

He raised the crop and with a swish brought it down with modest force. Eve let out a little cry followed by a gasp, and as the following blows fell, the pain for her was overlaid with pleasure as she felt a sensuous wetness between her legs. Then it was over and Nathaniel left the room while Mrs Pearson inspected the weals on her buttocks.

'I'll send Naomi to put ointment on those,' she said as she left the room.

Eve lay on her bed. There were tears from the shock of being punished by her father who had always been so kind and gentle to her, but the shock was mingled with rising desire from the flagellation. Her hand went between her legs and pleasure rose to new heights as she stroked herself within the lips of her vulva.

In imagination she was being loved first by Marcus then by Jeremy in turn, both with the force of Eli Brown. As she swam through waves of pleasure, she was oblivious to everything and her cries were mistaken by Naomi as permission to enter the room in answer to her knock. As her shattering climax subsided, she realised that Naomi was standing inside the room, blushing with embarrassment. She however relished the pleasure she had just given herself and was not embarrassed. Holding out her hand, she bid the maid walk towards her. When the girl came close, Eve took her hand in her own, drew her face down and kissed her gently on the lips. Naomi drew back a little in alarm, but Eve smiled up at her and turned over to receive her ministrations with the ointment.

As Naomi's hands gently stroked the weals on her buttocks whilst applying the ointment, Eve felt desire well up in her once more. Quite by accident, the girl's finger-tips touched where the base of her buttocks joined the tops of her legs in the proximity of her anus. The intensity of the thrill this sent to her genitals she could only liken to the thrill from a male phallus as it makes first contact with the vulva lips. She could feel moistness exit copiously from her. Suddenly she turned on to her back and pulling Naomi towards her, kissed her hard and long on the mouth, forcing her lips apart with her tongue and exploring deep inside.

Naomi was at first shocked, but by now had started to feel the first waves of desire herself. But she was frightened for she was but a young virgin girl, and when the kiss at length ended, she started to draw back. 'Oh, Miss Eve, I beg of yer,' she pleaded. 'This is wrong. I know I'm your servant, but don't force me to do this.'

'But Naomi, even if you are still virgin, you are at an age when you must feel these desires. Surely when you look upon young men you must wonder what they are like under their clothing?'

The girl blushed and nodded her head. She did not resist further as Eve drew her close once more, saying, 'Come. Don't be frightened,' she loosened her top clothing to expose the maid's firm young bosom, already with erect nipples.

Eve then loosened her own bodice and pulled out her more voluptuous

69

breasts. Turning the now pliant Naomi on to her back, she leaned over her until their bosoms touched nipple to nipple. Swaying gently side to side, she knew her maid was getting excited. Lowering her mouth to one of the girl's breasts, she first of all flicked the nipple with her tongue, then licked gentle circles around it just as she remembered Marcus doing to her some eighteen months before. She heard Naomi's breathing get heavier and started to gently suck her nipple.

'Now do that to me.' she said, and the girl, now thoroughly excited, did her best to imitate.

Eve then embraced her once more and kissed her hard and long. This time Naomi responded and as they exchanged tongue for tongue, Eve gently raised the girl's clothing and worked her hand between her legs, gently massaging her vulva lips.

'Do the same to me,' she commanded Naomi.

At first the girl hesitated, so with her free left hand she took her maid's right and guided it between her own legs. Before long they both exploded in simultaneous climax–for Naomi the first time in her life. Eve then kissed her again, this time more gently. The girl was crying. She spoke softly to her. 'Naomi, our bodies need men, that is natural, but they keep us from men, so we must needs amuse ourselves.'

Naomi got off the bed, attended to her clothing and started towards the door.

'Naomi,' Eve called to her. The girl stopped and turned. 'Come to my room tonight at midnight when the household is asleep.'

The maid smiled and nodded, then incongruously curtsied out of habit. Eve was, after all, her mistress. Eve knew she now had a fresh outlet for her desires.

***

Jeremy returned to his duties in the parish office at the presbytery. Reverend Jones, the pastor, was determined now to maintain a more active role in the administration of day to day affairs of the parish. He realised that the scandal of Dowdy's abuse of power had shown himself as a weak character, and if he was to maintain his position he must restore the confidence of the congregation that elected him. Jeremy was glad of this change and relieved that he would no longer have to take orders from Obadiah Dowdy. He settled down to work with a will, although he realised that sooner or later another strong personality from among the brethren would emerge as their unofficial substitute leader due to the frequent absences of Mr Person on county affairs.

Jeremy also knew Dowdy was still not without the odd friend or two among the stricter of the brethren who felt that he had been harshly punished, and that these men had antipathy towards himself. These were in general those brethren and their families hostile towards Eve.

***

Obadiah Dowdy turned after walking about two hundred yards from the

70

boundary of Brentham at the first bend in the road. The two soldiers who had escorted him to the village limits were still watching his progress. This was as he hoped, because he had asked to be set out on the road to Sudbury. He did not doubt that he would be spied on for the first few miles, and he wanted to give the impression he was making his way to London to start a new life.

But he was a man with hatred in his heart, bent upon revenge against four people. That morning he had stood by the whipping post and had the satisfaction of hearing Tobias Winscombe scream as he received his twenty-five lashes. But he was determined that the cowardly turncoat should suffer more at his hands for his betrayal–someday, sometime, along with the others.

Then he had been asked to make his choice, and he had entered into an agreement for his own voluntary exile from Brentham for all time. He was allowed to take a clean spare set of under-linen, a spare suit, food for one day and three pounds in money. By stealth he managed to secret some small hand tools, a large piece of soft leather, and a piece of russet-brown cloth in his baggage, along with a few sundries such as yarn and buttons.

He did not doubt as he entered the town of Sudbury that his progress would be noted and reported back to Brentham, but once he crossed the River Stour just outside the town, he would be in the county of Essex. Making a point of crossing and taking the road that led to Braintree and London was all part of the deception he planned. He was conscious of the fact that he was little better than a pauper now, and survival was his most pressing priority. Both this and revenge, he considered, would be more readily achieved by not moving too far from the area, whilst giving the impression that he had done so.

About six miles or so south-west after crossing the river, making sure no one saw him, he turned off the road and entered a small forested area to his left. Picking his way through the trees and bushes, he came to a clear area near the other side of the wood with a stream running through. It was now near to two o'clock in the afternoon, so he sat down and ate a little of the food he had brought with him.

The nearby fields were deserted, so no one was likely to disturb him in his next strange activity. Taking the soft leather and russet-brown cloth from his baggage, he proceeded to make himself breeches, tunic and soft hat. By sundown he was finished and well satisfied with his work and ate the remainder of his food. Having packed his normal black clothes and hat in his baggage, he lay down to sleep in his newly created attire, assured that he would now pass for any country craftsman as he made his way. It now remained to attend to having his hair cut and think of a new name. Obadiah Dowdy had ceased to exist, at least for the time being.

He rose early in the morning, washed in the brook and drank of its water, shaved and rough-cut his hair as best he could. Taking the rising sun

71

as his guide, he struck out in an easterly direction until he arrived once more at the River Stour where it changes once more from its south-south-east course and resumes its flow eastward.

In spite of the sun he had been obliged to divert from a straight line several times, so it was around noon by the time he located the south bank of the river. He was now hungry and thirsty but judged it wise to avoid human contact yet if possible, so resisted the temptation to divert into a nearby village to buy bread and ale. Instead he prayed to the Almighty to give him strength as he followed the eastward course of the Stour on the Essex side keeping as near to the bank as possible. Progress was slow, but before sunset he was within sight of the large village of Dedham. Here he decided to rest by a hayrick for the night, and for his sustenance chewed grass and drank from the river.

In the morning he needed to waste a little time before entering the village, so busied himself tidying his appearance after his cross-country trek.

Soon after nine o'clock he entered Dedham and found himself a barber, for he now needed to finish having his hair cut. Like so many of his kind, the barber was an inquisitive fellow who indulged in much chatter, throwing in the odd question or two aimed at finding out who the stranger was.

Dowdy grew tired of this. 'I do declare, but you're a nosy fellow,' he said with asperity. 'I did but come in here to have my hair cut, not to be plied with idle gossip and questions. But since you are so inquisitive I'll tell you my name and condition, in the hope that you'll then pursue your craft with greater despatch. My name is Joshua Harding and I'm a new assistant to Mr Matthew Hopkins of Mistley, where I am now bound. I'm in great haste because I said I would arrive there before noon, and I'm in great hunger because I had to leave Needham Market this morning at crack of dawn, without breakfast, because some knave had stolen my horse.'

At the mention of the name of the witchfinder general the barber became obsequious. 'Indeed sir, I crave your forgiveness, but from your attire I didn't know . . .'

'My attire is none of your concern,' snapped Dowdy.

The barber was now keen to make amends. 'Indeed it isn't, sir, but you shall not go hungry. I'll bid my wife set you a breakfast to eat when I'm finished. Also I'll saddle my mare for you while you eat. You can borrow her. She's old but will carry you quicker and in more comfort to complete your journey. I'll walk to Mistley next Sabbath in the afternoon to bring her back.'

With that he went out of the door to make arrangements with his wife, and returned a few moments later to continue working.

Dowdy's spirits rose at this, and as he ate the meal provided, he hoped that Matthew Hopkins would give him the employment that he had told the barber he already had. 'If not,' he told himself, 'I'll simply steal this garrulous fool's horse and go somewhere else.'

Matthew Hopkins was working in a back room of the Thorn Inn that he used for his business affairs, when his ostler rapped on the open door. 'What is it?' he snapped.

'A fellow, name of Joshua Hardin' is askin' to see yer', replied the ostler.

The witchfinder paused a moment to think. He knew no one of that name, but his instinct for cunning told him that this was something which might be better if not generally known. He sighed and adopted a forced demeanour of resignation. 'And how does he conduct himself today? Is he clean and sober?'

'Indeed he is,' replied the ostler. 'Quite sober an' clean, an' dressed like a country craftsman of good standin'. He spoke in the manner of one who hev a right to call.'

'Which indeed he does,' replied Hopkins with a forced smile. 'Bring him in.'

While the ostler was gone he checked the loaded and primed pistol that he always kept near at hand. He did not know a Joshua Harding, but he had many enemies, and a man like himself had always to be on the look out for his own safety.

The ostler ushered Dowdy in, then left at a wave if dismissal from his employer. Hopkins stared at Dowdy and felt he ought to know the vaguely familiar face. 'Your name is not Joshua Harding, for I don't know any man of that name. Yet I have encountered you somewhere in the past.'

'I'm Obadiah Dowdy of Brentham near Sudbury in Suffolk,' said his visitor.

'Ah! Of course,' exclaimed the witchfinder. 'Now I recognise you. But your appearance has greatly changed. Why the disguise and false name?'

Dowdy related the events in Brentham since the burning of Rebecca Brown.

'I do declare, you look in fine condition for a man who has recently received three-hundred lashes,' remarked Hopkins. 'Many of your age would have died under such a punishment.'

'But the flogging was suspended on condition that I entered into a voluntary agreement to exile myself from Brentham. Since they had confiscated most all my possessions and prohibited me from trading, there was nothing else I could do but agree.'

Hopkins let out a chuckle. 'So in seeking to become the first you became the last, as it says in the scriptures. But what do you want of me?'

'I did your bidding over the burning of Rebecca Brown, a matter for which I might even yet be called to account if it was known I was still fairly near. Now that I'm nigh to being impoverished, I ask your help in giving me protection and employment.'

The witchfinder general thought for a moment, stroking his beard. 'It would not be about the tavern that you sought employment of course, but in my work in cleansing the country round about of witches?'

Dowdy indicated his assent.

'You can assist me from time to time in the ferreting out of witches. It will not be regular, and the payment may be slight, but your bed and bread will be secure. For other money, well, I hear that you are a tailor by trade. I will let you a small workroom cheaply at the rear of these premises, where with industry, you can earn more.

'Tomorrow I go to Colchester castle for the day. You can come to watch me at work. I'll lend you a horse until you can get your own. Divert yourself via Dedham on the way to return the barber's horse, for I don't want him calling here. You can catch up with me at Colchester castle.

'Next week we shall be going to several places in north-west Essex, then up into Cambridgeshire. The whole trip will take two or three weeks. When you return, you must look for lodgings. For the next three nights I can accommodate you here.'

Dowdy felt well pleased. It was not much, but it would serve as a springboard from which to start to partly restore his finances and to work out his strategy for revenge. Meanwhile he had arrived at his starting point to claw back with only a few coppers of his original two pounds spent.

CHAPTER 9

Jeremy looked up from his work attracted by the sudden sensation of light. After several days of rain, the late summer sun had started to filter through the windows of the parish office. The long dry spell that had lasted from just before he came home from Cambridge in early July until after mid-August, had been followed by a couple of weeks of unsettled weather. Now as the sun returned on this early September evening, the grass outside had already started to lose its yellow tinge.

It was the end of his labours for the day and he walked across the green to call on Samuel Bloom in his forge before going home. Since the blacksmith's injuries a week before his own arrest, and since his release, he had made a point of calling there each day. Initially, his reason for such frequent visits had been to enquire after Samuel's progress. By now this was no longer really necessary. Although Samuel would carry some of the scars of his beating to his grave, he was fast becoming fit again, and had long since returned to work, although some of the heavier tasks had to be put off.

Another reason for frequent calling was to learn of news or rumours. The forge being the place where goods coming into the village were delivered to, and from where those going out were picked up, was naturally where information about the outside world, brought in by the wagoners, could be gathered.

Since the day when Marcus Kirby had pinned his brief notice about the great parliamentary victory at Marston Moor to an oak tree on the village green, more details of that battle had filtered through. One name was on most lips–Cromwell, the rising star of the parliamentary cause. Jeremy thrilled to stories of how his Ironsides had snatched victory from the near defeat of Fairfax, and had gone on to turn that victory into a rout. From these stories the seed was planted in his mind that one day he would like to become a soldier and join the famous Ironsides. However, he was concerned about deserting his employment after the efforts of Mr Pearson in getting it for him, also the sacrifices of his parents with his education.

But his real reason for daily calls at the forge of late, although he was loth to admit it to himself, was a desire to see Bessie as often as he could. He was still besotted with Eve, and troubled by erotic thoughts of her and memories of lost opportunities. In the weeks since the trial he had come to realise that he must expunge her from his thoughts. Apart from this, Eve was seldom seen in the village now for she was under much stricter supervision.

As he approached the forge there was the unmistakable sound of double hammering. No doubt Samuel had obtained some casual help from the village as a striker. Jeremy was a little put out because Samuel knew he was always willing to give help with that in the evenings.

He stood in the doorway until they were finished. Samuel, who was facing him, looked up and nodded to his striker to look in Jeremy's direction.

The striker turned round and recognition dawned on his face. 'Jeremy!' he exclaimed in his broad Suffolk dialect, advancing with outstretched hand. ''Tis over a year and a half since I last saw yer. How you've growed!'

Jeremy took the hand of the blacksmith's son and responded to his hearty shake. 'Joseph, glad to see you! Have you left the army?'

'No. I was wounded at Marston Moor. Spent a few weeks in a hell-hole called a hospital where a surgeon caused me more pain than the enemy. Wonder I survived his work. A lot di'n't, poor sods.'

Joseph raised the left side of his shirt and loosened his breeches to show his thigh and side. Jeremy gasped at the vicious scars revealed.

'Part grapeshot, but mostly surgeon's work,' said Joseph as he re-buttoned his clothes.

'So how do you happen to be here if you're still in the army?' asked Jeremy.

'Well. Soon arter I got out of that there hospital–an' the Lord be praised for that,' Joseph clasped his hands, and raised and tilted his head to look towards the forge roof, 'my company was sent down this way into reserve and to make up some numbers with new recruits. Not that we lost that many in battle, you understand–most of the dead bein' Royalists. But several of the lads reckon they can sod off home arter a year, which of course some can, the way things are bein' run at the present. Then there's them what go home anyway when they ain't s'posed to, 'cos the pay is late, silly sods. They're likely to be punished if they get caught. An' they will get caught, 'cos there's press gangs all over the place now. The army jus' gotter hev more men.'

There was a break in the talk as Samuel passed round tankards of ale drawn from a barrel he kept in the forge.

'Anyway, as I was sayin'. Our company got sent down this way in reserve. Close by Newmarket. Now they reckon I've been a good soldier,' Joseph smiled and raised his tankard above his head in self-salute, 'an' I've agreed to stay in the army until the war is over. So they sent me to that trainin' unit in Bury. If I do all right I'm gooner be made a sergeant and given my own platoon to help train as musketeers, and take back to the company.

'It was when I got there that I heard how there had been trouble here in Brentham, an' how father had been hurt, so I asked for some time to come over. Jus' for a week. I got here today, an' I'm gooner help him get some of the heavy work done.'

'I'd started to think I might like to be a soldier,' said Jeremy, 'but I rather fancied being a cavalryman. You hear such good things about the Ironsides.'

'Cromwell's Ironsides!' exclaimed Joseph. 'Thass a fine ambition Jeremy. Mind you, you'd hev to behave yourself in Old Noll's mob. Strict discipline an' no swearin'. But fair, 'cos he's a fair man, an' of course as a trooper you'd get more pay than a musketeer or pike man.

'I'm glad you're thinking about bein' a soldier though, 'cos among a number of things, this war is bein' fought for the rights of the common man.'

Joseph then started to launch himself enthusiastically into a long oration about the new Leveller movement and its leader, John Lilburne. He was interrupted by Samuel. 'Now you've started on your favourite subject, we best knock off for today and go into the cottage, or we'll still be here when that get dark.'

Samuel and Joseph emptied their tankards of ale in one draught. Jeremy found that too difficult but tried his best to imitate the older and thirstier men with the result that when he had finished he felt over-full, with his stomach awash with liquid as they walked away from the forge.

As they entered the cottage a smell of mutton broth hung heavy on the air from a pot simmering on a fire in the kitchen. Trying his hardest to stifle the belch that was wanting to escape, Jeremy felt that it would be hours before he dared attempt to eat again. Bessie blushed as soon as she set eyes on him, and he prayed silently that he would not disgrace himself in front of her.

'You'll stay and eat with us?' asked Samuel's wife.

'Thank you kindly, Mrs Bloom, but no. I must soon be getting home.'

Bessie left the room and came back with three tankards of ale and set one before Jeremy. Already suffering from the extra strong brew he had drunk in the forge, he would like to have declined, but out of politeness he did not. Instead he started to sip the ale slowly. He realised that it would take some time.

Between mouthfuls of food Joseph continued to talk about the Levellers and the rights of the common man.

'This sort of talk make me nervous,' said Mrs Bloom. 'Ordinary folk was allus ruled by their betters.'

'If you believe that mother, an' think it just, then you're wrong, an' things will never be put right. Hundreds of years ago, afore the Normans made serfs of the English, every man had common right to land with others, an' had a say how things was run in his village.'

'Ain't no serfs nowhere now; ain't been for a long time,' argued Mrs Bloom.

'That be as it may,' said Joseph. 'But it ain't much good to a man bein' able to move around if he's poor. An' poor is what ordinary folk will allus be as long as they don't hev a say in how things are run an' free access to land. Them who already hev plenty of land are enclosin' more, whether they own it or not.'

'But Parliament is mostly landowners an' merchants they say,' put in Samuel, 'an' you're fightin' for the Parliament.'

'Ay, that I am, an proud of it, but it won't be no good if we win and the only thing what happen is they take some of the King's power away and keep in to the selves. If this country is to be ruled by Parliament alone, then all men should hev a say in who sit there.'

77

'Thass a very forward ambition,' observed Samuel, shaking his head slowly. 'Can't see that happenin' in our lifetime.'

Jeremy wanted to turn the conversation away from politics, in which he did not have much interest, to the army. 'Is Cromwell in favour of the Levellers' aims?' he asked.

'No one don't really know yet,' replied Joseph. 'Some reckon he might be. Accordin' to the lads that come from up the fens, he stuck up mightily for the poor fenlanders afore the war when they were bein' evicted from their marshes, where their forbears had made a livin' for hundreds of years–all common land mind yer–so as the land could be drained.'

'Yes, I know about that,' said Jeremy. He had heard all about the fenland riots when he was at Cambridge.

'Anyway, he's quite popular, partly 'cos of that, partly 'cos he believe in freedom of worship, but mostly 'cos lately he seem to hev the knack of winnin'. Make no mistake, he's goin' right to the top afore this war is over. Sooner the better I reckon. There's already discontent about the way the Earl of Manchester in runnin' the Eastern Association. Thass rumoured that him an' Cromwell been quarrellin' 'cos Marston Moor ain't been followed up proper. They say Manchester wanted to talk peace with the King now that we've thrashed him in a really big battle, but Cromwell an' Fairfax reckon Parliament must go on and beat the Royalists thorough like all over the country afore the King will talk sense. Some even say that privately Cromwell favour this country bein' a republic, though others say not.'

'That might not be a popular idea,' put in Samuel. 'Anyway, let's not get into talk like that. Now young Jeremy here tell us he want to be a soldier afore too long. Got ambitions to be one of the ironsides. What do yer think of that, wife?'

'Mercy, surely not!' exclaimed Mrs Bloom, 'an' you so young to put yourself in such danger. Are yer still not satisfied with your work, even though that terrible Mr Dowdy is no longer around to bother yer?'

'I shall become eighteen in December, Mrs Bloom,' said Jeremy. 'As far as my work is concerned; yes it is more pleasant now Mr Dowdy's gone. Yet I'm much troubled by the vicious falsehoods being circulated about Mr Pearson's daughter. It's most unjust to her, and my name is still being linked to her even though we were proven innocent. One or two of Mr Dowdy's former friends think that he was harshly treated.'

'But Jeremy, yer know that God see all an' He know yer to be truly innocent as well as bein' proven so. What do it matter what a few waggin' tongues say?'

'It's worse than that, Mrs Bloom. There's one of the brethren in particular–Jonas Simpson–who is very hostile. Then there are the men who Mr Pearson had tried and punished at the whipping post for helping Mr Dowdy in arresting us and putting us in the bridewell. They hate Mr Pearson because of that. Sooner or later I fear they will try to make trouble for Miss

Eve, and maybe me. It would be better for both of us if I were not here.'

The conversation faltered and Joseph started on his favourite topic, the Levellers, again, so as soon as good manners would permit, Jeremy made to take his leave.

'See Jeremy to the gate,' said Mrs Bloom to Bessie. She and Samuel looked to Jeremy as a possible match for their daughter and were keen to throw them together.

It was growing dusk. At the gate Jeremy turned to face Bessie. She lifted her face to him, and there were tears in her eyes. 'Don't go to be a soldier Jeremy.'

'Would that make you so unhappy Bessie?'

'Yes,' she said in a whisper, nodding her head gently. 'When yer was accused with Miss Eve, I was unhappy and jealous in case it was true. Then when yer was proven innocent I was glad an' thanked God in my prayers that we got yer back free agin.'

'But Bessie, you heard what I said to your mother. I fear some might make trouble for Eve again and try to drag me in. You wouldn't like that would you?'

Bessie burst out crying and shook her head. Jeremy took one of her hands gently in his and squeezed it before turning and walking away.

After a few steps he returned to the weeping girl. With a hand on each of her shoulders he drew her towards him and gently kissed the top of her head. 'Very well Bessie. I'll try to stay.' She lifted her face towards his, and he found the courage to kiss her lightly and chastely on the lips before again turning and leaving for home.

It was the first time they had kissed. Indeed it was the first time he had kissed a girl at all, for even on that memorable afternoon when the naked Eve had left the lake glistening wet and led him by the hand to the summer-house with her invitation to love, he had fled the challenge before even a first kiss. He found it pleasant to kiss Bessie for there was but little challenge in it. Unlike the fierce sexual feelings which nearness to Eve evoked in him, contact with Bessie was controllable. With her the natural sensation in his loins was mild. No danger here that he would forget his strict puritan upbringing and fall into sin.

He contemplated the future with a little more contentment as he walked home. No doubt there would be more such chaste and pleasant kisses over the coming months as he paid court to Bessie. Maybe the danger of his name being linked to Eve again was not so great after all. If Bessie wanted him to stay in Brentham, that is what he would do. He vowed to redouble his efforts at work and push memories of Eve out of his mind.

✳✳✳

Obadiah Dowdy looked into the face of the witchfinder-general as he entered the room, but it was impossible to tell from that inscrutable countenance what the answer to his request would be. Nearly a week had passed since he made it and he did not doubt but that this was what Matthew Hopkins wanted to speak to him about.

'I've given much thought to your suggestion that you go out on your own in search of those who practice witchcraft, brother Joshua, and agree to it,' said Hopkins, addressing Dowdy by the alias he had chosen, and by which he was known in Mistley. 'I shall expect results however, even though it has been but a short time since you joined us to learn our methods. You have worked hard and learned well. It should save time that we might labour more productively in God's work and rid the world of a greater number of those wretches that have given their souls to Apollyon.'

The witchfinder general had taken some days to arrive at his decision. He had only known Dowdy slightly prior to that day three months earlier when he had turned up at the Thorn Inn under his assumed name of Joshua Harding asking for his help. There was no doubt that he had proved a most assiduous assistant, but Matthew Hopkins was, by nature, a suspicious man.

For his part, Dowdy had been quick to see how this employment might be his vehicle for revenge, or part of it. Nothing could be achieved without money in a greater quantity than paid to him by Hopkins. True, by being frugal, he had managed to survive on it so that the earnings that were now coming in from odd tailoring jobs could be put aside, but he needed to accumulate money faster for his aims.

On one of his early journeys in the witchfinder's company, the family of an unfortunate woman, who were rather better off than the average yeoman stock, had tried to buy Hopkins off to leave her in peace after she had been denounced as a witch. They did not succeed, for in his zealousness for his mission, he was impervious to bribes. The incident had set Dowdy thinking and planning. Realising that he must behave impeccably to earn the witchfinder's complete confidence, before putting forward his idea, he had worked very hard in his service, and been most punctilious with the rent on his workroom.

Therefore, Matthew Hopkins' decision came as music to his ears. It was now November. If his luck held, he would have a few weeks to try his idea before the worst of the winter set in to curtail his journeys.

***

Hannah Beck, cook to the Pearson household crept silently down the back stairs leading from the servants' quarters on the attic floor. Ahead of her, Naomi, unaware that she was being followed, tip-toed along the narrow passageway at the bottom until she came to the doorway leading to the central corridor that ran the length of the first floor, on to which the family and guest rooms opened. Clear in her mind was the excuse she would give if by misfortune Eve was not alone at this late hour.

Hannah had noticed a change in Naomi in the past few months. A mature woman, knowledgeable in matters of the flesh, to her eye it appeared that the girl was receiving sexual satisfaction. There was a new worldliness about her–a certain furtiveness which was not normal for Naomi. Yet there was an absence of men in the house. The sole manservant was the groom, Daniel. But he was almost middle-aged and displayed no interest in women. At one stage she had even wondered if Naomi was having a liaison with the master, but the idea was too monstrous to be worth more than a moment of thought.

Although normally a very heavy sleeper after a hard day in the kitchen, a few nights earlier Hannah had not been so deeply in her slumbers when she thought she heard the latch of Naomi's door click. It occurred to her that the girl might have admitted a lover to he tiny room even though it was but five feet wide and under a sloping roof. So she had waited a while before creeping to Naomi's door and gently lifting the latch. Even by the dim starlight that came into the room from its tiny window at floor level it was obvious that no one was there.

Hannah had tried to keep awake on following nights in the hope of catching Naomi, but alas sleep had overcome her.

Now, more than a week from that night, with supreme effort she had succeeded in staying awake, and on this occasion knew that if she heard the click again, it would not be a lover coming in but Naomi going out–but to where?

She left her bed quickly and silently, and lifted the latch on her own door slowly so as not to make a noise. Easing her door open in the same careful way she peered out in time to see Naomi almost at the bottom of the back stairs carrying a lighted candle which she shielded with her hand. The candle was extinguished just before Hannah gained the foot of the stairs, but it was followed by another faint glow and she was just in time to see Naomi pass through the door that led to the first floor corridor before she was plunged into total darkness.

Feeling her way along the passage wall, she came to the door and stopped to listen. Detecting no sound, with trembling hand she felt for the large knob and turning it lifted the latch. Having opened the door, she peered along the dim corridor lighted by six single candles spaced out three each along both walls.

There were eight doors. The next to her right she examined first because it was the long closet where the household linen was stored. The most likely place for an assignation and where a more plausible excuse might be given if she was detected. She had to be quiet because the next room was that of the master and mistress. The closet was empty. As the main guest room was opposite the Pearsons' room, Hannah gave that a miss. Next to that, and opposite the closet and passageway from which she had entered was a small landing leading to the main staircase down. Naomi would not have gone down there. Next along that side was the vacant room of Major John. She listened, and hearing no sound carefully opened the door to find the room empty. She followed the same procedure for the next two rooms along that side–that of the son who had been killed and the rear guest room.

81

Opposite that was another small landing leading to the back stairs that went down to the kitchen on the ground floor. Maybe Naomi had boldly used that way to get out of the house rather than use the outside staircase from their attic because it was night. Maybe she had even gone down there to steal food. Hannah crept down the stairs. There was no one in the kitchen, scullery or pantry, and the back door was bolted on the inside.

She climbed the stairs again and turned right. Apart from the two front rooms which she feared to approach, there were only two left. She entered the third guest room which was also empty. Next to that there was just Miss Eve's before she would come once more to the passageway by which she had entered the corridor. Standing in the empty room she could seem to hear voices and was afraid. She left the room hurriedly and paused outside Eve's room.

Here she was sure that she could hear a voice. Surely the girl was having a bad dream. But no there was another voice and be it ever so faint it sounded like Naomi's. What reason could a maid have for visiting her young mistress in the middle of the night, she wondered. Her curiosity heightened, she bent her ear closely to the door. Now she could hear laughter progressing to other sounds which to Hannah's ear seemed like lovemaking. But that could not be, for there was no male voice. She listened a while longer before curiosity overwhelmed her, and heart in mouth, she gently tried the latch. To her surprise the door was not bolted, so she eased it until there was just a crack she could see through.

She could scarce believe the scene that confronted her. Here before her very eyes were the master's daughter and Naomi–both naked–their arms and legs entwined, acting as if they were man and woman together. Oblivious to all else around them, their muted cries of ecstasy testified to the fact that they believed themselves unheard and unseen.

Hannah gently pulled the door to but did not drop the latch for fear of making a noise. She then made her way to her own bed, her thoughts in a turmoil as she lay mostly awake for the rest of the night.Their passion spent once more, Eve and her maid walked towards the bedroom door. Naomi was trying to find the words to tell her young mistress something when Eve stopped and caught her arm abruptly. 'Naomi, the door. It's not closed and latched!' she gasped. After fearfully opening the door and finding no one there she closed it again. 'Suppose we've been watched!' She paused and looked at the maid. 'But no, that could not be. There are only my parents, and they'd surely have burst in on us. It was but a draught. We must take more care in future to see that the door is latched securely.'

This alarm caused Naomi to leave the room without divulging her secret. The lovemaking that had taken place between her and Eve since that day four months earlier when Eve was beaten by her father, had so excited Naomi's sexual desires that she longed for proper lovemaking with the opposite sex. Only a few days earlier, on the Sabbath, when she had some time off, she had for the first time given herself to a boy from the village. She believed herself in love, and would certainly meet him again when she was free.

CHAPTER 10

The year 1645 dawned in Brentham to bitter cold, with a mixture of rain and sleet. Jeremy looked forward to the spring. His friendship with Bessie had rolled on in an untroubled and pleasant manner. They had kissed often, but always chastely. One day perhaps he would fall in love, but it would be a gradual process. He had not set eyes on Eve for over five months. The soothing effect of his gentle romance with Bessie had made his work seem less irksome although he still harboured a desire to be a soldier.

For the general populace of Brentham, there was an undercurrent of unease. The war, which back in the summer had been prophesied by some uninformed optimists would soon be over, seemed set to go on for ever. Although in Suffolk it made little difference to many unless they had kin in the army, for they were far from the battlefields, it was depressing trade. On the matter of religion they were being pressurised to conform to a presbyterian system, although some preferred to be independent–to worship God in their own way–to preach or pray at the roadside among like-minded souls. Rumour had it the Parliament wanted Presbyterianism just to please the Scots for the sake of keeping them as allies. To the ordinary folk of Brentham, Scotland was a far away land, of little concern to them.

For one young native of Brentham, the first week in January was a traumatic one. In spite of her inexperience, Naomi was now almost certain that she was pregnant. Out of her mind with worry, she turned to the only person she felt she could entrust her fears to–her young lover.

Alas for her, he was not the hero she imagined him to be. 'Naomi!' he exclaimed. 'you must tell no one of this, for they'd parade you around Brentham in a cart with a sign around your neck. As for me; they'd tie me to the whipping post and have the very skin off my back. You would surely not want that to happen?'

'No! No!' she cried, lifting her face to his for a kiss, 'But what are we to do?'

'Don't fear,' said this young charlatan who had eagerly sowed seed and feared to reap his harvest. 'I'll leave secretly tomorrow and go to London. There's an uncle there who has done much better than my father. He loves me as a son, for he has no children of his own. He'll give me money and more profitable employment. In a few months I'll be back to wed you and take you away.'

'How soon will that be?' she asked, anxiously.

He thought for a moment. 'Let's see. You didn't become mine until November. These matters take nine months, so you won't give birth until August. I shall return long before that–by May–or even April. We'll marry before the child swells your body and be away to where no one will know when we wed.'

So, believing the young knave, she allowed him to lead her once more to their secret love nest, where after his hands had caressed her into ecstasy, she willingly took him within her again, and he for his carnal pleasure deposited more seed into her already fertilised womb.

Satiated, he kissed her and took his leave for the last time. Too much in love to doubt him, she believed he loved her just as deeply and would be back. She would not tell.

✳✳✳

At the end of April, Eve began to suspect what Hannah Beck, the cook, had already suspected for some weeks–that Naomi was pregnant. That would explain her reluctance of late to fully undress for the girl to girl coupling that took place almost daily. Their lovemaking had been passionate. There was no doubt that they had fallen in love, the young mistress and her maid.

Yet since February Naomi had sometimes seemed less heated in her responses. Eve, fearing rejection yet again, started to become jealous. If Naomi were indeed pregnant, it could only mean that she had been unfaithful to her with a man. This would have to be settled.

Next time Naomi came to her room for their regular assignation, Eve wore a sombre and hostile countenance.

'Naomi, I believe you to be with child.'

'No, Miss Eve, for I've been with no man.'

'Don't lie Naomi. You've cooled towards me these past few weeks, whilst still declaring your love. This means that you must be with child, or if not that, then you at least have a male lover who has stolen your affections away.' Eve struggled to contain the jealous rage that was within her, for on no account must their own lovemaking become public knowledge or it would bring down the most terrible punishment on them both.

'But Miss Eve, I do love yer still, and allus will. I'm not with child. I don't hev no male lover. If I seem less ardent lately thass because I ain't been feeling too well. It'll pass.'

Naomi hated lying to Eve. When she had first met her lover, she had longed to share the secret with her young mistress. But as first one obstacle the another prevented her from doing so, and as time wore on, she started to fear that Eve would be jealous and especially so after she realised she was pregnant. Tomorrow was the first of May. Her lover had promised to come and take her away in May or even April. She would surely only have to keep the deception up a few more days.

'Then my dearest Naomi you must rest tonight and not come late to my room. Perhaps too much passion has drained your strength.' It suited Eve to let Naomi think she had accepted her explanation. No doubt the girl had deceived her. Eve wanted her out, but not to know she had a hand in it.

She let the matter drop for two more days Then one evening at dinner said, 'Naomi looks unwell, dont you think so Mother?'

'I hadn't noticed,' said Mrs Pearson, 'but will make a point looking at her tomorrow. Send her to me on some pretext. If she seems unwell I'll have our physician examine her.' Mrs Pearson was usually too preoccupied with her own ill health to notice the servants.

The next day when Nathaniel returned, she took him aside for she did not think what she had to say was suitable for Eve's ears.

'I looked carefully into the face of the girl Naomi today. In my view it is entirely possible that she's with child.'

Nathaniel felt he could do without trouble in his household at this time. Of late there was a great deal more work on the county committee for the war was building up. Meetings were more frequent. New messages and instructions were coming down from Parliament almost every day. He had to take his share of the work.

'I do declare. Before one problem is solved another presents itself. When is the physician next due to see you on his regular visit?'

'On Tuesday of next week.'

'Then I will write a note for you to give him, asking him to examine the girl and report to me privately.'

On the day that the physician called, Naomi was summoned to Mr and Mrs Pearson's bedchamber. The interval of a few days were sufficient to dispel any suspicion Naomi might otherwise have had that Eve had a part in the matter. She recognised the tall dark man as the regular physician to her employers.

'Naomi,' said Mrs Pearson, 'This is our family physiciam, Doctor Mills. In the last few days, you've looked unwell sometimes and I've asked him to examine you so that should you need any physic he can provide it.'

Naomi was alarmed at this prospect, but felt unable to object. But it could surely only be a day or two before her lover returned to take her away. She would stick it out and complain of wind and stomach cramps to explain the abdominal swelling that was now apparent when she undressed.

Mrs Pearson stayed discreetly in a corner while the physician did his work.

Doctor Mills waited until Naomi had left the room. He had examined her in such a way as to not cause her alarm or give the impression that he was looking for signs of pregnancy. 'This fluid will aid your digestion and help you get rid of stomach cramps,' he had said as he handed her the harmless but useless fluid.

He took paper from his bag. 'If you could favour me with a quill and ink I will write my report for your husband now, Mrs Pearson. It will save me much time.

'He asked me to report to him privately, but as his wife I can also tell you. No examination by a physician was needed to know that young female is with child. Insofar as I can tell, without an internal examination which would have alarmed her, she conceived between five and six months ago, in

86

November. All things being normal, she should give birth in August.'

The physician completed writing his report and sealed it before taking his leave.

When Nathaniel arrived home that evening from the committee at Bury St Edmunds, his wife imparted to him privately the news about Naomi.

'Such a matter at a time like this,' he said with exasperation. 'In my position we can't keep her in this house. There'll be some in the parish who'll want her charged with fornication. We must, for her own good, question her as to who is responsible, but not tonight for I have orders that have come down from Parliament to the county committee for the constables of all parishes. I must attend to those for the constable of this and surrounding parishes. It's imperative that the army has more men. Constables each have to make up lists of able bodied men not employed in agriculture or public service and ferret out any who have deserted.

'We'll attend to Naomi in the morning.'

Nathaniel had already done two hours work on county committee papers when the family sat down to breakfast the next morning. Pressure was too great to take his normal pre-breakfast ride around his land. If he was to have any time left for his own affairs he had no alternative but to work from the crack of dawn.

As soon as Eve sat down to join her parents, and they had given thanks for the food they were to eat, the Squire said to her, 'Promptly upon the completion of this meal, come with Naomi to my study.' He gave no reason, and Eve knew better than to ask, for she guessed what it was about.

'I worry about you having to work so hard these days,' said Mrs Pearson, to turn the conversation to other matters and forestall Eve from asking why. 'Couldn't Eve help you, or even young Jeremy Goodway in his free time, for you have done much for him.'

'For the present I've completed all, but ordinances are coming through thick and fast now and I must do my share with my colleagues. There'll be more, but hopefully it'll not be so much as to overwhelm the clerk as at present. It may be that Eve can help with the administration of our land too, since we have no son at home.

'As for Jeremy, I fear he may have his own hands full at this time. More and more orders are coming through about church administration and the need to conform to a rigid Presbyterian system. It's not long since an order went to all parishes requiring a book to be kept on church discipline and the names of any who had not yet signed and sworn the Solemn League and Covenant.

'It should all have been done long ago of course, but Reverend Jones has never been one to pressurise any of his flock who dissent into doing something they don't want to do. He values his living too much. Always yields to the most forceful persuasion, from wherever it comes. It'll not be popular of course, because we have a number of Independents in Brentham.'

'But why must ordinary folk be coerced into the way they worship. Surely that was the very complaint being made against the Anglican Church before the war started?' asked Mrs Pearson.

''Tis the price for the help of the Scots in this war. All the other matters about taxation, freedom, the rights of Parliament, and King Charles trying to rule without Parliament, mean nothing to them. Those are English causes. All they're interested in is church government throughout the two countries under a rigid Presbyterian system.'

'What do you feel about it?'

'I think it's unjust, but makes for some sort of order until this wretched war can be won. After that I think it'll fall apart. There are a very significant number of Independents in high places, particularly in the army. Cromwell himself is an Independent; that will influence the matter greatly, especially if, please God, the New Model Army is successful.'

As soon as breakfast was over, Nathaniel accompanied by his wife went to his study to await Eve and Naomi. Their knock came in a few minutes and he called them in.

'Naomi. Our family physician, Doctor Mills, states that you are with child, and have been so these last five or six months.'

The girl knew she must try to hold on, for her lover must soon arrive. 'Oh no sir, that can't be, for I've been with no man. I know I've been feeling somewhat unwell of late, but he give me some physic for it, which will cure me I'm sure.'

'Don't be foolish girl. The physician is not likely to be wrong. It is imperative that you tell the name of the one who has debauched you. You can't stay in the employment of this house and I can't conceal it from the brethren. There'll be those who'll want you charged with fornication before the parish court. I'll try to dissuade them, but can't go too far.'

Naomi was near to tears, for she began to realise the peril she was in, and the lateness of her lover in keeping his promise. 'No sir. I've been with no man. If I'm with child, then it must be by the happenin' of a miracle.'

'That's a suggestion you'd be most unwise to make if you're questioned by the brethren,' said the Squire, 'or some would want you charged with blasphemy as well as fornication. Be sensible and give the name. Then your punishment might only be to be shown round the village in a cart with a sign round your neck. If you persist as you are, it is likely to be more. Will you now give the name?'

Naomi shook her head, for the tears were welling up in her eyes.

'Very well. Does your father read?'

'Very little, sir. He ain't been properly schooled.'

'And your mother, of course, she doesn't.'

Naomi shook her head.

'Very well. I'll pen a letter to your father in simple language and my plainest hand. No. I'll address it to both your parents. Your father no doubt will have already left for his labours. Eve, see to Naomi collecting her things whilst I write the letter, which I'll leave unsealed. Then I want you to escort Naomi to her home. If her father isn't there, read it to her mother so that she may understand before her husband comes home.'

Eve returned shortly afterwards to her father's study, a weeping Naomi by her side.

'Here are two more letters about other matters. One for our constable which you can deliver to his house near the bridewell. The other for Reverend Jones, which you can leave in the parish office with Jeremy if the pastor isn't there.'

Eve received these instructions with some satisfaction, for now surely Naomi would pay the price for her infidelity to her and, if fortune held good, she would see Jeremy again. In the nine months or so since their trial she had been so closely supervised that she had only set eyes on him in church. Now that gossip about her had subsided, it appeared she was to be allowed out alone again.

Her craving for contact with the opposite sex had been assuaged by the substitution of her lesbian love affair with her maid, but now she would need another lover.

As she walked alongside Naomi to the girl's home she took care to conceal the hatred she felt, and was affable towards her. 'You must choose, Naomi, for you have a right to choose. If the father of your child be free, honourable and kind, keep his name secret, but tell him of your plight and run away together before the punishment of harsh people comes upon you. On the other hand, if he be a knave who has deceived you, then tell his name and so lighten your own penalty.'

Having delivered Naomi to her home and read her father's letter to the girl's mother, who alternated between tears of anguish and tears of anger, Eve bade them farewell. She did not doubt that Naomi had a difficult time ahead, for her maid had often said how strict her father was–never slow with strap or cane.

She then went to deliver the constable's letter. Sight of the bridewell where she had been confined caused her stomach to lurch, but as she turned to make her way to the parish office she was full of joyful anticipation. Jeremy was the better part of a year older now and hopefully not so gauche as the day he had returned from Cambridge, or when he was too timid to take her naked in the arbour. She had heard that he was paying court to the blacksmith's young daughter, Bessie. Cause for mild jealousy maybe, but she would soon sweep away competition from that little milk-sop.

***

Jeremy looked up from his work as the door opened and Eve came in. Deep in his bowels that same sensation which came whenever he set eyes on her in

89

church. But now they were alone in this room, and the sensation spread to his loins. In that moment he knew that the months without speaking to her had made no difference. The fire she lit in him was not the mild and pleasing flame of Bessie which he could control and with which his conscience was at ease. This was the flame of passion which made sin attractive. He knew he would not be able to resist her for ever if they were in contact. Had Obadiah Dowdy possessed the patience to have waited a few more weeks, he would have had true accusation to lay against them.

'A letter for the pastor,' she said, advancing with a smile further into the room than was necessary, before laying the letter on the table.

'T-Thank you,' he stammered for he was discomfited. As she walked towards him she appeared in his mind as naked as that day in the arbour, when she had advanced towards him out of the lake with water trickling around every delicious curve.

She held out her hand. He took it, and felt his sensations increase. She did not take it away, as modesty should have demanded, and he did not let go either. 'It's strange to see you out on an errand alone after so long,' he said.

'My father is somewhat overburdened with public affairs,' she replied, 'and has suggested that I might assist him in some tasks and with the administration of his land, there being no son at home. I think he feels that the tittle tattle has died down now, and that he cannot keep me a virtual prisoner indefinitely. For my part I welcome the opportunity.'

'I'm also much pressed with work here these days, said Jeremy.

'So I hear. But don't you have time to greet me with a kiss after all this absence, and all we went through together at that terrible trial? You felt tender towards me once, that was plain, even though my reciprocal desire led me to frighten you away with immodesty.'

He leaned towards her and placed a kiss upon her cheek.

'Jeremy you kiss me as though I were your sister. Do you no longer feel desire for me?'

'But I'm paying court to Bessie Bloom.'

'Is she enough for you Jeremy–little more than a child?'

He knew she was not. Leaning forward he kissed Eve once more; this time on the lips but chastely as he kissed Bessie.

'Is that a kiss Jeremy? Is that a kiss from one who desires me? If that's the way you kiss Bessie Bloom then I've nothing to fear, for you certainly don't love her.'

There was a faint mocking in her voice. It was a challenge. Twice before he had failed her challenge. If he failed again he could consign his latent desire for her for ever to the realms of fantasy.

He drew her gently towards him and placed his arms about her as he put his closed lips to hers. Her arms went about his neck and she kissed him back with a passion he had not experienced before as her tongue found its way into his mouth and he responded in like manner. He could feel her bosom pressing into his chest and was acutely aware of his rising phallus.

Memories came back of scholars in Cambridge jesting about female bosoms, and he drew back a little to let his left hand cup her right breast. His manhood was in full excitement, and he knew he had reached the point of no return. Suddenly she pulled back sharply and he thought he had offended her.

'Someone coming!' she whispered.

Jeremy moved quickly behind the table once more to hide the swelling in his breeches. The footfalls grew louder and Reverend Jones entered the room.

'Miss Pearson. Good morning?'

There was an implied question in his voice.

'I've just delivered a letter from my father,' explained Eve.

'Are you to wait for a reply?'

'My father didn't say so.'

The pastor quickly opened the letter. 'No reply required. This contains yet more instructions from the county committee on church affairs.'

'In that case I'll bid you "Good Day",' said Eve turning to leave without another glance at Jeremy.

But he knew now that she was back in his life. He had been unfaithful to Bessie and as his desire subsided he was repentant.

'One thing follows another to plague us,' said Jones. 'What I've long dreaded is now about to happen. We're to receive a visit from the Parliamentary visitor, William Dowsing, next week. I have long since removed valuables from the church and stored them. Fixtures I can't move. He of course will smash them and our fine stained-glass east window. Then he will charge us six shillings and eight pence for his pains.'

Jeremy had heard of William Dowsing–another son of Suffolk. A product of the times like Matthew Hopkins, but his speciality was not witchcraft. He had volunteered and been appointed by Parliament to tour the counties round about, smashing up or removing all forms of imagery.

Jeremy was not really listening as the pastor droned on, for he was still in a whirl after his encounter with Eve. When Jones left he fell to his knees and prayed. But he now knew that in the end he would not be able to resist Eve.

CHAPTER 11

A fortnight had passed after the return of Naomi to her home in disgrace, when the dreadful news of her death the previous day reached the Pearson household from Doctor Mills.

Her father, Job Field, in righteous indignation, had chastised his daughter several times. The first punishment was no more severe than might have been expected in the circumstances, but as Naomi continued in her refusal to name her lover, the beatings became more severe. She became ill and miscarried of a dead and very premature child. On hearing of this event, Nathaniel Pearson had immediately instructed the physician to give her every attention at his expense, but the good doctor's efforts had been to no avail.

Mrs Pearson was in tears at the news. Nathaniel was distraught that he should have sent her home to die. 'Yet what else could I have done?' he asked his wife.

'You only did what you must,' she replied. 'Had you let her stay here, some would have accused you of harbouring a wanton and brought up talk of our Eve again.'

'Yet Job Field should not have beaten her so severely, especially as he knew her to be with child. I can't let this matter be. I'll go now to bid the constable arrest him, and call a meeting of the committee of the brethren to enquire if they think he should be charged with murder.'

Eve also shed a tear, for although she had been angry at Naomi's unfaithfulness, and glad at the prospect of her punishment, she had not wanted it to come to this. Also her anger and hatred of the girl had softened over the last few days in the excitement of her new liaison with Jeremy. She had had occasion to visit the parish office again, and this time they had not been disturbed. His hand had found its way inside her clothing and toyed with her naked breasts. She had known him to be beyond the point of self-restraint. Much as she had wanted to yield, she had found the strength to bid him wait, for it would have been most terrible to be discovered in the act. She then set her mind to creating an opportunity in private circumstances.

✳✳✳

Hannah Beck in her kitchen received the news with emotion, but she was troubled. For months she had, with great difficulty, kept to herself what she had seen happening between Naomi and Eve. When she had first suspected the girl was pregnant, a dreadful suspicion entered her mind, for she was a simple soul who harboured a belief in witchcraft.

Now Naomi was dead, she could contain herself no longer. She needed advice from a friend.

It being Friday, Tobias Winscombe called with the meat. He had long since been forgiven by the Pearsons and reinstated as a supplier.

'I must talk to a friend, Tobias. I hev a secret and can't keep silent no longer.' Hannah then related in detail what she had seen happening in Eve's room on that November night.

'You did well to keep silent,' said Tobias with some amazement. 'I would that you hadn't told me now. Mention it no more.'

'But Tobias. It troubles me. Can you not see, the time fits?'

'Psh Hannah. Woman cannot get woman with child!' exclaimed Tobias.

'What if she be a witch with power at will to be as a man?' Hannah had at last unburdened her thoughts to someone.

Tobias was silent for a moment, then standing up turned round and lifted his shirt. 'Nigh a year ago I was foolish enough, through cowardice, to follow the loathsome Obadiah Dowdy in a false charge against Mr Pearson's daughter. Those marks on my back, which I shall carry to my grave, were my just reward, along with the loss of a lot of money, trade, and public esteem. I don't know if witches exist, or what powers they may have, but this I know; I will not go against this family again. They forgave me after my punishment and for that I'm grateful.'

'But don't I now have a duty to speak of what I saw, that others might judge if this led to poor Naomi's death?' asked Hannah.

'You've a duty to yourself to keep quiet. Think of your position here and the consequences. Isn't it possible that you imagined what you thought you saw? Persuade yourself that you imagined it for your own sake. In any case, with the girl dead, even if it were true, you wouldn't be believed. Eve Pearson would be unlikely to admit to such conduct.'

Hannah agreed to pay heed to the advice of her friend Tobias, but after he left, her mind was still troubled.

Two days later, after church, she forgot his advice, and mentioned what she had seen to her friend Elisa Reed. It was in the strictest confidence of course, and Elisa assured Hannah that she would tell no one.

Unfortunately, as Hannah should have remembered, Elisa was a notorious gossip, incapable of keeping a secret. So within days a rumour started among the lower orders in Brentham that Eve Pearson might be a witch, able at a whim to grow and use male genitals, and to impregnate her own sex.

∗∗∗

The meeting of the committee of the brethren, hastily summoned to decide if Job Field should come before the parish court to be committed to the assizes on a charge of murder was a heated one. A few were in favour of that, but the majority felt that he had only exercised his parental duty. Had Naomi not fornicated in the first place, it was argued, the event of her death would not have arisen. However, it was decided that he had been too severe in his chastisement and that he should be charged with violence towards his daughter, a lesser matter which the parish court could deal with.

At his trial the following week, Job was sentenced to receive fifty lashes at the whipping post. Nathaniel Pearson acted as president of the court, so to him fell the duty of passing sentence, and in that moment he made an enemy of Job Field. It was a very bitter man who was cut down bleeding from the whipping post the next morning.

The rumours about Eve persisted among the labouring classes, and after a while started to creep up the social scale a little until at length one of the wagging tongues was brought before the parish brethren to explain the source of her information. This led to three more women in line being called until they reached Elisa Reed.

Elisa did not hesitate to speak up for herself. 'Why, good gentlemen, this ain't no invention of mine. I had my information from the best of sources. Hannah Beck, cook at the Grange, told me how one night last November, being suspicious, she crept upstairs and espied Miss Eve Pearson and Naomi Field naked and having carnal knowledge of one another as if they were man and wife. Miss Eve, it seemed to her, was acting the part of a man.'

Hannah was hastily summoned to appear, and it was with fear and trembling that she approached the meeting with her escort. Even if no account were taken of the witchcraft rumour, carnal knowledge between Eve and her maid, if believed, would bring down the most terrible punishment on Eve, no matter whose daughter she was. In misery she reflected on the advice of Tobias and wished fervently that she had taken heed.

Courage deserted her. Her friendship with Elisa would have to be sacrificed. After all, the woman had betrayed her by repeating what she promised not to tell.

'I don't know,' she declared when pressed, 'why Elisa Reed should say this about me. I've served that household for many years and consider myself fortunate. Is it likely that if I witnessed such a thing I wouldn't do my duty and bring it to the attention of Mr or Mrs Pearson? Or if I didn't know my duty, isn't it strange that I didn't mention it to the other servants?'

'You foul liar!' cried Elisa Reed.

She was sharply rebuked and bidden to hold her tongue.

The other servants were sent for, and they said, truthfully, that Hannah had not said anything to them about it.

Unfortunately for Eliza Reed, she had twice before appeared in court and been punished as a rumour-monger. So Hannah was believed and she was not.

At the parish trial a few days later Elisa and the other three women were judged guilty of scandal-mongering, and sentenced to be conveyed twice round the village with placards around their necks. Elisa, because it was her third time for the same thing, was also locked up in the village bridewell for a fortnight. Lesser punishments than they had all feared, but none the less which caused them to resent the Pearson family.

The rumours subsided, but did not quite die.

***

Throughout May, into early June Jeremy had seen Eve five times as she conveyed letters from her father to the parish office. Only on that first occasion had they been interrupted. At all other times their embraces had been mixed with intimate touches, stopping only just short of the final act.

'Just be patient, my love, and I'll create the opportunity,' she promised him on the last occasion. 'But we must be careful, for you know how speedy the bigots will hasten to accuse us at the slightest suspicion. Look how they were prepared to listen to the foul rumours of those labourer's wives that I had what is called a lesbian association with poor Naomi. Even that by some magic I could get her with child.'

Jeremy of course knew, because he had to attend every meeting of the brethren and every sitting of the parish court, to take notes which he then had to copy into the journal. He had been glad when the matter had come to nothing, although he never really doubted her.

'Jeremy, I trust that now we're so close you have stopped paying court to the little Bloom girl,' said Eve.

'I can scarce avoid seeing her. Her parents are friends of my parents. I have long been in the habit of calling on the blacksmith for a few minutes when I leave off work. As you say, we must be careful not to arouse suspicion, which is what might happen if I suddenly stopped calling.'

'You neatly side-stepped my question Jeremy. I don't count Samuel Bloom among the bigots. I asked if you were still paying court to his daughter while declaring your passion for me?'

'I haven't walked with her this last three weeks.'

'But have you kissed her?'

'As you said only a few weeks ago. You've nothing to fear from the way I kiss Bessie Bloom, for it shows I don't love her. It's ever so chaste. If I stop now before you and I can declare our love it'll certainly cause suspicion.'

Eve seemed partly satisfied with that answer. Jeremy was glad when she left for home, because her questions were getting too close. Three weeks earlier, he had taken Bessie for a short walk after work on a day when he had been well excited from fondling Eve's breasts. In a secluded spot he had drawn Bessie towards him and kissed her in the manner that he kissed Eve. Even that may have passed had he not so far forgotten himself, because of a troublesome erection, as to allow his left hand to touch the gentle swelling of her right breast.

Although this had been outside her clothing, Bessie had struggled free and rebuked him, for signs of his excitement were obvious, and she was alarmed. He had begged her pardon and she had given it and they walked back to her home in silence.

Since then he had missed calling two or three times and when he did call had been over-zealous in his propriety. He knew it was upsetting Bessie, because she loved him, and he was troubled in his conscience.

With effort he brought his mind back to work. He realised that this latest

95

encounter with Eve had put him behind again, so he stayed late to catch up. This earned him the approbation of Reverend Jones when he came into the room at the usual time to give permission to leave off. Nevertheless, the pastor mentioned that the work seemed to be getting in arrears of late and hoped that Jeremy was not worried about anything.

Jeremy did not call at the forge that evening because he was late, but did the following day at the usual time. Samuel was busy with a customer, so he waited a while outside. Mrs Bloom called to him to come on into the cottage for refreshment.

'Sam and me was remarkin' how yer ain't asked for leave to take Bessie out walking these last few weeks,' she said after some initial inconsequential conversation.

'Oh mother!' protested Bessie, blushing.

'I'm under constant pressure at work these days,' said Jeremy.

'Uhm,' said Mrs Bloom. 'Well I'm sure you're doin' useful work, and thass nice to hear you're kept busy. The devil find work for idle hands, they say.' Jeremy wondered if she had noticed Eve going to the parish office and staying a long time.

'Tonight I'm caught up with my work, which is why I've left off at my proper hour. With your leave, if Bessie wants to go walking, I'll be honoured to go with her.'

After more conversation, Jeremy and Bessie left for their walk. At first they strolled in silence. He was struggling with his conscience, knowing that he should admit about Eve, but fearful of the consequences.

In the end it was Bessie who broke the silence. 'Did I give offence when I rebuked yer last time we was out walking? You ain't asked me since, until mother reminded yer today.'

'No. It was deserved. I was too forward.'

'It weren't 'cos I don't care for yer Jeremy, but them things are only for married people.'

'Yes that's what we're taught.'

'Now I worry where yer learned to do such things.'

'The older scholars at Cambridge used to talk much on the subject,' said Jeremy. This was the only explanation that came to mind.

'But yer di'n't do them things afore, an' thass nigh a year since yer come back from Cambridge.'

'Then you were little more than a child. You've blossomed these last months Bessie. I've already said I was sorry. I don't know what came over me. Won't you leave it at that? The memory of it causes me discomfort.'

They walked on in silence or spoke of inconsequential things until nearly at the forge. Suddenly Bessie touched his arm and stopped. 'I must speak my mind Jeremy.'

'What is it?'

'I've become jealous of Eve Pearson again.'

'You've no need to be,' he lied.

'Twice these last three weeks I've seen her come to the presbytery an' be there more than half-hour.'

'Her father spends more time with the county committee now. She helps him by bringing messages for the parish. She does chatter more than she should I know, but sometimes it's with the pastor.'

'Tell me agin I ain't got nothin' to fear from her.'

'You've nothing to fear from Eve, Bessie.'

When they reached the cottage gate he kissed her chastely and made his excuses.

On the way home he was fraught with worry. If his affair with Eve came to light it would break Bessie's heart and might spoil the friendship and high regard the Bloom family had for him.

What he felt for Eve was carnal lust, and against everything he had been taught and believed to be right. That he knew. He was only too aware of the drastic teachings of Saint Paul on the subject. But he could do nothing to help himself. She occupied almost his every waking hour. Just catching a glimpse of her in church would stir his loins.

Desperate he had become to know the delights of a woman's body, so graphically described by scholars at Cambridge. Between them and Eve he had been brought to this pass. Yet he valued purity and his good name. His mind turned once more to the army. It should solve the impasse. Bessie would be disappointed, but not so broken-hearted as if his affair with Eve was discovered.

✻✻✻

Early in June Obadiah Dowdy, alias Joshua Harding, reflected with some pleasure as he made his way from Mistley on his increasing pile of money. As yet he had formulated no exact plan for revenge, but soon he would have sufficient to offer good bribes himself.

He had worked assiduously, hunting poor wretches suspected of witchcraft for Matthew Hopkins, and collecting bribes from those who were better off and could pay to be passed over. Taking care to avoid the south-western corner of Suffolk, or indeed any part of that county, he had widely dispersed his activities over other parts of East Anglia. Now he was headed up into the eastern part of Norfolk for which he had to pass through eastern Suffolk and the town of Ipswich. There was not much contact between Brentham and Ipswich. In his present attire he was not likely to be recognised there he thought–but by coincidence he was.

The narrow street down which he passed was crowded and it had started to rain. With head down against the weather he collided into the tall figure of Jonas Simpson, of Brentham! He muttered an apology and was sure Simpson had not recognised him.

A few more steps and he heard his name called. 'Obadiah!'

He tried to ignore it, but he was called again. 'Obadiah!' This time he heard Simpson scurrying along, retracing his steps until he came to his side.

'Surely you are Obadiah Dowdy? I thought the face was familiar when we collided but couldn't place it. Why didn't you acknowledge me?'

'I thought every man's hand in Brentham was against me. And I go in disguise especially in Suffolk. The Pearson arm is long in the county to make trouble for me.'

'But you are only denied entry into Brentham,' said Simpson. 'Not the whole of Suffolk. As for every man's hand being against you; there are a few of us among the brethren who feel you were too harshly treated, being only half wrong, and would scarcely have fared worse at the assizes. You were wrong to go to such lengths against young Goodway, for he was most likely innocent. The Pearson girl is undoubtedly immoral, and I believe not that you raped her unless she bewitched you to do it. Had you but been more patient you are likely to have had a clear and much more serious charge to level against her.

'But come, let's eat together, while I tell you news of Brentham if you have the time.'

Dowdy was eager to hear more, so they found a tavern with a quiet and vacant corner.

'How have you fared?' asked Simpson. 'I see that at any rate you haven't starved.'

'Thanks be to God, they couldn't take away my skill as a tailor. I rented a small workshop in Essex–I beg of you not to ask me to be more precise–but today I have come up here on a mission for a benefactor. If you are kindly disposed towards me, I beg you to keep silent about this chance meeting. After what happened I fear the Pearson influence, and wish only to be left in peace.'

Simpson, being a rather gullible character, gave his assurance of silence. In spite of his rigid and even bigoted Puritanism he was also very garrulous, and related recent events in Brentham with great detail especially the recent rumours against Eve.

'You're convinced the woman Hannah Beck lied to the brethren in denying what the Reed woman said she had told her she had seen?'

'Yes I believe she took fright to go against her employer's daughter, which is why she held her tongue for so many months until the maid died. Then only found courage to tell Elisa Reed in confidence. Unfortunately, as you know, Reed is a notorious scandal-monger, whereas Beck is of hitherto good character. Naturally Hannah Beck's denial was taken as truth by the majority.

'The new constable, Peter Scott, is more strict than even Hermon Stark was. He'll not act, especially in a suggestion of witchcraft unless he has at least three good complaints. Against the Pearson girl he might demand even more.'

After the two men parted, Dowdy went straight to fetch his horse from where he had temporarily stabled it and rode out of Ipswich back in the direction of Mistley. The news that rumours of lesbianism and possibly even witchcraft had been circulating among the lower orders of Brentham against Eve Pearson was an opportunity that must not be missed. If their wretched constable insisted on three or four complaints before he would do anything, then the complaints would have to be invented. As yet he had formulated no detailed plan for revenge for hitherto he had concentrated on making money from bribes. Revenge he had thought was some months at least away. Now he would have to formulate his plan against the Pearson girl as he travelled. Whatever that would be, would need more money than he had on him that day.

As he rode he pondered where to start. Among the vast details given him by Jonas Simpson was the snippet that John Merton, after his punishment at the whipping post for taking part in the unlawful arrest of Eve and Jeremy, had been dismissed by Squire Pearson and had lost his home. However he had been taken on at one of the Manor farms owned by the Marquess of Stourland and was living in an isolated row of cottages called New Row.

Turning his mind back to his knowledge of parish boundaries, he realised that New Row would be just outside the boundary of Brentham although probably only by a few hundred yards.

He reined his horse to a stop. If he was going that near Brentham, he would need better disguise. His present appearance had not deceived Jonas Simpson. Better go back into Ipswich and find a wig maker. Then he paused, for he did not want to encounter Simpson again. Recalling that the barber in Dedham he had visited on his second morning after leaving Brentham displayed a sign proclaiming himself to be a barber and wig maker, he carried on to a junction that would set him to detour through that place.

The day was well advanced when he reached the barber. There were no other customers. 'Mr Harding, sir.' The barber greeted him with some apprehension.

'Show me your selection of wigs,' commanded Dowdy.

The barber motioned him to follow into a back room. Most of the wigs on the shelves were of a type denoting profession. The practice of wearing this sort of thing was declining in these times but he picked out one that did not look too smart and was grey in contrast to his own dark hair. 'Now I want a false beard,' he said.

'Thass not easy, sir,' said the barber, 'mummery havin' sort of gone out of fashion these days.' He pulled out a large box from under a bench. 'But I got these from years ago.'

Dowdy fingered over the dirty objects with distaste. 'These are pretty foul. Do you not have stock of hair matching the wig to make one with?'

'I do sir and can make one in a week.'

'I'll call for it tomorrow morning early–an hour before your shop opens,' declared Dowdy.

'Tomorrow morning!' exclaimed the barber.

'Which you can do if you work through the night, for which I'll pay you one-third above your normal charge. And before you say you can't, remember who I work for.'

The barber yielded in the face of this generous offer combined with such an implied threat.

CHAPTER 12

It was getting towards evening when Obadiah Dowdy arrived near the cottages known as New Row just outside Brentham. All was quiet and, preferring not to have to resort to knocking on any door at random to enquire which was the Merton's, he led his horse into a nearby copse from where he could keep watch without being seen.

At length he saw Ruth Merton enter her house. He walked over and knocked on the door. 'I need to see you. Where can I leave my horse that it will not be stolen?' he asked. She obviously didn't recognise him.

'Round the back would be safe, but it ain't my hour for business. Husband will soon be home. Wouldn't be right.'

'Not that sort of business, woman!' exclaimed Dowdy. 'I want to talk to both of you, and,' he said, hearing the noise of children in the back, 'get rid of the children. My business with you is private.'

'That cost money with a neighbour in the row,' she said in her broad Suffolk accent.

Dowdy handed her fourpence. 'I don't doubt she charges you well to keep your children from the house while you do your *business* as you call it. Even so this should be above twice enough.'

She took the money. 'You go an' tie the hoss round the back while I take the young 'uns down.'

By the time he had collected his horse from the copse and tied it round the back of Ruth Merton's cottage, she was back at her front door to usher him in.

'I don't know yer, though the voice seem familiar,' she said.

'I'm Obadiah Dowdy.'

'God Almighty!' she exclaimed. 'You ain't half aged. Ain't you afraid of comin' here. You'll get three-hundred at the post if the constable know.'

'No I won't. This place is outside Brentham parish boundary. But I don't want it known that I'm here. That's why I'm disguised. My business is very secret.'

'Well, what d'yer want with us. Last time yer wanted me to do somethin' yer was all powerful like. Called me a whore an' adulteress. Threatened yer could hev me stripped an' caned all over, then denounced as a witch.'

'I have no power in Brentham now, that's true. As for the names, does truth really offend? The furnishings in this house are not bought from the wages of an agricultural labourer. And I do still have the ear of the witchfinder general, even more so now. But let's not trade in abuse and threats. For what I want I'm prepared to offer good money.'

'Money would interest me of course, said Ruth, 'but as I recall, you was kicked out with jus' yer clothes, small tools an' two pound. Funds enough for poor labourers, but hardly enough for somebody as grand as you'd got.'

'People like me are not easily put down. What I had before was all earned. I started with nothing. I shall regain all, although not in Brentham. If I didn't have money I wouldn't be offering it. But I'm not a fool with it, so don't become greedy.'

Just then John Merton came in. He scowled at Obadiah. Although aware his wife's activities as a whore had increased since they moved, and was glad to share her earnings, he expected her to get her clients out before he came home.

'Do yer know who this is?' Ruth asked him.

'No.'

'He want somethin' for real money.'

'Don't they all.'

'Stop the tittle-tattle,' snapped Dowdy. 'Let's get down to business. I'm Obadiah Dowdy.'

John Merton gasped. 'The disguise is good, but I recognise the voice. What the hell d'yer want with us? The last time I did your biddin' I got my back badly marked an' spent a day in the stocks, an' lost my employment.'

'That was harsh and I don't doubt you hate Pearson for it. None the less,' said Dowdy, waving an arm around the room, 'you seem to have gained in accommodation.'

'Thass true; but I wouldn't go aginst them agin except for a lot more money than you was likely to be able to pay. Ain't a year yet since yer was nigh broke–by your standards.'

'What are yer offerin', and for what?' asked Ruth.

'I want you to persuade, or bribe at least four women–ones likely to be believed, to swear that the Pearson's cook, Hannah Beck told them directly months ago that Pearson's daughter was having regular carnal knowledge with her maid. I want you to find at least two other women who will swear that their husbands have been seduced by Eve Pearson. Further I want one, or if possible two, who'll risk punishment by admitting to having lesbian relations with the Pearson girl and that she seemed to grow a male organ while thus engaged.'

'Thass nigh impossible!' exclaimed John Merton, 'an' too risky.'

'What sort of payment are yer offerin'?' asked Ruth.

'Ten shillings for each of you now, just for agreeing to try. Ten shillings more for each of you if you get the number of people here for a meeting plus two shillings for each one. Ten pounds between you if she's put on trial as a witch. Finally, twenty pounds between you if she's convicted and executed as such.'

Dowdy was not surprised that John Merton was speechless. He would have to work two years to earn that much as a farm labourer. Dowdy was also aware that with similar bribes being needed for the false witnesses, his new resources would be dangerously depleted unless he cheated in the end.

'After you've recruited the people you'll need someone of standing willing

102

to put pressure on the constable to act,' said Dowdy.

'That'll be the easy part,' said Ruth.

'Who do you have in mind?' asked Dowdy.

'Jonas Simpson.'

'Simpson! A straight and righteous man. Are you sure he will take account of you.'

Ruth laughed. 'Ha! He ain't so righteous when he lay atween my legs. That surprise yer Mr Dowdy I bet. Thass somethin' the bigots on the parish committee don't know–or his wife.'

'So you'll take it on?' asked Dowdy.

'Yes,' said Ruth, 'but we'll need some more cash in front to tempt folk with.'

He handed them two bags. 'Each of these bags contain silver coins. The one is the one pound advance payment for you two. The other is six pounds to start your own bribes. I shall want you to keep strict account of amounts spent.'

'Seven pound. Thass a lot of money to trust us with,' said John Merton. 'How d'yer know we won't just keep it and do nothin'?'

'Let me explain, so you won't need ask that question again. Since I left Brentham I have become a close companion of a man called Joshua Harding. He works for Matthew Hopkins, who you have heard of, hunting witches. Should you cheat me, you would almost certainly find yourselves going to the gallows as convicted witches.'

'Do we use your proper name when we ask folk to come and meet yer?' asked Ruth.

'No!' exclaimed Dowdy, thinking of another alias. 'Call me Jonathan Bentley.'

'Practice another voice,' said John Merton. 'That might give yer away, but the disguise is perfect.'

'I'll come next week again on this day at eight o'clock in the evening. Do you think you can get all together by then?'

'Most likely,' answered Ruth.

***

In mid June, the news of Eve's arrest came to Jeremy in the course of his work. 'A special general meeting of the brethren has been called for this afternoon at two o'clock at the insistence of Mr Nathaniel Pearson,' said the pastor. 'His daughter has been arrested by the constable acting upon a complaint by two of the committee, Mr Jonas Simpson and Mr Luke Smith, supported by eight witnesses. You'll need to write two notices for the the congregation in general, and post them up in prominent places. Then go round to as many of the committee as you can trace, to tell them.'

Jeremy was shocked. 'What's the purpose of the meeting?' he asked.

'To question the witnesses and assess the validity of their evidence and decide if Miss Pearson should appear before the parish court with a view to being committed for trial to the assizes.'

'On what charge?'

'Witchcraft,' replied Reverend Jones.

Jeremy's heart sank, but he did as he was bidden.

The meeting was very fully attended. All the witnesses were forced to attend, as was Hannah Beck, once more. Eve was seated between the constable and a deputy.

The four women who claimed Hannah Beck had told them she saw Eve and Naomi having lesbian sex made their statements. Hannah was questioned again and denied once more having said it or having witnessed such acts. Questioned by Nathaniel Pearson as to why they had not come forward when the brethren examined Eliza Reed on the same matter, the four women said they had been afraid to.

The witnesses on seduction and the two women who claimed to have had lesbian relations with Eve during which, by sorcery, she grew a male organ, were closely questioned by several of the brethren.

When all questions were done, the constable said, 'From all that I've heard, I won't charge her with witchcraft because only the evidence of the last two witnesses has any direct bearing on such a charge. That's not enough.'

Jonas Simpson and Luke Smith, supported by two others protested, and from the back of the room Job Field cried out in anguish, 'She caused the death of my daughter!'

'If you won't charge her on the evidence presented,' shouted Jonas Simpson, 'then we demand that you send for Matthew Hopkins, that he may question her and the witnesses, and present the charge.'

'Very well,' agreed the constable. 'I'll send for the witchfinder.'

Eve looked first at her father, then at Jeremy. There was terror on her face.

***

Mrs Pearson was distraught when her husband brought news of what had transpired at the meeting. 'This time I can't place Brentham under military jurisdiction because there's no disorder. I'll ride straightaway to the army headquarters at Saffron Walden to see if I can get a message to John. They'll know where he is, although what exactly I expect him to be able to do I'm not sure. I can reach there by nightfall. Then at crack of dawn I'll ride from Saffron Walden to Bury St Edmunds to see if my colleagues on the county committee will support me to request the intervention of the chief constable.'

At Saffron Walden he found all agog. News had been received that morning of a great victory at Naseby two days before. Major John Pearson's regiment would likely have moved on to Leicester now, he was told. He was able to send a message with one of couriers keeping in touch with the army in the field.

***

Jeremy was unable to concentrate on work after the meeting. Something had to be done for Eve. Though his feelings for her might be but sinful lust, after what they had been to one another, to stand by and do nothing would be cowardice.

He considered the desperate idea of breaking into the bridewell to release her, without formulating any plan. Then somewhere would be needed to hide her until . . . until what? Beyond that he could not envisage.

It would be foolish to expect to hide her in her father's house. Undoubtedly for love of his daughter Squire Pearson would conceal her and compromise himself doing so. But that would be the first place the constable would go, and should her father deny her presence, might make so bold as to attempt a search.

There was a place–he recalled from his childhood his secret way in. But he would not be able to use that if he rescued her from the bridewell during the night. He would need a temporary hiding-place.

He racked his brain during the evening as he helped his parents. Hay was very forward this year, and his father, who believed part of the crop should be cut early to provide a more nutritious winter feed for the beasts, had already begun to fill the loft space in a barn. With what was now going in, it would be as full as prudent to allow turning. No one else would go up there for two or more days.

At supper he found it difficult to eat or converse. A sickening sense of fear was overwhelming him. 'Are yer feelin' unwell Jeremy?' asked his mother.

He was alarmed. On no account must his parents suspect what he had in mind. 'No. No, I feel quite well. Just that I'm saddened because of what happened today. The reputation of Matthew Hopkins fills me with dread. I fear that poor Eve Pearson is doomed.'

'Ay,' said his father. 'That may be, but there's naught simple folk like us can do but pray, an' hope that Squire Pearson can do somethin' outside this village. He's a man what count for somethin' in wider an' higher circles.'

'Then I'll take your advice, and hope and pray with you,' said Jeremy, with a sigh and forcing a smile to his face.

He bade his parents 'Good Night' and made for the stairway, noticing the time as he went because he had no watch, and there was but one clock in the house. He lay on his bed fully clothed trying to measure time by counting seconds; he would not make his move until he judged it was near midnight.

His counting went on. Keeping his hands clenched he straightened a finger each time he reached sixty. Each time he had fully unclenched both hands he would memorise the number of times. Tiredness started to overcome him. Was that five times of six, he wondered. He dozed off.

Awaking with a start, he wondered if it was too late. Everywhere was still. If it was after three o'clock there would not be enough time. He crept downstairs quietly with a silent prayer and glanced anxiously at the clock. It was fifteen minutes after midnight. His prayer had been answered–he had not overslept.

No exact plan had as yet occurred to him, he only knew that he had to try to get her out. He picked up a short stout stick laying in the yard with feelings of guilt and foreboding.

The Goodway farmhouse was the northernmost dwelling in the parish, set well back in an isolated position. Keeping close to shadows as much as possible, he crossed the road that came out of Brentham at the north end, along the short stretch where the tortuous track ran almost west to east before turning north again. Entering Pearson pasture land at the same point that Obadiah Dowdy had used in his arrogance, it was tempting to make straight for the church, for the bridewell was less than four-hundred yards beyond. But that would have brought him to where there were a lot of buildings and greater danger of discovery. So he made a wide eastward detour keeping well away from places of habitation.

At the southern extremity of Brentham, he entered land belonging to the Marquess of Stourland and turned west until, in a few hundred yards, he reached the road that approached the village from the south. He turned north again until just below a fork where the road from Sudbury joined it. To his right stood the bridewell end-on behind a screen of trees, facing south, well back from another screen of trees.

Jeremy concealed himself in the trees to the side and slightly to the front of the building. The door, which faced south, was open, for it was a warm night and the sound of the guard snoring could be heard. He had made no plan of action still. Should he just walk inside and attack the sleeping deputy without warning? What if he was not hard enough or quick enough? He had never attacked anyone before.

As he turned first one plan then another over in his mind, the snoring stopped. The deputy came out of the door, obviously in a drunken state, for he belched loudly as he lurched towards the trees about thirty yards in front to relieve himself.

Get inside first. Attack from there for surprise and take his keys, was Jeremy's first thought as he dashed as quietly as he could for the door. All cell doors except one were open. He tapped on it. 'Eve, be ready!' he whispered. Carelessly the deputy had left the keys on his table–such luck Jeremy had not expected. He quickly swept them up.

'Is it you Jeremy?' cried Eve.

'Shush!' he cautioned her, as he turned the key. It was noisy. The door creaked also. Surely the man had heard that. She was in tears and wanted to embrace him.

'Be ready to run,' he told her. 'I'll strike him down when he comes back in.'

Jeremy went to the side of the open front door. The drunken deputy could be clearly seen facing away from them, still urinating into the trees. He pulled Eve out of her cell quickly. 'Out to the left, round the back and wait,' he commanded.

At least she was out. He shut her cell door locked it and put the keys back on the table. It would give time. The deputy had finished just as Jeremy reached the front door and was struggling to fasten his breeches. Jeremy slipped out and round the side where he waited pressed against the wall, stick in hand. He dare not move further until the guard was back inside because he was now returning and might notice. The man was very drunk, for he had now been awake several minutes yet was still lurching wildly. He failed to see Jeremy standing there and entered the building with another loud belch. Jeremy uttered a silent prayer of thanks, that he had not had to strike him.

Jeremy stayed frozen in the same place and shortly the snores of the negligent deputy could be heard again. He crept round the back to where Eve was waiting in the shadows. They embraced and kissed silently. She was in tears.

'We must move quietly now' he whispered.

He felt tender towards her as she accompanied him trustingly–and proud. Now he had done a manly thing, and the thought of it stirred his loins.

When they were safely out of earshot on the same detour by which he came, she asked, 'Where do we go?'

'I've a hiding place within my home, but can't get you in there tonight for fear of waking my parents. It's important they don't know, or they would be compromised. Tonight and some of tomorrow I must conceal you in the loft of a barn, then when all are out tomorrow, get you indoors.'

'Might you not wake your parents when you return after hiding me?' asked Eve.

'I must wait with you until day first breaks, then return openly and say I have been walking because I couldn't sleep.'

When they reached the barn and he had closed the door behind them, she threw her arms about his neck and broke down in tears. He held her close and felt the wetness of her tears on his cheek. He felt his manhood stir and knew he would not be able to resist the temptation.

They waited until their eyes became accustomed to the gloom. It was still a bright starlit night and a little of it filtered through the several holes and cracks in the building.

He took her hand and led her to the foot of the ladder and invited her to follow him up. After he helped her off the ladder at the top, she did not loose her hold on him as he led her further to the back of the loft. The air was heavy with the aroma of new-mown hay.

'I've placed two pitchers of water in the corner over there for cleanliness and drinking. Food I could not provide in the time. This hay was mostly put here last evening. No one is likely to come to turn it for two days.'

'Don't worry,' said Eve. 'A little hunger is a small price to pay for safety.

But come,' she drew him down to the soft bed of hay. 'So recently I was setting my mind to providing an opportunity. Now danger has presented one, and that danger makes me even more ready to receive you. I've waited long for this and I know now that you'll not back away again like a frightened boy.'

Jeremy, already beyond the point of no return, unfastened her bodice and explored her already familiar breasts as their mouths met and tongues entwined. Feeling her fingers fumble for the fastenings of his breeches, he could scarce contain his seed. He drew back a little to unfasten them himself.

'Would you love me fully dressed Jeremy? Are you so shy? You have seen me naked. Isn't it fair that I should see you thus, even though the light in here is poor?'

He made to loosen some more of her clothing.

'No,' she said. 'Don't try to undress me further. You are too heated for that I can tell. All will be over before we begin. Let's each remove our own clothing and stand before one another as nature intended.'

Shivering with excitement, he stood up and undressed hurriedly. This was the wonder the older scholars at Cambridge had described that he was about to experience.

She undressed more slowly as if to torment him. His excitement rose to new heights at sight of her shape in the gloom and highlights of her curves in the starlight that filtered through.

They stood for a moment facing one another, then flung themselves together in an abandoned embrace and sank to the floor. He felt her hand come down to his loins, but she had tormented too much for one so inexperienced. In a mixture of ecstasy and disappointment he felt the seed leave his body, to fall into the hay.

He started to weep, for he believed he had failed as a lover, and for nothing he had sinned. She restrained him as he started to move away from her. 'Lay beside me and let us still embrace. It will return.'

They lay a few minutes; he on his back, she on her side facing him, her caresses soothing away his doubts. He became acutely aware of a new stirring in his loins and a naked breast against his flesh. Without moving from his supine position, he brought a hand over to the other breast and traced light circles around the nipple. That he knew gave her pleasure for she had asked him to do it during their intimate moments in the parish office.

Her breathing was becoming harder and he heard a sound come from deep in her throat. 'With your tongue,' she croaked hoarsely. 'Do that with your tongue.' He made to turn towards her, but she pushed him gently down again and leaning further over lowered the breast to his mouth. As he circled the nipple with his tongue, she took his hand and put it between her legs. He stroked and probed, savouring these new delights, until he felt he could wait no longer. 'Not yet,' she whispered, as she gently restrained him from laying her on her back.

108

Pressing him down again, she brought a leg over and straddled his stomach. 'Now the other one,' she pleaded, lowering the other breast to his mouth and placing his hand on the first breast.

As his tongue circled that nipple, Eve lowered herself, straightening and closing her legs until she was fully on top of him, and he could feel his engorged genitals nestling in the valley of her thighs. 'Now suck,' she asked. 'Suck hard.'

As Jeremy sucked, moving from breast to breast, he heard her moan and felt her start to quake. Suddenly she straddled him again and, first raising herself then reaching down took his erect phallus and guided it where it was more than eager to go.

Her warmth enveloped him in a new sensation, and immediately she cried out as copious wetness covered his loins. He thought she was finished before him, but she seemed to grow in strength, as like some wild animal, she rode him fiercely and he thrust up to meet her with hands pulling down on her buttocks. Again she cried out and climaxed, but he was nowhere near finished. Now he was feeling fierce to her and used all his masculine strength to prise her off and turn her over. He entered her again in urgent need of his own fulfilment. But she was not yet finished, and as their bodies heaved and writhed in this final coupling, she returned to him as good as he gave. Then, in a moment of extreme ecstasy such as he had never dreamed possible, it was over for him, and he heard her shout and felt her explode in climax again.

They lay, still engaged, for a few minutes. There were no more words as they pulled apart and kissed gently. Jeremy felt a pleasant tiredness overwhelm him.

Her hands caressing his loins awakened him. He was erect again. His mind cleared suddenly and he sat up in alarm. 'The time!' he exclaimed.

'Don't worry. It's not yet dawn,' said Eve.

It was nearly pitch dark. Jeremy got to his feet, and prised open a gap in the wooden wall a little further. The stars had gone and the faintest glimmer of dawn touched the eastern horizon.

He turned around and in the faint light could just make out her naked form in the hay. 'Will you not love me again Jeremy,' she challenged.

Laying down, he took her again gently and in silence. But she was neither gentle or quiet, and her fierce response brought him to a speedy conclusion.

She begged him to stay longer, but he was keenly aware of her danger, for the light was now increasing in the loft. He hurriedly dressed and going to one of the pitchers of water, washed his face.

'Get dressed now, Eve, and be as quiet as possible through the day. Keep away from the front of the loft as others may come in, but they're not likely to come up here. I'll return for you during the evening while I'm helping my parents and they're still in the fields.' With that, he kissed her gently and made his descent of the ladder, ruffling up the hay at the front of the loft as he went.

CHAPTER 13

Jeremy spent an anxious and unhappy morning. After his night of danger and love, he was tired. With desire satiated, his conscience plagued that he had sinned and enjoyed the experience. That he had lied to his parents about having been out on an early morning walk, and that he had been so unfaithful to Bessie, compounded his unease.

Yet it was some comfort that he had proved himself manly and brave by getting Eve out of the village lock-up. Also, according to the older students in Cambridge, it was a manly thing to possess a maid; although that ran entirely opposite to his upbringing and the teaching of the church.

On the other hand, there was the nagging worry about Eve's security that day, for the barn loft was not as safe a hiding place as he had claimed to allay her fears. Also, he had not the faintest idea what to do next, beyond getting her to the secret hiding place in his home. No doubt once there, he would be tempted again and sin once more.

News of Eve's escape was slow to reach the parish office. Mid-morning Samuel Bloom popped his head around the door.

'Hello Jeremy lad. Thought you'd like to know. Stage wagon has jus' been. He brought news from town. There's been another big victory for Fairfax an' Cromwell at a place whass called Naseby. They say the King's army was routed proper.

'The other news yer already know I s'pose–about Squire Pearson's daughter?'

Jeremy put on an air of sadness for the blacksmith's sake. 'Yes. I know she's to be questioned by the witchfinder general, poor young lady.'

'No!' exclaimed Samuel, 'Not that. Ain't you seen nobody to tell yer. She's escaped.'

'Escaped!' exclaimed Jeremy, hoping that his affectation of surprise sounded convincing. 'I didn't know. I only saw Reverend Jones for a few minutes this morning. He said nothing, and no one else has been in.'

'They say the constable is in a rare state with the deputy wot was on guard. Seem he got no idea when she went an' di'n't miss her 'til eight o'clock a s'mornin'. Reckon he found her empty cell still locked, and say thass no more than should be expected from lockin' up a witch, 'cos she can get out by magic. Drunken sod, that one. Most likely don't know if he locked the door or not.

'Anyway, the constable is searchin' the village for her an' went straight up Pearson's place first to see if she'd jus' gone home. Thass all I know so far.'

The blacksmith returned to his work. Jeremy was glad, for he felt guilty in his presence because of Bessie. Now his anxiety was heightened further on hearing of the constable's search. Was he even now looking into the barn loft he wondered?

'This worry and guilt is too much for me,' he murmured to himself. 'Surely now I'm reaping the wages of sin.'

He bowed his head in prayer, and vowed that once this nightmare was over, he would go to the army, where he might atone for his sin by fighting for a just cause. In any case, it seemed from Samuel's news about Naseby, that if he didn't soon go, the war would be over and he would no longer have the chance.

✳✳✳

Nathaniel Pearson came back home in the evening to find his wife in a distraught state. 'Whatever more is amiss?' he asked her.

'Our little Eve again. She's disappeared and I'm fearful for her safety.'

'Disappeared!' exclaimed Nathaniel. 'How can anyone disappear when locked up in the bridewell, pray?'

'I don't know,' sobbed Mrs Pearson, tears flowing down her cheeks, 'but I fear some underhand work. That she may have been murdered by one of our enemies and her body buried secretly. The deputy who was on guard seemed a rough and uncouth fellow who would do anything for money.'

'He was here!?'

'Yes. The constable came with two men to search. The one that had been on guard was clearly feared of the constable's wrath, for he alleged Eve's cell was still locked when he discovered she was gone, and she must be a witch to have escaped through a locked door. The constable was in a rage and struck him a blow, calling him a negligent and drunken lout. He said if Eve was not recovered he would get the truth out of him at the whipping post, then send him to the army with the next impressment, that they might flog some sobriety and discipline into him.'

'One of the deputies is reputed to be a drunkard and was badly chosen,' said Nathaniel. 'Further allegations of witchcraft are the last things we want. Try not to worry about her being murdered. That is scarce likely. Probably the deputy was drunk, forgot to lock her cell and went to sleep, she just walked out and is in hiding.'

'Who would conceal her?'

'I don't know,' said Nathaniel. 'But I wonder if young Jeremy would? She may have run to him, for she seems ever eager to talk with him. I'll call on the Goodway's after I've eaten. But first I must call on the constable. I have a written order for him from the chief constable.

'How did your efforts fare, my dear?'

'As well as I could expect to do I think. At Saffron Walden I was able to send a message off to John straightaway. At Bury this morning my committee colleagues, among all the excitement about Naseby, found time to give me their support about a request to the chief constable. I then rode over to him with the committee's letter. He promised to do all he could, but pointed out that it was lawful for Hopkins to question her. However, concern was growing about his methods, so this letter to our constable is to instruct him

112

that Hopkins is to use no torture or swimming and that I am to be allowed to be present, and with my lawyer if I wish.

'He also said that, although he had no jurisdiction over what Hopkins did in Essex, he would write to the chief constable of Essex asking him to forbid Hopkins from questioning her in Colchester or anywhere else in that county, as it is a Suffolk matter.

'I don't think I could have asked more, and I fear that Eve's escape won't have helped her. Let's pray that John can do something.'

✳✳✳

Jeremy was glad to get home that evening. As expected, his mother was not in the house. She was still in the fields with his father and the labourers at this busy time. It would be over an hour before she came to prepare the evening meal and over two hours before his father returned.

He first walked a little way to be sure they were not returning, then went quickly to the barn.

Tearfully, Eve threw herself into his arms. 'It's been truly terrible,' she sobbed. 'You said no one would come, but people have been in and out below many times, and some did come up here. The constable's men.'

'What did you do?'

'Hid under the hay. They prodded around and kicked the hay about but mercifully missed me.'

'Did they remark on the pitchers in the corner,' asked Jeremy, anxiously.

'No. They just swore and went away.'

'I must move those as soon as I have you hidden in the house in case they remember them and become suspicious. But come, time is limited. I must get you into the house.

The Goodway farmhouse was very old. Originally it had consisted of one high room with an open landing on one side and one end, with simple steps, hardly worthy of the description of staircase, giving access. On this landing the occupants would sleep–a fairly common arrangement a hundred years and more before in homes that were one step up from the homes of labourers.

Some fifty years or so before, an outbuilding had been added as a scullery on the side, and on the end, another single-storey room had been built, to be used as a bedroom with interior door from the original building. It was in this room that Mr and Mrs Goodway slept; whilst the landing had been walled in at one end to make an enclosed bedroom. Here Jeremy slept.

The additional room was not as high as the original building although it had a ceiling and the apex of it came to just below the little window high up in Jeremy's room. The building of it must have damaged part of the original plaster work, because part of the end wall of Jeremy's room was made of wooden boards.

As a child, Jeremy, ever inquisitive, had discovered two of these boards which were beside his bed, could be easily dislodged, and to his childish

113

delight gave him access to the roof space under the thatch above his parent's bedroom. This had been his secret, where sometimes he would play at hiding from an imaginary enemy, replacing the boards behind him. He had never told his parents about it, for they would surely have stopped him.

He had not been in there for many years until he heard of Eve's distress. Now larger, he found that an extra board had to be dislodged to gain access. He did that and prepared the hide-hole as best he could.

It was here that Jeremy led Eve after bringing her from the barn. 'It looks dreadfully dark Jeremy!' she exclaimed.

'You won't have to spend too much time in there. I clean my own room. Mother never comes in here. Most of the time you can spend here in my room, only going into the hide-hole if you hear the voices of callers. If you feel very nervous you could go in there in the mornings when my mother is engaged in or near the house, and late in the evenings when we eat.

'At night you can sleep in my little bed. I'll sleep on the floor. The most important thing is to be silent when anyone other than myself is in the house.'

'Supposing in the end they don't find me, what are our plans?' she asked.

'I must confess I have no plan except to hope that your father can use his influence to save you from a witchcraft charge. If he can, I will hear about it in the course of my work. If he can't, then all that is left to us is to run away together. But come, eat now. You must be famished.'

Jeremy handed her a large piece of bread with portion of cheese and a tankard of ale. She ate ravenously.

'This is the best fare I'm able to offer at the moment,' he said. 'I'll try to do better. There'll always be water in this room.'

'Dearest Jeremy. You've taken such risks for me. It'll suffice,' she assured him.

He showed her once more how to get in and out the hide-hole, making all look as if nothing had been disturbed. 'Now I must go and help my parents for a short while or they'll wonder at my absence. My mother will soon be coming back from the fields to prepare the evening meal.'

They embraced and kissed, and the by the way they did it he knew that this night he would be tempted to sin again.

After the evening meal the Goodway family spent an hour in conversation. Jeremy felt ill at ease and hoped that it did not show. He had already learned from them that the constable's men had searched the house during the morning. When they had told him of the barn being searched, he had had to act as though he did not already know.

At length they retired to bed. In his room, Jeremy found Eve seated on his bed fully clothed. 'Is all safe now?' she asked in a whisper.

'It would be wise to be totally silent for at least half an hour,' he whispered back. 'I usually pray at this time,' he added, almost as an apology.

'As I'm also supposed to, but often don't,' she admitted.

Jeremy dropped to his knees. He prayed in silence for many things. For the state of the country and the village. For justice to all mankind. For Eve in her danger, and his parents in their unremitting toil. For Eve's parents in their worry, and asked forgiveness for the sins he had committed and for strength to resist the sin of lustful gratification in future.

As he prayed, he felt Eve kneel beside him and after a while her hand came over to rest on his crotch. In that moment he knew his last prayer would not be answered.

The following morning while the family was still at breakfast, the constable and his men called at Goodway's farmhouse for the second time.

'One of my deputies thinks he remembers that last time we searched your barn there were two water pitchers standing in a corner of the loft. He may have imagined he saw them, but in case he did, we demand to search every corner of your farm again, including this house. We've already searched the barn and found no pitchers there, or anything else amiss.'

'I can't stop yer doin' what yer must,' said Silas Goodway. 'But please leave things in order afterwards.'

They went up to Jeremy's bedroom first. His heart was in his mouth. He hoped the terror he felt as he heard them thumping around did not show on his face.

They came down, apparently satisfied, searched the rest of the house, then left. Jeremy could scarce restrain himself from running up to his room. He prayed Eve would have the sense to stay in the hide-hole until his mother left the house, because she was bound to want to go and see if the men had left his room in a good state.

The moment of anxiety passed when his father said to him, 'You best go an' see they ain't done no damage in yer room. If they hev, I gooner complain to the constable. Ain't right to disturb honest folk.'

Jeremy walked up to his room as calmly as he could. 'No they haven't damaged anything,' he reported when he came down.

Three more days passed from when Jeremy had concealed Eve in the house. Those three days had each been preceded by nights of unbridled passion in which their naked bodies had writhed together. He had lost count of the times he had entered her and with difficulty restrained her from crying out as she climaxed over and over again. Each time it had been her craving which had taken the initiative. She was insatiable, and he powerless to resist her.

During that time he had stolen from his mother's pantry or concealed some of his own food to keep her from starvation. He wondered how much longer he could keep her secret from his parents. Yet he had to go on because he had already found out that all Squire Pearson had been able to do for his daughter was to secure her from torture if questioned by Matthew Hopkins.

115

The fourth morning, walking to work, he saw Major John Pearson ride into the Grange driveway. He thought for a little while, then decided to ask for his help privately. For the sake of propriety he waited an hour, then left his work to walk to the Grange.

'I wish to speak with Major John Pearson please,' he asked the maid who answered the door. 'I saw him arrive here over a hour ago.'

'You mean Colonel Pearson,' said the maid. 'Back from Naseby an' Leicester, promoted it seem. Whass yer name now?'

'Jeremy Goodway.'

'I know. From the little farm. You're the one whass courtin' the blacksmiss' daughter. Work in the parish office. I'll ask if he'll see yer.' She flashed him a smile and a look which indicated she would like him for herself.

The Colonel came to the door. 'What's this about Jeremy?' he asked, rather impatiently. 'This house is in distress over the disappearance of my sister, and I must needs ride out again very shortly.'

'I wanted to see you, sir, to ask advice about joining the army–the Ironsides.'

For the sake of anyone who might be listening, Jeremy had spoken in an unusually loud voice. Then before the Colonel could answer he continued in a whisper, 'I want to speak to you privately. I have your sister in hiding.'

Colonel Pearson took the cue. 'That's a noble ambition young man,' he said out loud. 'Let's walk awhile to the end of the drive and talk about it.'

Jeremy related details of how he had got Eve from the village bridewell, how he had hidden her and where. He explained that he had felt unable to inform Squire Pearson because, being involved with upholding the law, he would be compromised.

'You did right not to tell my father. That would have put him in an impossible situation. What you did was very brave, even though it's complicated the little he has managed to do for Eve.

'What I have already promised my parents I would do is to ride to Lieutenant General Cromwell and, as a special favour, ask for his intervention. In fact I was just about to start out. He isn't a law officer, but now has very strong influence in the highest circles. I may be lucky in that respect. However, it will take several days–time which we might not have had, were she still locked up.

'I want you to continue hiding my sister and not confide in anyone while I do my best. If I should fail, I will send a courier with a message to tell you, but if I succeed, I will try to return in person.

'It wouldn't be wise, I think, for me to go and see my sister. My presence at your father's farm would cause suspicion. Sadly, I also can't tell my mother that I know where Eve is, to relieve her worry.'

'I'll do my best to continue hiding her until you return, sir,' said Jeremy.

'May God be with you in your efforts,' said Colonel Pearson, 'and me in mine. What you've already done lad will not be forgotten by me or my family, and will not go without reward. Now I must be on my way.'

With that, the Colonel turned on his heels and returned to the house.

* * *

It was two days after he left Brentham that Colonel Pearson located Cromwell and was ushered into his presence. He explained all the details of Eve's arrest and escape and asked the favour of the Lieutenant General's intervention.

'I'm willing to help where I can an officer who has served so well and bravely, but this is a legal matter and outside my jurisdiction. What I *will* do is give you a letter to Mr John Bradshaw in London asking for his intervention. He serves as Attorney General for Parliament and has the power to stop prosecutions of this kind.

'Whether he will do so or not I can't say, but I'll make my request an earnest one. Due to our recent victories and your part in them, he could well be willing to grant me this favour.'

'Thank you, sir. I'm very grateful,' said Colonel Pearson.

Cromwell took paper and began to write while the Colonel waited.

'This matter seems to need speedy action. Therefore, what I've asked John Bradshaw to do, if he agrees, is to write instructions separately to the chief constable of Suffolk, your local constable, and this man Hopkins. Take at least two troopers with you so that you can be done with it quickly. The army needs you.

'Take also a junior officer to gather replacements from the training camps for your losses.

'We're on the move to aid General Waller by attacking the King's forces in the west now that we've severely defeated his attempt to invade the counties of the Eastern Association. As soon as you can, try to rendezvous with us at the town of Marlborough. Let the officer you leave in charge of your troops know that you'll be away a few days longer, and that he is to keep with the main body.'

'I'll do that sir, and thank you again,' said Colonel Pearson.

As he made to leave, Cromwell called him back. 'Colonel. That young man who showed such courage and initiative in rescuing your sister; he appears to be of the stuff good officers are made of. Speak to him about it.'

Colonel Pearson picked a cornet from his regiment and instructed him to ride to the training camps and collect twenty-six replacement troopers. Then told him to meet him at Brentham. If he had accomplished this before he himself was returned to that village, he should billet them there and wait, so that they could all return to the army in the field together.

After instructing his second in command and picking two reliable men to ride with him, the Colonel set out for London.

* * *

117

In London, John Bradshaw studied Cromwell's letter. 'He says here Colonel, that you'll tell me details of the matter. Pray do so now.'

Colonel Pearson then related once more about Eve's arrest and escape, and the slight easement of the situation that his father had already secured before her escape became known. He felt apprehensive, for it seemed by Bradshaw's attitude that he was reluctant to grant Cromwell's request.

'It seems to me,' said Bradshaw, 'that I, a senior law officer, am being asked to take a partial attitude in this matter. What makes it more difficult is that I am asked to do it to favour one who has already committed a crime by escaping from lawful custody. Pray give me more time to think this over. Return in two hours for my answer.'

After an anxious wait, Colonel Pearson returned full of apprehension. John Bradshaw's face was solemn. The Colonel feared the worst.

'Normally I would have turned down such a request as this,' said Bradshaw. 'for I've been asked to act in a most irregular fashion. However, I have a high regard for Lieutenant General Cromwell and his efforts in our cause. Here therefore are the three letters requested. I've also apologised to the chief constable of Suffolk for writing direct to your constable in Brentham due to the haste needed.'

'Thank you indeed, sir,' said the Colonel, taking the letters from Bradshaw's hand.

The one for Matthew Hopkins he bade one of the troopers deliver to the Thorn Inn, Mistley, if possible into the witchfinder's own hand. Then come to Brentham.

Taking the other trooper with him he rode off to Brentham himself, and arriving one evening, went straight to the constable's house.

The constable examined the letter. After first remarking that it was extraordinary for a simple village constable to receive instructions directly from so high an authority, he accepted its validity.

'This was done because of the need to hurry,' Colonel Pearson assured him. 'I have another here for your chief constable, who will be confirming the order to you within a day or two. Now I'll get my sister out of hiding and return her to our mother.'

'You can be assured that in the face of such an order as this, she has nothing to fear from me,' said the constable. 'No reason is given. Nor is one needed. But you know where she is hiding?'

'I discovered that several days ago,' said Colonel Pearson. 'Before I set out to ask for help from persons in high office.'

'Did your father the Squire know?'

'No. I kept my discovery secret so as not to compromise him. Neither will I disclose where she is, but merely see that she returns home before this day is ended.'

As he rode through the village, Colonel Pearson was met by his cornet, who had just come into Brentham with the new replacements for his regiment. 'You'll need to billet them for two to three days,' he said.

He next called at the parish office, where he found Jeremy working alone. 'Charges against Eve will not proceed on the orders of the Attorney General at the request of Cromwell. Is she still safe and well?' he asked.

'Yes,' said a very relieved Jeremy. 'Although in need of more variety in food.'

'I'm sure she's come to no harm through that,' said the Colonel, with a chuckle. 'How soon do you finish here?'

'In a little less than an hour.'

'As soon as you get home, send her to us. Now I go to comfort my mother with the news. Also to ask my father to instruct my courier where he may find the chief constable at this time. As for yourself, you have done very well. In fact it won the admiration of Lieutenant General Cromwell himself. Are you serious about wanting to join the Ironsides?'

'Yes sir. Indeed I am,' said Jeremy.

'I think I may be able to persuade General Cromwell to grant you a commission as a cornet to train as my aide in the field. You'll need a horse and money. After what you did, I feel sure my father would help you there. Continue working here quietly and prepare. I'll send a courier to fetch you when it's approved. I shall be leaving Brentham probably the day after tomorrow to catch up with my regiment which is even now moving to the west.'

CHAPTER 14

For Jeremy, Colonel Pearson's promise had been music to his ears. He was ashamed at the enjoyment from his affair with Eve. What could be better than to remove himself from his present confusion; from temptation and his infidelity to Bessie; and at the same time become one of the famous Ironsides.

The very heat Eve's responses and her initiative with variations in the art of making love was at last casting doubts in his mind as to her purity. He knew of course that she had been forcibly taken by Obadiah Dowdy. But that was the unwelcome attention of a old man. She had not learnt such things from that dreadful experience. Had there been other secret lovers? Could it be true what the bigots had been saying against her?

Three days after Eve went back to her family, Jeremy, to his own great disadvantage decided to do a gallant thing for her. Colonel Pearson had departed from Brentham with his soldiers the previous day. They had no sooner gone than some of the bigots began to say how unjust it was that Eve should be let off by people in high places without explanation, through the influence of her family; and without revealing by what black arts she had found it possible to escape from a locked cell.

Of course everyone now knew that Jeremy had been hiding her, because it was impossible to keep that a secret. Already they had been to the constable complaining that Jeremy had been harbouring an escaped prisoner. However, the constable had refused to act against him for that. He argued, since a higher authority had dictated that Eve was not to be charged, Jeremy had not hidden her from justice.

No one in Brentham knew Jeremy had set Eve free from the village bridewell apart from himself, Eve, the Squire and Mrs Pearson, and Colonel Pearson. After all, Eve was safe now, rumours of black arts could not harm her and would probably have died away in time had he let matters be.

Jeremy, however, knowing that he was going to walk away from Eve, decided to do one last gallant act for her, to kill the rumours once and for all. He went direct to the chief bigot–that remained after Obadiah Dowdy–Jonas Simpson. Miss Pearson had not by magic walked from a locked cell, he explained. It was himself who had got her out under the nose of a drunken and negligent deputy, locking the cell afterwards to give more time before discovery.

***

Nathaniel Pearson came bursting into his house. His wife could see that he was in an unaccustomed rage. 'What's amiss my dear?' she asked in alarm.

'I declare,' he said with exasperation, 'I shall never understand the folly of youth. Never!' He was almost shouting. 'I called in at the parish office to see young Jeremy Goodway. There I was met by Reverend Jones who informed me that earlier today he had been arrested by the constable. I went straightway to see Constable Scott. He told me that Jonas Simpson, Luke Smith, and two others, had laid formal complaint against Jeremy for breaking Eve out of custody.'

'How did they know that?' asked Mrs Pearson. 'I thought only us knew of it; and that only three days since.'

'You may well ask,' declared Nathaniel. 'Would you believe it; the young idiot told–yes, told–Jonas Simpson, of all people; and that in the presence of one of his clique.

'These bigots are smarting under their defeat about Eve and have turned on Jeremy in revenge. Apparently they had earlier tried to lay complaint against him for hiding Eve, but the constable resisted that on the grounds that she wasn't a fugitive.

'This has put me in a most invidious position. Breaking a prisoner out of jail is a serious crime under any circumstances. There'll be some who'll say I was tardy, and reluctant to act against him as I should.'

'Will our little Eve be in trouble again on that score?' asked Mrs Pearson. A look of anguish had come over her features.

'No. The order from the Attorney General covers that. He'd already been told of her escape when he made it.'

'Could you not argue that the same should apply to Jeremy.'

'There's no harm in that. I'll instruct our lawyer to act for him and do so. But I fear it'll not succeed. The order that Eve was not to be charged was the discretionary act of powerful man. It had no legal basis.'

'Can you do anything else for the poor young man?'

'I have given thought to that,' said the Squire . 'He can't possibly be judged innocent, since he has admitted it. The best I can do is make sure that I'm here to preside at his parish trial. I may be able to prevent it being sent to a higher court, and use my influence for the lightest possible sentence. Maybe I can get just a day in the stocks accepted. I will do my very best to avoid further imprisonment or the whipping post for him.'

'The whipping post!' cried Mrs Pearson. 'Could that happen, and he so refined and educated a lad?'

'I fear so,' said Nathaniel; 'and it would fall to me to speak the sentence. None the less I must preside, to try to keep it down. Some of the brethren are vengeful.'

✳ ✳ ✳

Jeremy had not realised what great trouble he was in until the lawyer had visited him and explained.

'I'll do my utmost to argue that justice demands the charge be dismissed. However, I fear I'll not succeed in that. Next I'll argue that the matter can be judged in the parish court. In this I expect to be successful. Then I shall plead for a light sentence.'

'What sentence am I likely to get?' asked Jeremy anxiously.

'There may be some who will want you locked up here for another six

121

months or more and suffer fifty lashes into the bargain. However, Mr Pearson will be presiding and doing his best for you. He may be able to get you away with a just a day in the stocks, but I think you should prepare yourself for a little experience at the whipping post. Say a dozen strokes.'

So Jeremy, although fearful, was not surprised when a few days later, at the end of his parish trial, he heard the Squire pronounce sentence; a dozen lashes and sit for a day in the stocks. The lawyer's prediction had been accurate. He heard Bessie and Eve, who were both in the court, gasp and sob.

He resolved to take his punishment like a man; not to scream or cry–and he kept that resolution the next day as he suffered. But he made another. Without waiting to hear of Colonel Pearson's success in getting him a commission, he would leave Brentham and enlist as an ordinary soldier. As long as he stayed in the village he would never be free from the temptation of Eve, or the hostility of the bigots. Obadiah Dowdy still had a few friends. Now by spite they had shown themselves for what they were.

After the whipping was over and the constable put him in the stocks, Doctor Mills came to dress his stripes. Constable Scott turned a blind eye.

'I don't usually get this commission,' said the doctor. 'Wrongdoers normally have to rely on the ministrations of their women folk, after much more punishment. Even having to wait for that until after they have been released from the stocks.

'Mr Pearson engaged my services. I'm to tell you that he wishes to see you after this is over. It'll be to your advantage, and he trusts you don't think ill of him for doing his duty.'

When Jeremy was released in the evening, his father was waiting. 'Come over to Sam's,' he said. 'Your mother is waiting there.'

Still sore from the whipping, Jeremy's back and legs also ached from sitting long hours with his ankles held in the stocks. He did not relish meeting Bessie, for he felt guilty towards her; but he was glad of the chance to sit in a more comfortable position for a while.

His mother hugged and kissed him, forgetful of his sore back until he winced.

'You need this no doubt,' said the kindly Mrs Bloom, handing him a tankard of ale. He thanked her.

'Thass a sore reward yer got for a good deed,' said Samuel Bloom. 'Sometimes I think our Joseph is right in wot he say. No good come from helpin' the gentry.'

'Oh, I don't blame Mr Pearson because he had to pass sentence. I could have fared much worse without him there. I've no doubt who was really responsible. In any case, it was my own folly for telling Jonas Simpson about getting Eve out.

'It won't happen again. I shall be out of reach of their spite. Tomorrow I'm going to leave Brentham to join the army.'

'But Jeremy!' exclaimed his mother, tears coming to her eyes.

'I thought yer wanted to be a trooper,' said his father. 'I only got one hoss thass barely suitable for that, an' I can scarce afford to let it go.'

'That doesn't matter. I'm content to volunteer as a foot soldier and train as a musketeer, like Joseph.'

'So thass how our sacrifice is to end,' said Silas Goodway, growing rather angry.

'I must be going,' said Jeremy, changing the subject as he finished his ale and stood up. 'With your permission Mrs Bloom. The Squire has asked me to see him this evening.'

He noticed that Bessie was missing and could hear her sobbing in the kitchen.

Silas and Mary Goodway left at the same time, all the way trying to talk him out of his decision. He had not changed his mind when they left him at the Grange gateway.

'I was glad to hear from Doctor Mills that you don't think ill of me,' said Nathaniel after the maid had ushered him in. 'I did what I could.'

'I realise that, sir. Much was my own folly for telling Jonas Simpson' said Jeremy.

'Indeed it was,' said the Squire . 'It seems an appropriate time to reward you for what you did for Eve. Without that, my son would not have accomplished what he did in time for her to be saved from the assizes.'

As Nathaniel spoke, a wicked thought crossed Jeremy's mind. That Eve had already rewarded him in full measure. Then sharp awareness of his sin returned.

'I did but do what seemed necessary,' he said, 'and caused more problems by locking the door.'

'Never mind about that,' said Nathaniel. 'All is now safe.

'John told me before he left that you had ambitions to become one of the Ironsides, and that he had promised to try and get you a junior commission to train under him.'

'Yes. That's correct, sir,' said Jeremy.

'For that you'll need a good horse. I'll help you there when the time comes. Cavalrymen have to provide their own mounts. Come around tomorrow and pick yourself a horse from my stables, and practice your riding while you wait to hear from John.'

Jeremy hesitated for a moment; his resolve weakened, then recovered. 'Tomorrow I leave Brentham to volunteer as a foot soldier. After what has happened, I won't stay here another day.'

'Please let me persuade you against that course,' urged Nathaniel. 'John could do a lot for you in the army. He's in high good favour with Lieutenant General Cromwell, and through him with the Commander in Chief, Sir Thomas Fairfax.'

'I truly believe he would, sir, and I must seem ungrateful, but Brentham has turned sour for me. I cannot wait.'

'Then at least come in the morning, and choose the horse I have offered you, that you may enlist as a trooper; and a little money also, for the army I hear is in arrears paying its soldiers.'

'Thank you very much,' said Jeremy, a smile coming to his face. 'I accept gladly. It's a cavalry soldier I really want to be.'

'Then be round tomorrow at eight-thirty,' said the Squire , showing him to the door. 'And think overnight of the benefits you would gain by waiting.'

In the morning, Eve waylaid him as he approached the Grange gateway. 'You're out walking early, Eve' he called to her, for want of something better to say, because he felt guilty about leaving her.

'As well I might be,' she snapped back. 'What's this folly I hear from my father. That you are off to join the army today. And without even waiting to see if my brother can get you in as an officer.'

'You must understand. After what's happened there'll be no respite for me in Brentham from the spite of the bigots.'

Her tone softened. 'Doesn't our love mean anything to you Jeremy? For all you know I could be with child. You possessed me above a score of times with passion. Will you now run away like a coward? I doubt my father would be giving you a horse if he knew what had passed between us.'

As she spoke, she rested her hand on his forearm. At once he felt his loins stir and was tempted to take her in his arms; but they were within sight of the house now.

He found the strength. 'I must go, Eve,' he insisted. 'If you are with child, and your father permits it, I'll do the honourable thing and wed you when I return. Though what I could give you I don't know.'

Her anger rose. She stood before him, making him stop. 'After surrendering my body to you over and over, you still cannot decide between me and the little Bloom girl,' she hissed. Then turning on her heels in a temper, ran crying into the house.

So Jeremy chose his horse and accepted another gift of fifteen pounds from Eve's father. After saying farewell first to his parents, then to Samuel Bloom and his wife, and a nod to a weeping Bessie, he rode out of Brentham looking forward to whatever adventures lay before him.

***

Eve had shut herself in her room after her encounter with Jeremy. She stayed there for an hour so that her parents might not see her distress.

Her ploy to stop him going had been a lie. Nature had already told her that she was still not pregnant. She doubted now if she ever would be. Marcus had been the first. It was said women did not conceive the first time, but he had taken her twice that night. Obadiah Dowdy had raped her, or she thought he had managed to, but that was the feeble effort of an old man, and he had no family. But the common Eli Brown had already proved himself with another before he took her, and Jeremy had deposited his seed within her nigh thirty times. She judged herself barren.

Turning her mind to what life might hold for her in that condition, she resolved that if she was not to have family she would try to have great riches should the opportunity arise again from the Marquess of Stourland. None but herself knew she might be barren. Union with him would not last long, and a rich widow might have many lovers.

Would the callous Jeremy Goodway, spurn her riches as well as her love, she wondered? She might yet get him from the blacksmith's little daughter.

She pulled herself back from her day-dreaming, and went down to help her father. As yet the Marquess hadn't repeated his offer.

✳✳✳

Obadiah Dowdy had stayed well away from Brentham for three weeks. He felt that to be the wise course to give his plans time to hatch. Deciding to see if he could glean any information from Matthew Hopkins before going over there to see Ruth Merton, he lingered after giving the witchfinder general his latest batch of names. It would not do to let Hopkins know that he was curious about Brentham.

'I can see how you came to grief in your old parish,' said Hopkins, with an unusual willingness to give information. 'You pitted yourself against too powerful a family it seems.

'Two weeks ago, I went to Brentham at the behest of their constable to question one, Eve Pearson, daughter of the Squire, who the constable had locked up, she having been denounced witch by several common people, and one not so common. Yet the constable required more evidence!

'When I arrived, I was told she'd escaped by some magic from behind a locked door. I was also told by the constable that when she was apprehended, I wouldn't be able to coerce her into giving the answers I sought, on the orders of the chief constable of Suffolk.

'Some days after I returned from this fool's errand, I received a letter from the chief constable of Essex forbidding me to have her brought into this county for questioning because it was a Suffolk matter. Yet a few days more and I received this, brought by an army courier from the highest authority, that I was not to attempt to bring or assist in the bringing of charges against her at all!'

He handed Dowdy the order from John Bradshaw.

'This appears to be direct from the Attorney General!' said the incredulous plotter, aghast at the failure of his plans.

'It not only appears to be from him, but is. I'm satisfied of that,' said Hopkins. 'Apart from the wasted time of this wicked farce, I care not. There are other witches a'plenty. I'll not move against this one again.'

Dowdy left the room deflated. The Mertons had failed him, they would not get the rest of the money. He rued having given them any. There was

125

nothing more he could do now but settle down to keep making more money from bribes. Some day, if there were justice, he would have his revenge.

CHAPTER 15

January 1646 found Jeremy in Abingdon and he was bored. His unit had been sent there in December as part of a force to garrison the town; a task until recently performed by auxiliaries from London, until they went home.

Little was happening at Abingdon, although it was not far from the Royalist headquarters at Oxford. Apart from keeping his horse well groomed, weapons and equipment clean and uniform smart, there was little to do except patrol and guard duties. In fact those were almost the only things he had been doing since he finished his training, wherever he had been.

Occasionally they had been sent to quell minor disturbances here and there, but had not been engaged in any fighting as such. His pistols had as yet fired at nothing in anger, or his sword slashed at anything other than dummies.

The war had moved on as the King's forces, reeling from defeat after defeat at the hands of the New Model Army, sought to make a last desperate resistance in the west country.

It was all but over, Jeremy reflected, and he had missed it. All his training had been for nothing; his ambition to be one of the famous Ironsides would not be achieved. True he was a trained trooper and they were all starting to be referred to as Ironsides now, but had he had the patience to remain in Brentham a few more weeks, he would no doubt have been sent for by Colonel Pearson and been long since in the thick of things.

Lately he thought occasionally of Bessie and Eve again. If the war was shortly to be over, he wondered if he would be forced to leave the army. Although the bitter distaste for Brentham that had overtaken him at the time of his punishment had mellowed, he knew he could never return there to live as long as Eve was around. Just thinking of her would even now cause his phallus to stir. He wondered if she was by now heavy with child as a result of their copulation, and fervently prayed that she was not. Although he had a good education, it had not been quite completed; and he was from a humble background. Marriage with a daughter of the minor gentry–and one of dubious purity at that–would not make for a happy future. He began to day-dream of going to Brentham and taking Bessie–the virgin–away somewhere and getting married.

In the second week of February, the call that Jeremy longed for came. His troop was ordered to join, as replacements, the main body of the army under Sir Thomas Fairfax in the west. Campaigning this year had started early and it was said that Exeter was already under siege by units of the New Model Army.

They rode hard, and although impeded somewhat by muddy roads, made rendezvous early in the afternoon of the fourth day near the little village of

Chulmleigh in Devon. It had been raining and they were tired.

Rumour was that they were going into battle next morning to attack Torrington. However, they had scarce had time clean off the mud of their journey and to eat a meal before they were ordered back into their saddles. It was already growing dusk. The sound of cannon and their muzzle flashes lit up the gathering gloom. Jeremy had never imagined it would be like this; in darkness and so sudden. He had not even heard which regiment they had been attached to or the name of its commanding officer. As he rode he prayed silently that his courage would not fail.

They lined up to charge, just as they had been trained. Their troop formed part of the second line. The guns stopped. The first line moved off at a steady trot. Shortly Jeremy heard shouts and the clash of steel through the gathering darkness. 'Be ready,' called the troop commanders in his line. He heard a ragged volley as the first line discharged their first pistols. 'Move off,' came the command to his line. They moved at a walk and another ragged volley came as the first line discharged their second pistols.

The first line passed through them on their return. They closed back up and at a command broke into a steady trot. They were only yards from the enemy now and the ground was difficult. Jeremy heard shots passing through their line and the scream of a nearby man as he fell. Now they were upon the enemy and he was slashing and stabbing as he had been trained. Sometimes he made contact but mostly he missed. Visibility was bad now–the enemy were faceless shadows. All was noise and shouting. The Royalists were putting up a stiff resistance, but he sensed that they were pushing them back a little. The order to fire came and they discharged their pistols at close range into the enemy. Screams were heard, and at a command they fired their second pistols.

'Retire' came the order. Turning about they were soon passing through the third line coming forward to attack an enemy not yet recovered from their own assault.

They passed through to the rear of the first line who had just finished reloading their weapons. At a command they started the lengthy process of reloading their own pistols. Jeremy sensed, but could not see for the darkness, the first line moving off again.

Now they, themselves had finished their reloading and the returning third line was passing through them. Soon it would be their turn again.

Time and time again the cavalry lines attacked the determined enemy, relentlessly pushing them back. Now they were where the houses started. Too difficult to fight with proper formations as the streets narrowed. Men fought in little groups; infantry as well as cavalry. No room for large hedgehogs of pike men protecting the musketeers as they loaded their cumbersome weapons. Some were using them as clubs.

There was much confusion in the dark streets, only illuminated by the occasional building on fire. Jeremy struck out when he could find an enemy in the melee. It was difficult to tell friend from foe. Then there seemed to be few, if any, enemy. They were retreating fast.

Suddenly the sky lit up as a thunderous explosion rent the air. The noise was so loud that it alarmed Jeremy far more than his first assault on the enemy lines. Masonry started cascading down. There were screams in the crowded streets as men were hit. Now he was going to die–he could feel it coming. He felt the blow to his head–then nothing more but blackness.

He recovered consciousness, realising he was almost upside down with a foot caught in his stirrup. His head ached from the blow and his shoulder from the fall. With difficulty he pulled himself up and freed his foot. He appeared to be not seriously hurt. Incredibly his horse was still standing more or less where it had happened. The street was littered with rubble. Dead and wounded lying all about. He removed his turtle-pot helmet. There was a significant dent in it. With sudden gratitude, he knelt by his beast and gave thanks to God; for his first battle was over, and he had survived.

He had no idea how long he had been unconscious, but it was still dark, so it could not have been long. Also he did not know where his troop was, and there was no point trying to pick his way through the rubble in the dark to look for them. So he just sat in a recessed doorway, reins in hand, to wait for dawn.

He must have either fallen asleep or passed out again, because when he came to, the morning was already well advanced, but his horse was gone. He found his troop about an hour later drawn up in a square surrounded by many damaged buildings. They were about to be addressed by the troop commander. The officer looked at Jeremy. 'Where have you been, Goodway?' he asked. 'We didn't find you among the dead and wounded. You look a terrible sight.'

'I was hit by falling masonry, sir, after an enormous explosion.' Jeremy pointed to his damaged helmet. 'How long I was unconscious I don't know, but I came to, hanging with my foot caught in my stirrup. It was dark and I was confused by the blow, so sat down to rest in a deeply recessed doorway with my horse's reins in my hands. Whether I passed out again or fell asleep I don't know, but when I came to again, about an hour ago, my horse had gone!'

'Your horse is here,' said the officer, pointing to a group of beasts being guarded by two troopers at the end of the square. 'Are you injured?'

'Nothing but a bad head and aching shoulder from my fall, sir.'

'Well, after we get you billeted, you can rest up for the remainder of the day. I'll command one of the doctors in the town to take a look at you. Both surgeons are leaving with the main army.

'The rest of you will take parties of townspeople and make them clear up all the rubble

'The explosion was caused by a retreating enemy soldier setting fire to their magazine in that church.' The officer pointed to a nearly demolished building. 'It was devil's work, for there were about two-hundred of our own men held prisoner in there. All were killed.'

'As for this troop, we have lost seven killed and ten wounded.

'Because we only arrived late yesterday after a long ride and were thrown straight into action, the colonel of our new regiment has directed that this troop be left here with some from other units to garrison this town. The main body of the army is even now starting to pursue the retreating enemy army of the west to its destruction.

'When that is done they will call back this way and we can join them for the final assault on the King's headquarters base at Oxford. Back almost from where we came but a few days since.'

'Who's regiment are we in, sir?' called out one of the troopers. 'Being sent into battle so quickly, we weren't told.'

'The name of our regimental commander is Colonel John Pearson,' said the officer. 'A veteran of nearly the whole war. Edgehill; Winceby; Marston Moor; Second Newbury; Naseby and a score of others. A hero, and one of the original Ironsides. It'll be an honour for us all to serve under him.'

Jeremy received news of this coincidence with mixed feelings. Now he was a real Ironside. But what would Colonel Pearson say to him when they met. Would he understand his reasons for leaving Brentham, or would he have taken offence at this seeming rejection of his offer?

A month passed at Torrington during which news arrived of the surrender of the King's army of the west. The war, it seemed obvious, was drawing to its end. Jeremy's troop rejoined Colonel Pearson's regiment as it moved back with large sections of the army heading to complete the siege of Oxford and force a final surrender.

News came that the King's last field army under Lord Astey was headed in their direction, hotly pursued by Parliamentary units under General Brereton moving south, having captured Chester. Colonel Pearson's regiment was diverted from its march to assist in the entrapment of Lord Astey's forces and it was at Stow-in-the-Wold on 21 March that trooper Jeremy Goodway had his second taste of battle.

The fighting was fierce and the heavily outnumbered forces of Lord Astey resisted stoutly before bowing to the inevitable. While senior officers were negotiating surrender, Jeremy and his comrades were engaged in disarming and marshalling prisoners.

'Trooper Goodway!'

Jeremy turned around to see his troop commander beckon him from a little distance. He walked towards the officer.

'Goodway. Colonel Pearson wants to see you.'

'The Colonel!' exclaimed Jeremy. Alarm showing on his face. 'What for?'

'How would I know that?' asked the officer with asperity. Then with a twinkle in his eye. 'Perhaps it's about losing your horse at Torrington.'

Jeremy turned around, worried, and started to walk towards a group of senior officers a few hundred yards away.

'Trooper Goodway!'

Jeremy turned around. The troop commander was calling him back.

'I don't think it's too bad, Goodway. He asked me how you performed in battle. I told him you did your duty well. I understand you were some sort of hero before you joined the army. Liked to rescue maidens in distress.'

'Sir?'

The officer waved him away and he turned to go.

'Trooper Goodway.'

This time when Jeremy turned, the officer was frowning.

'I trust that's all you did to his sister, Goodway. Rescue her. Off you go.'

Now Jeremy's stomach was turning over as he approached where Colonel Pearson was standing. It was about Eve, he was sure. She was pregnant and the Colonel knew. What would he say when accused of dishonouring the Colonel's sister? He dishonour her! That was unjust; she dishonoured him; she was no maid. Would it be right to save himself by explaining that to his Colonel, he wondered?

He stood respectfully a few yards distant from the group of officers waiting to be noticed. After a while they broke up and Colonel Pearson walked towards him. Jeremy looked at his face. The expression was neutral, Could not tell anything from that.

'Trooper Goodway.'

Not "Jeremy" he noticed. But of course he was an Ironside. An officer would never address a trooper by his Christian name. Bad for discipline.

'Sir.'

'So you were too impatient to wait to see my offer come to fruition?'

It was a bad start.

'I was feeling humiliated after being flogged and made to sit in the stocks. I wanted to get away from Brentham.'

'That I understand, though whether a mere twelve lashes can be called a flogging, I don't know. I think my father, the Squire, did quite well to get you so little a sentence. And then only after you got yourself into trouble by boasting to your enemies of what you had done.'

'I realise I could have fared much worse, sir, and it was due to my own indiscretion, but I was only trying to protect Miss Eve's good name.'

'A task which becomes more difficult by the day,' said Colonel Pearson.

Jeremy was astounded by that remark, and it gave him the courage to ask, 'How is Miss Eve, sir?'

'You mean, the Marchioness of Stourland.'

Jeremy's heart plunged to his boots.

'Sir?'

'Yes. I dare say you *are* surprised. My sister married the Marquess of Stourland last December. It was a simple ceremony. I was there. It seems the

Marquess renewed an offer which he made back in forty-four then withdrew when you two were in trouble together. Though by what guile she caused him to make it, I don't know. Personally I'm not in favour of spring marrying winter; or in her case perhaps I should say "high summer" marrying winter. However it seems she jumped at the chance, and it will not be at all a bad thing. She's been a worry to my mother by her erratic behaviour these last three or four years, and my father's rivals have ever been ready to use her to his disadvantage, because of her beautiful but immodest looking features. Now she's no longer their responsibility.'

Jeremy was so overawed by the news and the Colonel's frankness about his sister that he did not take in what he said next.

'What is your answer?' he heard him say as he came back to life.

'Sir?'

'You were day-dreaming, trooper. There is but little room in this army for an officer who day-dreams,' said the Colonel with some asperity.

'Officer, sir?'

'If you'd been listening, instead of mooning over my sister, you'd have heard me say that your troop commander has given me good reports of your performance in battle and your conduct as a soldier in general. I had to make sure of that before I approached Lieutenant General Cromwell again on your behalf.

'Today is the twenty-first of March. Do you still wish to become an officer if I can get it approved? Eight months since, I promised that as *my* reward for your efforts in saving Eve, and I'd be glad if you would now, at last, allow me to keep my word.'

'Thank you, sir.' I'll do my utmost to live up to the honour.'

'Good. Return to your duties with your troop. We're moving against Oxford now. Leiutenant General Cromwell and the Commander-in-Chief, Sir Thomas Fairfax are likely to be there with us at some stage for the final show-down. I'll try to take you to them.'

As he walked back to his duties with his troop, his emotions were mixed. Elated at the prospect of becoming an officer. Pleased that his interview with Colonel Pearson had gone well. Pleased also that if he ever had the chance to return to Brentham he would be free from the temptation of Eve. Yet he felt jealous–wretched and jealous.

***

Jeremy was in buoyant mood as he rode out of Cambridge, heading for Brentham, for he was going home with something to boast of. Although it was not yet 7 o'clock, the early morning sun was already lighting up the countryside on this late July morning. A year had passed since he left Brentham, angry and humiliated by his public whipping and day in the stocks. Now he was returning, resplendent in uniform with orange sash, a junior officer who had seen action in three places; Torrington, Stow-in-the-Wold, and Oxford.

The terrible civil war was over it seemed, although he had been told a negotiated settlement with the defeated King had still to be reached. But those were matters for older men of higher rank and station in life. He was young, still with five months to go before his twentieth birthday. His attitude to Brentham had mellowed during his year of service. Now with a fortnight's leave of absence before him, the world seemed a bright and pleasant place.

He was going back to Brentham where he had been tempted of the flesh and failed. Where he had paid in some measure for those sins at the whipping post and in the stocks. He had, by God's mercy, completed his atonement in the fire and battle of a just cause. He had served with comrades imbued with a spirit of righteousness and clean living, who prayed before and after battle and sang psalms of praise for victory; where drunkenness was forbidden and where a man could lose the skin off his back for taking the name of God in vain. Not among these men was the levity and incitement to sin of the Cambridge scholars he had known. For this was the great New Model Army created by Fairfax and Cromwell which, by discipline and training, had in eighteen months, transformed an endless war of attrition into complete victory. And he was one of Cromwell's famous Ironsides, the very backbone of that army.

His mother and father would be proud of him. He would be able to show Squire Pearson that he had kept the horse he had given him in prime condition. Samuel and Mrs Bloom; they would be pleased to see him–and Bessie. He had been unkind to Bessie, for she had shown her love for him, and he had not returned it as he should, so besotted had he been with the fleshly delights of Eve.

At that thought he stopped his horse, leaned his head forward and uttered a prayer of thanksgiving that God had allowed rational thoughts to come into his head. The jealousy that had overtaken him in March, on hearing of Eve's marriage, had long dissipated in the face of sound reasoning. There could never have been any future for him with her. She had chosen to wed riches and age. She was of the aristocracy now–a marchioness. As the daughter of Squire Pearson, she had been above him in the social order; as the Marchioness of Stourland, she was remote indeed. Temptation had been removed.

He remounted and rode on, his thoughts now of Bessie. Now she was seventeen. By the time he was twenty she would be eighteen–of marriageable age. He hoped she had not given her love to another suitor while he had been away.

It was about 5 o'clock in the afternoon when Jeremy approached Brentham. He could have covered the distance quicker, but like all good cavalrymen he had thought of his horse as well as himself. The day had been hot so at noon they both stopped at an inn for two hours, where he bought himself a meal, after first grooming down and stabling his beast and attending to its feed.

There were also two or three shorter stops of a few minutes.

At the end he made a slight detour round the village, so as to come in from the north and thus to his parents farm. It was only right they should see him first. A few hundred yards short he stopped once more under the shade of some trees and gave his horse a final rub down and dusted himself off. This fine beast, he thought, has carried me today over thirty-five miles and looks as fresh as when we started this morning.

His mother was out, no doubt around the farm with his father, so he went to look for them. His mother saw him first and thought it was a stranger approaching. Then recognition dawned and she called to Silas and ran to embrace her son.

'Oh Jeremy, we've been so worried about yer. We ain't heard nothin' since yer wrote an' said how they was gooner make yer an officer.' She released him. 'Look there's me not thinkin'. Can't muck up them smart clothes with my dirty hands.'

'Paper is not too easy to come by on active service,' he excused himself, 'and I know what a problem it is for you to read letters.'

Just then his father came up and took him by the hand. 'Good to hev yer back son. Where hev yer jus' come from?'

'Cambridge. Our regiment moved there soon after the fall of Oxford on twenty-fourth of June.

'Come. Let me stable yer hoss. Then we'll go in the house an' yer can tell us all about it. I can take a couple of hours off my labours to speak to my son.'

Jeremy told them in greater detail that he had been able to write of his training, of his time at Abingdon, of Torrington, and of Stow-in-the-Wold.

'Then we moved on to Oxford. That was when I wrote to you at end of March. We started to help with the encirclement. Part of our army had been there some time, but the place wasn't properly sealed off. By the time it was tightened up, it was end of April, and we later learned the King had slipped away three days earlier and gone to Newark to surrender himself to the Scots. Rumour has it that he did that because he thought he could get a better deal from them by agreeing to their demand about Presbyterianism and maybe turn them against the English Parliament.'

'I heard a rumour that the Scots are giving him up to the English,' said Silas Goodway.

'Well, selling him,' said Jeremy. 'Of course. I'm only a junior officer, so Cromwell doesn't tell me things direct. I get my information third hand, usually from Colonel Pearson whose aide I am. It appears that after the Scots had the King they decided they couldn't trust him, so being in need of money, they offered him to the English Parliament for as great a sum as they thought they could extract. I hear it hasn't been settled yet.'

'Thass a rum carry on,' said Mary Goodway.

'Did yer get to speak to Cromwell at all?' asked Silas.

'The Colonel took me in to see him when he sought to have me made an officer. The Commander-in-Chief, Sir Thomas Fairfax was with him.'

'You met them both?'

'Yes. The Lieutenant General had most to say. He's a very direct man, not very handsome. Refers to scripture and God a lot in his speech. They do say that he studies scripture for guidance and justification of all his decisions. Sir Thomas is tall and good looking. Seems quiet and doesn't say much.'

'But what about the fightin' round Oxford. You ain't told us much about that?.'

'Our forces made several attacks trying to break in, but without success. I wasn't in all of them. Apart from that it was mostly exchange of gunfire by the artillery and patrols for us. In the end of course they had to surrender because there was no help coming.'

Jeremy then went on to tell details of various attacks he had taken part in, by which time two hours had passed.

'Thanks be to God thass all over an' you've been spared,' said Mary Goodway. 'Now thass time I was preparin' our evenin' meal.'

'While you're doing that, mother, I'll just pop round to see Squire Pearson. I have a message from his son.'

'What about Sam Bloom?' asked his father.

'Samuel will want to have all the details. There won't be time tonight after we've eaten. I'll go down the village straight after breakfast tomorrow,' replied Jeremy.

In the morning he called at the forge. He was in happy anticipation of meeting Bessie, for his parents had already told him over supper that Bessie was not courting anyone.

'Well, an' look at this fine gentleman,' cried Samuel. 'Bessie! There's somebody here you're gooner want to see. Thass a fact.'

'Bessie's helping you in here?' asked Jeremy somewhat surprised.

'Yes. With some of the lighter things, an' the goods wot come off the stage wagons. She allus did a bit, but now she do more since I was took badly ill last winter an' can't work such long hours. Some say that ain't right work for a maid, but I can't manage much longer without Joseph, unless I can get a man from somewhere. Trouble is, most men wot ain't on the land or in service hev been took by the press for that big army you're in. Thank God thass over.'

'I was sorry to hear you'd been ill, Samuel,' said Jeremy.

Just them Bessie appeared from the back with a blush and a smile. Obviously she had been trying to tidy herself because she had made a smear just below her hairline. Jeremy thought it made her look rather sweet. She had blossomed out some more. The old clothes she was wearing did not detract much from her virginal beauty. 'Jeremy. Nice to see yer.'

'Come on in the cottage. I'm gooner shut up for an hour,' said Samuel. 'I gotter hear all about wot you been doin'. You an officer. Who'd hev thought it?'

In the cottage, Mrs Bloom greeted him with profuse admiration. He gave answer to all their questions, for the blacksmith wanted to hear all his experiences.

'Is it true wot Joseph said once that Cromwell might favour this country bein' a republic?' asked Samuel.

'Almost certainly not I should think,' said Jeremy. 'That's an idea put about by supporters of the Levellers. According to Colonel Pearson, he's only too keen to negotiate with the King for a more democratic monarchy. His son-in-law, Commissary General Ireton is working on some ideas.'

'I allus said Joseph was talkin' through his hat gettin' mixed up with them Levellers,' said Mrs Bloom.

Changing the subject, Jeremy asked, 'Do I have your permission to ask Bessie to go out walking this evening?'

'Thass alright by us an' allus will be. Ain't that right, wife?'

'Yes,' said Mrs Bloom.

Bessie had just returned. She had been away to clean herself up and look more presentable for Jeremy.

Duing the two weeks he was home, Jeremy and Bessie went out walking most evenings. They were growing closer gradually; the kisses became more ardent; the touches more intimate; but still not inside clothing. His manhood would stir and although he was tempted to go further, he could resist, because this was Bessie.

On the morning of his departure, Jeremy rode out on the road that went south from the village before, at a fork well beyond the boundary, it turned westward towards Cambridge.

At this fork stood the main gate to the Manor House and by that gate, wandering or waiting, was the Lady Eve, Marchioness of Stourland.

He stopped at her signal and out of courtesy dismounted. 'Your Ladyship?'

She let out a giggle. 'It's right that you should address me thus in company, and I address you by your rank. But when it's just us, I shall ever be Eve and you Jeremy. My husband, the Marquess, would be pleased if you could spare him a few moments.'

He wanted to ask how she knew he would be passing at that time but did not, because the son of a tenant farmer did not question a marchioness–and he was Jeremy and she was Eve.

He also wondered why a servant had not been sent to intercept him, but did not ask, because she was Eve and he was Jeremy.

Instead, he just followed her.

CHAPTER 16

Jeremy waited anxiously on a May evening in 1647 for Colonel Pearson to return from his meeting with Cromwell, praying fervently that his request for the life of Joseph Bloom, Bessie's brother, to be spared from hanging would be granted. If it was, he prayed that it might go some way to atone for his weakness in the face of fleshly temptation. For when she had tempted he had fallen, just as Adam had fallen before the temptation of that other Eve.

In spite of his growing fondness for Bessie; in spite of his resolutions to put thoughts of Eve from his mind; in spite of his doubts; when she had beckoned, he followed. Followed even when she had confessed that after all the Marquess was not at home. Followed when she led him to a summer-house, that they might be private from the servants. Followed her summons to gratify an urgent need that did not even grant time to undress as they copulated against a wall. Followed again as she stayed his departure, and there in the woodland on the warm summer grass, careless of discovery, took her naked while her cries of ecstasy rent the air.

He, Cornet Jeremy Goodway, had committed adultery with Eve, Marchioness of Stourland; he had partaken of forbidden fruit. God had not accepted Adam's excuse that that other Eve had tempted him. He was as guilty as she.

Nine more months of army life had passed for Jeremy since his return from Brentham without much happening, except patrols and putting down the occasional minor disturbance, to relieve his consciousness of this latest sin. The only news of significance during that time was that the King had been handed over by the Scots to representatives of Parliament at the end of January, and was now living at Holmby House in Northamptonshire while negotiations for a settlement progressed.

Meanwhile, vast numbers of soldiers with nothing to do were encamped in many parts of the country. Large concentrations especially were around Newmarket. Pay for the men was in serious arrears and being withheld by Parliament, which, after the enormous expenditure of the war and the large bribe paid to the Scots to hand over the King, was hoping to disband a lot of regiments without paying them. Discontent of the soldiers at their wretched conditions was endemic and Leveller agitation abounded.

Colonel Pearson's regiment had been ordered to Newmarket Heath to quell a mutiny there. When they arrived, they found that the core of that mutiny had already been dealt with by another unit, who had arrested twenty men for incitement to disobedience. The remainder of the soldiers were in a truculent mood, but violent disobedience had ceased on the promise that Lieutenant General Cromwell was coming to speak to them about their grievances.

Cromwell had come and assured them that both he and Sir Thomas

Fairfax were with them in their grievances against an ungrateful Parliament, and would not suffer them to be disbanded without the pay due. Being thus assured by one they respected, the men had calmed down; but Cromwell would not have breaches of army discipline at any cost, so had ordered immediate courts martial for the twenty. They were all condemned to hang at sunset.

Jeremy had been appalled to learn that Sergeant Joseph Bloom, brother of dear Bessie, was among the condemned. He had gone to his colonel and begged him to use his influence with Cromwell to have Joseph reprieved. 'It's none other than the son of Samuel Bloom, the blacksmith, of Brentham, whom you know,' he had explained.

'Ah, that Bloom,' Colonel Pearson had said. 'Then it's a case of, "Like father, like son", for I recall hearing that in his young days, Samuel was ever one to oppose authority with his tongue. However, he's a stout fellow, so I'll do my best to save his son; but don't expect too much, because the Lieutenant General will have discipline, for that is the basis on which he built this army which won the war.'

Jeremy waited and prayed for what seemed hours. At length Colonel Pearson came back. 'I've prevailed on the Lieutenant General to be merciful to Joseph Bloom. In fact, he relented and looked at all the cases again whilst I was with him. That's what took so long. Now only the six worst offenders are to hang tonight. The other fourteen are all to receive various doses of the lash in the morning according to their involvement. In Bloom's case this is to be three dozen. He is also to lose his rank of sergeant. I tried in vain to get the Lieutenant General to change his mind about that last. He said that although Bloom had a record as a good soldier up to then, to leave him with his rank would be a licence for others to mutiny.'

The next day, Jeremy sought out Joseph to see how he fared after his punishment.

'Sore but alive,' said Joseph, 'Thanks be to God–and to your colonel I hear.'

'Yes. That's so,' said Jeremy. 'Have you managed to visit Brentham lately?'

'Went for a few days couple of months ago. First time for over two year. Then only 'cos there ain't been nothin' for us to do for months. What with that an' the pay bein' so far behind, small wonder some hev jus' done a flip.'

'Could I say somethin' without causin' offence. You bein' an officer, like?'

'Of course,' said Jeremy.

'I heard when I was there as how yer saved the Squire's daughter, an' got yer back marked for it. Well might they hev made yer an officer. What I want to say is this. I'm a man of the world an' I hope I ain't presumin' if I say it was a miracle if she di'n't offer yer reward herself in all the time you hid her, if you get my drift. An' it would hev been a bigger miracle if you'd hev refused.

138

'Oh I know wot they prate to yer in church, an' the army chaplains too, but a man is a man. Thass how God made us; weak vessels all. An' the devil had a hand in the buildin' of that young woman, for she's growed with looks that a man wot get close to her must find it terrible hard not to sin with.'

Jeremy started to stutter. Joseph raised his hand for him to stop.

'No need explain to me, Jeremy—or must I call yer "sir" now? I ain't gooner say nothin' to nobody. Wot I was gooner say was that now she's been an' gone an' got herself married to the Marquess, thass good for yer. They do say that when a man do that to a woman an' she like it, she can't leave him alone. Now she's out of the way an' thass good. She'd be no good as a wife. You'd never keep her satisfied, allus be fightin' off other blokes.'

Jeremy was embarrassed. 'There never was any ambition by me to marry Miss Eve,' he protested.

'Good,' said Joseph. 'Wot I meant was, don't hanker arter her at all an' grieve 'cos she's out of yer reach now.'

Jeremy was too ashamed to admit his terrible secret—that Eve had already proven willing to go to great lengths to get within his reach.

'When I was home, my sister Bessie was on about yer the whole time. "Jeremy did this. Jeremy did that." Thass obvious she love yer. She'll be nineteen afore the year is out, an' if I remember right, you'll be twenty-one. A man has bodily needs, an' could do worse than marry young to save his self from "sin" as they call it.'

'I've heard from the scriptures that it's better to marry than to burn,' was the only remark Jeremy could think of to terminate this embarrassing line of talk.

He then turned the conversation to other matters, but after leaving Joseph he decided to take his advice as soon as possible as a means of saving himself from further sin.

***

Not wanting to bother Colonel Pearson with yet another special request so soon after saving Joseph, he left matters another month or more until late June.

'I know it's a year since you last had leave of absence,' said Colonel Pearson, 'but the granting of the month that you have asked for, so that you may court and propose to your maid, is too much at this time. Relations between Parliament and the army are deteriorating fast, and I have been warned to hold myself in readiness for some kind of movement within a few days notice. You can take three days, starting tomorrow. That will have to suffice.'

So Jeremy made the most of his time, though it left him little more than a day to do what he must. Bessie blushed and said 'Yes'. Samuel and Mrs Bloom were delighted at the prospect of having him as a son-in-law. His own parents were pleased too. It was agreed that he and Bessie should marry as soon after his twenty-first birthday in December as he could get away from his duties for a week or more.

✳✳✳

Eve heard the news of the impending marriage with dismay, for Jeremy had been in Brentham so little time that he had gone before she knew of his visit. In private she wept and raged. Had this stupid ungrateful wretch not believed her when she told him of her love? Did he not realise that she had only wedded an old man so that he would have riches and security in her after he was finished with the army? Her husband was already seventy-eight. The longest would not be long.

She vowed that she would stop this foolish marriage somehow, and heedless that the Marquess might question her movements, had the coach prepared and went with all speed to Cambridge, then to Newmarket Heath. In both places she was told the bulk of the army had moved in the direction of London because of trouble.

Her journey had involved an overnight stay at an inn and she did not have the slightest compunction in lying to her husband.

'I heard from my father, the Squire, that my brother, Colonel John Pearson, is moving back into some danger in London. So shocked was I after thinking all was now peace, that out of sisterly love, I wanted to see him once more.'

'Indeed,' said the Marquess, 'I've heard a rumour that mobs have rioted in London in favour of the King, and yet another rumour is that they were incited to do so by some members in Parliament, most of whom want Presbyterianism, while most of the army are Independents. Because of this and not having enough to pay the soldiers, enmity is developing between Parliament and the army. All, it appears, may not yet be over.'

'My father, the Squire, told me only a few days since, that apparently the army last month, by a ruse, removed the King from where he was living at Holmby into their protective custody in his palace at Newmarket,' said Eve.

'If war does break out again,' said the Marquess, 'I shall remain neutral once more. Some say, as an aristocrat, I should support King Charles, but I believe him to be the architect of his own troubles by his obstinacy. Yet I'll not, like some others of my class, go so far as to support Parliament. My job is to safeguard this estate and my family line from extinction by producing an heir.'

✳✳✳

After Jeremy returned to duties following his brief visit to Brentham and proposal to Bessie, it was not long before his regiment, along with others from the area had orders to proceed to Hounslow. There they assembled with many other regiments under Sir Thomas Fairfax and soon the bulk of the army marched on London.

By early August Cromwell had taken over the Tower of London, and the city was under virtual martial law. Jeremy heard it said that some members of Parliament who had been working against the interests of the

140

Independents and the army, wisely fled; others who had earlier had to flee from them, were escorted back by the troops.

All was in ferment. Jeremy hoped that this new trouble would not prevent him having leave of absence to marry Bessie when December came.

***

One day in mid-August, Obadiah Dowdy, alias Joshua Harding, returned to the Thorn Inn, Mistley, from a two week foray. There, a strange and unbelievable rumour that Matthew Hopkins had died, came to his ears. The obsequiousness with which he was normally treated seemed to be missing.

He decided to seek out Hopkins' chief assistant, the lawyer John Stearne, also a prosecutor of many witches. Dowdy didn't like Stearne although they had much in common, for he was, like Obadiah, a religious bigot. Hopkins he had found easier to get on with, although like most others, he was afraid of him, in spite of being now sixty-two and Hopkins only twenty-eight.

'The rumours of Matthew's death are true, though it is with sorrow I say it,' said Stearne. 'I had him laid to rest in Mistley churchyard a few days since—on the twelfth.'

Dowdy realised his money-making was probably now coming to an end without his protector, 'How did this come about?' he asked.

'You may as well know for your own caution,' replied John Stearne. 'He was set upon by a lynch mob near Halstead and swum. Because he saved himself they then hanged him from a tree. I was powerless to prevent it.

'It would be as well not to say this around Mistley. I'm putting about a story that he died in his bed from consumption. He had the sickness as you know. If it becomes general knowledge that he was murdered by a lynch mob with impunity, it may embolden some here to do it to us. For several weeks Matthew and I have been questioned by local worthies on our methods. There have been complaints to them from lower orders.

'Not everyone it seems appreciates our service in the Lord's cause. There have even been monstrous rumours that we've been partial in our search for witches, by taking bribes from those able to afford to pay us off. If such an evil falsehood takes hold, we could be in grave danger.

'For my part, I'm giving up the search for witches and may seek another place to live. You must please yourself of course.'

Obadiah Dowdy needed no more prompting. In the three years since he came to work for Matthew Hopkins, he had accumulated a small fortune in bribes. He had saved it all, except the little he had wasted on the Mertons; living on what he honestly earned from odd tailoring jobs, and the pittance given him by Hopkins. He was comparatively well off. Another year or so, he reflected ruefully, and he would have been as wealthy as he was before being forced out of Brentham.

At nightfall he collected all his possessions and left Mistley secretly, heading north away from East Anglia and danger of retribution.

Jeremy's regiment remained in the London area for the remainder of 1647. King Charles during that time had been moved and lived now under the army's house custody at Hampton Court.

As riots had been curbed early in the army's occupation of the city, Jeremy felt by mid-November that things were sufficiently peaceful, at least on the surface, to approach Colonel Pearson about leave of absence to get married.

'Things are now as quiet as they're likely to get,' said the colonel. 'That in spite of dissensions and splits emerging between our main commanders, who favour a limited monarchy, and the extremists among us agitating for people's rights and a republic.

'Now I've just received worrying news; the King has escaped from Hampton Court. How he escaped and where he's gone, I haven't heard. I fear it could mean trouble, although I don't know yet. No doubt he received daily intelligence of our sad divisions and feels he might profit from them.'

The colonel thought for a moment. 'Look cornet,' he said. 'It takes but three days to get married. One to go; one to wed; and one to return.'

'Sir!' exclaimed Jeremy. He hoped the colonel did not really mean that. No man could ride nearly seventy miles in a day unless he was able to change horses.

A smile crossed Colonel Pearson's face, and a suggestion of a twinkle in his eye. 'Are you sure you want to get married so young, and in times as troubled as these? You're as yet barely twenty-one. I'm thirty-four and not yet wed. I don't see the urgency. Have you thought it through and made sure of your reasons for wanting to marry?'

Jeremy almost wanted to tell his colonel that the urgency to get married was because he had failed to contain his vessel as commanded by scripture; also as advised by scripture, it was better to marry than to burn. Instead, he just said, 'Yes sir. I am indeed sure.'

'Well,' said Colonel Pearson. 'I suppose we must be kind to you. If trouble is destined to break out, it is unlikely to do so in depth of winter. You can have a month's leave of absence from twenty-first December to twentieth of January.'

'Thank you, sir,' said Jeremy. This was more than he had dared to hope for.

'There's a condition. You're to keep in daily touch with my father, the Squire. He gets all the communications that come down from Parliament to his county committee. If I send for you through him, you're to return immediately, married or not. Also, if you hear from him that fighting has broken out, you're to return with all speed.'

'Thank you again, sir,' said Jeremy, all smiles.

He made to leave.

'Cornet Goodway.'

Jeremy turned round.

'Will I be welcome at your wedding, if things should still be sufficiently peaceful to allow me the time?'

'Sir. We'd be honoured, Bessie and I,' cried Jeremy. Then thinking a moment, became bold. 'Sir. Will you consent to be my groom's man?'

'That's a surprise and an honour, cornet. I consent, but you must remember I may not be able to get there. You would be wise to find a reserve.

'That wasn't the request I thought you were going to make. Do you not have another?'

'I can't think of one, sir.'

'Wouldn't you like me to speak to Joseph Bloom's commanding officer to ask that he might be allowed a few days off to attend?'

'That would be wonderful, sir!' Jeremy thought how fortunate he was to be serving under a man like John Pearson. Momentary elation then dissolved in doubt. 'But he's a foot soldier, sir.'

'Indeed he is,' said the colonel. 'How else did he get to London but upon his feet?' He waved a hand as if dismissing the problem. 'We can lend him a horse of some sort. He can ride I know. I've often seen him ride my father's horses home from being shod when he was but a child.'

* * *

It took Jeremy two days to cover the sixty-eight miles from London to Brentham. He called first on his prospective bride. Mrs Bloom was all a fluster.

'Sam an' me went to see Reverend Jones, an' fixed the date for the thirty-first of December. He was a bit dubious about lettin' Bessie marry in white, 'cos some of the bigots don't approve of that sort of showy thing. His allus frightened of somebody. But I say to him as how my Bessie's a virgin an' it's only meet that she's be in white.

'I do declare, there's some as don't want us takin' pleasure in nothin' no more.

'Anyway, he want to see you an' Bessie alone for a talk as soon as yer can.'

'Who are yer gooner hev as groom's man?' asked Samuel.

'Colonel Pearson is willing; but he advised me to have a reserve in case he couldn't get here,' replied Jeremy.

'That'll be my brother George,' declared the blacksmith. 'He won't mind playin' second fiddle.'

'Lor' lumme alive,' cried Mrs Bloom. 'My Bessie marryin' an officer, an' with a high rankin' officer in attendance. Thass somethin' wot yer might call a step up. Be expectin' the Squire an' his lady to come next, I shouldn't wonder.'

'Perhaps they might like to be asked,' suggested Jeremy.

'You surely don't think they'd accept?' asked Bessie's mother.

'I think they very well might,' replied Jeremy. 'They could take offence if

143

not asked. Would you like me to raise it when I see Mr Pearson tonight? I have to report to him every day in case of recall.'

'You go an' do that, Jeremy lad,' said Samuel. 'Then if they accept, we'll hev to ask some of the better folk in the village, so as they won't feel too embarrassed.'

During the days leading up to his wedding, Jeremy called on Nathaniel Pearson every day for news, as he had been instructed. He and his wife accepted the invitation to his nuptials with pleasure.

On one of those visits Eve was just getting into her coach to depart after one of her occasional visits as he arrived. She smiled but did not make any overt gesture which might have betrayed what they had been to one another.

Jeremy had stayed for nearly thirty minutes, and was surprised when he turned out of the gate to walk in the direction of the village, to find her coach still standing in a secluded spot.

'Get in,' she demanded, opening the door.

'My Lady,' he said loud enough for the coachman to hear. Then in a whisper, 'It's not meet . . .'

'Get in, Cornet Goodway,' she interrupted him.

Jeremy could see the look on her face. He did as she asked to avoid a scene. Eve looked out and called to the coachman, 'The track that skirts the village please.'

She placed a hand on Jeremy's knee as soon as they moved off. He felt that sensation she always aroused in his loins. 'Why do you seek to break my heart after all we've been to each other that you plan to marry the blacksmith's little daughter?'

'But you're married to another,' he protested.

'An old man who has but little life left,' she said. 'Is your love for me so shallow that you couldn't wait?'

'But it's wrong for me to love you.' he said.

'After the way I've opened my body to you, and you have delighted in it, isn't it just as wrong to break my heart?' she pleaded.

He was fighting against his inclinations, for he was already erect from her touch. 'We can't for ever keep risking the immortality of our souls. Let's pray that we may be forgiven for what we've already done.'

'Do you think that little Bessie Bloom will satisfy you as I've done? Do you think such an insipid little creature can respond as I've done to your mighty thrusts or will she for ever plead to be left alone? Are you so naive that you believe all women to be the same? You're destined for an unhappy marriage if you go through with this. Then will the force of your passion cause you to seek another, and once more you'll cry "This is sin". Have the sense to follow the instincts of your body. Soon we'll be able to marry, then no more will you be worried about sin.'

She pleaded with him and argued, but he struggled mightily against the temptation bursting in his breeches. She seemed to give up as they arrived near the Manor.

'I can walk from here,' he said.

But she tapped on the roof and called to the coachman, 'Drive into the village.'

She tapped the roof for the coachman to stop right outside the forge. Jeremy alighted, sickened in his heart that Bessie most probably witnessed it.

* * *

The wedding day came. Dry, with hoarfrost and wintry sunshine. Colonel Pearson had arrived the day before with six troopers, which he billeted at home. 'So that my junior officer and his bride might have a fitting arch of drawn swords to walk under,' he explained.

'Thass a great honour he's accordin' yer,' declared Silas Goodway as they prepared for the ceremony. 'Me an' your mum are real proud of yer, son. Ain't that right Mary?'

Mary Goodway could not speak, for she was in tears as she threw her arms around Jeremy's neck and kissed him.

'I jus' wish I could give Sam a help with all the money his spendin' on this,' said Silas. 'Trade is so bad.'

'I shouldn't offer,' advised Jeremy. 'He might feel insulted. The Squire gave me a message to offer him help when we invited him. Samuel sent a polite message of thanks back, but said he only had one daughter and he wanted to do his duty by her, unaided.'

The ceremony went off well. There were about thirty guests. Reverend Jones preached a sermon about the sanctity of marriage.

As the happy couple passed with arms linked under their ceremonial arch of swords, several of the local maidens were there to watch and cast envious glances at Bessie and her handsome officer. Jeremy felt his wife squeeze his arm tighter, as if to say, 'He's mine. All mine.'

A few yards further on, as they walked to the inn where the wedding breakfast was to be held, the Marchioness of Stourland leaned from her coach, strategically waiting by the pathway, and blew Jeremy a kiss from close quarters. He felt Bessie jerk and gasp. Squeezing her arm tighter to reassure her, he silently cursed Eve for trying to spoil his Bessie's day.

The wedding breakfast was a fine affair. Jeremy made a little speech saying how lucky he was to have Bessie for a wife. Samuel said how he was pleased to have Jeremy as his new son, and Silas said how happy he was to have Bessie as his new daughter. Joseph Bloom, who was there with his wife, welcomed Jeremy as a brother and told Bessie how lucky she was. Colonel Pearson made a speech extolling Jeremy's worth as a soldier, saying he had a great future ahead of him. Nathaniel Pearson the Squire, said the bride and groom should have a good future since they both came from such law-abiding and hard-working families, and that when army days were over for Jeremy, he would make sure there was a good cottage for them to live in. Everyone seemed happy although it was noticed that Bessie had looked a little upset at first.

It had been decided that Bessie should continue to live with her parents until Jeremy left the army, as they had sufficient room. Therefore the wedding night was spent under Samuel's roof. Jeremy was a little concerned that their lovemaking might be noisy and cause embarrassment. He was remembering the trouble he had subduing Eve's noisy reactions as they copulated under his own parents' roof.

Bessie was shy and hesitated to undress. Jeremy assisted her to start. From there they each removed an item of clothing slowly in turn until at length she was completely naked, and he nearly so.

The sight of her smooth white flesh and firm young breasts drove his already erect phallus to even greater hardness. He could scarce contain the seed within his body.

Bessie uttered a little gasp when he revealed himself. They fell into each other's arms and kissed. Jeremy picked her up and laid her on the bed, and having pulled the blankets up, extinguished the candle and got in beside her.

As he started to caress her intimately, she began to cry. He wiped her tears with his hand and assured her that it was natural, and he would be gentle. He was desperate to be within her.

'It ain't 'cos I'm feared to take yer inside me that I'm cryin' Jeremy. I love yer too much to be frightened of yer. Thass 'cos of that Eve an' what she done today. I jus' know yer must hev done these things with her when yer had her hid. An' she'll try an' get yer agin, even though she's a fine lady now.'

Jeremy tried to assure her that she had nothing to fear, but guilt had come upon him and he felt himself losing his erection. So they didn't copulate then, but lay in each other's arms; she weeping from time to time; him with a tiny flaccid phallus and seed still wanting to get out.

At dawn things seemed better and he took her for the first time. A gentle, quiet and pleasurable event, but lacking the fire and satisfaction he had achieved with Eve over and over again.

Lovemaking improved over the remainder of the time Jeremy was at home and they became used to one another. But great passion was still missing, and he prayed fervently that what they had between them would be enough to stay him from falling into sin again.

***

Laying in bed beside her old husband on the night of Bessie and Jeremy's wedding, Eve was angry and disconsolate. She raged inwardly that her life should have come down to this. At last she had found one she could love as she had loved Marcus; one that could satisfy the sexual craving that Marcus had first awakened in her. Now she had lost him to the blacksmith's little daughter; and for what reason? Because of arrant nonsense about purity and natural desires being the work of the devil. He had even expressed those fears to her, so thoroughly had he been indoctrinated.

Could not her brother have prevented it? He was her love's commanding officer. What brotherly love and regard did he have for her, that he should presume to reprimand her in her own coach, in front of village oafs for what she did today?

The Marquess had just taken her, as he often did in his frantic need for an heir. The fumbling of an old man spilling seed into her from a member that would not harden properly, and it filled her with loathing. She would have borne his attentions gladly had Jeremy waited for his death. But now she would bear it no longer.

She would hasten him to his end.

CHAPTER 17

'Well, Cornet Goodway, does the world appear different now that you're a married man?' Colonel Pearson waved Jeremy to take a seat soon after he reported back.

'The world seems the same, sir; but I myself am uplifted by the love of my dear Bessie,' said Jeremy. 'Thank you again, sir, for coming to my wedding, and the great honour you did Bessie and myself. Also for helping her brother to be there.'

'Hm. Then let's pray that your Bessie doesn't all too soon become a widow,' said the colonel.

'Sir! Are matters again getting worse?'

'They never really got better in the first place. Just quietened down a little. Isolated riots started again around the time you left. I almost didn't come to your wedding. In fact I was on the verge of recalling you. There was a particularly bad one on twenty-fourth of December, but General Fairfax snuffed it out by sending a large body of troops to occupy Whitehall.

'After that it was quieter for a week or two, which allowed me to get away. There are a few smaller riots even now. As long as they remain just riots they can be easily dealt with. But I fear them to be the precursor of another conflict. You're too young to recall, but before our country sadly slid into civil war in forty-two, London was plagued by riots.'

'Do you no longer believe there'll be a settlement with the King, sir?' asked Jeremy.

'I have ceased to hope for such a miracle, since he escaped in November. As you know, he went to Carisbroke on the Isle of Wight, expecting the commandant of the castle to favour him; but he's more a prisoner now than he was before because his guard has been doubled. Yet he still works his intrigues from there, playing one side against another and all against the middle. You've kept abreast with most of the news by calling upon my father, I trust?'

'Indeed I have, sir. Only last week he read me a long letter you'd written to him. It related how in December, Generals Cromwell and Ireton, suspecting the King of underhand dealing, had gone to a tavern dressed as troopers and removed a letter by stealth from his messenger, which illustrated the mischief he was about.'

'Yes,' said Colonel Pearson, 'the *Blue Boar* tavern in Holborn. An inn already getting a name as a place of Royalist intrigues. While the King's messenger went to his ablutions, they slit his saddle bags and took the letter. I'm not clear to whom it was written, but the gist of its contents were that the King was leaning favourably towards the Scots in the hope they would be his salvation. He also clearly stated that he'd no intention of keeping any promises made under duress.'

148

'Does General Cromwell still favour trying to reach a settlement with the King do you know, sir?'

'I hear not. It seems he has lost patience with the duplicity. I'm told that, like Fairfax and Ireton, he still favours a monarchy, and is dead set against the republicans. Yet he says it can't be with this King, and another must be found to replace him. There's talk of trying to negotiate with the Prince of Wales in an effort to get him to accept the idea of constitutional monarchy put forward by Commissary General Ireton.

'Meanwhile divisions and factions arise everywhere. New pamphlets appear on the streets nigh daily, advocating first one viewpoint then another. The Levellers with their futuristic ideas on universal suffrage and people's rights and liberties are but one.

'Yet others in London who don't care a fig about politics, eagerly embrace the Levellers call for "Liberty" and misinterpret that as licence. Some of our wealthier former supporters are aping the morals of the cavaliers and sleeping with one another's wives or husbands. Apparently to cuckold a friend, in some circles, is coming to be regarded as an achievement; to the utter disgust of the religious fanatics.'

Jeremy winced at this, imagining that the colonel must have found out about him being intimate with his sister since she married.

'If real warfare starts again sir, from which direction do you expect it to come?' he asked, changing the subject.

'Maybe the north, since it appears the Scots are turning against us, but I think we must be vigilant everywhere. Now to future work. Orders have come down from deliberations with the Parliament that we are to start reducing our strengths for economy, whilst keeping the same structure. In our case that'll mean a few men from each troop. Get from each troop commander a list of men we could discharge. It's a foolish order I think at this time, and one we needn't be too hasty with in execution.'

✳✳✳

The Marquess of Stourland became ill with fever in mid-January. The sickness dragged on for three weeks and Eve began to hope there would be no need to try and kill him. The physician said it was a normal matter of ageing, and there was little could be done except prayer. Nevertheless, he prepared some concoction which he instructed her to give him daily.

As far as prayer was concerned, she decided not to. She did not want to pray for his recovery and could not bring herself to ask God, in whom she still retained a small remnant of belief, to kill him for her.

Long since had she pardoned herself for fornication, self-gratification, lesbianism and adultery, on the grounds that God had made her as she was–aided and abetted by Marcus Kirby. Yet she retained some regrets to grate her conscience; having gleefully led poor Naomi to her death at the hands of her father; the accidental killing of Eli Brown; and worst of all, her failure to admit what she had done and thus save poor Rebecca Brown from death at the stake.

Now she was into something even worse. She contemplated killing her husband. It would be so much easier if God did it for her.

But He didn't–or so it appeared–for the Marquess recovered in mid-February. As soon as he did, he returned to his attempts at breeding with her.

She wanted an end to that. 'My dear, why tax your strength? My monthly cycle didn't come whilst you were ill. Truly I believe myself to be with child. You've achieved your goal. You're to have an heir,' she lied, knowing full well that she was almost certainly barren.

But the Marquess was a man who liked to make sure, so Eve had to endure more nights of having him dribble seed into her from an ineffective member. Whether or not she liked the prospect of direct killing, she would have to take action.

She knew little or nothing about poisons, but she had heard that certain fungi were deadly. She scoured the park lands until she found evil-looking specimens growing on some of the older trees.

Her next problem was how to administer the fungi without being discovered. After chopping and chopping again the specimens until the pieces were tiny enough to be sprinkled. She then wrapped them in a fragment of cloth and put that inside a small drawstring bag which she usually carried on her left wrist.

She had some not too definite plan to sprinkle a little of the chopped fungi in his soup at dinner. However, this proved easier to accomplish in thought than in deed. Ten days or more passed in these attempts before lack of privacy from the servants at meal times, or the sharp eye of the Marquess himself, forced her to give up.

Then, late in February, the Marquess fell ill with a fever once more. The physician shook his head, gave some more of his concoction and prescribed bed and hot broth. Goody Fran was somewhat offended that she, the longest serving and most senior staff member of the household, was not allowed to spoon him his broth. Eve insisted it was a wife's duty to nurse her husband.

Two days running, Eve surreptitiously sprinkled the desiccated fungi into her husband's broth. Then he became violently sick. Goody Fran took it upon her own initiative to send urgently for the physician. By the time he arrived the fever had gone and the Marquess was well on the road to recovery. 'By the grace of God, he has found the strength to expel the evil from his stomach!' exclaimed the doctor. Eve was aghast. All the fungi had done was to make him sick.

Two more weeks passed and once more the already weakened Marquess went down with yet another fever. The physician said to Eve, 'These repeated fevers. Each one weakens him further. I fear you must prepare for the worst.'

This time she didn't put fungi in his broth for a whole week. Instead she added a little spice each time that she had taken secretly from the kitchen, in the hope that this would keep the fever going and further weaken him. Then she started to add the fungi in smaller doses that the stomach might not expel. The fever raged on for several more days as she gradually increased the dose of fungi. Then one night she added a little of one of her cosmetic creams. She had heard tell, though didn't know the truth of it, that some of those preparations were made from the plant called Belladonna.

The next morning, 28 March 1648, they found the Marquess dead in his bed. The doctor clicked his tongue and shook his head. 'Sad. Very sad,' he said, 'but no more than I expected. No frame so old could stand those repeated fevers.'

So Eve did not know whether or not it was she who killed him.

After the funeral, Eve recalled something the Marquess had said two months earlier . . . 'If war does break out again, we'll be wise to hide about half our silver and brass. This time the sequestration will not stop at Royalist supporters, but will extend to those of us who, having declared neutral, haven't contributed to either side.'

When she had asked why in that case they should not conceal the lot, he had replied, 'If we do that they'll say we have given it to the King's side, declare us malignant, and perhaps take some of the lands, or even this house. Make no mistake, if they win again, there'll be little sympathy for those who supported the renewal of war. They'll be angry. I must resign myself to losing some of my plate, even though I've done nothing to deserve it.'

So, trusting only the stalwart Goody Fran, Eve, Marchioness of Stourland, secreted valuables in long unused attics and roof spaces, and under floor boards. They even lifted the boards and dug a pit under that same summer-house where she had once stood against a wall with raised clothes and parted thighs, like a village girl with her swain, and eagerly copulated with the then recently appointed Cornet Jeremy Goodway.

***

During March two pieces of interesting news reached Jeremy in London.

The first was of general interest. The father of Sir Thomas Fairfax had died. Their commander-in-chief had therefore now become Lord Fairfax of Cameron, and should be addressed as "My Lord", and be referred to as "The Lord General".

The other piece of news was of more personal interest. The Marquess of Stourland had died. 'I do declare,' said Colonel Pearson when giving him the news, 'my sister has gained more from just over two years in her bed, that I have from the better part of six years on the battlefields. Or for that matter my father, the Squire, from all the years he has devoted to his land and holdings; or his public service. That's, of course, if she can keep her gains from the sequestrators.'

This was the second time Jeremy had heard the colonel make deprecating remarks about Eve. Clearly he didn't have a very high opinion of her.

Early in April news of more national importance started to come in. A disaffected Parliamentary officer Colonel Poynes commanding Pembroke Castle had changed sides in late March, and declared for the King. Chepstow Castle also declared.

'Is this what you expected, sir?' asked Jeremy of Colonel Pearson when he gave him the news.

'Something like it. Trouble is also brewing in the far north near the border with Scotland. We may be invaded from that direction. Local forces are trying to deal with these situations, but Cromwell is about to start out with a large force to capture Pembroke and Chepstow.'

'Aren't we going with him, sir?'

'No. Lord General Fairfax expects trouble nearer home. London cannot be left unprotected. The Lord General is maintaining a large army here to deal with whatever revolt arises in this part of the country. A Scots army under the Duke of Hamilton is assembling ready to invade England on behalf of the King, and already Cromwell, our best commander, is drawn away to deal with a rising in South Wales. Other diversions are expected, aimed at tying down our forces so they can't meet the invasion.'

As April progressed into May, news filtered through of revolts and mini-revolts in towns all over the country. Local forces were left to mainly to deal with them aided by some detachments from the main army. But most of Lord Fairfax's large force stayed near London waiting to see which revolt developed most.

'All these revolts at the same time can't be coincidence,' declared Colonel Pearson. 'Now we see the result of the intrigues which I forecast. Royalist agents have whipped up disaffection to cause us to dissipate our forces when invasion is in the offing. I had a letter from my father this morning Apparently there has even been a revolt only ten miles from home at Bury St Edmunds involving over five hundred people rioting on the trivial complaint that they want their maypole back. Two hundred of our soldiers have been detached from elsewhere to deal with it.'

On 26th May Jeremy's regiment received orders attend a general muster of the army on Hounslow Heath next day. Over the previous few days news had come in of revolts in Kent which were hardening into a general rising. The town of Rochester had been seized. The following day the whole force under Lord Thomas Fairfax marched to deal with the crisis. By the last day of the month they had reached Gravesend.

'Intelligence has reached us that Lord Goring with the larger part of his force is in Maidstone,' said Colonel Pearson on his return from a conference of senior officers. 'As he's undoubtedly the leader of this Kentish revolt, the Lord General has decided our whole force is to attack him there.'

'What about Rochester, sir?' asked Jeremy.

'We're to leave that for now, and Dartford which has also been taken by the Royalists. Our immediate aim is to defeat their main force and capture Lord Goring if we can.'

By the following afternoon, most of them had reached Maidstone which was immediately stormed. After many hours of bitter street fighting, the town was captured. There were some prisoners taken, but not Lord Goring. Thus did Jeremy once more experience battle.

'He's given us the slip,' said Colonel Pearson the following morning. 'No information of his intentions has been obtained from prisoners, but his force is reported to number between five and six-thousand, not all of whom are properly armed. It hardly seems sufficient strength to attempt London, though he's arrogant enough to try anything. Anyway we're having to split some of our army to look for him, but in the main we are to set off for London.'

Two days later they arrived on the outskirts of the city where information came that the attempt had been made on London the previous day and failed.

'It appears,' said Colonel Pearson, addressing an assembly of all the officers of his regiment, 'that after some success and seizing Bow Bridge they were stopped by the London trained bands. It is said they hoped the population would rise in support but that didn't happen, so they retreated. Intelligence is confused because the trained bands didn't pursue. Some say Goring's forces left London southwards, others that they marched into Essex, probably aiming for Chelmsford. The Lord General favours the latter report but cannot leave Kent until the other has been explored.

'As for us, we've been given an important task. We're to ride as fast as we can to Tilbury, cross the river there and proceed to Billericay. There we must found a camp from which to probe around for Goring. If we find him we are to keep on his tail, sending twice daily reports, or more, to the Lord General. He then will bring the majority of his forces out of Kent to rendezvous at Billericay.'

'Do you have any idea what he might be aiming for in Essex, sir?' asked one of the officers.

'There are about four possibilities,' replied the colonel. 'One, there has been a rumour of some sort of trouble brewing in Colchester; he may aim to reinforce that. Two, he might turn north at Chelmsford and drive into our heart lands; possibly to capture the Isle of Ely, or maybe even to march right up into the midlands to meet and assist the Scottish invasion when it comes. Three, he may be aiming to capture and fortify Chelmsford, or even double back and attack London again from the northern quarter. Four, he may be just retreating with no clear idea what to do except to lead us a merry dance and prevent this army moving towards Scotland to meet the invasion.'

153

'Is there any fresh news of the invasion sir?' asked an officer.

'As you know, news from the Scottish border takes several days. Latest reports from our spies are that Hamilton is still assembling his army in Scotland. The situation at Carlise and Berwick is being contained by our local forces. They'll not be able to stop the real invasion when it comes. We must all hope and pray that either this army or Cromwell's will be free to meet it.'

'Any news of General Cromwell, sir?'

'As you already know, Chepstow had surrendered to forces in the area by the time he arrived. Pembroke is still holding fast against his furious assaults.

'Now, for us, speed is of the essence. We're a small regiment of only five squadrons of four troops each, but an efficient one. Four squadrons will ride immediately with all haste to Billericay. The fifth will come up the rear escorting our baggage wagons.

'When we get to Billericay, I shall leave Major Lehan in charge with two squadrons and the baggage, while I take three with me. If Goring has been to Chelmsford and gone by the time I get there, I shall leave one squadron in that town to do what they can and promptly report to Major Lehan if he doubles back that way on London. With the other two squadrons I shall follow whichever way he goes and split my force if he does likewise trying to deceive me.

'Remember, our work is not to engage in hopeless combat at this time but to ensure that accurate intelligence reaches the Lord General speedily, so that he knows which way to go with the main forces when he gets to Billericay.'

Two days later Jeremy was with Colonel Pearson and three squadrons on the outskirts of Chelmsford when scouts reported that what seemed to be the whole of Goring's force was in the town threatening to fortify it if the populace did not give them provisions and arms.

Jeremy was bidden to fetch two couriers. 'Ride with all speed to Billericay and request Major Lehan to immediately send this message to Lord General Fairfax; "Contact made with the enemy at Chelmsford".'

A few hours later scouts reported Goring's forces were leaving the town heading northwards, taking members of the Essex county committee with them as hostages. Colonel Pearson immediately sent two couriers off with a despatch to say that the enemy had turned away from the Colchester road and was heading towards Braintree.

They followed Goring, keeping sufficiently far behind to be out of sight, relying on scouts in ordinary dress, like men about their daily business, to approach closer and pass back intelligence.

They had covered about five miles when a scout came galloping in at a furious pace. 'Sir. The enemy have stopped outside the next village!' he cried breathlessly, addressing Colonel Pearson.

Holding up his hand to command the two squadrons to halt, the colonel studied his map. 'That village is called Leighs. It seems strange they should stop to rest so soon.' Then as if something had just come to his head, he extracted another paper from his saddle bag. 'There's a magazine there at the house of one of our supporters!' he exclaimed.

Even as he spoke, the sound of musket fire could be heard. 'It'll be but barely defended, if at all, and there's nothing we can do,' he said to Jeremy. 'Go and request all troop commanders to get their men into as much cover as they can find off the road. The enemy came this way to raid the magazine. They may return if it's their intention to try London again better armed; this time from the north-east.'

Jeremy returned to find only the colonel and two squadron commanders still in the road. The four of them then went into cover. The sound of musketry stopped and all was silent for a while. Then they could see smoke rising from burning buildings.

The colonel stepped into the road to intercept a galloping scout. 'Enemy has left the village, heading north towards Braintree, sir,' cried the man.

Colonel Pearson beckoned Jeremy and the two squadron commanders to come out of hiding. Jeremy also brought the colonel's horse. 'Get your men out on the road into formation again,' he ordered the commanders.

'Do you think now he's heading for the Isle of Ely or Cambridge, sir,' asked Jeremy.

'We can't come to conclusions unless he keeps going north after Braintree,' replied the colonel. 'There he could turn right along the old Roman road and head due east again for Colchester; or he could turn left and by a detour come down on London from the north. I don't think there is much chance of the latter, and we can probably dismiss both possibilities after Braintree.'

'If he does keep going north after Braintree, sir, might that not be his intention to lead us north and not veer north-west at Halstead to head for the Isle of Ely at all?' asked Jeremy.

'No. To keep going north through Sudbury, then our own village of Brentham, then Bury St Edmunds, then Thetford would lead him to wide open country where he would be at disadvantage from the strength of our army. Even if he out-paced the Lord General further than that he would sooner or later reach the coast near Lynn and have to turn and fight with the fens to his right to block easy escape.

'No he wants a place he can fortify and hold us down for a long time. If he doesn't change direction at Braintree, the possibility of Colchester recedes, and the Isle of Ely looms large.'

They paused briefly in Leighs to inspect the burnt house and outbuildings which once housed a magazine. There were no bodies. 'The defenders either ran away or have been taken prisoner,' remarked Colonel Pearson. 'As for the enemy; though some of them might have been deficient in arms, that is certainly not their condition now.'

As they approached Braintree, a scout came riding back. 'Enemy left the town heading north still, sir,' he reported.

'Then it's almost certainly the Isle of Ely he's heading for. Fetch me a pair of couriers. This message is important.' He stopped to write his report and opinion, and handed it to the couriers who galloped off together at speed.

Not more than five minutes later he stopped to examine his map. 'I rue sending that message,' he said to Jeremy. 'Goring's move may be a ruse. The Lord General need not come this way to get to Ely. He could pass several miles to our left to save a few miles. Here take this note. Ride as you've never ridden before and catch those couriers. Tell them to replace their letter with this.'

Jeremy read the note before it was sealed. It simply said 'Enemy heading north out of Braintree.'

He rode, spurring his horse to greater effort than it had ever made. In a while foam started to blow past him from the beast's mouth. Even so, though the couriers had only seven or eight minutes start, it took over ten miles to catch them, almost back at Chelmsford.

Having delivered his message, he was anxious to get back, but it was vital for his horse to rest a few minutes and drink. He led it to a stream and when it had quenched its thirst, removed his saddle and rubbed the animal down.

Half an hour later he saddled up again and started back at a walk, breaking every now and again into a canter. He caught up with his comrades stopped a mile or so short of the little town of Halstead. Darkness was soon to fall. 'My spies inform me that the whole force is stopped in and about that little town, apparently for the night,' said Colonel Pearson when he reported. 'There seems to be some indecision about what to do next.'

'Did you catch the couriers?'

'Yes, sir,' replied Jeremy.

'Good. Now go get some rest. I've posted men to watch on all roads out of Halstead.'

Jeremy found himself a spot and laid down. Reflecting on the events of the day he was tired but exhilarated at the part he had played. His thoughts turned to Brentham, now only about thirteen miles away. What if the enemy should go that way, he wondered? They were rude and coarse cavaliers; would poor Bessie be raped? The thought startled him and he prayed. Then his thoughts turned to Bessie and rape and, before tiredness overwhelmed him, of Eve.

He woke just after dawn to a strident erection, interrupting a vivid dream in which he had been thrusting wildly into, not Bessie, but Eve, while her breasts, as big as houses, engulfed and smothered him.

He walked over to Colonel Pearson, who was awake. They chatted for an hour before a junior officer came running, 'Enemy leaving, sir,' he said.

'Which road?'

'My man was posted where the south-east road crosses the River Colne, sir'

'The Colne Valley road!' exclaimed the colonel. 'Was this all of them?'

'It seemed so, sir. I went to see for myself.'

'He turns part back on himself. We may never know if yesterday was a ruse or if he changed his mind.' Then turning to Jeremy. 'Get me couriers quickly. Then tell the squadron commanders to order saddle up and come to see me.'

To the first courier that reported he gave a simple verbal command. 'Ride at your greatest speed to Billericay. If Lord General Fairfax is not yet there with the army give this message to Major Lehan to be immediately sent on, "Colchester. Enemy moving on Colchester from Halstead." Tell Major Lehan that I am sending a longer report.'

As he was speaking another courier came. 'Did you hear that?' the colonel asked him.

'Yes, sir.'

'Then ride along with this man. This message must not fail to get through.'

To the squadron commanders when they arrived he said, pointing to his map, 'We trail Goring along the Colne Valley road to this fork near the village of Lexden, the last village before Colchester. It's at this junction we'll wait for the Lord General as he comes with the army straight from the Chelmsford direction. May it please God that he will not be long.'

The date was 10th of June. They arrived at the junction later that afternoon, but it was not until the night of the 11th/12th that Lord Fairfax arrived with an advance guard of 1,000 horse. Lord Goring's forces were camped outside the gates of Colchester

On his return from meeting Fairfax on the morning of the 12th, Colonel Pearson said to his assembled officers, 'Reliable intelligence numbers Goring's force as five thousand six hundred. In addition, Sir Charles Lucas, a Colchester man, in violation of the parole he gave when taken prisoner at Stow-in-the-Wold back in forty-six, has garrisoned the town with some of his adherents. He's also prevailed upon the trained bands and some of the foot soldiers stationed there to change sides and join him. How many that makes we don't quite know.

'The Lord General knows that Goring is negotiating with the burgesses to be let in, and wants to defeat him outside the town. As yet we're not strong enough, but others are coming. As soon as more arrive we are to attack without waiting for our full army to arrive. Later today or tomorrow morning we go into battle again. Meanwhile the Lord General is setting up his base camp at Lexden.'

CHAPTER 18

Jeremy had ridden the twenty miles or so from Colchester at an easy pace. It was surprisingly hot on that late August day, considering the amount of rainfall over the past days and weeks of seige. Road conditions were bad, and he was glad to be arriving at his destination. The Manor House driveway seemed so different from when he had last seen it, two years before. With lower branches not lopped, the avenue of elms in places met the tops of the unsythed grass. Underfoot occasional unfilled pot holes had to be avoided, whilst weeds were sprouting unchecked.

Reining his horse to a halt, he dismounted in the welcome shade from the canopy of neglected trees overhead. The news he had to impart was sad, so he felt it would be more easily delivered after cooling down.

Continuing on foot at a steady pace with easy hand on bridle, he paused again at the driveway end before stepping into the sunshine in front of the house. Had he done right to come here, he wondered, as he surveyed the imposing red brick facade of the building with its fine stone porch and tall ornate chimney stalks. After all, she had chosen to wed age and wealth. But he owed it to her brother, his colonel, fallen on the last day of the siege, just three days after they received news of Cromwell's victory against the invaders at Preston. He smoothed out his orange sash with pride.

Round the side of the house Jeremy sought in vain for a groom to take care of his horse. At length, Matt, the old retainer appeared. 'Mister Jeremy,' he exclaimed overjoyed. 'Ain't no men folk here 'cept me. Press took 'um all when the war started up agin. Hosses too.'

'The master?' enquired Jeremy. 'I have news of Colonel Pearson for your mistress.'

'Master died six month since,' said the old man. 'Mistress is a might upset today 'cos the 'sessors was round a s'mornin'. So yer best see Goody Fran.'

Jeremy pretended to be surprised. He wanted to ask more about the assessors, but Matt went straight to a side door to call a maid.

The young girl came quickly at the summons, curtsied, and blushing, motioned Jeremy to follow her.

Walls in the side hall way were plain white. This entrance was unfamiliar to him. But when he was ushered into the same room at the front where he had been before, he noticed once again that new fashion of the wealthy, of wall paper covering the top half of the room above the wainscoting. Nevertheless something was different. Yet it was the same paper. He moved to a window seat to wait upon the goodwife. What was missing? The heavy oak table, the chairs, tallboy, console table, ornate settle. These were the same as he remembered–and yet–that was it! The carved wooden figure in the centre of the table. There used to be a pair of solid brass candlesticks there. His eyes moved to the console. The silver and brass were all gone!

After a few minutes Goody Fran walked into the room. 'Jeremy Goodway. A fine officer. Can this be the nervous lad who came to see the Marquess without his tunic, when was it? Four years ago?'

'Just over,' said Jeremy. 'July of forty-four.'

'And you haven't been here since of course.'

He did not know whether that was a question or a statement, so he let it pass, but his guilty conscience reminded him that although he could have truthfully said 'No' as a passing remark, he would be making a fine distinction between the house and the grounds. Could it be that the goodwife had heard Eve's cries of ecstasy from the woodlands.

'I was sorry to learn that the Marquess died,' he said.

From the look the goodwife gave him, he thought that perhaps she did not believe him.

'I have a personal message for your mistress.'

'The Marchioness is somewhat upset today.' She waved an arm, pointing around the room. 'As you see, much silver is missing. Parliamentary assessors were here this morning and confiscated it because the late Marquess had not contributed to their cause. Neutrality it seems is now frowned upon. You could give me the message.'

'It wouldn't be proper to give you such a message first. If her ladyship pleases, there's no reason why you shouldn't hear it at the same time, but not before.'

The goodwife clicked her tongue. 'I'll ask if she's willing to see you.' She reluctantly turned and left the room.

Jeremy was glad he had made that last remark on impulse. It could be the means of saving him if Eve allowed the goodwife to stay. He had tried to fool himself that he had called here because it was the first house on his way into Brentham. The real reason, he knew, was his remembrance of *her* and his sexual fantasies over the long weeks of siege and combat. Already his loins were astir merely at being here.

Eve came into the room with Goody Fran following. He could tell she had been crying, and she looked more beautiful for it. She wore her hair loose, and was dressed in a pink silk gown with low-cut bodice. As he took the hand she offered him to kiss, his eyes were drawn to the valley between her breasts, and his phallus moved in the first stirring of an erection.

'Cornet,' she said. 'You have a message for me?'

'Lieutenant now.' He immediately regretted speaking of his promotion at a time like this. 'Your Ladyship, I beg your pardon. That was ill spoken. I have sad news. Your brother, is dead. Killed by escapees seeking to avoid capture yesterday. The very day that Colchester agreed to surrender. I've been commanded by Lord Fairfax to tell his family that a burial party will be bringing his body back to Brentham tomorrow afternoon.'

She effected a tear. 'It was bound to happen sooner or later. So it's all over at Colchester. Have you been to my father with these tidings?'

159

'No, I came here first because it was on my way in.'

She turned to Goody Fran. 'Leave us while the lieutenant tells me all the sad details.'

He was taken aback. Half of him hoped she would not do that; the other half was pleased she did. His phallus moved a little further towards erection.

He started to tell her details of her brother's death and what seemed like the end of the war as soon as the goodwife left the room, but she interrupted him.

'I've but little interest in the war, Jeremy. As for John, it's sad, but we weren't very close.

'Now my heart is glad because you've come back to me first, before seeing my father or your wife. You didn't call here because it was the first house on your way, but because what we are to one another cannot be denied.'

He tried to speak but couldn't find the words as she took his hand and placed it on her bosom. Without thinking of where he was, he let his fingers undo her top button and thrust his hand down to hold a naked breast. He felt himself grow and harden, and knew there was no turning back.

'Not here,' she croaked, moving his hand. 'Come with me.' He followed where she led, because he was Jeremy and she was Eve.

'What about the servants?' he asked, in a moment of unwelcome caution as they mounted the main staircase.

'There are no man servants except old Matt now, and he never comes up here. Neither do the maids at this hour of the day. As for Fran, she's all discretion, and will not.'

His sexual excitement rose to new heights as she closed the door of the luxurious bedroom behind them, and he caught sight of the huge four-poster bed on which he was soon to deceive his wife. No longer the boy that needed leading, he seized her in close embrace, while mouth to mouth their tongues entwined.

They pulled apart panting and urgent, and hurriedly started to undress, carelessly casting aside their clothes. He was finished before her, and like a man possessed, pulled and ripped away at her remaining undergarments. She had never known him like this, and cried out in delight at his ferocity when, at her pretended restraint, he roughly knocked her hands aside.

As they embraced and kissed again her arms were about his neck and she started to raise herself. Realising what she wanted, he put both hands beneath her buttocks and lifted; she clasped her thighs around his waist and he could feel her pubic region against his midriff, tantalisingly close to his throbbing erection.

Pulling back a little, he slowly lowered her until she was fully impaled. He walked around the room carrying her and made towards the bed. 'No. The mirror,' she whispered. He walked over to the full-length mirror standing in one corner. Their reflections joined together drove him to further frenzy, and in response to his touch she started to raise and lower herself slowly on him. Then carrying her over to the bed, without disconnecting, lay down with her, pulling them both up by the bedclothes. The movement brought him to his climax, and she responded with hers.

'Don't get up,' she murmured hoarsely.

They lay still and he felt himself shrinking inside her, until after a little while, with gentle movement of her hips and flexing of her muscles, she started to harden him again. He toyed with her breasts until her movements became frantic; then took her once more with deep, hard thrusts.

'Does it go so hot with little Bessie?' Eve asked, as they lay, with passion spent, side by side. She raised herself on one elbow and looked down into his face. 'You remain silent because it doesn't.'

'Bessie was a young virgin. It wouldn't have been proper for her to be skilled in these things.'

'Meaning that I was not virgin!' she flared angrily. 'How many lovers do you think I had before you? Did you imagine I learnt how to respond with passion from an assault by Mr Dowdy? It's as I told you last time you were here. All women are not the same. Those born with passion in them will respond fiercely to their chosen love, even though they be virgin. Those that aren't born with passion cannot.'

'It was pleasant enough with Bessie,' he said defensively, getting up from the bed to dress.

'Pleasant enough! Pleasant enough!' she exclaimed sarcastically, springing from the bed and standing still naked before him. 'And is that why you came to see me before her on the spurious excuse that this is the first house? Your wife is but a mile away at most. You could have been in her arms as soon as mine.'

'I freely admit I was tempted and fell,' he said, 'but what we've just done was wrong. I'm married to Bessie.'

'It was just as wrong last time, while I was married to the Marquess. Yet you came again. Why do you imagine I married the Marquess?'

'I don't know. It surprised me when I heard.'

'It was because I love you and knew there was but little comfort ahead for us that I gave myself to an old man of wealth, with only a short time to live. John was then alive; he would have inherited most of what is my father's. You've no wealth, and what's your prospect after the army? You say the war's all but over once more.'

'We're taught that the Lord will provide if we obey His will.'

She laughed. 'But you haven't been obeying His will, have you, Jeremy? Wouldn't it be better now to end the mistake of your marriage, and secure yourself a rich future as my lawful husband?'

'The law doesn't permit putting aside marriage.'

'Money may secure much, Jeremy, and the law turn a blind eye. Your marriage could be annulled if Bessie agreed.'

161

'Bessie has never expressed any ambition for wealth,' said Jeremy.

'But you will mention it to her?'

He hesitated awhile but she persisted.

'I shall confess our love,' he promised. 'Now I must be going. I've much to do before nightfall.'

Without waiting for her to dress, he left the house and fetched his horse. The enormity of what he had just promised Eve, and what he had done, troubled him. Now it was not just the flesh. She had offered him a rich future as owner, with her, of all the vast Stourland estate; and now she would inherit Mr Pearson's lands as well. He was sorely tempted, but as he rode, his mind turned to his upbringing and the scriptures. *The devil taketh him up into an exceeding high mountain and shewed him all the kingdoms of the world and the glory of them; And saith unto him; all these things will I give thee if thou wilt fall down and worship me.* He stopped his horse and with bowed head, prayed forgiveness and the strength to resist.

✳✳✳

'Jeremy. Thank God you're home an' well!' exclaimed Samuel Bloom, as he dismounted outside the forge. 'Is all well, or is aught wrong?'

'Colchester surrendered yesterday after twelve weeks of siege,' he replied, 'and I believe the whole war may be finished again. Four days since, we received news that Cromwell had smashed the invasion with a great victory at Preston in Lancashire.'

'Then I pray that our Joseph is still alive. But you'll be keen to see Bessie, come on. She's in the cottage. Leave yer hoss in the traverse. I'll put him away.'

Jeremy followed Samuel with trepidation. How could he face Bessie? How could he confess? It would break her heart.

As soon as he entered the cottage, Mrs Bloom threw her arms about him and cried. 'I'll fetch yer a tankard of ale,' she said, releasing him as Bessie came in from their room. 'Then me an' Sam'll go outside a while. You two'll want to be alone.'

Bessie fell into his arms as soon as her mother left, and they kissed a long lingering kiss. She pulled back. 'Whass wrong, Jeremy? I'm so joyful to see yer back, but somethin's wrong; what is it?'

This was the moment he dreaded, and he could not face it. 'It's the sad news I must go and give the Squire. Colonel John has been killed,' he said, by way of explaining his reserve to his wife.

'Then yer mus' go an' tell him now, afore yer spend time with me, though I need yer very much. How long are yer home?'

'A week, but I should be able to get home more soon, for the war seems to be over again.'

'Then go an' do your sad duty now, an' go an' tell your poor mother you're safe afore yer come back to me, for I know her to be worried sick.'

He was relieved to get away and postpone the inevitable.

162

'You off so soon,' said Samuel as Jeremy made to pass him and his wife in the garden.

'I shall be back shortly,' said Jeremy. 'I must go and tell the Squire that Colonel John has been killed.'

Mrs Bloom let out a gasp. 'Oh poor gentleman, an' his lady. Thass both sons they're gone an' lost in this war.'

✳✳✳

Nathaniel Pearson was alone in his study when the maid ushered Jeremy in. He rose and offered his hand. 'How are you, and how are things at Colchester?'

'I'm well enough, sir,' said Jeremy. 'Colchester surrendered yesterday–three days after we passed them news that Cromwell had smashed the northern invasion at Preston.'

'Yes. Thanks be to God. I'd heard that briefly from the county committee; but no details. When did it happen?'

'On the eighteenth and nineteenth, but the news took five days to reach us. The battle lasted two days they say. But sir, it wasn't about the war that I came to see you. This is a duty I wish hadn't fallen on me to perform.'

The Squire had a resigned look on his face as if he expected bad news. 'You've called to tell me something's happened to John?'

'The colonel was killed yesterday, just as Colchester surrendered. Lord General Fairfax commanded me to bring this news, for he held him in great esteem, as did Lieutenant General Cromwell. A burial party will be bringing his body back to Brentham tomorrow and staying for the funeral.'

'How did it happen after the surrender?' asked the Squire.

'For several days before, odd numbers of the defenders had been deserting and trying to make their way through our lines.

'We were patrolling north of the town just as the surrender was made, when we came upon a party of about thirty making their way through to the woods. All were armed. Two or three were officers. There was a sharp skirmish. Some of them we killed. Ten we took prisoner. The colonel made to chase some who were getting away, when one, an officer, turned and shot him.'

'So he met his death at the hands of a terrified and hungry man, determined not to be sent as a slave to the New World,' said the Squire. 'A sad epitaph for a brave man after years of conflict.'

'How is Mrs Pearson, sir?'

'Alas my poor Judith. She's sick and at this time in her bed. I must find a quiet moment to tell her of our son's death tonight. I fear it will do her no good. After you leave here and have seen your parents, pray call on Reverend Jones, and bid him come to me early tomorrow about John's funeral. I daren't leave my wife, for she'll be in great shock.

'But give me some details of Colchester. John's letters were sparse in information after you arrived at Lexden, although some details came through

163

to our county committee. There was a nasty fight at the beginning I believe.'

'Yes,' said Jeremy. 'We arrived at a fork road near Lexden on tenth of June. Lord Goring's forces were still camped outside Colchester gates. It was not until the night of eleventh twelfth that Lord Fairfax arrived with an advance of one-thousand cavalry. He would have liked to have attacked them on the twelfth, but they numbered five-thousand-six-hundred and we not much more than twelve-hundred horse and no foot. By the next day, the thirteenth, more reinforcements came and we numbered about eighteen-hundred cavalry and seventeen-hundred foot.

'Lord Fairfax was keen to attack while Goring was still in the open, so we went into battle that morning and had some success. We started to rout the enemy, who fell back behind the Headgate but were still outside the town in the suburban areas. So the next day we attacked in an area outside the walls known as East Hill while Suffolk auxiliaries, who had just arrived, attacked from the Hythe end to meet us. All the enemy then retreated into the high town within the walls.

'The enemy lost two-thousand to us in those two days counting killed, wounded or prisoners. For sake of morale, our casualties were announced as one hundred, but I fear we lost over five-hundred.

'That evening, Lord Fairfax started siege arrangements. In the early days, as more of the army arrived, other attacks were made on the walls but they were all repulsed with losses, so from then our efforts were aimed at keeping the enemy in.

'It took until second July to complete the forts. As you probably know, eight were built, but it took until twentieth July to completely seal in the town.'

'Yes. I heard about the forts through our committee,' said Nathaniel. 'Did the defenders attack the Suffolk auxiliaries at one of the forts before it was ready?'

'That was on twenty-third of June at a fort called Suffolk at the Mile End. The auxiliaries were chased into a wooded area known as High Woods. It fell to us, under Colonel John to chase the enemy back into Colchester town.

'There were several sallies out in the early days. Sir Charles Lucas went with twelve-hundred horse well on the way to Harwich foraging for provisions and more men. Then on another sally out, the enemy emptied a warehouse on the Hythe of provisions.

'But by the end of July we started to hear from deserters of privations, because nothing more was getting in. Stories of looting and rape against the civilians by the defenders. By mid-August we heard of people eating cats and rats; and of a woman who asked what she was to feed her child on, being told to boil and eat the child which would make much good meat; and of a maid protecting her mistress from rape having lighted sticks put under her fingernails.'

'In war, the base will ever find excuse for cruelty,' remarked the Squire.

'I believe the townspeople suffered terribly,' said Jeremy. 'The defenders burnt down some six-hundred homes near the walls, to give themselves field of fire against us. Although I haven't been into the town myself, because I came away too soon, I hear disease is ravaging the starving and weakened populace

'There was one distressing incident I witnessed a week before the end, which surprised me. I was returning from Lord Fairfax's headquarters camp at Lexden, when several hundred hungry people were let out of the town by Goring to beg food of Fairfax to save them from starving. The camp guards fired on them and drove them back into the town. Some were killed.'

'War is a dreadful, terrible thing, Jeremy,' said Nathaniel, 'and when it's civil war within a nation, more terrible still. Now I must let you get back to your wife, while I find words to break the sad tidings about John to mine.'

✳ ✳ ✳

It was after 8 o'clock in the evening before Jeremy returned. Bessie had been getting anxious because he had been gone over three hours.

'After I told the Squire about his son, I had to tell him about Colchester,' he said. 'Then at my parents, my mother made a great fuss over me and wanted me to eat with them, although I told her you'd be expecting me to eat here. Then I had to relate all about Colchester again. After that I had to see Reverend Jones for Mr Pearson.'

Bessie thought he looked ill at ease, and a little suspicion, born whilst he was out, tormented her.

'Well, you're here now, an' thass what matter,' said her mother. 'Could yer eat a little more, even though you've eat with your parents?'

Jeremy assured Mrs Bloom that he had left room for some of her excellent cooking.

'I'd like to hear all about Colchester,' said Samuel during the meal.

'Oh Sam,' said his wife. 'The lad's had a hard day. I don't 'spect he want to go through all that agin.'

'That's perfectly all right,' Jeremy assured her.

So they sat and listened to all the horrible details; then spoke of the war in general again, and of his promotion only given that morning. Bessie noticed that Jeremy did not look at her much, and thought he was trying to stretch the conversation out. She started to cry a little.

'Whass yer cryin' for, Bessie?' asked Samuel.

'Thinkin' about all them poor people hevin' to eat cats an' rats, an' gettin' sick, an' soldiers bein' cruel to 'em, an' hevin' their homes burnt,' wailed Bessie, giving part of the reason for her tears.

'War is a cruel, hard thing,' remarked Samuel.

'Amen to that,' said his wife. 'Now I think thass time we all went to bed.'

Bessie was sad. It should have been a joyful day of reunion for her. Instead, there was something wrong between her and her dear Jeremy, and she dreaded finding out the truth.

In their bedroom, she faced him seeking to be kissed. He held her close, leaning over her shoulder like one troubled, then after a while, without speaking, kissed her tenderly on the lips. But there was no fire and he did not attempt to undress her, as he had during the last time he was home.

In bed after the candle was extinguished, they lay side by side in silence. She longed for him to take her, and held out her hand to touch his. He squeezed it as if to reassure her. She turned towards him and expected him to reciprocate, but he did not. She was tempted to stoke his body, but it would not be meet to do so. That was what she believed. It was for the man to make the first move.

He was not sleeping, she could tell that. Now she had no doubt that her suspicions were correct. She burst into tears.

'What's amiss, dear?' he asked.

'I might well ask you that, Jeremy,' she sobbed. 'Now I know what I suspected earlier. There was somethin' wrong when yer first got home. Then yer told Dad tonight as how yer left Colchester durin' this mornin', but he di'n't seem to notice how long that took. You di'n't come straight home to me, did yer, Jeremy? Neither did yer do what was meet yer should hev done first; gone an' told the Squire about his son.'

He turned towards her and seemed as if he was going to mutter something.

'You went to her first, di'n't yer Jeremy? Lady Eve, the Marchioness. I can smell her on yer. She took yer to her bed and you've been doin' private things with her, so don't want to do 'em with me.'

He turned towards Bessie and put his arms about her. She could feel him crying softly. At last he spoke. 'I'm so ashamed Bess. I don't know what came over me. It's as if when my seed is up I can't resist her.'

He then confessed all about his encounters with Eve.

'But she di'n't stand outside to stop yer ridin' by this time, Jeremy. You went in of your own free will; thass whass so heartbreakin'. You must hev been thinkin' of her, as yer rode along, instead of me, an' jus' went in there.'

They talked and talked most of the night. Jeremy assured her that he didn't want Eve or the money for that matter. But Bessie would not be consoled, and at last cried herself to sleep.

In the morning, they resolved to talk over their problems, and after breakfast walked and talked for two hours without coming to any conclusions. In the afternoon the burial party arrived, bringing the colonel's body. 'I must go with them to see the Squire and Reverend Jones about the funeral arrangements,' he told her.

That night Jeremy attempted to make love to her, but she repulsed him. 'No Jeremy. I gotter think this all through. You're only comin' arter me 'cos your seed has come back agin. If yer really loved me, yer wouldn't hev done what yer did. Thass jus' lust what I can feel pressin' against me.'

The funeral was set for the following day, in the afternoon. A large number attended out of respect for the Pearson family. Bessie noticed that Eve, although in black, was still dressed to flaunt her sexuality. The top half of her bodice was of black lace, through which part of the valley between her breasts could still be seen. Her lips had been artificially moistened and made to look thicker, and her golden hair had been allowed to hang free. As she passed by, the heavy aroma of her perfume lingered.

Bessie paid more attention to her than the funeral service, and several times noticed her look towards Jeremy. At the graveside, Bessie and most of those who attended had to stand well back from the immediate family. She noticed that Eve manoeuvred herself until she stood near to Jeremy and his soldiers.

After the burial she saw Eve make to speak to Jeremy, but her father, the Squire, had got to him first. Apparently he had something to say, so Eve showed the discretion to turn away and return to her coach.

Bessie had been crying off and on, so when her mother had her on her own she tackled her. 'Now whass all this cryin', Bessie? I know funerals are sad, an' sometimes we all hev a little tear, but it ain't meet that a young woman, an' married, should weep so much over a gentleman she di'n't hardly know.'

Bessie cried some more.

'This ain't 'cos of the funeral is it? There's somethin' wrong atween you an' Jeremy.'

Bessie nodded.

'Then jus' you tell your ole mum about it afore Sam an' Jeremy come back. Thass wot I'm here for.'

Tearfully, Bessie related all about Jeremy's infidelities.

'Now thass a rum job,' said Mrs Bloom. 'But I ain't too surprised at it. You only gotter look at that there young woman to know she got the curse of Jezebel on her. Somethin' must hev happened to her early to make her like it. It would hev been a marvel if she hadn't hev tempted him into that all the time he had her hid. An' somebody like that was never gooner be satisfied with wot a man over seventy did for her in bed.

'Trouble is, most men ain't got no strength against that sort of thing if thass freely offered. Ain't no good the church tryin' to tell 'em different. They're all over-equipped in their breeches. Thass been the same ever since when that first Eve offered Adam that there apple wot the Lord God told him he mustn't eat.

'Now whass to be done, thass the problem. Do yer still love him? Or do yer want to be rid an' let her pay yer money?'

'No!' cried Bessie. 'I love him an' want him. I don't want her money. I'm jus' heartbroken that he could do that.'

'Then yer gotter fight to hold him my girl, 'cos she'll keep tryin'. But one thing in your favour. Yer won't hev to fight too long. A body like that can't manage without a man, an' will take up with the first one whass anything wot come along.

'Now; did yer do it with him last night, or did yer jus' wail an' feel sorry for yourself?'

'No. He wanted to, but I refused.'

'That ain't no way for a woman to fight. Wot about the night he come home?'

'No. He lay there all spent it seemed. I touched his hand an' he squeezed mine back, but di'n't do nothin' more. Thass when I questioned him about her.'

'You'd hev done better to get hold of his cock . . .'

'Mother!' cried Bessie, blushing.

'I ain't gooner mince my words. Cock, thass wot they call the thing they got in their breeches, though yer mustn't say that outside, or them there bigots whass at it, an' not only with their wives, will be hevin' yer caned or paraded around in a cart. He weren't spent. Don't take a young man like him more than a couple of hours to recover. He was jus' ashamed 'cos of wot he'd done.

'You take my advice. Don't be shy to make the first move. If he seem too quiet, get hold of his cock an' stroke it an' squeeze it. It'll soon grow hard in your hand. If it don't at his age, he's ill. An' if he still seem slow comin' on to yer, get on to him.'

'Mother. Thass not proper!'

'Everything's proper in private atween a man an' woman whass lawfully wed. An' put some fire into it. That way you'll soon hev a little somethin' in your belly; an' when that happen an' his got a little 'un, he'll be proud an' most likely won't stray.'

CHAPTER 19

Jeremy made a wide detour across fields to avoid passing the Manor House on his way back to Colchester. He had made a promise to Bessie that he would make a fresh start and he intended to keep it. On the last four nights following Colonel Pearson's funeral their lovemaking had been both tender and passionate. Bessie seemed to have lost some inhibitions, and although she was still not so passionate as Eve, she had climaxed on two of the four nights. Jeremy felt there was nothing lacking in his marriage.

Any small anxiety he might have had as to what he would do for a living when eventually discharged had also been solved. The Squire had told him that he would find him something worthwhile in his commercial enterprise.

He was deeply conscious that in a moment of weakness after he had made love to Eve a week earlier, he had left her with the false impression that he was interested in her proposals. She had tried to speak to him after her brother's funeral, but had been thwarted by her father, the Squire. No doubt these last few days she had been expecting him to call. When she discovered that he had left without contacting her, he did not doubt that all her latent passion would find expression in fury.

As soon as he arrived at his camp outside Colchester he reported back to Major Lehan, who he discovered had been promoted to colonel during his absence. 'Welcome back lieutenant. Before I assign you to your duties, I'll fill you in on what has taken place here at Colchester. Our casualties have been high, as have the enemy's, some of whom died of fever along with the unfortunate townsfolk. Would you like to read this list, lest there should be someone you know?'

Jeremy took the paper. 'Thank you, sir.'

'The total number of Royalist prisoners taken at the surrender was three thousand-five-hundred-and-twenty-six, of which two-hundred-and-eleven were officers.'

'What is their fate, sir?' asked Jeremy.

'Sir Charles Lucas and Sir John George Lisle have been shot by firing squad for breaking the parole they gave when taken prisoner at Stow-in-the-Wold back in forty-six. Lord Goring, and the other lords and gentlemen, have been sent to London as prisoners of Parliament, who will determine their fate. All other officers, also soldiers ranking sergeant and above, are being sent to the galleys or the plantations of the New World. Soldiers below sergeant have been disarmed and sent home.

'The Lord General has been less merciful here than is his usual nature. No doubt it's because Colchester held us off for twelve weeks and cost dearly.

'As far as the town itself is concerned, he has fined it fourteen-thousand pounds as a guarantee against looting and pillage by our troops. He has little sympathy for the ruin that has befallen the leading citizens and traders, who he blames for letting in the Royalists in the first place.

'Many of the general populace have tried to leave, but have been forced to remain living in their disease-ridden streets. The Lord General said that empty houses would be an invitation to looting.'

'Has there been trouble with looting sir?' asked Jeremy.

'Not much. Of course, there are always a few ruffians willing to risk a firing squad. But mostly we've had trouble with our soldiers being unwilling to go into the town for fear of disease. Several have had to be punished for refusing orders.'

'Are we staying here, sir?'

'For a few weeks. Mainly on patrol work and keeping order. There is much to be done in dismantling siege works, and I hear the town walls are to be pulled down so that Colchester can never be a place of siege again.

'Now that you've been promoted, you must take charge of a troop. A cornet could do the same, as you know. Not too many are promoted to lieutenant; it's only a stepping stone. It means you've been singled out as a possible future captain. Take care to keep your good record going.'

✳✳✳

Jeremy's regiment stayed around Colchester until October, but he did not have the chance to go home in spite of being so near. Then they were moved to London because, he was told, there was further disagreement between Parliament and the army. Then he heard that the army had gone and taken the King from the Isle of Wight and finally held him as their captive at Windsor.

Soon after, he saw Cromwell return, having completed his campaign in the north. From then things moved quickly. He heard that the King still refused to agree to a constitutional monarchy or anything else that diminished his powers to rule by divine right.

Then he heard of demands by the army, and those who supported it in Parliament, that the King be put on trial for treason. When a certain Colonel Pride, acting under orders, turned all the Presbyterians who wanted to continue negotiating with the King, out of Parliament, Jeremy heard many say that the tyranny of the King had now been replaced by the tyranny of a minority Parliament.

So for Jeremy ended the year 1648. A momentous one for him and for an England still not significantly nearer freedom and justice after over six years of conflict and bloodshed.

✳✳✳

When Eve realised that Jeremy had returned to army duties without calling, her natural passion manifested itself in the fury of a woman scorned. Shutting herself in her bedroom, she tore off and spoiled the bed cover on which she so recently had made love with him. Then, taking a heavy fire iron, broke the

170

free-standing full-length mirror in which she had seen herself riding his erection. That the ungrateful coward should go back on his word was something for which she meant to be avenged. She resolved to give herself to the first worthwhile lover that came along. Yet she still wanted Jeremy and meant to have him, even if it meant murdering Bessie to achieve her objective.

But even she could not survive just on anger and desire for revenge. She flung herself into regularly checking on how the vast Stourland estate was being managed, a task sorely neglected since the late Marquess had fallen ill. As small numbers of pressed men started to be released, and men were again in service at the Manor, she had the neglected gardens and park land attended to. She also started to interest herself a little in the affairs of Brentham; a development which did not please everybody.

Though still a sexual desert, her life became very full, and at the end of the year, when her mother died, the sadness also helped to push ideas of revenge and other lovers to the back of her mind for a short while.

✳✳✳

For Bessie the first few weeks after Jeremy departed from Brentham following Colonel Pearson's funeral were ones of hope. She had taken her mother's advice. Life and lovemaking with Jeremy in the final four days had taken on a new flavour, when, casting off inhibitions, she responded to him with ardour. As she had bidden him farewell she felt certain that she already carried a child within her.

A few weeks later, nature told her that she did not. In answer to her mother's enquiry, 'Hev yer got a pea in the pod, now yer doin' it proper? I only asked 'cos I care about both of yer,' she revealed her disappointment.

'Now thass somethin' what yer might call a rum job,' said Mrs Bloom. 'Of course thass early days yet, an' it don't allus happen straight away. Then it could be that his seed ain't no good. Arter all, his been . . . '

Bessie realised what her mother had just stopped herself saying. 'What you was jus' gooner say, mother, was that he'd been doin' it with Eve all the time he had her hid, an' off an' on since, and she di'n't get pregnant.' She wiped a little tear away.

'Now, now. Don't you go upsetting yourself agin about whass gone. Thass in the past. As I told yer afore, men hev the curse of Adam on 'em. They're most all over-equipped in their breeches, an' sometimes a woman hev to forgive an' forget. Things is all right atween yer now, yer say?'

Bessie nodded and sniffed as she wiped another tear. 'Yes,' she said.

'Now we could wait an' see what happen arter he come home next time,' said her mother. 'You might hev a problem though, so thass best if somebody can look at yer an' help. 'Of course until four or five year ago there was several widders in Brentham helpin' women wot had problems. Then when they accused poor ole widder Potter of bein' a witch an' drowned her in the pond, the others took fright an' stopped.

'You don't hear so much round about of witches gettin' swum or hung since last year when that there witchfinder general, Hopkins, got his self strung up on a tree. Now I hear there's a widder Carter the other end of the village wot has started agin. I don't know the woman, 'cept by sight, but we'll go and ask if she can help yer.'

So they went to see the widow Mrs Carter. Bessie judged the woman to be nearing sixty, and noticed that her home was little better than the hovels occupied by farm labourers, and that her clothes were well worn and mended in several places. Both Mrs Carter and her little house, however, were clean. This woman obviously needs money, thought Bessie.

'You do realise I hev to make a charge for my services?' she asked, when told of Bessie's problem.

'No need to worry on that account,' said Mrs Bloom. 'My Sam's a hard workin' an' sober man, even if he do let his tongue run away sometimes.'

'Thank the good Lord we can start helpin' agin,' said Mrs Carter. 'I've been a widder since forty-three an' hev a rare job keeping a roof over my head.

'Soon as I heard that cruel sod Matthew Hopkins was dead, I started tending my herbs agin an' lookin for the wild things wot I know cure people of all manner of ailments. At first I was a bit careful because I heard as how that friend of his, Stearne, had come to live right near here at Lawshall, atween here an' Bury. Then I heard as how he'd give up witch huntin', so, 'specially as we won't see that ole sod Dowdy in Brentham no more, I thought it might be safe to start agin, though there's a couple of others I need to watch. I wonder what happened to ole Dowdy arter he got forced out?'

'Thass funny yer should ask that,' said Bessie's mother. My Sam get a tidy bit of news an' rumour off the drivers when the stage wagons call. It was said that there was a man callin' his self Joshua Hardin' wot had been goin' around findin' so-called witches for Hopkins though he never come near Brentham. Thass said that if anybody who was rumoured to be a witch give him enough money, he'd not give their name to the witchfinder.'

'Do you reckon thass Dowdy then?' asked Mrs Carter.

'A man wot used to live in Brentham, caught sight of this Joshua Hardin'. He reckon that was him, though well disguised. It would explain why he never come near Brentham. It seem he disappeared off the face of the earth round about the time Hopkins was strung up; or died. I don't know if you heard that other rumour, that he weren't lynched at all, but died of consumption?'

'Who care? He's dead, thass wot matter,' said Mrs Carter. 'I s'pose this Hardin', or Dowdy, if that was him, ran away to save his skin once he di'n't hev the witchfinder to protect him.'

She turned to address Bessie. 'Now young woman. We best see whass the matter. We won't help yer get babies standin' here natterin.' She motioned Bessie to go and lie on her bed.

'Can't feel nothin' wrong,' she observed, after prodding and poking Bessie inside and out. 'You ain't been opened up long hev yer? Whass he been doin'; leavin' it?'

Bessie blushed and stammered an incoherent answer.

'There might be nothin' wrong with yer; an' there's allus a chance his seed ain't no good yer know. That do happen. Ain't allus the woman.'

Bessie wished people wouldn't keep suggesting that awful possibility.

'Still, you want to make sure.' she handed over a bottle of liquid and a jar of ointment. 'Take this potion regular, every night an' mornin'. Then when he come home rub a little of this ointment on yourself an' some on his . . er . . '

'Cock,' interjected Bessie's mother.

'Yes, but we mustn't say that word outside, or goodness only know what they'll do to us,' said Mrs Carter.

'She already know that,' said Mrs Bloom.

✳✳✳

Jeremy's regiment continued to serve in London throughout the early months of 1649. It was a time of high drama. The King, having been tried for treason and condemned was executed on the penultimate day of January, and it fell to Jeremy's troop to be part of the guard that surrounded the scaffold shoulder to shoulder, two deep, facing the crowd. In a nervous reaction, he jerked as he heard the thud of the axe behind him, and the gasp of the throng he faced.

Bile rose in his throat to burn him. Had the powers that be done right, he wondered? Who would be the next king? Like so many other ordinary people, he had no conception of a country without a monarch.

Events followed in rapid succession. A week later, the whole regiment was called on parade to be addressed by Colonel Lehan. He was flanked by his squadron commanders. Troop commanders like Jeremy were ordered to stand well in front of their men and turn and repeat the colonel's words to them sentence by sentence.

'This is a momentous day. . . . The monarchy has been abolished. . . . England is now a republic. . . . The republic will be governed by a Council of State aided by what is left of Parliament.'

Most men received the news in silence. A few cheered, and shouted, 'Agreement of the people,' and taking the green ribbons of the Levellers from their pockets, stuck them to their shoulders. Leveller support in Jeremy's regiment was not so strong as in many others, and did not include any officers.

A few days later, Colonel Lehan called all his officers together. 'News has just come in that the Scottish Estates refuse to recognise the republic and have proclaimed the absent Prince of Wales as King Charles the second.'

'Could this lead to war again, sir?' asked Jeremy.

'As yet they lack the strength to attack us, but the threat is recognised. So

173

no cavalry will be discharged, or any more foot. There is talk of a strong force being assembled to finish off the Irish Royalists and Catholics once and for all, before trouble starts from the north.

'Meantime we have been asked to convert by persuasion, or by discipline if that fails, away from the more outlandish aims of the Levellers, any of our men so affected. I want each troop commander to make up a list of names of any Levellers they have with special note of the more outspoken ones. The activity of this movement is growing again and is a threat to the stability of our new republic.

'Assure them that their legitimate grievances over pay are being attended to; that will quieten the moderate ones. Make no mistake, our leaders mean to quell by force any mutinies that break out.'

In April, Jeremy watched while a Leveller mutineer was hanged outside St Paul's Cathedral and saw a large group of his comrades, defiantly with green ribbons in their hats, carry his body away to honour it with a military funeral. Then in May his regiment formed part of a numerous force under both Fairfax and Cromwell that went to Burford in Oxfordshire and very firmly put down a large Leveller mutiny. After that, there seemed less turbulence from the Levellers within the army.

Later that month Jeremy was relieved to find that their regiment was not one of those earmarked to go to Ireland. Much as he would have liked to serve under Cromwell, who had been appointed to lead the campaign, the prospect of Ireland did not appeal, for there were evil rumours of that country.

Also, he had not been home in the last nine months and was missing Bessie. Although Colonel Lehan was a pleasant enough officer to serve under, he was not a Suffolk man, and news of home was more sparse than had been the case in Colonel Pearson's time. Then, as his aide, he had received a steady stream of information out of Brentham; also he had been privy to his superior's personal opinion on many matters; both these he missed.

He was therefore overjoyed when, in early June his regiment was posted to Newmarket.

***

Joseph Bloom, hearing hoof beats enter the forge yard, straightened up from the plough he was mending. 'Lor' lumme alive!' he exclaimed. 'Look who's here.'

'I'm just as surprised to see you, Joseph,' said Jeremy, dismounting from his horse. 'Are you nearby now, that you can get home easily?'

'No, back here workin'. Finished with the army altogether, I hope.'

'I thought no regiments were getting disbanded now,' said Jeremy.

'Ours weren't disbanded, explained. 'Jus' a few of us whass been servin' a long time got discharged. But we was told we could be called back agin if need arose. I got the impression we was bein' weeded out. It might hev been 'cos I was involved in the mutiny at Newmarket a couple of year ago.'

'Newmarket is where I am now,' said Jeremy. 'I should be able to get home often if peace lasts. Now I must go to Bessie. I'll come out to talk with you and Sam later. Is she in the cottage or the forge?'

'Might be in the goods shed; she look arter all that now.' Joseph craned his neck towards the shed. 'No. Thass shut. She'll be in the . . . Oh hec!' He dropped his voice to a whisper. 'The blasted Marchioness.'

Jeremy turned his head to see Eve, elegant and beautiful as ever, approaching and only a few yards away. In a panic misjudgement, he slapped his reins into Joseph's hand and made for the cottage gate, hoping to get there before her.

When he smelt her aroma, and felt her hand on his arm, and heard her address him as, 'My elusive Jeremy,' he realised, too late, that he would have been better going into the forge.

His phallus stirred. It would never be over.

✲✲✲

Eve smiled to herself as she made her way home. She felt a deep sense of inner satisfaction from her brief encounter with Jeremy near the forge. Almost as much as if they had made love.

He hadn't turned away as he could have done. But then he wouldn't, she reflected. With his strict upbringing he would always be polite and deferential, and act with scrupulous propriety–until his privy member stiffened. She chucked at the memory of how he had addressed her as 'Your Ladyship'; he who at feeble excuse had not hesitated to feast on her body many times, and then each time repent because he had sinned.

She had sensed his rising heartbeats as she laid her hand on his arm. He seemed awkward and uncomfortable, almost as gauche as that day five years ago when he had come back from Cambridge. But then he would, for they were in clear view of the cottage where his wife lived. She hoped little Bessie had seen them. She had deliberately turned so that one of her breasts touched his arm as she bade him farewell.

Certainly that oaf of a brother of hers had seen them, she knew, for he had glowered at her with a face full of hatred as she passed. No doubt he would tell of it even if she had not seen, for was he not a big-mouthed fellow like his father?

It was customary, she knew, for ladies of her rank to ride almost everywhere in their coaches, and until three months before, she had done so. After her mother died, she made a practice of calling on her father, the Squire, three times each week, always in her coach.

Then as the first shock subsided, thoughts of revenge returned. She had considered murdering Bessie, but there was little opportunity, and in any case, she did not know how to set about it. She was never quite certain if it had been she who caused her husband's death or if he had died from a natural cause.

So she contented herself with harassment of Bessie, and a determination to take Jeremy from her eventually. Whenever the weather was fine and it was dry underfoot she would walk to her father's, even though it was a good two miles plus the not inconsiderable length of the Manor driveway. Her route to and fro always took her past the smithy, although she could have detoured round the green; past the church and parish office, where once she and Jeremy used to feel one another.

Always, as she passed, she would be exquisitely dressed and made up, but not to attract men. Her purpose was to flaunt her wealth and beauty in a woman's face–Bessie's. Would she think, each time she saw her, of Jeremy lifting her under her thighs while she rode his erection before a mirror? Had Jeremy told her of that, she wondered? Or of the park, or the summer-house, or the loft in his father's barn, or of the near three weeks of nightly bliss in his own bedroom?

She was sure that he had, for that would be Jeremy; repent, pray, confess, get it off his chest. And surely Bessie would be counting. They had been married over eighteen months and been together barely three weeks. She would know that her Jeremy had possessed Eve more times than herself, and be tormented by it.

Now today she had triumphed, for she had shown, before little Bessie's eyes, that for all his regrets and repentances, when she beckoned her husband he would turn to her; because she was Eve and he was Jeremy. Sooner or later little Bessie would give up.

She reflected with regret, that she would be somewhat hampered in her enticement by lack of information. Since her brother had been killed, news of the activities of Jeremy's regiment had ceased to come to her father. However, two days later she did discover from the Squire, that although Jeremy had been home for little more than twenty-four hours, he had made a short courtesy call on him. He was stationed at Newmarket.

This was excellent news; she would go to him. Her dull life would liven up again.

And it had been a dull life for her these last three and a half years. She often regretted having married the Marquess in the first place. He had been a solitary figure having only the occasional guest calling. Those of his class in East Anglia who were not themselves Puritans and had not already been fined for supporting the King, were careful to live quiet and sober lives, to protect themselves from spiteful charges of malignancy and consequent loss of property.

Her hard work with her estate, whilst giving her an interest in life was doing nothing to alleviate her sexual craving. Neither was the self gratification which she had long indulged in, or the lesbian affair which she had once more started with one of her maids proving effective remedies. She needed a man on a long term basis; a husband. Reflecting that in only four months she would become twenty-five, she decided that unless she could

176

very quickly get Jeremy away from Bessie, much as she loved him, she would have to look elsewhere. Her present life buried here deep in the country and alone would not do.

This brought her again to an idea she had conceived before her mother died, then given up. Sell the vast Stourland estate, or a very large part of it, and take up residence in London. She had heard that although there were no longer organised entertainments in the capital, the wealthier citizens were entertaining themselves with free love in each other's homes, cocking a snook at restrictions.

CHAPTER 20

Eve's heart sank as, looking from her bedroom window one bright summer evening in 1649, she saw troopers approaching down the long drive. She had a premonition that this might be what she had been dreading, and against the possibility of which, among other reasons, she had been considering selling up.

'Your Ladyship.' She heard the sound of a maid calling and tapping on the door. 'Your Ladyship.'

Eve called 'Wait.' She could have let the girl come in straight away, but it was not good to give staff the idea that her bedroom was a place of quick and easy access.

After two minutes she called, 'Come in.'

The maid bobbed a curtsy. 'Your Ladyship; Goody Fran say there's a Captain Tripp want to see yer.'

'Did she say what he wanted?'

'No, yer Ladyship.'

Eve wanted to waste time to get her thoughts together. 'Then pray ask the goodwife to see me immediately.' She waved a dismissal at the maid.

Tripp? Not at all a common name, yet it seemed familiar. She had already decided what dress to wear to meet him and had laid it out by the time the goodwife knocked.

'Come in Fran,' she called.

'You should have come yourself in the first place,' said Eve in mild rebuke.

'I told the maid he was from the sequestrators, but I don't suppose she could say such a big word. Also, I didn't think it right to leave an armed soldier alone in the drawing room,' explained the goodwife.

'One wonders what you'd have done had he drawn his sword or aimed his pistol at you,' said Eve with a smile. Never mind. I was merely seeking to gain time to think. Help me change my dress. His name, Tripp, has a familiar ring. Have you an idea where I might have heard it.'

The goodwife took a while to answer as she helped Eve off with her dress, wondering why she was doing a personal maid's job, and one that Eve often did on her own. 'Tripp. Let me see. Don't know anyone of that name . . . but wait. I seem to recall five years back. You remember when your father had some soldiers down from Bury because of disturbances, when the constable was murdered and that poor woman was burned?'

'Yes.' Eve was glad that Fran was considerate enough to have omitted to mention herself being tried for fornication. Good, loyal Fran. What would she do without her?

'Well. Now I come to think of it, I seem to remember one of the servants mentioning that there were soldiers in the village and the name of their officer was Tripp. Cornet Tripp I believe.'

Eve recalled a handsome young officer who had constantly looked at her in the court with eyes that seemed to undress and ravish her. No doubt he was as afflicted with desires as herself.

He was a man she would have liked to meet again had her father not confined her to her home and garden for several months after her release. By the time she had been allowed into the village again, he and his men were gone. The officer who was in charge on the day of her trial was a Captain Williams; she remembered that well enough. Now her memory had been jogged she recalled her father saying, just once, that he had ridden back to Brentham with a Cornet Tripp.

'Tell the captain, I'll be pleased to see him and will be down in about fifteen minutes.' She spent the time adding her most expensive fragrance, tidying her hair and adjusting the provocative dress she had just put on.

Eve recognised Tripp as soon as she entered the room. Older, more weather-beaten, but the same man who had ravished her with his eyes five years earlier. As she offered her hand, she noticed his gaze hold on to her bosom, trying to discern the valley beneath the fine black lace that concealed from casual glance, but not from keen inspection. She would defend her wealth with what she had.

'Captain Tripp. I believe this isn't your first visit to Brentham?' said Eve, giving a subtle opening for Tripp to think of her in a sexual context.

'Indeed it isn't, Your Ladyship. Nearly five years ago at the request of Mr Pearson, a member of the county committee, as a young cornet, I was sent with a party of soldiers to quell disorder in Brentham.'

Eve could tell he was pretending not to have recognised her, so offered another lead. 'Ah, yes. Now I remember seeing you in the parish courtroom.' She sensed from his expression that the unspoken invitation had found its mark.

'Now I realise where I've seen you before,' said Tripp, pretending that he had only just recognised her. 'A just result from a monstrous charge brought against a virtuous young lady.'

Eve thought to herself, You're an accomplished liar Captain. You don't believe me virtuous at all. You have been feasting your eyes and wondering how you might get between my legs without discovery. With you I can trade favour for favour.

'What of the young man that was charged with you?' asked Tripp.

Now you're feeling out the competition, thought Eve; but she replied, 'Young Mr Goodway? He's in the army these last four years nearly. A lieutenant of horse.'

'Ah.'

He made no further reply, and Eve, believing he sought further information, said, 'Married eighteen months ago to the blacksmith's little daughter.'

As soon as she had said it, Eve regretted using the word "little", for that betrayed her jealousy of Bessie. She saw just the trace of a smirk cross Tripp's face. The self-assured expression of a man in the presence of a deprived and sexually orientated woman. An easy conquest. But Eve did not mean to be too easy. She wanted to trade.

'You've already been told that I've been sent by the sequestrators,' said Tripp. 'I'm under orders to search this house. It's felt that you weren't entirely honest with the assessors last year as to the extent of your late husband's wealth and therefore the amount levied was less than it should have been.'

'But the Marquess was a neutral,' said Eve.

'So it was claimed,' said Tripp. 'But apparently not always believed. Even neutrals were supposed to pay levies towards our cause, according to their wealth. It seems he paid little or nothing when he was alive. If it's now found that the assessors were grossly deceived last year, it could be presumed that he was a secret Royalist, and you with him. That could then lead to a charge of malignancy and the possible sequestration of some or all of your property to pay the huge penalty which would be imposed.'

Eve started to be frightened. Perhaps, after all, this man would put his duty before sexual gratification. 'But my brother, the late Colonel John Pearson, was a hero in our cause, highly thought of by both Fairfax and Cromwell,' she said. 'Surely that must count for something.'

'The pesky politicians thought too little of live soldiers to pay them properly,' said Tripp. 'Dead ones may not expect more than lip service.

'Of course, much will depend on my report. Make no mistake, there's much bitterness due to the second war. Our people mean to beggar all avowed Royalists who took part in it or supported it with money, whether openly or secretly. I have to visit all large houses in the area unless they are proven supporters of our cause.'

He made a gesture with his hand around the room. 'The voluntary offer of a comfortable billet for my men and a base to work from would go in your favour.'

Eve took the cue. 'How many men do you have?' she asked.

'Apart from myself, a cornet, a sergeant, and eighteen troopers.'

Eve turned to the goodwife. 'Fran. Take the captain's soldiers to the rear rooms of the house. Make sure the cornet and the sergeant have a room each with a bed. The troopers can share a couple of rooms. I fear we may be short of bed linen for so many.'

'Don't concern yourself on that score,' said Tripp. 'The troopers will fetch for themselves in that respect.'

'As for you, Captain Tripp,' said Eve. 'Whilst Mrs Francis attends to billeting for your men, I'll find you something better at the front of the house. Come with me.'

She led the way up the main staircase until she came to the room next to her own. 'This is the dressing room that the late Marquess used. He also used

180

to sleep in here on those occasions when I wished to be alone. Will it suffice for your needs?'

'It will be adequate,' he replied.

She saw his eyes move to a door in a side wall.

'My chamber is next door. Normally that door will be locked,' she said, with just a little emphasis on *normally*.

She knew he had taken the cue.

'I don't have to decide until the morning whether to start with this house or another, as we'll be using this as a base,' he said.

Eve knew what he meant.

Long before Captain Tripp retired to bed that evening, Eve quietly unlocked the connecting door between their rooms. She looked forward with relish to the pleasant sacrifice she would soon make to protect her wealth and property.

Later, after undressing for bed, she gazed at her naked form in the full length mirror. A new mirror, a new man. Would he take her in front of the mirror like Jeremy, she wondered. How she wished it was Jeremy she was preparing for. She stroked herself sensuously, admiring her own beauty; her golden hair hanging about her shoulders.

And yet, she thought, so favoured, I still lost him to the blacksmith's little daughter with the tiny breasts. Now I give myself to another, but will have him yet; she shall not win.

She sat on the edge of her bed, and, taking a hand mirror from her side table, placed it between her legs. With her left hand she stretched her vulva forward, then flipped the lips apart to examine every anatomical detail. Her thoughts flowed on. Men have all strength, all power; yet to possess this small piece of flesh, so insignificant, so ugly, they will risk all.

Selecting her most odoriferous fragrances and creams, Eve anointed herself. Toying at first with the idea of getting into bed naked, she decided instead to don her most voluminous and unattractive night-shift. The aroma to tempt; the night-shift to bar the delights and trade with.

As darkness fell, Eve drew back her curtains before getting into bed. It was the time of a full moon; before long the room would become a pattern of soft light alternating with shadows.

Almost an hour passed. She had wondered how it would be and guessed he would be over confident. Even so, in her pretence of sleep with one eye open, as he came through the connecting door she was surprised enough to leap from her bed. A slightly shorter but more muscular man than Jeremy, he advanced towards her, naked with full erection. The moonlight played on his splendid torso, highlighting his biceps and making his phallus seem enormous.

'How dare you come into my room thus!' she exclaimed.

'I dare because you invited me to come and trade favour for favour. Your

181

offer couldn't have been clearer had it been made directly. Am I supposed to trade on a promise without sampling the merchandise?'

'I am no whore to be bought. If you wanted to become my lover I'd expect a more gentle approach. You offend by appearing before me suddenly as you are.'

He gave a little chuckle and flicked his phallus. 'If the sight of what I have offends, then turn away, that you might not see it.'

Eve turned around. In a flash he was upon her, bending her over the bed. The night-shift was pushed up to her shoulders, her legs pushed apart and she was filled with him. She could have struggled, but she did not, preferring to enjoy the humiliation he was inflicting upon her, as, with a breast in each hand, he rode her like an animal. Then, stopping for a while, he lowered one hand to between her legs and with the other still holding a breast, flicked around a nipple.

They finished together. As he disengaged, he pushed her arms up and removed the night-shift completely. She slapped him hard across the face. 'That was rape!,' she hissed. 'What would be your punishment if it was known you raped me?'

He laughed at the slap. 'I've been in battle these many years. Am I supposed to collapse at a slap from a woman? As for rape, if it were known, at the very least I would be reduced to the ranks and lose the skin off my back. At the worst I could face a firing squad.

'But it's not going to be known is it, because you don't want to lose what you've got? Vent your anger if you must, but you enjoyed it. The first sample was good, but I'll stay the rest of the night for another. I don't think I'll have to order my men to take up your floor boards or search your attics tomorrow. We'll talk trade when I've sent them elsewhere. Tonight is for fun.'

He took hold of her arm and pushed her gently into the bed. She pretended to resist as he climbed in with her. Turning her back on him, she lay in anger, fuming that she had already submitted without gaining anything, and enjoyed the experience.

After a little while he burst out laughing. 'I was just thinking. I can hardly keep calling you "Your Ladyship" now that I've fucked you. Can I call you "Eve"; it's your name, I believe?'

She turned suddenly and raising herself struck him full across the mouth then grasped his hair in both hands. 'Isn't it enough,' she hissed, 'that you treat me like a farm animal, without descending to the language of the gutter? Beware, I may yet prefer to sacrifice the Stourland wealth to see you punished. My father, Squire Pearson, from whom I shall also inherit now that my brother is dead, is a member of the county committee as you know. A complaint to him would find its way to your highest commanders.'

She knew her threat had found its mark because he fell silent as they lay side by side.

'Then if I've offended with oafish behaviour, I apologise,' he said at

182

length. 'I'm not an oaf by nature, but a man with some education who has been brutalised by this war which I've fought from the beginning. My wife was raped and killed along with our baby by marauding cavaliers. My home burned. I hate Royalists with a hatred that will not be assuaged. I've lost everything.'

Eve felt a sudden tenderness towards him. 'Then I begin to understand,' she said, touching his arm. 'But *we* are not Royalists. My father a county committee man; my late brother a hero who fought under Fairfax and Cromwell. As for my late husband, the Marquess, he was strictly neutral; his only ambition was to produce an heir so that the Stourland title might survive.'

'But you didn't produce an heir.'

'He was approaching eighty, and could scarce perform the deed.'

'Therein lies your danger. Had the Marquess not married, the government would now own the property and lands. They are desperate for money. You're but a young woman with many years of life ahead and standing in their way. They won't give a fig about your dead brother's heroism. If they can find cause to declare you malignant they will. Only the thin veil of your father's influence at county level protects you. You need my good offices. Why did you marry the old Marquess in the first place?'

'A sacrifice of love,' replied Eve. 'At that time, my brother was alive and would have inherited from my father. I needed a well-placed husband, but the young man I loved was far from wealthy. It would have been but a short wait.'

She fell silent, and he did not speak for a few moments either.

'I think I understand,' he said slowly. 'The young man who was tried with you. But he's married to another now. Won't I do instead? I'm educated, and an officer.'

Eve let out a little laugh. 'The man I marry will at least act like a gentleman. Had you ambitions in that direction, you made a very poor start. No, I love Jeremy yet and mean to get him. He was very brave; broke me from prison and suffered for it.'

'What I may do for you carries a deal more risk than breaking a person out of prison.'

'You won't go unrewarded. Ours will be a trading arrangement. Meanwhile I've agreed to take you as a lover. You may call me Eve in private. What is your name, Captain Tripp?'

'Henry.'

She leaned over and kissed him lightly on the cheek. 'Then Henry, let ours be a happy association.'

He put an arm round her shoulder and drew her towards himself until their mouths met and tongues entwined, while his hand traced the curve of her spine and buttocks.

Another hour had passed before Eve fell into an exhausted sleep, knowing in her own mind that if she failed to get Jeremy, she might very well come to love this man.

In the morning, Tripp sent his men to search another suspected house a few miles distant. 'We need to do all in seven hours,' he said to Eve. 'You trust me. Tomorrow we shall search this house. It's important that valuables hidden in attics are removed; also anything under already loose floorboards. I must appear to do my duty in front of my men. Who can you trust completely in your household?

'The goodwife, Mrs Francis.'

'Then bid her set the maids more work than they can do in a day in the kitchens and below stairs. Then let us collect all the valuables from attics and below floorboards and bring here.'

Eve knew she had no alternative but to trust Henry Tripp. She would, after all, be no worse off if he proved false than if she was discovered in deception.

'Do you also have hide-holes behind walls?' he asked after they had gathered together the valuables from around the house.

'Only one; behind the wainscoting in your room. That has nothing in it.' She took him and showed him the hidden spring that released a panel.

'This will do for some,' said Tripp. He examined some pieces and put them in the hide-hole. 'I won't let the men search my room. Let's wrap the rest of this in a large cloth. Do you have anything concealed outside?'

Eve hesitated.

'If you want us not to find it you had better trust me,' said Tripp, sharply.

'The summer-house.'

'Let's go there then.'

He followed her, carrying the silver valuables which he had wrapped.

'There's a pit under the floor,' said Eve.

He took up some of the boards and removed the lid off the pit. 'This is already full, and not too well concealed,' he said. 'I'll cover it better.' He replaced the lid and covered it with more stones. 'I'll make sure my men don't search here tomorrow.' He replaced the floorboards. 'Now tell me where I might find a spade in order that I can bury this surplus from the house?'

'In the shed next to the stables.'

'Now I think you should bide in the house while I find a suitable place.'

Eve made to demur.

'Go,' Tripp said, sharply. 'Go I say!'

Eve did as she was bidden. She knew she was in this man's power as well as falling in love with him.

Henry Tripp did not return to the house for several hours. No more than a few minutes before his men returned. Eve wondered what he could have been doing in all that time. Not having eaten since breakfast, he was ravenously hungry. The rest of the evening was taken up with eating and doing business with his soldiers.

Any small doubts as to his reliability were dispelled during a night of furious lovemaking. Four times he took her. On each occasion he brought her to several shattering climaxes. She was satiated as she had never been before.

In the morning, Eve stayed in her bed for an extra hour or more. Henry Tripp had not been by her side as she woke. She could hear the noise of soldiers searching other parts of the house. Louder noises started coming from Tripp's room. She sprang from bed and made for the connecting door.

Realisation that it was not his voice caused her to stop, leave her own room and approach his from the landing. She opened his door. Her heart sank. The cornet and two troopers were thoroughly searching his room. He had said he would not let them do that. She nearly fainted when the officer found the spring catch and revealed the hide-hole. It was empty!

'If it's convenient for your Ladyship,' said the cornet, 'we'd like to search your bedroom now.'

'Yes. Yes of course.' She was too bewildered to speak coherently. She had seen Tripp put valuables in that hide-hole.

She sat down in her room while it was being searched. Although thorough, the soldiers were polite, and she was grateful that they left everything in good order.

The search lasted several hours. It was mid-afternoon before she heard Tripp give his men orders that now they had finished in the house they were to search all outbuildings thoroughly. The men split up into three groups. Her nerves were on edge as she realised Tripp wasn't going with the smaller party making for the summer-house. He merely seemed to be walking about outside. she went out to him.

'You said you wouldn't allow them to search the summer-house.'

'On reflection, to stop them would have seemed suspicious.'

'But if they find the pit!' she exclaimed.

He smiled at her slowly but didn't speak. He was enjoying her panic.

'What if they find the pit?' she demanded.

'They won't.'

'How do you know that?'

'Because it isn't there. I filled it in. It was an unwise place to hide your things in the first place.'

'What have you . . . .'

He interrupted her. 'I must make sure my men are doing their duty.' With that he strode off in the direction of the summer-house.

She did not see him any more until the evening meal. Then they were not alone long enough for her to ask the question that was on her mind.

He came to her room that night, as of a right. She had not started to undress.

185

'What have you done with my valuables?' she demanded, knocking away his hands as he came close enough to fondle her.

Without answering, he put his hands behind her head and brought his mouth down on hers. She tried to close her mouth, but then responded as she felt herself melting. 'What have . . ?'

She shuddered as he nibbled her ear. 'Don't fret. They're all safely concealed,' he whispered, sliding his hands down the nape of her neck and loosening the top two buttons of her bodice.

'You should tell me.' As she spoke she felt him undoing more buttons.

'You must tell me.' She was trying to be firm with him, but now he was loosening her under garments, and she could feel his hands on her naked flesh. He drew all her upper garments together over her arms, and she helped him.

'If you won't tell me where you've buried them, I shall search the . . .' Her voice was growing hoarse as he traced his tongue around one nipple. '. . . . and have servants help me. Then . . .' She took his hand and placed it on her other breast. '. . . . all will be discovered.'

He took his mouth from her breast. 'Search away for their burial place.' He started to pull the remainder of her clothes down over her hips and she helped him. 'You won't find it.'

She stepped out of her clothes and started to undo his. 'Would you cheat me?'

'You'll get your valuables back, or most of them when we have successfully traded.'

'What do you want?'

'First, submission and humility.'

'Humility?'

'Kneel.'

Eve, now desperate for him, did as she was commanded. Neither did she object when he took a cloth and blindfolded her; or when he gently bound her hands behind her back.

'I fear lest you offer me violence.'

'I offer no violence.'

She heard him walk to the other side of the room and sensed that he was undressing. His naked footfalls could be heard padding towards her and his pungent male smell filled her nostrils. She felt his hardness press against her lips. After a moment's hesitation in the face of this new experience, she opened her mouth. He bent over her and removed the blindfold.

But he was becoming too eager and she feared she would choke. She shook her head. He withdrew and untied her hands. 'You must tell me if I press too hard,' he said, softly.

Her hands freed, she put them behind his buttocks and drew him to her again. After a while he pushed her gently away and stood still. 'It becomes too much.'

He raised her from the floor and guided her to the bed to lay. She felt his tongue encircle both breasts then slowly trace its way across her abdomen. Realising his intentions, she opened her legs wide. She cried aloud at the pleasure he was giving her and exploded it her first climax.

'Now you know I return deal for deal,' he whispered in her ear as he took her conventionally.

Afterwards they lay side by side. 'Will you now tell me the substance of the trade that you want?' Eve asked.

'For a goodwill token, just two-hundred pounds for now. It'll help me bear the burden of my arrears of pay.'

'A bold demand, yet modest enough since you are risking your life for my benefit. Anything else?'

'I would have you to wife.'

'There you ask too much. I've already said that I love Jeremy Goodway and will yet have him away from his wife.'

'For a woman that loves another, you certainly put fire into your responses to me.'

'That's how I'm made. I admit that in the few days we've been together I've found you a good lover. Had I known you longer, and had my heart not already been set on Jeremy such an idea might not have been out of the question. But I must have him. I was his first love. I won't be bested by that little wife of his.'

'You won't succeed. From what you tell me of him, his strict upbringing will prevent him from leaving her, however he feels about you. Oh I know you may be able to tempt him between your legs–you could exercise that power over any man. But he'll always feel shame afterwards and pray about it. That's how it is now in the army. It's been drummed into them. If they have too much to drink or say a swear word they repent and pray about it. That's unless their officers know, in which case they get the lash and really have something to repent about.'

'You're an officer; do you have men flogged for such small offences?'

'I have to. It's orders. Especially when serving under Cromwell. He's kindly and just, but he will have discipline and piety. Do you know, they say he looks in the bible to find justification for every decision?'

'I'd heard that from my father.'

'Which gives you some idea of the risk I'm taking. But I can't eat piety, and I've lost everything in this war except my life. When my wife and baby were killed and my home burned, my parents farm, which they were buying, was destroyed. They were too badly injured to continue, so the land reverted to the lord of the manor in their area. They died broken hearted soon after.

'I could coerce you into marrying me. I know where your valuables are hidden and leading my men on more diligent search would discover them.

'But I'll not have you to wife by force. You'll grow to love me when you give up this silly idea of getting Goodway from his wife. Until then I'll be patient and settle for a good farm.'

'A farm?'

'You have many farms belonging to this estate. You could well afford to make one over to me; especially as it would come back into the estate if we married.'

'There's one farm where the tenant grows old. But it's a bold demand you make, which I need time to think about.'

'So long as the transfer is made before we leave here in about six weeks. Until then your valuables will remain hidden. I shall need to see the farm and approve it of course.'

$$***$$

In the morning, Tripp declared his intention of going with his men, but at the front gate turned back. Skirting the park land until he came to the most densely wooded part, he tethered his horse.

Making sure he was alone, he climbed a tall elm and from its upper branches untied one of several sacks hanging there, concealed by the foliage.

By the time his horse had reached the front gate, he had decided on Colchester. Being in the next county it would be a little safer. It was also close enough to get to and return in the day.

A goldsmith in that town, with the embryo of a bank, bought the silverware, opened him an account and placed two-hundred-and-sixty pounds to his credit. Tripp drew a little of that for his immediate needs.

Somewhat more than the lady agreed last night, he reflected as he rode back. Still, I may return the excess to her when I get the farm.

CHAPTER 21

'Welcome home, Jeremy. Thass nice to see yer agin.' Mrs Bloom was all smiles, throwing her arms about him as he walked into the cottage. 'Go through to Bessie. She got somethin' important to tell yer.'

Bessie was in their bedroom. Even in the dim light from the small window that late November afternoon, Jeremy could see she was glowing with excitement. She jumped up and threw her arms about him. They kissed long and passionately.

'What's all the excitement, my love,' he asked her, although he already guessed the answer.

'Jeremy; oh Jeremy. I do love yer so. I'm gooner hev a baby. We been an' talked to Mrs Carter, whass an expert in them things, an' she say thass gooner come in May if that run true to time.'

Jeremy kissed her again. 'I'm so glad Bessie. You must take care of yourself and get plenty of rest. Who else knows?'

'Jus' the family. Dad won't let me lift nothin' heavy now over the goods shed. Thass why I'm finished early. He sent me in to rest. An' your parents keep bringin' down extra milk for me.'

They talked and planned of all the wonderful things they would do when he was out of the army. Jeremy was happy. Now he should at last be able to put Eve from his mind.

Eve had come to search him out at Newmarket soon after he arrived there in June. Once more he had been unable to resist her. They had walked in the woods and made love standing against a tree. She had promised to visit him often. At that time, believing he would never be free from her temptation, he had resolved to tell Bessie it was no good their going on. He would have to go to Eve.

It would break Bessie's heart and cost him the friendship of Samuel and Mrs Bloom, and Joseph; shame his parents; possibly even cost him the esteem of Squire Pearson. Nevertheless he had meant to do it. But Eve had not called on him again, and when next he came home, he learned about Captain Tripp being at the Manor.

I'm truly ashamed of myself he had thought. Relieved at being free of her temptation, yet jealous that she beds another. There had been no doubt in his mind that she was bedding Tripp; nor, he could tell, in the mind of Squire Pearson, when he had told him of it.

He had spent a rather unsettled few months with these mixed emotions. Now all that was over. Dear Bessie was pregnant. There could be no question of leaving her now. He was happy.

He went out to the forge. 'Here come the man whass done it,' cried Joseph, slapping him across the shoulders.

'That call for a drink,' said Samuel, going to his barrels of forge brew and drawing three tankards. 'Now what shall we drink to; the baby ain't due for another six month?'

'We'll jus' hev to drink to his ole knob,' chuckled Joseph pointing his thumb at Jeremy.

'Now, thass enough of that there army talk,' chided Samuel. 'This is a God-fearin' forge.'

They all laughed. Everyone was happy.

In the morning Jeremy called on Squire Pearson. 'Indeed I'm pleased for you and Bessie,' he said, shaking him by the hand.

There was a certain sadness in his eyes as he spoke. Jeremy realised that the sad shocks of recent years; Colonel John; his wife; Eve's behaviour, and the overwork were taking their toll on him. He was starting to look older than his fifty-eight years.

'I promised you a good cottage. It stands alone on the corner of Bear Pit Road and Sandy Lane. There's work needs doing on it, but I'll attend to having that done. It's bigger than the average cottage and of higher quality. Fit for a farm manager. Would you care to learn to be my farm manager if and when you can get out of the army?'

'I know the house sir. Your farm manager! You favour me so much again.'

'It's because I think you're worth it lad,' said the Squire, patting him on the shoulder. 'And the respect I have for your hard-working parents and their sacrifice in having you educated. I think you worthy to train to do the job dear John would have done had he not been killed.'

Jeremy could see the tears in his eyes as he spoke. A lump came to his own throat. Shame was in his heart. He had deceived this fine gentleman with his daughter; as he had deceived his own wife and her family; and his own parents. Thank God it was now over.

***

'There's no chance of getting out of the army at this time,' said Colonel Lehan, when Jeremy approached him. 'Trouble is expected from Scotland during next year. They don't recognise England's republic. Ever since they proclaimed the Prince of Wales their King Charles the second, their commissioners have been visiting him in Holland negotiating terms. It's believed he might grant their every Presbyterian whim to secure their help in regaining the throne of England.

'As a matter of fact, I'm informed that this regiment is getting some more men in January. You're to be promoted to Captain in charge of a new squadron.

'When you take over your new men, ride them hard. They come ready trained, but train them more. Let's get this trouble settled once and for all. Then perhaps it'll be right to talk of leaving the army. Hopefully General Cromwell will have put down the Irish in time to be with us.'

Jeremy was disappointed at not getting out, but honoured at his promotion. He hoped trouble would not start until he had seen his new baby in May.

During the next few months Jeremy was able to get home several times for short stays. Also when out training with his new squadron, for one of the longer rides he would take in Brentham.

'Lor' lumme alive!' exclaimed Mrs Bloom the first time he did that. 'My Bessie married to an officer whass in charge of all them men. Thass somethin' what yer might call a marvel.'

Jeremy watched Bessie swelling more as the months went by and when he came home on twenty-fifth of May he found that he had already been the father of a fine baby girl for two days. Reverend Jones was persuaded to hold the christening ceremony the next day. They named the child Jemima Elizabeth, which was the nearest Bessie could think of to their own names. Nathaniel Pearson stood in as Godfather and Samuel's sister-in-law as Godmother. There was merriment among family and friends, to the disapproval of the more bigoted in the community. The baby's head was metaphorically wetted so many times that, had so much ale and wine actually been poured over the infant's head, she would surely have drowned.

And that was the last time Jeremy came home while he was at Newmarket. He did manage to stop in Brentham for less than two hours the following week while on exercises with his squadron.

'Do take care of yerself Jeremy,' said Bessie with a tear in her eye when he told her that civil war appeared to be imminent once more. 'Jemima an' me need yer.'

'You'll win now "Ole Noll" is gooner be with yer,' declared Joseph Bloom, when Jeremy informed him that Cromwell had returned from Ireland.

✳✳✳

It was about this time that Eve had to bid farewell to Captain Henry Tripp. Although he had only been billeted at the Manor House for six weeks from the time he arrived there the previous July, she had become very fond of him. When she had made a farm of his choice over to him, he had straightaway secretly returned most of her valuables as he promised. In spite of diligent searches, she had never discovered their hiding place, though after he had gone she noticed a lot of scratches on a tree trunk and believed she understood.

He had kept her free from malignancy charges and sequestration at a risk to his own neck. When he returned the sum of sixty pounds to her, saying he had over-estimated the amount of silver plate he needed to sell to get the two-hundred pounds they had agreed, she gave it back to him.

Although he had to move on while he worked more distant parts of the county for the sequestrators, he continued to come and see her often. Their affair developed passionately. When the time for parting came at the end of

May 1650, Eve did not know whether it was Henry or Jeremy she loved the most. But in Jeremy's case she was resolved to be revenged on Bessie for stealing him. Even if she failed to get him back, she was determined that he would be unfaithful with her again and Bessie know about it and suffer torment.

As far as she was concerned, both Jeremy and Henry were good lovers, but Henry Tripp was more unruly, forceful and experienced than the considerate Jeremy. She smiled in anticipation of Jeremy's reaction to some of the tricks of love she had learned from Henry Tripp. That would most certainly give him something to repent and pray about.

Now both the men she loved were off to battle. 'To finish the bloody Royalists once and for all, be they English or Scots,' declared Tripp, who did not hesitate to use profane language in private, though he was obliged to flog his men for doing so if he heard them.

★

In the third week of June Colonel Lehan had special news for his squadron commanders. 'We are to put ourselves in readiness to march when the order comes. It's been decided that we are to invade Scotland without waiting for their attack. Lord General Fairfax declined the command and resigned. General Cromwell has been promoted to command all the forces of England and will be leading us.'

When this information was given out to the men on parade, they let out a mighty cheer. Jeremy was proud and in high spirits, for now he was a captain of Ironsides directly under Cromwell.

Early in July the order came for them to march. Their destination Berwick-on-Tweed, where in the third week of July they joined all the other troops making up Cromwell's invasion force.

At Berwick Jeremy was approached by an officer of his own rank from another regiment. He had noticed the man looking at him. Slightly shorter, but more muscular than himself, his face was vaguely familiar, though Jeremy could not quite place him. 'Would you perchance be Captain Jeremy Goodway from Brentham in Suffolk?'

'Yes. To whom do I have the pleasure?' but Jeremy was already guessing the answer as he spoke.

'My name is Captain Henry Tripp. I was on duty in Brentham six years ago as a young cornet when you were in trouble.'

'I thought I'd seen your face before, but couldn't recall when or where,' said Jeremy.

'I was in Brentham more recently.' A smirk played round Tripp's mouth as he spoke.

Jeremy could sense hostility. 'So I've heard.' he said, coldly.

Tripp was about to say something else when a couple of Jeremy's troop commanders came to him.

'I shall see you again one day,' said Tripp taking his leave.

On 22nd July, the army crossed into Scotland. They advanced to the little port of Dunbar where a base was established so that they could be supplied by sea. From there they marched towards Edinburgh, making their forward camp at Mussleburgh. They were faced by strong entrenchments and earthworks over a broad front. It was not going to be easy to take Edinburgh.

The weather turned bad with heavy rain every day. One attack was attempted without success. The ground was sodden, supplies short and men were falling sick. At the end of August they fell back on Dunbar, the enemy harrying their rearguard as they went.

By the 2nd September, the enemy had occupied ground to their south cutting off their only escape route. The Roundheads were outnumbered two to one. To some of the dispirited soldiers it seemed likely that the great Oliver Cromwell might suffer his first serious defeat, unless they could be evacuated by sea.

But the Scots on their southern hillside, were too confident that it would be they who attacked next day. Oblivious that their position was not good for defence, and as if time was on their side, their infantry extinguished matches for the night.

But Cromwell's army worked all night and attacked at four o'clock in the morning. The Scots had a burn to their front falling down from a deepening and closed valley to their left.

Jeremy heard the start of the attack by part of the army on the unprepared Scottish centre. Then his regiment, with the bulk of the Ironsides, received their order to ride. Cromwell led them in a wide arc until they crossed the burn at its lower end near the coast. Then turning right, they headed up the mouth of the valley, falling on the enemy flank. The Ironsides stabbed and slashed. As the Scots fell back before them, the valley became narrower, the burn deeper. The enemy were retreating into a trap.

The battle was over by six o'clock when ten-thousand Scots surrendered as prisoners. Three thousand of them lay dead. No more than fifty of Cromwell's army had been killed.

It was in the confusion of the later stages of the battle, that Jeremy was struck by a shot. It did no harm except to shake and alarm him as it ricocheted off his shoulder, narrowly missing his neck. It seemed as if the shot came from his right across the burn, But there were no enemy over there–he must be mistaken. He offered a silent prayer of thanks, and put it from his mind.

In the confusion, some of the enemy had escaped up the narrow ravine or across the hills. Before Cromwell would allow pursuit, he had the army stand and give thanks for their victory by singing psalm one-hundred-and-seventeen.

O praise the Lord, all ye nations;
praise him all ye people.

193

For his merciful kindness is great toward us;
     and the truth of the Lord endureth for ever.
Praise ye the Lord.

It was during the chase for those that ran away that Jeremy was shot at once again. At first he thought it was the group of Scots they had cornered. But they turned out to be unarmed, having thrown away their weapons as they ran from the battlefield. Jeremy became unreasonably suspicious of his own men.

Edinburgh fell soon after the victory at Dunbar, although the castle did not surrender until 24th December. Meanwhile there had been a miserable autumn of skirmishing in appalling weather, for the Scots were not beaten, although they were far from united.

By no means all the Scots were hostile to the English invaders. Indeed, there were several weddings between Scottish girls and Cromwell's soldiers, including one in Jeremy's squadron.

But Cromwell was not able to win the Scottish nation over, for they mainly supported their Kirk; and the Kirk was determined in its Presbyterianism. Though they loathed the Church of Rome and the Anglican Church, they would have no dealings with Independents either. The English Parliament had accepted their help in the great civil war and promised to enforce Presbyterianism, a promise they had been unable to keep. Now the soldiers of Cromwell, the arch-Independent in religion, were preaching in their kirks and streets as if they were ministers.

Early in January Colonel Lehan had some news for his assembled officers. 'Charles Stuart, who the Scottish Estates back in early forty-nine proclaimed King Charles the Second, has humbled himself before the Kirk. He's admitted his late father's mistakes and apologised, discarded his support for the Anglican Church and taken the Oath of their Covenant. His cavalier followers have done the same.

'They crowned him at Scone on the first of January. With this stroke he's united most of Scotland against us. It's the opinion of General Cromwell that he'll raise a new army here to invade our republic. We must beat him on his own ground.'

The Scottish campaign ebbed and flowed indecisively over the next few months hampered somewhat early on by the illness of the Roundheads' great commander. It was after a victory at Inverkeithing in July, in which another two-thousand Scots were killed, that the mystery of who had been taking occasional shots at Jeremy became known to him in desperate circumstances.

His squadron had gone out searching for Scots who had fled the field. Other units were engaged in the same work. Jeremy momentarily left his men to look over the rim of a wooded dell not much more than a large pit. He started his horse down the slope.

'Captain Jeremy Goodway!' The call came from his right.

Jeremy turned to see Captain Tripp half concealed by a tree, pointing a pistol at him.

Jeremy made to move.

'Don't move Jeremy, or I'll kill you straight away. I've taken several shots at you and missed. I don't know why, because I'm a good shot. It must be because I hadn't given you time to pray. God, if there is one, won't let you die before you've prayed. Pray now Jeremy. I know you like to pray. Eve tells me you prayed each time after you'd fucked her.'

'Don't use profane language. General Cromwell would have you reduced to the ranks and flogged if he heard you.'

'I don't give a damn about Cromwell's bloody piety. I've had enough. Lost everything in this war. Nine years now, off and on. Nine long bloody years. How long have you been in the army Jeremy?'

'Since August of forty-five.'

'Where did you first see action?'

'At Torrington.'

'Ha! Torrington. I was at Torrington. Quite a little fight, that. February of forty-six. But the big one was nearly over then. Know when my first taste of action was? Powick Bridge, September of forty-two, when the Royalists ambushed and cut our patrol up; a month before the war started properly. Lost count of how many battles since. Know what happened to my family in forty-three while I was away fighting?'

'No. But you can tell me.' Jeremy tried to keep the conversation going in the hope that Tripp's moment of madness would pass.

'My wife was raped by marauding cavaliers, then killed along with my little one. My home burned. My parents injured and broken so they died later. Lost the farm; everything. The enemy hasn't set foot in Suffolk, has he Jeremy?'

'No. We've been fortunate in that respect. Where do you come from?' Jeremy was hoping that Tripp would lower his pistol.

'Leicestershire. Know this Jeremy Goodway, I intend to have Eve, Marchioness of bloody Stourland. She's my future.'

'I understood you were already doing very well with her.'

'Oh, I've been inside her times enough, but she loves you still. She told me so. You're in my way Jeremy. In the way of my future.'

'She means nothing to me now, Captain Tripp. Believe me, I'm glad she's found you. I'm happy in my marriage.'

'So you say, but she'll get to you again and you'll fuck her once more and pray about it. Pray now Jeremy; pray before you sin again; pray while you've got the . . . .'

Jeremy's heart jumped as the shot rang out. He thought Tripp had fired, but he saw his pistol drop to the ground. Tripp seemed to sit silent in his saddle for a moment, then fell.

Jeremy looked up and saw a young trooper, one of his own men, smoking pistol in hand on the rim of the dell. He started down.

'He was going to kill you, sir,' said the lad. 'Is he dead?'

Jeremy dismounted and went to look at Tripp. 'Yes.'

'Will you report me now sir, for killing an officer? Will I hang? He was using devil's words.'

Jeremy looked at the lad. Probably not yet nineteen. He still had freckles. 'No, lad. Go back to your comrades and pray silently, but say nothing. You did right.'

He slapped Tripp's horse across its haunches. The beast made off. 'Someone will find him and believe he died a brave man against the enemy.'

'Who was he, sir?' asked the lad.

'Just a man brutalised by the war and all the cruelty, and driven out of his wits. Please God that it may soon be over for good.'

* * *

A few weeks later, during the first week of August 1651, as Cromwell had predicted, the Scots invaded England again. This time they were led by Charles who they had crowned Charles the Second.

'He starts with only twenty-thousand,' Colonel Lehan told his officers. 'Not a great number for such an enterprise, but our spies tell us that he has confidence that English Royalists will rise and flock to his banner in large numbers. This I doubt, for England has had enough of war, and General Cromwell's reputation is so great that even those of Royalist persuasion will doubt they could win against him.

'Meanwhile, we number not more than twelve-thousand, having had to leave some behind to finish the Scottish campaign. However, our armies are mustering in England; both regular and malitia. The plan is to let the enemy invade England and not bring them to battle until they are exhausted and far from home.

'They are advancing down the western side. Our army is to follow, but down the eastern route. If he changes his mind and starts to retreat, we are to move over and bar his way.'

The army under Cromwell pushed on in boiling heat, and by 19th August had reached Ferrybridge in Yorkshire, where they were rapturously welcomed by ordinary people. As they had advanced, spies reported that on the other hand Charles was not being at all well received by the English people. Very few English Royalists were joining him. As a result a few of his less enthusiastic commanders had started to leave him piecemeal to go home. There were also individual desertions.

'We hear that he's changed his mind,' said Colonel Lehan when they were at Ferrybridge. 'Due to the desertions in his own ranks and the growing strength of our armies to his left, he has abandoned the idea of fighting us somewhere near Coventry then marching on London. Now he's keeping well to the west. Presumably he feels that the south-west and Wales where his father's staunchest supporters were would be his most likely recruiting ground.

'From here we are to change course to the south-west and rendezvous with our other armies at Warwick. It is thought he may stop somewhere near Worcester. All our armies will concentrate in an arc east of that city to block his way to London.'

Another five days were to pass before they reached Warwick. They were days of brilliant sunshine. It had been that way since they left Scotland. The men were well disciplined and in good spirits. There had been little for Jeremy to do on the long ride apart from the daily assembly with Colonel Lehan, and occasional conversation with fellow officers. The harrying of the enemy was left to the other armies to their right. He had much time to his own thoughts.

As news of the wastage of the enemy through desertions and skirmishing reached them, it became fairly obvious that their were riding to the final battle. Jeremy's mind as he rode, often turned to Brentham and Bessie; and for that matter to Eve also. Though eager to get back to his wife and child, if he thought of Eve his loins would stir; just as they had stirred on that other hot summer day seven years before, when he rode home to Brentham on a juddering stage wagon.

His thoughts turned to Henry Tripp. It was a pity he had died. Though to his shame he had felt jealous of him with Eve at one time, the man had been some sort of shield. No one had remarked at Tripp's death. Presumably he had been recorded killed in action.

Jeremy made his mind up that if he survived the coming ordeal, he would petition for discharge. No one in Brentham was likely to ask him about Tripp, unless he ran into Eve. Then he would deny knowing of his whereabouts. After all, they had been in different regiments. There was no reason why they should have met among all those thousands of men.

When they reached Warwick on 24th, information was received that Charles was indeed in and around Worcester where he had arrived two days earlier, with not much more than fifteen-thousand of his original invasion force left. It was reported that he was scouring the area for recruits without any great success. At that time Cromwell had over thirty-thousand to engage him with.

From there they moved to Evesham and thence to the area of Worcester. Plans for the battle and capture of fugitives were carefully laid, especially the capture of one in particular. On the evening of 2nd September Colonel Lehan addressed his assembled regiment.

'I am to caution you against over confidence. The enemy's position may seem hopeless, for we out number him about two to one. We fight tomorrow; one year to the day since Dunbar, where they outnumbered us by two to one. Our position seemed hopeless with our backs to the sea. Yet we trounced them thoroughly.

'Weary they might be, and dispirited by lack of support. Yet they will fight desperately, for they have nowhere to go. They cannot return to Scotland. And their leader, who they have crowned Charles the Second, knows well what capture will mean.

And the enemy did fight desperately. It was the hardest battle Jeremy had been in and lasted five hours. But the end was inevitable. Outnumbered as they were the invaders stood no chance against Cromwell's superbly trained and disciplined army. After the carnage, nearly three thousand Royalists, mainly Scots, lay dead. Ten thousand were prisoners. But unlike Dunbar, it had not been a victory of minimal casualties on the Roundhead's side. Some units were sent to capture fugitives but the most important fugitive, Charles the Second, a king without a kingdom, escaped.

After the battle, there were the usual services of thanksgiving. Jeremy heard Cromwell's chaplain address the militia soldiers before sending them on their way. *When your wives and children shall say unto you, "Where have you been and what news:" then shall you say that you have been at Worcester where England's troubles began and where they have now happily ended.'*

He recalled what Tripp had said about the first fight at Powick Bridge before he died. Powick was just down the road. England's civil wars had indeed ended where they began nine years earlier.

* * *

'I wish to petition General Cromwell for my discharge, sir,' said Jeremy to Colonel Lehan.

'I was going to recommend you for promotion to Major now that we sadly have a vacancy,' replied the colonel.

'Indeed I'm honoured, sir. None the less, the army is not for me. The war is over now.'

'I'll take you to him, but it's not a good moment, I must warn. Charles Stuart has escaped. He'll be anxious about that unless and until our patrols catch him.'

The colonel took Jeremy to Cromwell's temporary headquarters in the captured city. 'The General's on his knees at prayer,' warned the young aide outside his door.

They waited for some time before being admitted. The great man looked tired, but in a fairly happy mood. Colonel Lehan explained Jeremy's request.

'How sits this with you, colonel?, asked Cromwell. Can you spare him? Did you have many casualties?'

'We lost no squadron commanders, sir, but we've been short in the ranks since before we left Scotland and have lost several men here.'

'Then could you not repair your losses by dispersing his men among your other squadrons. A reduction of one squadron will do no harm at this stage.'

'Very, good sir,' said Colonel Lehan.

'But not until we get to London, colonel. Some of us, including your

198

regiment will be leaving for London soon. It'll keep until then. Now if you won't be offended, I would like a private word with this young officer.'

Jeremy was apprehensive, wondering what it could be Cromwell wanted to say to him in absolute privacy. Could it be that Henry Tripp's death was not regarded as death in action?

CHAPTER 22

Cromwell looked at Jeremy in silence for a full minute as if reconsidering what he wanted to say. 'You've done very well as a soldier and vindicated the late Colonel Pearson's faith in you. He was a brave man of sound judgement. You were a clerk, were you not; is that the work you wish to return to?'

'No sir. I'm to train as the farm manager to Mr Nathaniel Pearson, father of the late Colonel Pearson.'

'Splendid. An honest man loyal to our cause. A member of the county committee for Suffolk I believe?'

'Yes he is, sir.'

In return for my granting your discharge, would you be prepared to give some time to our service in your life as a citizen?'

'I'll do my best, sir.'

'And will you give me your word to keep what I say next a secret if you don't accept?'

'Yes sir.'

'Good. As you know, after the great civil war ended in our victory, we were plagued by Royalist plots and intrigues until we had a second war on our hands. Riots and little uprising broke out simultaneously all over the land because they were provoked. We were largely unprepared because we lacked pre-knowledge.

'We're determined this shan't happen again. An intelligence network is to be set up in the charge of a lawyer prominent in our cause; Mr John Thurloe in London. You would be required to pass on information you hear of plots and intrigues around the markets you visit. Only if you accept this service can I grant you early discharge.'

Jeremy gave his agreement.

'Then I'll write you a letter of introduction to him. Seek him out in London before you go home.'

***

Jeremy was deep in thought as he rode home to Brentham from London. He was anxious to see Bessie and little Jemima, for it was now almost fifteen months since he was last there.

The last ten days or so since the battle of Worcester had been momentous ones. His regiment had been among those which had accompanied Cromwell to London. The pace had been leisurely and their leader had been stopped and feted by local dignitaries in towns along the way.

In the capital, Cromwell received a hero's welcome. It had been fairly easy for Jeremy to seek out John Thurloe without drawing undue attention to himself. Appointed a secret agent in his area for the government, he was given information as to channels through which to send reports each week and at any other time he deemed urgent and necessary. Also, he would be expected to visit London every few months, or when summoned. It was obvious that John Thurloe was setting up a very sophisticated organisation to gather information on the activities of the republic's enemies both at home and abroad.

***

For Bessie, Jeremy's homecoming seemed the happiest day of her life. To her eyes he seemed the fittest and most handsome man in the world. He bent down to greet his sixteen-month-old daughter, but the child shied away and clung to Bessie's skirts.

'I fear it'll take a little while for her to become used to me,' he said.

Bessie agreed. 'It'll come,' she said, looking at him tenderly. 'Are yer really home for good, Jeremy? Is it really over this time?'

'Yes, I'm home for good, but to secure my early discharge, I had to give a undertaking that I would serve again if the need arose. Also I have to explain another commitment I've made, otherwise my movements may seem strange to you. Needless visits to strange markets and taverns.'

Jeremy explained the small part he had undertaken to play in Thurloe's intelligence network.

'Will this be dangerous for yer?' asked Bessie, anxiously.

'The danger is very slight indeed, Bess. I've only to pass information; not apprehend plotters. But it's best that as few people as possible know of my activities. Your parents, bless their hearts, are great talkers. We must keep it from them. For this reason, I want us to move into the cottage Mr Pearson has provided as soon as possible.'

'Oh, my dear, so do I!. But I think we'll have to let Jemima get used to you first, or it'll upset her.'

'Then I'll woo and win Jemima in say . . . a fortnight.'

'What about me?'

He took her in his arms and kissed her again, whispering in her ear, 'Such lack of privacy. However are we to restrain ourselves until tonight?'

'I don't know Jeremy. I jus' don't know how I'm gooner wait 'til tonight,' she murmured.

But night did come, after seemingly endless greetings with family and friends. Bessie gave herself with a passion she did not know she possessed. All the long months of waiting and worry melted away in his arms, and in the morning her instinct told her she was pregnant again.'

***

Over the next few months, Jeremy thought he must be the happiest man in the world. Two weeks after he came home, he and Bessie, with little Jemima, moved into their well-appointed cottage. Soon after, Bessie was able to tell him she was pregnant again. Mrs Carter had forecast she would give birth the following June.

His work with Squire Pearson was going well and he enjoyed it.

Gradually he was given more responsibility. He had found it necessary to confide in Nathaniel about being a part-time agent for John Thurloe, and was astonished that the Squire did not seem at all surprised. In fact, after a short time he helped matters along by entrusting the bulk of the market work to Jeremy.

There were just two worries—like two small black clouds in a blue sky. Distant but still there. One was Eve. So far he had managed to keep out of her way except on one occasion. Then the Squire was with him. He was sure he could resist her now, but did not want to be asked if he knew what had become of Captain Tripp. She must soon start to wonder why he had not contacted her. The other was a vague feeling of insecurity. Although Squire Pearson was only fifty-nine, the years were weighing heavily on him. It occurred to Jeremy that his employer would probably not live to a very great age. Presumably Eve would inherit, since as far as he knew there were no other relatives. Unless Eve were satisfactorily wedded by that time, the situation would be impossible. He had heard there had been another lover while he was away, but had seen nothing of such a person, so it may have been just a rumour. Tripp would not be coming back. Eve could still be a danger to his security and happiness. Eventually he might have to look for a career outside Brentham.

For the time being, however, life had an halcyon quality, as each day he did a good day's work, and heard his child's laughter, and watched his Bessie's belly swell. It was in the last month of her pregnancy that this fragile framework of happiness shattered.

It was part of Jeremy's duties to write up a report and take it to the Squire each day provided both of them were there. They would talk over progress and market prices. Nathaniel would listen to Jeremy's opinions, and with his own greater experience, decide whether on not to act on them.

Towards the end of May the Squire fell ill. Doctor Mills attended him, and pronounced it a fever caused by the heat; a cover-all diagnosis based on lack of knowledge. But after the first few days there were pains which the doctor could not explain. He could only give potions which made his patient want to sleep.

Jeremy had still called with his report most days after the Squire fell ill and discussed business with him at his bedside. One afternoon early in June he was about to enter Nathaniel's bedroom, when he met Doctor Mills coming out.

'I fear he's too ill today to be worried with business matters,' said the doctor. 'He's asleep now. I'm going to find two women from the village, so that someone can sit with him day and night. Will you tell that to his daughter, the Marchioness, if you see her.'

The doctor started to descend the staircase. Jeremy followed. 'I'm unlikely to see the Marchioness,' he said.

'She comes for a short while each day since he's been ill,' the doctor began.

Jeremy was surprised to hear that. Although he had been keeping an eye open for her coach, so that he could avoid her.

'In fact, she was here not many minutes ago. She bade me farewell and left in rather a hurry, which seemed strange.'

After the doctor left, Jeremy decided to leave the papers in the Squire's study until he was somewhat better. He went to the large room that his employer used for this purpose, and striding over to the big oak table in the centre, laid them on it. He heard the door slam shut behind him and turned sharply.

'Hello Jeremy at last. You've been avoiding me.'

'Whatever are you doing here, your Ladyship?'

'Am I not allowed to visit my sick father?'

'Pardon me, your Ladyship. I was merely surprised his daughter should feel she needed to hide behind his study door.'

'I saw you coming to the house from the landing window, papers in hand. For sure I knew Doctor Mills wouldn't want you to bother him this afternoon; and where else were you likely to leave papers? And for pity's sake stop this "Your Ladyship" nonsense, after all we've been to one another in the past. Eve I am, and Eve I'll ever be to you.'

She had spoken the last sentence in a seductive tone, and his phallus, which had stirred when he first saw her, was already partly erect.

'Doctor Mills asked me to tell you he's sending women to sit round the clock with your father,' said Jeremy, trying to stop their conversation developing along intimate lines. But even as he spoke, he could not fail to notice the smile at the corners of her mouth as her eyes dwelt on the growing bulge in his breeches. And he, noticing in particular those full and moist lips, slightly parted, became more erect.

'That's good. Very good,' she said softly and seductively. It was in answer to what he had said about the doctor, but sounded to Jeremy as if she was admiring him.

'I must get back to my work now,' he said, trying to sound casual. She was standing with her back to the door. He hoped she would move to let him pass, but she stood her ground.

'Are you running from me so soon, after all we've been to one another?

'What we did in the past was wrong and sinful. It would be even more sinful now. I've nearly two children. In any case you have a lover.'

She thought he referred to Henry Tripp. 'Oh Tripp you mean. It's true we made love, but ours was a business arrangement. Without his help I might have been declared malignant, and suffered sequestration. He wanted to marry me, but I told him it was you I loved.'

So it's true what Tripp said before he died, thought Jeremy. 'You should have married him,' he said. 'The two of us can't be together now.'

She was still barring his way. He didn't want to talk about Tripp. Moving towards her, he gently put an arm on her shoulder to move her aside. Just this small physical contact stirred his loins further. She didn't move aside, but brazenly lowered her hand to the crotch of his breeches. He was hard as iron. She put her other hand to his cheek and raised her head offering her parted lips.

Her fragrance overwhelmed him and all his resolution melted away as their mouths met, and tongues and arms entwined in an abandoned embrace. She broke away and started to unbutton her bodice. But he was feeling fierce towards her now. She had led him on again, and he was in no mood to give quarter. He started to try and rip her clothing.

'Have a care my love,' she said, urgently. 'Don't tear me. I've no change of clothing here! Be patient. It will be all the sweeter for delay.'

They helped one another undress until they stood naked together, then fell into each other's arms again. He picked her up and carried her over to a rug by the hearth; the only part of the floor which was covered. He made to lay her down, but she knelt upright.

'Why do you kneel?' he asked.

'To humble myself before my lord and master.' She touched his leg to bid him come nearer.

Her head bowed and he felt her kiss each of his knees. He ran his fingers through her hair as she traced her tongue up his thighs. When she took him in her mouth, he thought he would explode. It was a new experience for him. But he was getting too excited and started to thrust. She pushed him gently away. 'It will end too soon,' she croaked.

He made to lay her down, but she resisted. 'No; you lay down.'

Jeremy lay on his back. He thought she wanted to take the masterly part, like that first time in his father's hay loft. But she had other tricks to show him that she had learned from Henry Tripp.

She turned the opposite way to him and straddled his face. He felt her take him into her mouth again. Her vulva was only inches from his face and her pungent odour filled his nostrils. She tapped his side; he knew what she expected of him and did it. At first it was distasteful, but he began to enjoy it, until he felt her shudder in her first climax. He felt he could go on for ever.

Eve turned around and impaling herself on his phallus, rode him fiercely until she climaxed again. He prised her off and pressing her over on to her knees took her like an animal. He was feeling fierce and did not want to finish. He withdrew briefly, then threw her roughly on to her back. Time and again he made her change position, until finally he exploded in the greatest climax he had experienced.

They lay together in silence for a few minutes, then Jeremy got up and started to dress. 'Do you still think we should stay apart?' she asked. 'Will you not tell Bessie that you love me best and must have me?'

But the fire had gone out of him, and he did not answer. She started to dress herself. 'What will you do then Jeremy; pray forgiveness again; just until next time?' There was a hint of mockery in her voice.

'No. I'll not insult God by asking His forgiveness yet again. I know my weakness in your presence, and it is only with you. For fifteen months I was not in contact with any woman, without too much discomfiture. It may be that you'll drag me down to Hell with you, but I'll not mock God. And I'll not tell Bessie, for that would break her heart and be an even greater sin. Maybe I do love you in a perverse sort of way, but my love for Bessie is the greater, for it embraces every aspect of my existence. Between you and I there is nothing but lust. When near, you have some dreadful power over me which I can't resist. If I can but keep out of your way I shall live a virtuous life.'

Eve started to grow angry. 'Then what will you do? My father ails. When he dies I shall inherit. Then you'll be my manager, and we shall be in contact every day.'

'No. When your good father gets better, or if he dies now, and my next child is a few months old, I'll seek employment away from Brentham. Start a new life with Bessie and my children. If all else fails, I'll return to the army.'

Eve pretended to accept defeat. She changed the subject. 'Do you by chance know what's become of Captain Tripp? I know he went to Scotland with you.'

Jeremy's heart sank. At first he was minded to deny all contact, then remembered several had seen them talking in Berwick.

'Went to Scotland with me!' he exclaimed. 'So did thousands of others. We met by chance at Berwick-on-Tweed where the army assembled before crossing into Scotland. I saw nothing of him after that. We weren't in the same regiment. There was no reason for us to keep in touch.'

Jeremy knew he was safe in saying that, because the young trooper who saved his life was later killed at Worcester. He reflected that he had now added lying to his several sins. 'Anyway, I thought you said you cared nothing for him?'

'I don't. Ours was a business arrangement. It's just that the last communication I had from him was dated July last year. I'm looking after something of his and begin to wonder what I must do.'

'Communication is difficult when on service. In any case, some units were left up there to deal with Stirling. Perhaps he's still there.'

'My father told me that was over.'

Jeremy shrugged his shoulders. 'I'm afraid I can't help you any more about it.' He did not want to discuss Tripp.

With that he left, to spend the rest of the afternoon in misery as he worked, reflecting on the impasse he was once more in.

***

But Eve had no intention that Bessie should be left in ignorance of what had occurred. She had vowed to avenge herself on her for marrying him. Now she would do it.

She ordered a housemaid to keep watch on her father until one of the women from the village should arrive from the doctor. Then she set out for Bessie's cottage.

✳✳✳

Bessie heard a knock at her door and waddled to answer it. She was very heavy now, for there were only three weeks or so of her pregnancy left.

Her heart lurched as she opened the door. Eve, Jeremy's mistress from before they were married and with whom he had been unfaithful in the first year after, was the last person she wanted to see. None the less, out of deference to her rank, she stood aside to let her enter, and tried her best to curtsy. After all, her father did own the house.

Eve sat down without invitation. 'No need to look so surprised, Bessie, or be obsequious. I wasn't born to the Stourland title; only married it. I don't mind using my own feet when the weather is fine; and I don't need a lackey to announce me.'

Bessie remained silent for want of something to say.

'I've come to talk to you as woman to woman, because we both love the same man.'

Bessie caught her breath in an audible gasp.

'But that same man doesn't love us both equally. He told me so.'

'Thass my Jeremy you're talkin' about.' Bessie had a quiver in her voice. 'Oh I know yer was his mistress afore we married, an' I know he was unfaithful to me with yer the first year on his way back from Colchester. Rememberin' it is bitter to me. But I hev forgive him. Now thass all in the past, an' we're happy, an' hev this dear mite an' another nearly.' She put her arm round the head of little Jemima who was clinging to her skirt.

'But this afternoon, Jeremy and I made love, passionately. And not for the first time since he's been back. He said he loved me more than you but stays with you because of the children,' said Eve, mixing truth and untruth together.

Bessie started to cry as Eve related details of the afternoon's events.

'What future do you have with an unfaithful husband, Bessie? My father ails. If he doesn't die this illness, it will still not be long. Then I'll inherit and Jeremy will be my manager. What peace of mind will you have when we're in contact day after day?

'Be sensible and give him up now. I can make you rich by your standards, Bessie. No need to worry about money for the rest of your life. Many a likely country lad would jump at the chance of having you, especially if I gave you a good farm as well. Stourland means nothing to me. I'm minded to sell it off. Far rather I took my father's place with a husband I loved.'

But Bessie was sobbing her heart out and could only whisper, 'Go. Please go.'

After Eve left she knelt down by a chair. She had not knelt down to do her praying for the last few weeks because of her condition. But this was a special prayer, so she struggled to kneel, not knowing how she was to get up

206

again.

Still sobbing, it was a few minutes before she could say her special prayer, 'Please God strike her dead. For the sake of the peace of me an' Jeremy, strike her dead. For the sake of my little ones, please strike that wicked woman dead. An' hev mercy on me for askin' such.'

She was still on her knees sobbing quietly twenty minutes later when her brother Joseph walked in. Little Jemima was also crying with her mother. He had stopped by on his way to his own home to see how she was.

'Whass the matter, Bess? You shouldn't kneel down no more afore yer hev yer baby.' He helped her up and into a chair.

'I was prayin',' she wept. 'I ask God to strike her dead, an' thass dreadful.'

'Who?'

'The Marchioness.'

'Oh, her. Whass she done now?'

Between sobs, Bessie related most of what had passed between her and Eve.

Joseph's face became flushed with anger. 'No need to ask God to strike her. I'll do for the whore, that I will, though I hang on the gallows for it arter.'

Just then Jeremy came in. Bessie bust out crying again.

'What's the matter?'

'Well might you ask whass the matter,' shouted Joseph. 'That whore of yours has been round upsettin' Bessie. Boastin' that yer fucked her this arternoon an' how yer loved her more than your own wife. Is that true?'

'I was tempted, I admit, but Bessie and I . . . ' Jeremy started to say.

'You bloody rat. Bessie an' you nothin'. I'll do for the pair of yer, though I swing for it an' go to hell for foul language.'

With that Joseph advanced on Jeremy and struck him in the chest. Jeremy tried to push him away only to receive a fist in his face. He reeled back putting his hands up to deflect the blows.

Bessie was screaming for them to stop. As Jeremy retreated, the fight continued in the back yard. Jeremy was trying to persuade his brother-in-law to desist, but as blow after blow landed he was obliged to try and defend himself. But guilt made his own fists light, and he was getting the worst end. Soon Joseph landed a mighty blow to his jaw and he fell to the ground unconscious.

Bessie was still screaming and Jemima crying as Joseph brushed past them panting and saying, 'Now for the bloody whore.'

Bessie fetched a bowl of water and bathed Jeremy's face over and over. It was a full ten minutes before she could bring him round and he was still bleeding from cuts. He started to get up but fell back again.

'Oh, Bess what can I say? I'm so . . .'

'Don't worry about that now,' she cried. 'Oh, what are we gooner do? His gone to the Manor. Reckon his gooner kill her. He'll hang.'

'Don't panic they won't let him in.'

207

'But he got an ole army musket an' pistol in his house! Oh fetch Dad an' go arter him.'

'No. Don't involve Sam. Just give me a minute.'

'But he jus' give yer one hidin'. Yer won't be able to stop him.'

'He thrashed me because I was feeling guilty. I can stop him if I must, don't fear. Just give me a minute to recover.'

Jeremy waited about five more minutes to get his breath back, washed his face once more, then stood up to leave.

Bessie was sobbing. 'He'll kill you too. Don't go alone. Don't go alone.'

CHAPTER 23

Jeremy set out after Joseph on his horse. Although his inclination was to urge the beast into a gallop, he decided to let it walk, in order not to draw too much attention to himself. He doubted if Joseph would take a musket if he intended to force entry into the Manor House, because the weapon would be too cumbersome. The pistol would either be wheel-lock or snap-chance which could be used in a confined space, but he could only use it once, without lengthy reloading. Therefore he was unlikely to boldly seek admission through the front door, because Eve would not answer it herself.

From this reasoning, Jeremy deduced that Joseph either intended to conceal himself until Eve should appear; or break into the house. If the latter, he would have to wait until well after dark, so there would be plenty of time. He must already be in, or seeking a place of concealment near the house. It would not be the stables, for there he would be in danger of discovery by a groom.

Jeremy was only familiar with the front and left side entrance to the house. The latter opened on to a yard across which stood the stables and coach-house. He cast his mind back four years and thought hard. There had been a large clump of bushes backed by the first of the smaller park land trees right opposite to the entrance of the stable yard, not more than about thirty yards away. A slightly further distance away to the right, but not more than forty yards, was the front door.

It was an ideal place to lay in wait, since if Eve decided to go riding she would exit through the left side door, but if she intended to walk or go in her coach she would come out the front. This was the most likely spot, but Joseph was not familiar with the grounds and would have taken a little while to select it. Jeremy was confident he would find him in time.

He ventured as far as the main gate. No one was in sight, so he entered and turned immediately left into the park land until he came to a secluded spot. Here he dismounted and tethered his horse. From there he made his way on foot in the direction of the house, keeping hidden and taking care to keep as silent as possible, moving from tree to tree as he drew closer.

Then Jeremy saw Joseph, and knew he was well in time, for he was just securing the musket rest to the ground and sighting the unloaded weapon on the front door of the Manor House. Apparently satisfied, he pulled out his pistol and was about to start the process of loading that when Jeremy stepped forward and put a hand on his shoulder. 'Joseph . . .'

Joseph turned sharply in alarm. 'What the . . . ?'

'Stop this madness, man. I'd not be able to save you from hanging a second time.'

'I don't care.' He pushed Jeremy roughly. 'Get away, unless yer want another thrashin'.'

Jeremy knew what he must do. He wrenched the pistol from Joseph's hand and threw it away.

Joseph bellowed with rage and head-butted Jeremy so hard that it winded him and he fell to the ground. While he lay there in pain, Joseph seized his musket and using it as a club, tried to strike him. But it was heavy and slow to use. Jeremy rolled out of the way as the blow struck the ground. Joseph raised the musket and tried again, but by now Jeremy's pain had gone. He stuck out his leg and tripped him as he came forward with the raised musket. Joseph crashed to the ground.

Both men got up simultaneously. Joseph bent to pick up the musket but as he did so, Jeremy kicked him on his hip with the flat of his boot. Joseph fell again and rolled away. Now Jeremy was between him and the musket. Joseph got to his knees and made a dive for Jeremy's legs. But Jeremy anticipated him and stepped out of the way, raising a foot a little; but that missed Joseph's chin and scraped along the side of his face, making a cut.

Joseph sprang to his feet and aimed a blow at Jeremy. But his aim was bad and the blow just glanced off Jeremy's left shoulder. Jeremy landed his right fist in Joseph's face. Joseph staggered back away from him, bleeding from both the nose and the cut in his cheek.

Jeremy stepped towards his opponent but stopped suddenly. Joseph had drawn a dagger from his clothing and was pointing it at him. Jeremy retreated a few paces. Joseph advanced with a murderous look in his eyes. He made a swipe with the dagger which Jeremy dodged. Jeremy retreated further. Joseph swiped again. Once more Jeremy dodged the blow and retreated further. Now he had reached the spot where the discarded pistol lay. Jeremy picked it up by the barrel and just as Joseph made a third swipe, struck his elbow with the butt. Joseph let out a cry, and the dagger fell from his grasp.

In pain, Joseph grasped his right elbow with his left hand, and while he was off guard Jeremy struck him a hard blow with his fist to the jaw. No pulling punches this time. Joseph crumpled to his knees. Jeremy struck him hard again and he collapsed unconscious to the ground.

Jeremy picked up the dagger and pistol and put them inside his own clothing. Then collecting the musket and rest, he took them a fair distance to hide them in the undergrowth, making a mental note where he had left them.

Joseph still lay unconscious when he returned. Jeremy was relieved that no one had come to investigate the commotion, for they had been making a noise as they fought. He got one of Joseph's arms round his shoulder and half carried, half dragged him back towards where he had tethered his horse. Just as they got there, Joseph started to come round, so Jeremy hit him back into unconsciousness once more.

Jeremy laid Joseph across the saddle and led the horse out of the Manor House grounds. They looked a strange pair and he hoped they wouldn't meet the constable before they reached his house.

Bessie opened the door and cried as she saw them. Joseph had started to come round and staggered in with Jeremy's help. She brought water to bathe his cuts. 'Did you stop him,' she asked Jeremy, anxiously.

'Yes.'

'What about you?'

'Not hurt this time.'

'You bloody rat,' said Joseph. 'Stopped me killing yer whore. What hev yer done with my weapons?'

'Hidden them.'

'Give 'em back.'

'Not until you've learned sense. This is the second time I've saved you from hanging. Now go to your own house.'

Jeremy had been afraid that the shock would cause Bessie to give birth prematurely and harm the child. However, she went to her full time a bore a healthy son. They discussed their problems. Nathaniel Pearson had started to get better and Jeremy said he would tell him of his intention to seek work away from Brentham as soon as he was fully recovered.

Meantime he and Joseph had patched things up, although Jeremy had still not returned Joseph's pistol and dagger. Soon after the new baby was born, he had occasion to go to Colchester on business. Before leaving Brentham, he called to pick something up from the forge and happened to mention to Joseph and Sam where he was going.

✷✷✷

Less than an hour after Jeremy had left, Joseph saw Eve approaching the forge on horseback. His hatred of her still burned fiercely.

She stopped and dismounted. 'I fear that this horse has a loose shoe,' she said.

Joseph grunted; he had no intention of being polite to her because she was a marchioness. It was customary for people of her rank to send a groom on such an errand. As he led the beast into the traverse, he wondered what she really wanted. There proved to be little wrong. It was obviously a frivolous request. Joseph tapped the shoes all round, removed a loose nail from one shoe and replaced it. A job her own groom could have done in the stables in a few minutes without a forge.

'I saw your brother-in-law riding out of Brentham in great haste,' she said. 'Where does he go that's so urgent?'

So that's it, thought Joseph. She's after Jeremy again. He paused for a moment and was almost on the point of telling he he did not know, then changed his mind. 'London. He told me he was goin' to London.'

Eve thanked him and left in the direction of the Manor.

Samuel Bloom, who was just inside the blacksmith's shop, had heard this exchange. 'Why did yer tell her Jeremy had gone to London?' he asked. 'You must hev heard him say Colchester.'

'Jus' 'cos I hate her,' replied Joseph. 'No other reason.' He turned away and went back to his work.

Samuel shook his head and wondered. He and his wife had seen the cuts and bruises on both Joseph and Jeremy the day after they had fought. Both men had refused to explain. Neither would Bessie or Joseph's wife tell what had taken place. There was a conspiracy of silence.

'They'll tell us in their own good time,' Samuel had said to his wife. Both Joseph and Bessie were precious to them. Four other children had been born to Mrs Bloom in the ten years that separated these only survivors. Two had died being born; the others within their first year of life.

***

Eve urged her horse on faster, when she was out of view of the forge. She had seen Jeremy gallop by the Manor House gateway earlier on while she was still in her own driveway. She had attempted to follow, but he had been much too quick for her, and by the time she came to a fork in the road a mile away, she had lost him. She had started to ride back towards her father's house, then decided to save time by asking at the forge. The Bloom's usually knew most of Jeremy's movements.

She had not seen Jeremy alone in the month that had passed since they made love in her father's study and she had told Bessie of it. She wondered if the marriage would hold. The marks on both Jeremy's and Joseph's faces indicated that there had been some sort of family fracas; but on the important issue of whether Bessie and Jeremy were reconciled she had no information. With her father now rapidly getting better, if she was to make one more attempt at getting Jeremy before he carried out his threat to leave Brentham for good, she would have to act soon.

It seemed strange that Jeremy should be going to London, and she wished it could have been somewhere nearer and smaller where he would be easier to find. However a trip to London would also enable her to try to kill two birds with one stone, for she must start enquiring about Henry Tripp. The tenant of the farm she had made over to him had now died and she had felt obliged to put someone in charge and pay the labourer's wages as if it were still part of the Stourland estate. If she failed in this attempt to get either of her lovers, then clearly she had to seriously think about her future, for in a few months she would become twenty-eight.

As soon as she arrived at the Manor she called for the groom who also doubled as coachman. 'Have the coach and horses prepared to start within the hour for London,' she commanded him. He was a surly fellow of medium build, still in his twenties, single and without a family. Eve had taken him on a few months before to replace old Matt who had died. She was not entirely satisfied with his work and had had to reproach him twice for uncleanness both in his person and the coach. His employment hung by a slender thread.

'Won't get far today,' he grumbled without addressing her as "Your

212

Ladyship." 'Be gone eleven when we get started.'

Eve was in no mood to take argument from him. 'Chelmsford we'll get to tonight if time's not wasted on mid-day refreshment.' She heard him grumbling as she went to the house to get herself ready.

Jeremy, for the sake of himself and his horse would not have continued at the pace she saw him going, and Chelmsford could possibly be where he stopped over.

The afternoon of the second day was well advanced by the time Eve's coach arrived in London. Some further time was spent negotiating the narrow streets and seeking directions to the *Blue Boar* inn Holborn. She had no knowledge of London inns, but she had heard the name of this one mentioned somewhere–perhaps it was by Jeremy or her father–and it had stuck in her mind. She hoped she would find respectable lodgings there, and sent her coachman to enquire.

The coachman was in a truculent mood, not having yet forgiven his employer for yesterday. He had been made to drive for over seven hours without respite or refreshment over the appalling thirty-five miles from Brentham to Chelmsford. The road had improved slightly after Chelmsford and he had been able to cover the thirty miles from there to London in six hours, including a stop for one hour of rest and refreshment.

Eve grew impatient waiting for the coachman's return, and ventured into the inn herself. Although not yet evening there were about twenty people within the room she entered. Some were soldiers. Two girls, looking like whores, were seated at a corner table giggling with two men. She caught sight of her coachman drinking at a table with a tidy but hard-faced man. Flushing with anger she went over to him. 'How dare you refresh yourself before completing the errand I sent you on,' she said sharply. 'Get out to the coach at once.'

The coachman drained his tankard, rising slowly in dumb insolence to obey her command.

'I already told 'im as 'ow I did 'ave a fine chamber I could accommodate you in m'lady,' said the inn keeper, coming over. 'But I told 'im as 'ow I couldn't accommodate your coach, 'avin' no coach 'ouse, as it were, and but little room in the yard. Then I pointed out my friend Tom Slater 'ere, who might be able to 'elp. But I told him to bring you into my best room first to talk, which would be more fittin'.'

The hard-faced man rose. A smile played on the corners of his mouth. 'Tom Slater, at your service m'lady. I've already told your man I can house your carriage and stable your horses. He should 'ave brought you in to the other room to talk terms. It was most uncouth of 'im to seek 'is own refreshment first. 'Ow long do you intend to stay in London?'

'That's difficult to say,' replied Eve. 'There are two gentlemen I seek but have lost contact with. I think they may both be in London, and my plan is to ask in coffee houses and taverns until I locate them. One is a Captain Henry Tripp. The other is a Mr Jeremy Goodway.'

One of the soldiers at a nearby table stood up and came over. 'About Captain Tripp, your Ladyship. Do you recognise me?'

'Your face seems vaguely familiar,' said Eve, in a condescending tone.

'We were billeted at your home under Captain Tripp back in forty-nine.' The soldier indicated his two comrades still seated. 'The captain was killed fighting the enemy, I'm sorry to say. About a year ago now. Just after Inverkeithing.'

The soldier went on to relate how Henry Tripp's body had been found in a dell, shot through the neck. It was presumed by fugitives from the battle, who were still armed.

Eve thanked the man and rewarded him with a coin. So now it was only Jeremy to seek out just once more.

Tom Slater led her to the better room to discuss with him the accommodation for the carriage. They agreed terms. 'My establishment is barely fifty yards away,' he said. 'Me and my brother are starting an enterprise for the conveyance of the public by coach on request. I've a small room over stables that will do for that uncouth coachman of yours. Now I'll wait while you arrange your own accommodation with the landlord, then help your man with your baggage.'

Eve thought that was very civil, and thanked him. The landlord came in and he led her to inspect his best chamber and agree terms. When they came down, Tom Slater, true to his word assisted in the unloading and carrying of her baggage to her room.

'It's a fine coach you 'ave m'lady,' he said. 'No doubt you would like to come with me to see where it will be housed?'

Eve agreed to this, and they rode together in her coach the few yards to his premises. It consisted of a large yard surrounded by a row of stables, three open-front sheds each roomy enough to hold a coach, what appeared to be a feed store, and a house. Some of the stables had horses in.

Tom Slater explained that theirs was a livery stable. 'Hiring horses is our business. But more recently we've started to try to meet a demand that's growing for public travel. Two coaches we 'ave at the moment, both bought off noble houses that had been sequestered. Mostly at present we operate within twenty miles of London, but my brother's gone on a very long run to Exeter. The other coach is out with a hired man. We could find business for a third coach.'

Eve confirmed her satisfaction and paid Tom Slater four days in advance. With that she made her way back to the *Blue Boar* and ordered a meal to be sent to her room.

She had scarce finished eating when there was a commotion outside on the landing, heavy footsteps and a loud knock on her door. She opened it to be confronted by an officer and three troopers.

214

'You are the Marchioness of Stourland?' enquired the officer.

Eve was too shocked to speak, so just nodded.

'You will come with me, m'lady,' commanded the officer in tones which brooked no argument.

'But who are you?'

'Intelligence. There are questions. Come,' he commanded once more, ushering her out of the room without giving time to pick up any belongings. She was taken down to the street and ordered to get into a plain coach.

Eve didn't know what "Intelligence" meant. Hitherto she had regarded it as a state of cleverness, but she was too nervous to ask. They rode along in silence.

When the coach stopped she was ordered out. They were in the quadrangle of what was obviously some public building. The officer took her up a broad staircase and into a large room. He bid her wait in front of a large oak table. Two troopers guarded the door through which they had entered. The officer went to another door knocked and when opened announced her presence.

A middle-aged man in civilian dress and small beard sat down at the table. 'Pray be seated, your Ladyship.' He indicated the chair she stood by.

'Your Ladyship,' he began. 'Our nation has many enemies within and without our shores. The *Blue Boar* in Holborn is a notorious haunt of Royalist spies and plotters. Why did you choose such a place to stay?'

'Because I'm unfamiliar with London and it was the only inn I'd heard of.'

'By whom had you heard it mentioned?'

'I don't remember. Maybe my father, Mr Nathaniel Pearson, Squire in Brentham, Suffolk and member of the Suffolk County Committee. Or perhaps I heard it from a friend of mine in Brentham, Mr Goodway, Jeremy Goodway. At one time he served in the army in London.'

'Ah, yes. That was one of the names you were enquiring after. Why do you seek him in London if he's a Brentham man?'

'Because I'd heard he came here.'

'When?'

'This morning.'

'Uhm. The other name you were enquiring after. Captain Tripp. You didn't know he was dead?'

'No.'

'What did you seek him for?'

'Because I sold him a farm back in forty-nine, which he said he would come back to after the war. I agreed to supervise its running until that time. Now his tenant is dead.' Eve felt uncomfortable with that answer because to cover up the gift of the farm she had lent Tripp the money to buy it from her on the understanding that he need never repay. For his own security she had given him a note to that effect. She hoped it would not be discovered.

'You sold him a farm! Marchioness, Captain Tripp was killed in Scotland.

215

He had no relatives so his papers came back through his regiment. Among those papers was the copy of a will naming you as his beneficiary. Since it is our duty to safeguard the nation against those who would steal from it as well as its enemies, we felt it our duty to find out what a man in his position had worth leaving. To our amazement we found that he had a little fortune of nigh two-thousand pounds. Now you tell me he also bought a farm from you.

'Exhaustive enquiries at every goldsmith and would-be banker in the county of Suffolk where he worked on sequestration have revealed no case where he banked valuables in exchange for money. Had we found such a case we would have confiscated it as stolen from us. The deposits he made here in London were also made in cash, so we have no proof of theft.

'Now, Marchioness. While I listen and my clerk takes careful notes, relate in detail all that transpired throughout the time Captain Tripp and his men were billeted at your house.'

Eve's heart sank. She did her best, leaving out all that could lead to trouble. She was past worrying about losing the Stourland wealth now and she didn't care about Tripp's bequest. However, she was most anxious not to find herself in prison, or even on the gallows, for assisting Tripp to defraud the nation.

'Very well, your Ladyship,' her questioner said after she had finished. 'We shall want to speak to you again after we've checked your story. Either tomorrow or the next day.' He nodded to the officer, who motioned Eve out of the room.

In the closed coach she thought she was being taken back to the *Blue Boar*, but when told to alight, found herself in a filthy enclosed courtyard surrounded by barred windows. It was getting dark. What's this place?' she demanded.

'Newgate prison, m'lady,' said the officer. 'Only for two nights at most. Don't make problems.'

The troopers moved closer to her and she was escorted to an open doorway. The officer went ahead and she was obliged to wait in a corridor with the troopers while he shouted and argued with a gaoler in a closed room further on.

Then the officer and gaoler complete with manacles came out.

'Will 'er Ladyship be peaceful, or will she need these?' asked the gaoler.

'I'll be peaceful,' said Eve. She went with the gaoler unfettered.

He led her down steps, along dim corridors until he came to a large barred room from which issued screams, curses and laughter. 'Fraid this is best I can do ternight. Might be able to find somethin' better in the mornin'. It depends.'

Eve had a few coins tucked in her dress. She handed these to the gaoler, since they would probably be stolen in this hell-hole anyway. He unlocked the barred gate and gently touched her shoulder to go in.

The place stank with sweat, stale urine and excrement. She was nauseated. There was barely any light and the room seemed to be peopled with demons, male and female. These were the human refuse of London, and they clawed at her dress as she tried to find a clear spot.

'Over 'ere. There's a space 'ere,' croaked a female voice. Eve made her way towards that voice. She could barely make out the form of the woman laying in a corner patting a bed of straw near to her. It was the only clear space she could see. She did not welcome the thought of laying on straw on a hard floor but had no choice.

She spent a sleepless night, without privacy even for the common office, troubled by rats and the noise from other inmates, who mercifully seemed to leave her alone. As the early morning light filtered through a grating high in the wall above, she could see that the woman she had laid next to was covered in sores. She was in despair.

The gaoler called her name. She hoped that the soldiers had come for her. 'Not yet yer Ladyship. I promised somethin' better an' I'm a man of me word.'

He led her up two flights of stone steps. 'This 'ere place was built under the orders of a famous Lord Mayor of our city; His Honour Mister Richard Whittington.' This he said with pride, but Eve reflected in that case the dreadful place must already be well over two-hundred years old.

They came to a solid door, 'A lady of yer own rank in 'ere,' he said motioning her inside. This room was lighter, with its own window and two beds. The door slammed shut behind her and Eve saw the emaciated figure in the other bed. 'I'm a countess,' mumbled the wraith.

Eve spent that day and two nights with this half-demented companion who, when not in recurrent fevers, never ceased rambling on about her misfortunes. Strange circular blotches disfigured her neck. The woman never ate her food the second day, and on the third morning Eve could tell she was dead.

'Oh dear,' said the gaoler when he came in with the food. He quickly went out again and came back with two companions. All three had kerchiefs tied over their mouths. They wrapped the body in a sheet and took it and her bed away.

After spending another night there, Eve began to panic in case she had been forgotten, but in the morning they called for her. The officer upbraided the gaoler when he saw her condition, for she had not been able to wash since being in Newgate. A bucket of water was fetched and a comb found, and in a side room she was told to tidy herself as best she could before being taken for more questioning.

On the journey Eve was apprehensive, for she had concealed a lot she could have told. When she arrived there were two men behind the table. The new one seemed more senior but did not speak.

'We've checked what you told us, your Ladyship. First of all, we know that the Mr Jeremy Goodway you were seeking is not and has not been in

London in the recent past. In fact he's in Brentham still. We sent a courier to check. That's why we had to detain you longer than expected.'

Eve wondered why they had gone to all that trouble to check on Jeremy, but was afraid to ask.

'As far as the bequest from Tripp is concerned. We are satisfied that we've no proof that he came by his money dishonestly. Therefore there is no reason why you shouldn't have this.' He pushed Tripp's will towards her.

'However, we're not satisfied about some of the returns from Captain Tripp's time in Suffolk. In your case, although as far as we can see, no fault attaches to yourself, this doesn't mean that estate can be entirely exempt from penalty. Although your late husband, the Marquess, declared himself neutral; the brother from whom he inherited in forty-three most certainly was not, and had he lived would have been declared malignant.

'You're free to leave now. Go back to Suffolk. Assessors will call on you again shortly. Don't attempt to sell any more property without permission. Leave London within twenty-four hours, otherwise you'll be arrested again.'

Eve undertook to do so. After this experience, she wanted only to get back to Brentham. She didn't care if they took all the Stourland estate lands. She would happily go back to live with her father. The officer was instructed to convey her back to the *Blue Boar.*

There Eve found that her room had been let. 'We didn't want no trouble,' explained the inn keeper. 'Tom Slater 'as took care of yer bags.'

She walked up to Slater's premises. He was in the yard. 'I've to get out of London right away, or be arrested again,' she declared.

'How will you do that?' asked Slater. 'That cowardly coachman ran off as soon as he knew you were arrested.'

'Not with my coach and horses?' asked Eve with alarm.

'Nar, 'e wanted to, by I stopped him.'

Eve thought for a moment. 'Will you drive me? Any price.'

'Oh I don't know about that,' said Slater. 'Mean I'll 'ave to leave this business for the missus to run. That'll mean trouble for me. Still come over to the 'ouse.' She followed him into his house and into a little room used as an office. He pulled out a crude map of East Anglia. 'Where you say you live, Brentham; where's that?'

'A few miles the other side of Sudbury.'

Slater traced a finger across the map and found Sudbury. 'A tidy journey. Any price, you say?'

'Within reason.'

'Your coach.'

'What!'

'Your coach. That's my price.'

'That's unreasonable!'

'It would be a sight less reasonable in Newgate again as I'm sure you'll agree. In any case, 'ow am I supposed to get back without? Take it or leave it.'

Eve was about to say that she imagined he would take a spare horse to come back on, but remained silent. It looked as though she was about to lose much of her property anyway. She agreed and wrote him a note transferring ownership of her coach to him in return for carriage home.

'Not until the mornin' at nine o'clock though,' said Slater. 'Other things to do today. We can put you up in the 'ouse an' give food, so it ain't all bad. You best not go near the *Blue Boar* again.'

CHAPTER 24

In the morning, about fifteen minutes after the coach started, it stopped outside a prosperous-looking house. After some vibration, which seemed like the loading of additional baggage, Tom Slater opened a carriage door and motioned to two women and a man to get in.

'Who are these people?' snapped Eve, putting out a hand to restrain them from entering. 'I understood I would be travelling alone.'

'I gave no such undertaking, m'lady,' said Tom Slater.

'Considering the exorbitant price you extracted because of my plight, it was a fair assumption.'

'Does your Ladyship wish to stay in London longer? The bill you gave me mentioned no date for travel.'

'Rogue! You know I can't.' Eve sighed and moved over to make room for the other passengers.

The faces of her travelling companions indicated to Eve that the exchange with Tom Slater had made them hostile to her.

'It seems that we travel with one of the aristocracy who deems a merchant and his family who made their way by honest toil, unfit companions.' The words were spoken by one of the women, well past middle age, hawk-nosed and thin-lipped. The other woman, around the same age, bore a resemblance, but was a little plumper. The man was fairly stout. All three wore the customary Puritan clothes. Predominantly black with white collars, in contrast to Eve's rather more colourful attire.

'I'd have expected a person like her to have her own coach,' said the woman.

Eve became annoyed with them talking about her as though she was not there. 'This *is* my coach,' she snapped. 'Or at least it was until yesterday when that rogue took advantage of my distress and need to leave London urgently after my rascally coachman deserted me.'

'So!' exclaimed the man. 'That's why he came to us yesterday saying he could convey us three days earlier than first arranged for extra payment. He had won himself another coach, the knave. Your need to leave London must have been desperate to give him your coach and horses in exchange for the journey.'

Eve made no comment. Although her face remained solemn, she was smiling inwardly at the mention of horses, for she believed that she had outwitted the audaciously greedy Tom Slater. Faced with his outrageous demand, she had, as a desperate ploy, written him a bill transferring ownership of the coach but making no mention of horses. She had scarcely been able to believe her luck when he failed to notice the omission. On arrival at Brentham she fully intended to inform Tom Slater that the horses were not his. He would then be given the opportunity of purchasing the beasts at a grossly inflated price, or selling her back the coach very cheaply.

He could, of course, just laugh in her face and drive off; but that would be horse stealing and it would not take long for the constable on horseback to catch a lumbering coach. Eve was a very intelligent and keen-witted young woman. When confronted with sharp practice, she could return like in full measure.

The man in the coach was still inquisitive. 'What was your reason for having to leave London quickly? I trust we're not travelling with a fugitive from justice.'

'You are impertinent, sir,' cried Eve. 'Because an army officer purchased something from me and didn't claim it I came to look for him, not knowing he'd been killed. Again, in my ignorance I stayed at the *Blue Boar* inn, not realising it was a meeting place for Royalist spies. I was taken for questioning. There is nothing against me, but because my late husband was a marquess although neutral in the war, I was, in the dictatorial manner of our masters, told that if I didn't leave London within twenty-four hours I would be arrested. Now, sir, I trust that your idle curiosity is satisfied and you will leave me in peace.' She thought it best not to mention Newgate.

'So we're travelling with a malignant,' said the thin woman, sarcastically.

Eve ignored the remark. The man removed his hat and closed his eyes to go to sleep.

From then, things started to go even worse for Eve. The coach stopped for lunch at Brentwood. When Eve's travelling companions discovered where they were, the man asked Tom Slater why they were on that road since they were going to Norwich. He was obliged to tell them he would be striking across country after Chelmsford to get Eve home and then go on until he picked up the Norwich road.

'So that's why we've been charged extra!' exclaimed his disgruntled passenger, 'For the privilege of travelling further, over worse roads, for much longer. You're a dishonest knave Slater, and a sinner.'

Now they were even more hostile to Eve, and hostile to Tom Slater as well.

They stayed overnight in Chelmsford. Tom Slater advised them to get a good night's rest as he planned to get further than Brentham next day and progress would be somewhat slower.

Eve slept only fitfully that night, for she was disturbed by the hostility she had experienced in the coach. She awoke very early with a fever. Eventually the fever subsided, but she began to be troubled by a nagging pain in her left armpit. Water had been left in her room overnight so she got up to wash. Feeling for the source of the pain she became aware of a slight swelling that had not been there before.

Her travelling companions were hostile as soon as the coach started out of Chelmsford. 'Such a disgrace that godly folk should not only be cheated by a rogue, but now it seems we are obliged to travel with someone who has over indulged in strong drink. Did you not see her before we boarded the coach; unable to walk a straight line?'

It was the thinner of the two women who spoke–probably the sister of the man's wife. Eve did not feel like answering their carping as the others grunted their assent and added their own barbs. It was true that she had felt somewhat unsteady as she walked from the inn to the coach, but it was due to an attack of dizziness, not strong drink. She felt utterly tired and closed her eyes to try to sleep.

She started to feel a pain in her left groin as the coach juddered along the rough track called a road. Unable to keep fully awake, she was surprised to be shaken gently by Tom Slater and told it was a luncheon stop at Halstead. Her travelling companions had already alighted. She had been so drowsy that she had not noticed their passing through Braintree.

After lunch, of which she had eaten little, Eve felt nauseated. Seeing she looked unwell, Tom Slater asked her if he should seek a physician. 'No, we can't be long now,' she replied. 'I'll wait upon the comfort of home and call my own doctor.'

He assisted her as she walked to the coach, for she was very unsteady. She was already dozing when her unsympathetic companions returned.

Eve's fever mounted as they travelled and she started to feel a pain behind her left ear. Tracing over the spot with her fingers she could feel a lump. After about an hour she was sweating profusely and her travelling companions were carping about having to journey in the company of a sick person. The man beat on the roof of the coach with a stick

'What's amiss?' asked Tom Slater, as he came to the door of the stationary vehicle.

'This person. This marchioness; she's sick and a danger to us all. We insist that you eject her from this coach.'

'I can't do that,' said Tom Slater. 'She paid handsomely for the journey. We're not much more than an hour from her home and her own physician. 'Tis but a little fever, I suppose caused by the anxiety of being in Newgate a few nights.'

'Newgate!' cried the man. 'Is there aught else you haven't told us, you cheating rogue? We ride with a gaol bird! Make no mistake, my lawyers will deal with you Mr Slater, when we return to London.'

'That's for the future if you wish,' said Tom Slater. 'None the less, I won't turn her off. It would be inhuman and likely against the law.' He remounted the driving seat and started off once more.

The women inside the coach were starting to panic. 'Do something!' they screeched at the man. 'See now the inflamed carbuncles that start upon her cheek.'

The man reached in his bag and extracted a pistol and powder flask. He proceeded to load and prime the weapon.

As in a fog, Eve saw what he was doing and started to become alarmed, which sharpened her mind a little. 'What are you about to do?' cried the man's wife in alarm. 'Shoot her?'

'No. That would be murder. 'Tis but to threaten Slater if he becomes difficult again. Here; hold this.' He handed the loaded weapon to his wife. Without more ado he opened the door between himself and Eve; then grasping her roughly by the arms, pushed her to the opening. She tried to resist, but was no match for him, especially in her present state.

It was a hard landing on the verge for Eve, although the coach was only doing about five miles an hour. She was too weak to get up. The coach was still going on as if Tom Slater was in ignorance of what had happened. Then about forty yards on, she saw him look round as if he had just realised something was wrong, and stop the vehicle.

He jumped down from his seat and started back towards her. 'Stop!' commanded the man from the coach. Tom Slater turned round to find himself facing a pistol. 'Leave her,' said the man sharply. 'Drive on.'

'Don't be a fool, man,' said Tom Slater. 'You can't do this. Put the gun away while you yet 'ave time. I'll pick her up.' He turned to walk towards where Eve lay, but before many paces a shot rang out and he collapsed to the ground.

The man mounted the driving seat of the coach and drove off unsteadily.

Eve could tell Tom Slater wasn't dead, because after a few seconds he tried to move, but couldn't get up. He crawled towards her, wincing in pain. 'Only my right leg I think. Stay calm. I'll try to get help. That must be Sudbury? He pointed to houses less than a mile away.'

'Yes, that's Sudbury,' croaked Eve from a parched throat.

Tom Slater tried to stand, but fell over again. He crawled towards a thicket, drew a knife and cut out a rough staff. Then he pulled himself up and started to walk on one leg with the aid of the staff. 'I'll get help,' he called.

And those were the last words Eve was to hear in her life. She made a gallant effort to crawl but was too weak with fever. Her last vision was of Tom Slater hobbling along one hundred or more yards ahead, and far in the distance the coach crossing the River Stour towards Sudbury less than a mile away, and only six from home. Then she became unconscious as the mists of time enveloped her.

✳✳✳

It was in the main street through Brentham village that the luck of Eve's erstwhile travelling companions ran out. They need not have gone that way, but being unfamiliar with the district had followed Tom Slater's drawn plan.

Constable Scott had been to the forge, and was standing outside in conversation with Samuel Bloom when the coach came into sight. The driver seemed uncomfortable with the horses. 'That coach being so ineptly driven by a stranger looks identical to that owned by the Marchioness,' said Constable

Scott. 'But what, I wonder, is the contraption on the roof, holding luggage?'

As the coach approached, the constable stepped into the road. 'Hold. Hold I say.'

'Who has the impertinence to bar a law-abiding citizen on his journey,' demanded the indignant driver.

'My name is Scott. Constable of this parish. I have a right. This looks like the coach belonging to the Marchioness of Stourland. And you sir do not speak like nor drive like an experienced coach driver.' He turned to the blacksmith. 'Sam. Can you help?'

Samuel Bloom looked at a bracket on the back of the coach which he had recently repaired. Then he lifted up a hoof of one of the horses.

'Yes. Thass our work.' he called out.

The constable looked inside the coach and saw the two strange women. Both of whom seemed to be in a nervous state.

'This is grave impertinence,' said the man. 'Of course this coach and horses belonged to the Marchioness of Stourland. I bought them from her in London three days since.'

'That seems strange,' said the constable. 'I have heard the Marchioness is in London, yet you handle the coach badly for one who has driven nearly seventy miles. If you will show me your bill of sale, and tell me your destination, I can let you go.'

To say 'Norwich' considering where they were, would have been very suspicious. The man just said 'Of course,' and fumbled in a box beside him as if looking for a bill of sale. Then he pulled out the ready pistol which he had just cocked, fired at the constable, then tried to urge the horses on.

It was a desperate move by a desperate man. The shot missed. Samuel Bloom held the horses' heads, and Joseph who had heard the whole exchange, picked up a pole and pushed the man off his seat by the time the constable had drawn and cocked his own weapon.

The constable aimed a kick at the man laying on the floor. 'Get up!,' he ordered. Then he called to the blacksmith. 'Sam; keep an eye on the coach and these women while I get this one locked up. I'll be back soon.'

'That way,' he commanded, giving his prisoner a push in the direction of the bridewell. 'Whatever the truth is about the coach we'll find out later. Now I'm arresting you for shooting at a law officer.'

A few minutes later two horsemen came along at a gallop and pulled up by the coach, both with drawn pistols. 'This looks like it,' said one. Then turning to Sam and Joseph, 'We're from the Sudbury constable with orders to stop this coach and bring back two women and a man we should find on it.' He looked in the coach and saw the women. 'Which of you two is the driver?'

'Neither,' said Joseph. Our constable jus' took him to the lock up. We're the blacksmiss of this place.'

'Here come the constable now,' said Samuel, pointing across the green to Constable Scott striding in their direction with a deputy. 'What's this?' asked

Scott when they reached the coach.

'We're from the Sudbury constable and . . .' began one of the men.

'I know,' said Constable Scott, impatiently. 'I recognise you.'

'We're under orders to stop this coach and take it back to Sudbury with two women and a man driving it.'

'You can't have the driver,' said Constable Scott. 'I've just arrested him. He shot at me when I stopped the coach because I recognised it as belonging to the Marchioness of Stourland.'

'But it's our orders sir. A fellow hobbled into town, wounded in the leg, from across the river. Claimed the coach was his. The Marchioness was one of his passengers same as these others coming in from London. She came over very ill with a fever. They took fright and pushed her out. When he stopped to get her back in, the man shot him and made off with the coach. Constable's gone to find a doctor and go down to where the Marchioness was left.'

Constable Scott turned to his deputy. 'Go and tell Mr Pearson what's happened. If he's well enough, he'll want to come. Best tell his physician, Doctor Mills as well. He's sure to want him along.'

'I'll tell the doctor.' volunteered Samuel. 'It'll save time.'

'Thank you Sam,' said Constable Scott. 'I'll go and get my prisoner manacled and mounted. I suggest you two start with the coach. We'll catch you up. I'll talk this out with your constable. He remains my prisoner meantime.'

Constable Scott with his prisoner, hands manacled and mounted on a horse attached by a rope to his own, accompanied by a deputy caught up with the coach just before Sudbury. Nathaniel Pearson had been able to travel faster, not having a manacled man with them, and had passed the coach a few minutes earlier.

***

Nathaniel Pearson and Doctor Mills rode straight through Sudbury and took the road across the river where they had been told the incident took place. They came across the Sudbury constable and a doctor standing with their backs to Eve who was laid on the ground. The constable recognised Nathaniel and acknowledged him. 'I'm afraid she's dead sir,' he said.

'Plague,' explained the doctor.

'Plague!' exclaimed Nathaniel. He dismounted to look at his daughter's corpse. Doctor Mills did the same. Afraid there's no doubt about that,' he said.

'I've sent back for men to bring a litter to pick the body up,' said the constable.

There were tears in Nathaniel's eyes. 'Then she wasn't murdered,' he said.

'No,' answered the constable. 'I can't charge them with that unfortunately. Cruel it might be to put a sick person off a coach, but it's not a crime. The only thing I can charge them with is theft of the coach and wounding the driver. And only the man at that.'

'What's this I hear about a wounded driver? Was it her regular coachman?'

'No sir. He's a London man. Name of Thomas Slater. I'm satisfied the coach was his. He had a bill of sale from your daughter, although he seems to have struck a hard bargain. He gained the coach a the price of a journey back from London because her coachman had deserted her.'

After a little while, they saw the coach coming up the hill from Sudbury with the two men who had fetched it from Brentham. It was being driven by Tom Slater. Constable Scott was in attendance with his prisoner still tethered.

'What's this?' demanded the Sudbury constable. 'I sent for a litter to take a body away.'

'With your leave sir,' called down Tom Slater. 'I undertook to convey the lady to Brentham. Let me complete the commission, though she be passed away. And I fear I shall need a helping hand when I get there.' He pointed to his leg and crutch.

The Sudbury constable looked enquiringly at Nathaniel Pearson, who nodded his agreement. 'It will be meet, so that I can give her a decent Christian burial among the family.'

'What have you done with the women?' the Sudbury constable asked his men.

'Locked them up sir.'

'You can release them when you return. Now Constable Scott. Why is my prisoner tethered to you?'

'Because he's my prisoner on a more serious charge. He shot at me with his pistol.'

'A serious charge indeed, Constable Scott. Shooting at a law officer. A matter for the assizes. But I've two charges against him. Stealing the coach and wounding the driver.'

Constable Scott looked around him towards the river and the town of Sudbury. 'Tell me. On this spot are we not in the county of Essex?'

'By a whisker,' admitted the Sudbury constable grudgingly. 'It's an Essex matter and I have a duty to inform our schief constable so that he can inform the chief constable of Essex. Yours on the other hand is a Suffolk matter. Guard the villain well and speed him on to the assizes and the gallows.'

He turned to his men. 'Cancel that order to release the women. The Essex chief constable may want to charge them with something.'

While the constables were having their discussion, Nathaniel Pearson, aided by Doctor Mills laid Eve's body in the coach. Nathaniel tied his horse to the rear because he wanted to ride seated beside Tom Slater as he drove.

'Now, Mr Slater. Pray tell me all you know of what befell my daughter in London.'

Tom Slater told all he knew in detail.

'So,' said Nathaniel. 'She'd been in Newgate four days, which is no doubt where she became infected with the plague, and under further threat if she didn't leave London. Added to that her coachman had deserted her. In her distress you took advantage by demanding her coach in return for getting her home. Don't you think that was sharp practice, bordering on dishonesty?'

'It was a business deal,' replied Tom Slater, defensively.

'So you say. Will you show me the bill of sale please.'

Tom Slater handed Nathaniel the document. The Squire looked at it long and hard until they arrived at his house in Brentham. 'Let me hand you down. It's too late now to start out for London.'

Nathaniel carried Eve's body into the house. He then went back out to Tom Slater. 'Tell me, Mr Slater; how do you propose to return to London?'

'I shall drive my coach of course.'

'Your coach needs horses, Mr Slater. The horses aren't yours. Look again at the bill of sale. No horses are mentioned as included in your exorbitant reward.'

Tom Slater tore the bill of sale from his pocket to read again. His face showed disbelief that he could have allowed himself to be outwitted.

'My daughter was no fool about money, Mr Slater. It's easy to see what she had in mind to pay you back for your sharp practice. Now she's dead and no family, her property will become mine. Don't try to go off with *my* horses, Mr Slater, or I'll have the constable arrest you for horse stealing.'

'Then sell me *your* horses. I assure you, sir, I wouldn't dream of stealing them,' said Tom Slater, with asperity. 'I'm an honest man.'

'Very near the periphery of that desirable condition, Mr Slater. Dangerously near,' said Nathaniel. 'As to selling the horses to you. Pray let me first attend to my daughter's speedy funeral, for my heart is full of sorrow. After that I'll consider what deal is just, taking into consideration that you did, after all, try to get her back on the coach, and was shot for your pains. You'll not be fit to drive nearly seventy miles for a few days anyway.

'Now, unless you prefer to first park your coach on public land, I'll have someone park it in my grounds where it will be safer before he stables the horses. Then I'll escort you to our nearest inn for lodgings. It's no more than three hundred yards and on my way to see the pastor, and to buy my daughter a coffin. I trust you can hobble that far. I'll fetch you a stouter stick than you have, to use as a crutch.'

Tom Slater realised he had met his match in commerce, and thanked Nathaniel for his consideration.

CHAPTER 25

Because she had died from plague, Eve's funeral was arranged for the following afternoon. Samuel Bloom's brother George, the local carpenter, who also doubled as an undertaker, did not have a coffin ready made suitable for a person of her rank. He did his best, which was one that might have been ordered for a village shopkeeper, and worked all night to finish it off and put the corpse in.

At the funeral Bessie cried, as indeed she had with great frequency ever since Jeremy had told her of Eve's death the previous evening. She was still of distressed countenance and racked with bouts of crying after they arrived home.

'A funeral is a sad occasion, I know, Bess, but why do you cry to such extremes?' asked Jeremy. 'After all, there's no longer any need for me to seek employment away from Brentham. This sad chance has lifted that burden from our lives.'

'She died 'cos of me,' wailed Bessie. 'Such wickedness. Now I'll be damned for it.'

'Dear heart, she died of plague. You didn't infect her with plague.'

'No, but I asked God to strike her dead. On that awful day, arter she come to see me I was so upset I got on my knees an' asked Almighty God to strike her dead.'

'That was certainly a wicked request Bess, made in a moment of anguish. I doubt the Lord God answered it. Next time you pray, ask forgiveness for asking such a thing.'

'But I feel I must do somethin' towards puttin' it right.'

'If God wants you to atone for that sin, He'll present the opportunity. Just as He'll present opportunities for me to atone for my many more and greater sins. We have much life in front of us. Now dry your tears and try to be at peace with yourself.'

But Bessie would not be at peace with herself. It was like a great burden to her.

***

It was about a month after Eve's death that Squire Pearson asked Jeremy to make time from his labours for a private discussion on a subject other than his work.

'A wilful girl, my daughter. Ever loth to accept guidance. Believed she could take care of herself in all matters.' Nathaniel paused for a moment and gave a little chuckle. 'And in the end, in desperate case with her back to the wall, managed to outwit that rogue Thomas Slater.'

Jeremy knew the Squire had let Slater have horses for the coach but did not know on what terms. 'Could I presume to ask what you did about that sir?'

'Oh, after reflection I let him have horses at just a fraction above market price. After all, he had tried to help Eve in the end and was wounded for his trouble. He also insisted on completing the journey with her body, though he was still in pain. That was worth some reward.

'Now to what I really called you in for. Ever since you came to work for me, a year now, I've been concerned about your future, which seemed to rest upon my staying alive. Although Eve had adequate wealth of her own, to disinherit her would have been tantamount to disowning her, and I could never have done that. What to do was worrying me, bearing in mind her various attempts to attract you from your wife, which had not passed entirely unnoticed by me.'

Here Jeremy tried to intervene, but Nathaniel held up his hand. 'Spare me the details. Knowledge of the outline causes enough sorrow. Now that it has pleased God to call her home, the question of your future is straightforward. Quite simply I propose to make you my heir.'

'Sir!' exclaimed Jeremy. 'What can I say. I'm not worthy. Surely you have relatives? In any case, you may yet want to re-marry. There are years of life ahead of you.'

'You're worthy as any and more so than most. As for relatives. If I still have any, they're so distant as to be beyond my knowledge. I shall not re-marry. Next week I become sixty and I've had the first of those fevers which, after a time, combined with worry about Eve, took my dear wife Judith. How long we live is in the hands of God, but if I hazard a guess I would put my remaining span at the very most, five years, maybe as little as two or even less.

'You see, Jeremy, it's not just your future, but the future of Brentham I care about. My family founded Brentham.'

The Squire then embarked on the long history of his family. How five hundred years before they had carved out their original land from primeval forest and built the first small village. That original land comprised all of the present Brentham, down to where it abutted what was now the Stourland Estate at the southern quarter; as well as his cultivated fields and pastures to the north, west and east.

'So you see, Jeremy, how they built Brentham into a place of industry and farming which enabled some traders to buy their properties and plots.

'Now as to what your inheritance will comprise. All Pearson land and property and such money as I leave, after worthy donations.

'It won't include the Stourland Estate, although Eve left a will naming me. I've recently completed negotiations with the sequestrators. Because the Marquess before the one Eve married was an avowed Royalist who was still living when the war started in forty-two; also because, according to them, insufficient had been paid in levy by the last Marquess; they insist it was the estate of a malignant. They argued that they were entitled to levy a fine just as if the old Marquess had still been alive. The penalty was huge. It would have taken all the money Eve was leaving plus some of my own to pay it. Not needing such an encumbrance, I declined.'

'Does this mean that all Stourland Estate now belongs to the government?' asked Jeremy.

'Yes. All the vast amount of land and property have been sequestrated. Since that's worth more than their penalty, the actual money Eve left and her valuables come to me. By the time the latter are encashed it will increase my own personal money three or four fold. In addition Eve had been left nineteen-hundred pounds by that fellow Tripp, which surprises me. Also a farm which at one time used to be part of Stourland, though how he came to own it I don't know.

'I don't need all that money for my personal use Jeremy and neither will you when you inherit. I want to see some spent on Brentham itself and make sure that what my ancestors started continues. The first thing I've done is to offer to purchase back from the sequestrators at above market value, that small part of the Stourland Estate which lies within our present parish boundary. That will mean that whoever buys the Manor itself, which is outside, however influential, will have no proprietary right to interfere in the development and running of Brentham.

'This will increase your own influence and compensate somewhat for your lack of years. Are you willing to undertake such responsibility when I'm gone?'

'I'll certainly do my best to see Brentham is run as you would wish. But may you live long yet to have your own hand on the tiller,' answered Jeremy. 'I'm worried still that I don't deserve such trust.'

'Then you'll work all the keener to satisfy yourself that you do. That's good. Do you have anything in mind where money needs to be spent at this time?'

'Some of the labourer's cottages are in bad condition, sir.'

'That had occurred to me also. Make a start on that will you, and keep me informed if any are too dilapidated to be worth repairing. I had a mind to either give your parents their farm, or let them go rent free for the rest of their lives. It makes little difference since you will inherit that back when they go. How about Sam Bloom?'

'Sam would be too proud to accept a gift. You could offer to sell the property to him cheaply. He has some funds I believe. It would enable him keep his pride.'

'Good, and that will make one more property owner in Brentham. We'll discuss other plans as we go along. There's one piece of largess I'm indulging in which might disappoint you.'

'I'm sure you have the right to give to whoever you please, sir.'

'None the less I will tell you. Tobias Winscombe, the butcher. Eight years ago, the parish fined him a quarter of his worth, for his part in that trumped-up charge against Eve and yourself. He would have been unable to pay without selling his shop and dwelling. Effectively going out of business. He came to me begging for help. After searching our hearts, Judith and I decided to forgive him, especially as he had also received twenty-five lashes. He had merely been a foolish tool in Dowdy's hands. I quietly loaned him the better part of the fine on his honour to repay me over twelve years.

'Since then he has paid back promptly each quarter, and has been a model citizen. Now I'm told, he and my cook Hannah Beck are to marry. I'm remitting the final four years of his repayments as a wedding gift. How do you feel about that, as one who was plotted against?'

Jeremy paused for thought before giving his answer. 'I think you're an example of Christian justice to us all, sir.'

* * *

Bessie could scarce comprehend the news that Jeremy was to inherit from Squire Pearson when he died. 'That mean I'll be the Squire's Lady. I ain't fit arter that wicked thing I done. An' I ain't had no fine schoolin' like you. I sound common when I talk.'

'You were taught to read and write Bess,' said Jeremy, 'which was unusual for most village girls. Sam made sure of that for you. As for the way you speak, if you think that matters, try practising. It may be years before Mr Pearson dies, so there's time for practice. You won't lose the Suffolk accent entirely any more than I did, or for that matter the Squire himself has. Nor should you, it's naught to be ashamed of. You could try to get rid of some of the most extreme things such as "arter" for "after" and "allus" for "always". And if you can't avoid "thass" and "whass", try saying "that is" and "what is" then soon it'll become easy to say "that's" and "what's".'

'I'll try that Jeremy, dear. I really will,' said Bessie.

'So long as you never use one of your mother's expressions in public.'

'Whass . . I mean *what is* that?'

'"Lor' lumme alive",' replied Jeremy, 'because dear Bess, I'm sure the Lord does in fact love us and wants us alive to do good to our neighbours. In the end that's what will really matter. How we treat others when we have power.

* * *

Over the remaining eighteen months of his life, Nathaniel Pearson did all he could to promote Jeremy's status in the immediate district. He was anxious that Brentham should progress peacefully, untroubled by a power struggle such as happened between the Pearson family and a faction of bigots led by Obadiah Dowdy after the Royalist Marquess of Stourland lost his influence at the start of the civil war. Although the condition and administration of law and order was now more settled than in the uncertain days of 1644, the diversity of opinions was on the increase. This was especially the case in matters of religion.

Jeremy was elected to the committee of parish brethren. The Squire had been successful in his bid to purchase that small part of the Stourland Estate that fell within the boundary of Brentham itself, effectively giving himself the status of a lord of the manor, although Brentham was not a manor itself. This meant that when Jeremy inherited he would have an automatic right to preside in the parish court when it was used as a manor court on court leet matters.

The rest of the Stourland Estate, as it turned out, was not bought by one person, but split into four. Therefore Nathaniel's–and subsequently Jeremy's–new neighbour was much more on a par with him; and with no automatic say in the affairs of Brentham. He was, however, a magistrate like Nathaniel and Reverend Jones, so could preside in the parish court when it was used for criminal matters.

The important thing as far as the Squire was concerned was that he had created a situation where Jeremy, when he took over, would be the most powerful arbiter in Brentham in the matter of property, business, and public morals. He felt that the future good of the parish would be safe in his hands.

The outlying farm that Eve had originally given to Henry Tripp and had come through her to Nathaniel was sold to an independent farmer.

The Squire advised Jeremy not to get involved in the politics of the country, any more than he already was by being a minor agent for the intelligence network. 'I fear for this nation,' he said. 'The chance of a just society, bought at the cost of a hundred-thousand lives, is being cast away by the factious conduct of men, who believe only in their own opinions. The remnant of the old Parliament had to be chased out. Now we're ruled by a Lord Protector and a nominated Parliament. Even that last is failing. Soon it'll decline into rule with a strong hand by one man. That will doubtless be a just rule, because he is just, but when he dies, as all mortal men do, all will be chaos as factions vie for power. Then will all the spilt blood be mostly proved to have been in vain. Be content to see that Brentham is a just and peaceful place.'

But it was in his last illness in March of 1654 that Nathaniel Pearson spoke to Jeremy of more personal things. He said how he regretted having had to place Brentham under military jurisdiction ten years earlier. An act which culminated in the ruin of Obadiah Dowdy at the time. 'Yet it was necessary for the peace of Brentham to be rid of him,' he said.

'I heard a rumour that he more than recouped his losses by bribery later,' said Jeremy.

Then Nathaniel wanted to talk about Eve. 'She was ever a wilful child, but not wicked. It was just before her marriage to the Marquess that Judith and I came to suspect why she had turned out the way she did. I had for some time come to believe that she had been seduced by a young knave called Marcus Kirby; son of former friends of ours. When exactly I don't know, but it couldn't have been later that forty-two. From that time she developed a strong longing for him. Indeed for some time we came to think of him as her future husband.

'A dramatic change came over her after Marcus rode in with news of Marston Moor. If I remember correctly that was the day after you came back from Cambridge. The following morning he admitted at breakfast having married another, obviously because he had got her with child.

'The news upset Eve and she didn't come with us to market that day. There was nothing remarkable in that but . . .'

Nathaniel hesitated a moment. 'I must unburden myself to one I can trust. I can bear it no longer alone. When I had Judith we bore it together.'

'You needn't tell me anything that upsets you,' said Jeremy. 'All that is now past.'

'No. I must. It was shortly before Eve married that she had a nightmare. Her cries were so loud that Judith went into her room. My wife and I remained awake for the rest of that night trying to fathom out what Eve's disjointed cries about flames and washing away blood, and how she would burn, could mean. The realisation came in the small hours. It was something so dreadful we never mentioned it to our daughter.

'I believe that on that fateful day; the day that a labourer of mine died–Eli Brown his name–she killed him. Accidentally no doubt. Perhaps he tried to rape her–I can only guess at the circumstances–then became too frightened to admit it. This all fits. It was the day Dowdy first claimed to have seen her naked by the lake. She had gone there to wash away bloodstains and perhaps she thought, the act itself. Perhaps he *had* raped her and she felt dirty also.

'But as time went by, it became even more difficult for her to admit. Then came the awful day that Eli Brown's unfortunate wife was burnt at the stake by a lynch mob for his killing. I believe the horror of having to carry such a secret on her own turned her mind. She believed herself a damned soul. From that time all other sins were easy and paled into insignificance.

'Poor girl she was more sinned against that sinning at the start of it all. Remember her as kindly as you can Jeremy, and remember her in your prayers.'

Jeremy could see the tears roll down Nathaniel's cheeks. 'I'll do that sir and forever keep secret what you've told me. Now I must leave you to rest.'

The Squire died two days later and his funeral was on the second day of April. Jeremy, now aged twenty-seven, was the new Squire of Brentham. His lady wife, Bessie, twenty-five.

✳✳✳

Over the following six months Jeremy did his utmost to ensure that Brentham continued as Nathaniel Pearson would have wished. Where he was called upon to exercise minor judgements, he went out of his way to be fair. He was becoming liked and respected, as indeed was Bessie.

During those months little Jemima became four and Benjamin, their son, two. They were healthy. Bessie and Jeremy were blissfully happy, although a little troubled that they did not deserve the good fortune that had come their way. When they had first inherited, they had resolved to always do their best to help those less fortunate than themselves. Yet to Bessie, who was still much troubled that she had prayed for Eve's death, it seemed something more need to be done to atone for such a sin.

It took Jeremy three whole months to persuade Bessie to move into Brentham Grange, which she considered too grand. Although she would not admit it, the house and its associations with Eve troubled her, especially the study, which she pestered Jeremy to have refurbished. The two remaining maids had stayed on after Nathaniel Pearson died, although there was little for them to do since only the study was in use.

Hannah Beck, the cook–who married Tobias Winscombe, the butcher, a year before and became a widow six months later–left when Nathaniel died. She had ceased to live in when she married, but continued to come in every day to work, out of loyalty. With her employer dead, no longer needing employment, and being unpopular with some village women over the Eliza Reed affair, she left Brentham to live with a widowed sister.

Having finally given in to pressure and moved into the Grange, Bessie wanted to do her own cooking. Jeremy said that would not be right for the Squire's lady, but let her do so for the time being. After inspecting the servants' quarters, he had judged their condition bad and cramped. He therefore decided to have them renovated, and hired builders for the work. The outside staircase which permitted the servants access to and from their quarters without using the family corridor on the first floor was also in a bad condition. Jeremy ordered that to be rebuilt after they had finished the rooms. While this was being done, the two maids were sent to live with their families and told to come in daily. When the work was done, Jeremy informed Bessie, they would have to have a live-in cook.

CHAPTER 26

Obadiah Dowdy rode his horse out of Nottingham on his way back to Suffolk. It was a bright early morning in the September of 1654. More than ten years after he had been forced out of Brentham, and seven since he had fled East Anglia on the death of Matthew Hopkins. He was just starting his fourth day of travel and estimated that his journey was now half done.

His heart was full of hatred and he was relatively poor. Not destitute and hungry like a beggar; nor poor like an agricultural labourer who might toil a lifetime and never have twenty pounds to call his own. But by the standards of Obadiah Dowdy, one time master tailor of Brentham, prominent in local affairs, owner of his own premises and employer of labour, he was poor. He had just over thirty pounds to his name, his horse, a change of clothes, two pistols, and tools of his trade.

His condition need not have been so. When he had fled East Anglia and settled in Lancashire, he was almost as affluent through bribery as he had been before his fall from influence in Brentham. Had he been endowed with the slightest degree of humility; had he been endowed with any quality of mercy; had he been able to consider that he might in the slightest degree be wrong about anything; then his latest calamities might not have happened. But he could not, because he was Obadiah Dowdy. Certain of his own rectitude in the sight of God, and obsessed about witches, he had once more been in conflict with people more powerful than himself.

He had made many enemies and for his pains had been subjected to fines, a short period of imprisonment in a local bridewell, and two substantial civil claims. He had even had a first taste of the lash, with twenty-five at a whipping post.

That should have reminded him there were three-hundred of the same waiting if he ever entered Brentham again. But he was sure his latest crop of misfortunes was caused by the witch Eve Pearson, who from a distance of over two-hundred miles, with supernatural powers, had found his whereabouts and cast an evil spell. If he was to live, she must die, preferably slowly and painfully, for it was his duty to God not to suffer a witch to live–or so he believed. While he was about that necessary task, it was time he also avenged himself on her father, Nathaniel Pearson; on the cowardly turncoat Tobias Winscombe; and on that lickspittle clerk Jeremy Goodway–a tool of Nathaniel Pearson.

Three days later Obadiah Dowdy once more entered the county of Suffolk at Newmarket, which fifty years earlier had been a village smaller than Brentham–until the first Stuart King took a liking and built a palace there. There he stopped the night and, after thought, decided that in the morning he would take a route which would take him to Sudbury, that being close enough to glean information about Brentham without arousing undue suspicion. As his appearance had greatly changed, he should also be able to stay there the next night unrecognised under the alias of Jonothan Bentley.

He arrived at Sudbury during the afternoon of the following day. After trying three taverns he found one where the inn keeper was new–that was safer–and here he took a room.

Dowdy was not naturally given to friendly conversation with strangers, but that evening he made the effort. Striking up coversation first with one drinker in the tap room then another, he finally came to one who, being on his own, seemed to welcome conversation. They sat together at a table. Mostly the man talked about Sudbury. Dowdy wanted to turn the conversation round to Brentham without mentioning the place. The breakthrough came when the man related the instance of the Marchioness of Stourland abandoned and dying of plague by the roadside no more than a mile from town.

Obadiah at first did not make the connection with Eve, for although she had married the Marquess eight months before he fled from East Anglia, he had not been anywhere near Brentham in that time and had no knowledge of it.

'Let's see,' he said. 'The Stourland Estate, that's up Brentham way, is it not.?' At last the conversation had turned where he wanted it. 'Some years have elapsed since I was last in these parts, but I thought surely the Marquess was a bachelor?'

'He was, until right late,' said his drinking companion. 'Then he went an' married this young woman. Somewhat below his station though. Daughter of the Squire of Brentham. Name of Pearson. I know that 'cos that was the name they said when we apprehended the coach. That was the name of the man that come an' picked the body up too.' The man chuckled. 'The Marquess never lasted two year. Reckon gettin' married was too much for him.'

The shock revelation that Eve had been dead and beyond his revenge for over two years, numbed Dowdy so much that he only heard other things the man said as through a fog. At length he regained his composure. 'You said you were sent to apprehend the coach; who sent you?'

'The constable of Sudbury of course. I'm one of his deputies. Didn't I say so.?'

Obadiah shook his head. For a brief moment he was speechless. He had been asking questions of a minor law officer! He quickly turned the conversation away from Brentham and as soon as was practical, made his excuses.

Alone in his room, he upbraided the Almighty for robbing him of the opportunity for revenge. 'Now doth she persecute me from beyond the grave with the aid of Appollyon,' he declared, for he would yet have it that Eve had caused his most recent losses.

It would be obviously too dangerous now to ask more questions in

Sudbury. He would seek out the Mertons for information on the other three.

In the morning he waited once more in the copse opposite New Row, the cottages where Ruth Merton lived with her husband when he was last in the area. After a while she appeared, much the worse for the years, then went back indoors. Obadiah crossed over and knocked at her door.

'Yes?' asked Ruth when she answered his knock. Obviously she didn't recognise him.

'Don't you know me?'

'Can't say I do. Meet lots of men.'

'Johnothan Bentley.'

'Still don't know yer,' she said at first, but although she had lost her looks, her memory was intact. 'Wait a bit. Thass the name Dowdy asked to be called by last time I saw him. God Almighty, you're Obadiah Dowdy! Come in. You owe me money.'

Dowdy stepped inside. 'You wretched whore. I wasted seven pounds on you!'

'We was expectin' the other thirty. Or at least the other ten. She was arrested.'

'But not tried,' said Dowdy. 'You can't expect payment for failure.'

Ruth Merton grunted. 'Well, what d'yer want now? I know that ain't me.'

'Information about three people.'

'Don't give information. I can sell it. Who?'

'Tobias Winscombe the butcher for one?'

'That'll cost five shillin's.'

'That's five times as much as you get for your wretched body I'll warrant, you thieving whore.'

'Take it or leave it,' said Ruth, holding out a bony hand. 'You can't go in Brentham to find out.'

Dowdy handed her five shillings.

'Dead. About a year now. Died a respectable citizen once more.'

The news cut Dowdy to the core. Another had escaped.

'Who else?' asked Ruth.

'Nathaniel Pearson. The so-called Squire?'

'A really important man. Ten shillin's for that.'

'Seven shillings, whore.'

Ruth nodded and Dowdy handed her the money.

'Dead, April of last year.'

Dowdy was aghast. His dismay showed on his face. 'What of that clerk, Jeremy Goodway?'

'Now I got a real lot to say there. Not less than fifteen shillin's.'

'Ten shillings, whore. Five shillings in advance, and another five after, if I judge the information worth it.'

'He's the new Squire of Brentham. Pearson left him the lot. More than

Pearson used to hev his self until late, they say.' She went on to tell him all the details about Jeremy and his fortune; his wife and children; and how well they were thought of. 'If you're thinkin' about revenge or somethin' forget it. You can't take him on. Aside the money an' the influence there's him. Strong now. A real man. Was a captain in the Ironsides. Fought in battles. Take my advice; ride away. There's nothin' waitin' for yer here.   .   .   Except three-hundred at the post,' she reminded him as an afterthought.

Dowdy made for the door. Ruth tried to bar his way with outstretched hand for another five shillings. He gave her one more shilling and pushed her roughly aside.

He retrieved his horse from the copse and, heedless of advice, decided to take a chance and ride through Brentham. After all, she had not recognised him. He hoped he would catch sight of Jeremy Goodway, Squire of Brentham, the only enemy within reach.

No one signalled recognition as he rode along the high street of Brentham. Even Samuel Brown, toiling in the yard of his smithy, merely looked up from his work and nodded at this strange traveller passing through.

It was just before he reached the front gateway to the Grange that he saw Jeremy; mounted on a horse coming his way. They exchanged nods on passing one another. No recognition from Jeremy; and Obadiah almost did not recognise him. Older, powerful-looking, self-assured, no longer the timid clerk he used to order about. Outside the gate a young woman who he could barely recognise as a more mature blacksmith's little daughter, with a child on each hand waving farewell to their father.

Dowdy dismounted and removed his hat. Did that small frown mean the woman recognised him he wondered. 'I beg your pardon ma'am. Can you let me purchase a can of milk?' he extracted an empty can from his luggage.

'We don't usually at this door,' said Bessie in the clipped tones of one forcibly suppressing an accent. 'But if you go round the side, I'll send a maid out to get you some from the dairy.'

As he led his horse round the gable end of the house and Bessie walked to the front door with her children, an evil thought entered Dowdy's warped mind. Those three will suffice in place of the three who escaped me, and their deaths be fair revenge on the fourth if I should fail with him.

He had heard the sound of hammering. This ceased as he arrived round the side. Three building workmen came down the rickety outside staircase, lunch bags in hand. It was half past the noon hour. He noticed that they did not lock the door from which they came.

'You seem busy,' he said as the men passed.

Two of them ignored the remark, but the third stopped. 'Oh. We're a doin' up the servants' quarters. Makin' them real nice on orders of the new Squire.'

'No doubt you'll be soon done,' probed Dowdy more as a remark than a question.

'Gotter replace that there staircase when we're done indoors. Better part of another three week I reckon.'

Just then the maid Bessie had sent came up to them, and the man left to join his mates.

While the maid was fetching the milk Dowdy noticed that the workmen had gone round the side of the stables to eat their food; no doubt to catch the best of the mid-day autumn sun. He also studied the door the maid had come out of. There was no keyhole. Obviously this was secured at night from the inside with bolts, and must therefore be a scullery.

The maid returned with the milk. As he took the filled can, Dowdy turned on the charm—an unusual condition for him and only used to attain a particular goal. 'The workmen tell me your quarters are being refurbished. You are lucky to have such a considerate employer; though no doubt you have uncomfortable nights while the work is unfinished.'

The girl blushed. 'Indeed sir, Mr and Mrs Goodway are very kind, an' we don't suffer from the work 'cos they let us go home nights while thass bein' done.' She turned on her heels and made straight for the scullery door.

Good, thought Obadiah. Only the family at nights.

He rode a mile out of Brentham to think. On his way down from the north he had formulated a rough plan of how he intended to attack the Pearson family. A fire that could not be quenched—a suitable end for the witch he had been sure Eve was. But events had moved on; the Pearson family were all dead. The same plan would now do for the Goodways.

He was well satisfied with what he had learned on his short call at the Grange. It seemed to offer him a way into the house, and he believed he would be able to conceal himself in there for several hours. Although he had been inside the Grange once many years ago and remembered something of the ground floor, he had never been upstairs. Windows seemed to indicate there were eight bedrooms on the first floor. Almost certainly the Goodway family with two such small children would only use one or at most two. A lot of space for a former clerk, he reflected. There were most likely two staircases; one towards the front for the family and one near the back for service. Also there had to be some sort of stairs inside leading down from the servants' quarters to the first floor so that, in normal times, maids could attend a summons from their employers during the night.

He could almost guess the layout with fair accuracy. They could be trapped. Much depended however on the certainty that the workmen followed the same pattern with their mid-day meal every day. Not least of all, what they did if it rained. The maids and the family would probably all be attending to the preparation, serving or eating of food at that time. But Jeremy Goodway had not done so on this particular day. It would be necessary to watch the back of the house from noon until about 2 o'clock on three days, at least one of them wet.

There was also the question of the ingredients for a lethal Greek fire; quicklime, sulphur, saltpetre, naphtha, and pitch. It might arouse the suspicion of some knowledgeable person if purchased all in the same place. Naphtha and pitch might only be available where there were ships. He would visit both Colchester and Ipswich for those and split his other purchases along his route. Three days to watch the house and a two or three day round trip to buy supplies. He had plenty of time. Gunpowder for a fuse was also needed, but he already had that.

The weather was dry but not unduly hot. It seemed unlikely there would be rain in the next day or two, so Dowdy decided to do his purchasing round first. It was still no later than one fifteen. He could be well on the way to Colchester before he needed to find somewhere to stay the night.

First of all though, he decided to visit the arbour area of the Grange garden. He had given some thought as to where he was to watch the house from and where he was to secret his inflammables. He would have preferred to store them close to the house, perhaps in the stables, and watch from the side lane, but the risk of discovery was too great. The arbour was a good deal further away but safer. He doubted very much whether the blacksmith's daughter or the new Squire–the former clerk–had much use for such idle indulgence.

Some difficulty was presented by the enclosure hedge next the road, for it was now full grown and thick. He made a wide detour, but intended to cut his way through when the actual materials were being carried. Arriving at the rear of the domestic property, the wicket gate in broad daylight seemed an undue risk, being as it was on the house side of the screen of trees. So Dowdy wriggled his way through the yew-tree hedge, still not very thick, where ten years before he used to spy on Eve. The area had an unused look. Walking to the screen of trees he worked himself into the foliage. He could see the wall where the workmen had sat to eat, the stable doors, the outside staircase and the scullery door, though not a frontal view. It would suffice. He went over to look at the summer-house. Obviously it had not been used for a long time, for it had a neglected look. Here he would be able to mix his lethal concoction in peace and store it until ready. The only problem about this approach was the distance he would have to walk on the night, twice, and in full view of four bedroom windows. And he would need moonlight if he was not to trip over. Some thought would have to be given to that problem.

On his way back with the supplies he had purchased, Obadiah Dowdy pulled off the track where it was crossed by a stream. He was well away from any place of habitation and there were no workers in nearby fields. About two hundred yards away there was a small wood. Following the stream into the wood, he searched until he found a fairly clear area. Sometime in the past he had been told the secret of Greek fire, but had no practical experience. A little experiment was necessary.

After tethering his horse well away, he extracted a small amount of each of his ingredients, mixed them and wrapped the mixture in a rag. He then laid a long trail of gunpowder and cut a hole in the package so that some of the mixture dribbled on to the gunpowder. Using his tinder box, he lit a taper with which he started the powder trail.

The little package burst into flames with a WHOOF that startled him. The rag disintegrated and the mixture spread into a fiercely burning pool of flame. He walked over to the stream and filled an old wooden beaker; then from as near he dare go to the blaze, he threw the beaker into it. As soon as the water touched the fire, it burned even more fiercely. He was satisfied. Long ago he had been told that Greek fire could not be doused with water, but would burn even more fiercely.

Now followed four nights of discomfort for Dowdy, for he decided to live alone in woodland near Brentham while he watched the house. He had brought food enough for himself and there was grass and water for his horse. On Friday and Saturday the workmen did exactly as previously with their meal break. Dowdy prayed for rain. He needed to discover what they did when it was wet. Sunday could not be put to any purpose, but it started to rain during that night.

But he gave thanks for the discomfort because Monday was a rainy day. Prompt on half past noon, the three workmen came down the outside staircase again, but this time they went into one of the stables to eat. They returned to their labours as usual at one o'clock. No other person came into view between that time and half past one.

Tuesday morning Dowdy devoted to transporting and mixing his materials. Here lay some risk because the materials could not all be carried in one trip without his horse. If mixed in his hiding place there could be danger of spontaneous combustion during the journey. The choice lay between carrying them, still separated, himself in two journeys from his hiding place in the wood to the summer-house, or leaving them beside the hedge in the pasture while he returned his horse to hiding. He decided that the former, though more arduous, carried less risk of discovery.

On his first trip he was fortunate. No one came along the road as, with a small saw, he cut a neat clump out of the enclosure hedge, passed through with his materials and replaced it behind him. He did likewise with a branch of the yew-tree hedge. The second journey he was met by two travellers on foot, so had to continue a little way further, then stop until they had passed out of sight before returning.

By noon, secreted in the summer-house, he had made up twelve packets of the lethal mixture and put three of each in four bags. He walked to the screen of trees to watch the house. All was as on previous days. The workmen came down on time and went into the stable. There was no sunshine and although yesterday's rain had gone, there was a stiff breeze and a threat of more.

Having decided not to risk the main garden even as far as the wicket gate, he left the arbour through the yew-tree hedge and entered the lane at the bottom. In his hand was a can, just in case someone was around when he reached the side entrance near the house and he had to ask for milk again. But no one was there. Unobserved he crossed the yard and mounted the rickety outside staircase and gained entry through the door the workmen had come out of.

It was as he expected, and he quickly and quietly descended the servants' inside stairway to the passage which lead to the door on to the first floor corridor. He crept along silently, his heart beating fast for he was now approaching one of the moments of greatest risk. He listened intently before opening the door. Voices could be heard but they were muffled and obviously coming from the ground floor. Silently he entered the corridor, noticing at once that he was opposite the main staircase going down. He guessed that the family would use one or two rooms at that end, so tip-toed in the other direction. As he came to the head of the back stairs that led down to the kitchen, he could hear the servants chattering. He entered the guest room opposite and settled down to wait over twelve hours.

The single hand on his egg-shaped pocket-watch was three-quarters of its way between twelve noon and one o'clock. It was a fine instrument known as a Nuremberg Egg taken as part of a bribe during the time he worked for Matthew Hopkins. Made some fifty years before, it had no minute hand. It would not be until that hand had passed one o'clock in the morning that he could act, for it was said that then began the time of deepest sleep.

Now that the danger of gaining entry had passed he was seized with a desire to urinate and defecate. Tension and a wet night in the woods had done their work on him. He was obliged to relieve himself there and then like an animal, for there was no chance to get to a privy. The time passed slowly. He knew if he was disturbed by a maid he would have to kill her silently, for he could not afford to discharge either of the loaded pistols he had ready should he need to shoot his way out. But he did not expect to be disturbed, and was not. There were tense moments when he heard Bessie come to put the little ones to afternoon rest; again when she fetched them down; again when Bessie and Jeremy retired for the night. But this activity was by the main staircase. No one came near his end of the landing.

At last it was one o'clock. Dowdy listened at the door before leaving the room. All was silent as he crept down the back stairs, save for occasional sounds caused by the breeze outside, which helped him. In spite of some cloud, there was sufficient moonlight filtering through the window to enable him to see what he was about as he gained first the kitchen, then the scullery. As he had anticipated, it was secured by bolts top and bottom. First leaving his bag of gunpowder in a corner, he gently eased these back and raised the latch. Now he had a way in to do his work.

The two return trips via the lane to the summer-house caused him some anxiety about the possibility of spontaneous combustion although he had taken great care to keep the mixture dry. But the distance to carry each time was less than two-hundred yards and soon all materials were inside the scullery. Nothing had disturbed his passage to and fro the lane, although he had heard horses' feet shuffling as he passed the stables which backed on to it. Removing his shoes for the sake of stealth, Dowdy distributed ten of his packages of death in the house with three at the foot or under both main and rear staircases. A pitcher of water found in the kitchen he stood on the fourth step of the back stairs so that it just balanced. Then he laid his powder trails to the back door. The remaining two packages he placed under the foot of the rickety outside staircase. The powder trail from those he ran to the other at the back door. He cast a furtive glance all round. All was silent except for wind and the sound of horses shuffling in the stables. He took out his tinder-box and taper.

CHAPTER 27

Alone in his room over the stables, Daniel Peters, a cousin of Amos Peters, could not sleep. Employed a long time at the Grange, he had charge of all the horses, and the living quarters over the stables went with the job. Originally intended for a family, because it was a responsible position, there was more than one room. Daniel however was single, although aged thirty-five, not being very forward with the opposite sex.

For some time he had developed a passion for Maude, the elder of the maids. Although he had been too shy and slow to press his suit, she had often smiled on him. The young lady claimed the skill of a cook. It was said that the Squire's Lady would soon be engaging a new cook. No doubt they would prefer a mature settled person. Daniel dreamed of proposing marriage to Maude, and living happily over the stables as a husband and wife team in the service of the Goodways. All he seemed to need was the courage to pay court to Maude.

Through the fog of his dreams of the future, he was conscious of the wind. He had not realised it was strong enough to make a buffeting sound. Then his dreams faded as he realised that the sounds were not all due to wind, but the horses shuffling about below. That was what had woken him in the first place! It could be a prowler trying to steal one!

He got out of bed and quickly donned his breeches and boots. Then, arming himself with a large piece of wood that he kept by his bed, he crept down his staircase that led to the gloom of the area in front of the stalls. Fearing that he must have carelessly left a door unbolted, he believed he was too late and that one of his charges would already be gone, along with his job and dreams of life with Maude. Fearfully he peered into the gloom of each stall. None of the restless beasts were missing, thank God. Then there must be a prowler trying to get in! He knew his duty.

Daniel drew back the bolts on one of the outside doors and stepped outside with club raised. At that moment fire erupted at the foot of the outside staircase of the Grange. He saw the arsonist stare for a moment at his work before turning to attempt his escape through the opening to the lane. But the wind was blowing in that direction and the spreading pool of flame pushed out a fiery finger to bar his path. He turned to make his escape past the front of the stables in the direction of the private gardens, seemingly oblivious of the man with the wooden club moving towards him.

With a shout Daniel brought his club down hard on Dowdy, who collapsed like a stone. Then he ran towards the house shouting 'fire!'. Flames barred his path to the scullery door or round the left of the house, so he ran the other way round to the front door which he banged with his fists shouting, 'fire, fire!.' He could see flames inside so he smashed a window where there was no fire and climbed in. But when he opened a door into the main hallway he was met by a pool of flames which pursued his retreating footsteps. He climbed back out the window and ran round the back of the house again.

✳✳✳

Jeremy and Bessie awoke at the same time, startled by what seemed like a series of muffled explosions. As he went into the corridor he seemed to hear someone shouting out the back. Was it 'fire' the person was shouting? He could smell fumes.

'Bess, the children!' he cried, rushing into the children's room with Bessie on his heels. 'I think the house is on fire!'

Each carrying a child, they made their way to the small landing at the head of the main stairway, only to find the bottom steps already alight with flames creeping up. They heard hammering on the front door and cries of, 'fire, fire!'

Jeremy pushed Bessie back. 'Quick. The back stairs to the kitchen.'

They ran along the corridor and heard the crash of a falling bucket as they ran. The children were screaming. Flames were already three-quarters the way up here and the fire much more fierce. 'We're trapped!' cried Bessie.

'Stairway up to the servants' quarters,' shouted Jeremy, turning her round.

They made their way along the corridor into the dark rear passageway. As they entered it Jeremy saw the first tongues of flame from the back stairs reach that floor. He knew that the fire on the front stairs would not be long behind. Soon the first floor would be an inferno like downstairs as the ancient timber structure fed the flames.

Along the passage and up the narrow stairs to the servants' quarters where all was wood shavings and loose pieces of timber left by the workmen in the middle of their task. A faint flickering light told him that the flames had already reached the door they had come through on the floor below. He set Jemima down and unbolted the door to the outside staircase.

As he opened the door he saw Daniel waving his arms frantically and pointing to a body on the ground. 'It was him sir,' he called. 'I hit him.'

Jeremy stepped out on to the platform. As he did so, the rickety staircase, now with the support of its bottom steps burnt away, wrenched its rotten fixings from the wall and swung free. The platform started to give way and as Jeremy reached back to the doorway, collapsed under his feet. He almost fell to the ground but caught a door post just in time. He pulled himself back in with Bessie and the children. The fire had now reached the bottom of the indoor staircase they had come up and the situation was critical. Daniel seemed to have disappeared. Now it looked as if they were really trapped.

Daniel came out of the stables carrying a ladder. It was too short, but he climbed up as soon as he had it placed. His head and shoulders were only just above the threshold. 'A little one Mr Goodway. One of the little ones.'

Jeremy handed little Benjamin to Daniel who took the screaming child in one strong arm. Bessie was anxious lest he should fall, but he did not.

'On daddy's back Jemima,' Jeremy bent down and Bessie put the child on his back with her arms round his neck. 'Try to follow me down Bess.' He gained the ground and left Jemima in the care of Daniel. Looking up he saw Bessie hanging from the threshold by her hands, unable to reach the ladder. 'Hang on Bess.' He went up the ladder until she straddled his neck. 'Let go one hand at a time and hold the sides of my head to steady yourself.' Slowly Jeremy carried his wife down.

Bessie clutched the little ones to herself. They looked up at the doorway. Already flames could be seen there.

'Now for the arsonist,' said Jeremy; but when he and Daniel turned round Dowdy had gone.

'Must hev gone through the garden,' said Daniel. 'Couldn't hev gone out the side. Thought I'd hit him too hard to ever get up.'

They both ran down the garden but could see no one. 'I think it's more important to stop the fire getting to the stables,' said Jeremy. They went back and found that Bessie had sensibly moved back away from the house to the dairy. The pool of fire that had been started outside was now barely twelve feet from the stables. Daniel picked up a pitcher of water and threw on it. Suddenly it flared higher.

'Scrape dirt to contain the fire, Daniel. I've heard about this. There's a special mixture from ancient times that can't be put out with water.'

They worked hard to scrape a little earth barrier to stop the pool of fire reaching the stables. But now it started to die of its own accord as all the lethal mixture was consumed, leaving only the blackened earth. The house itself continued to burn, fuelled by the ancient timbers, flames now through the roof and reaching for the sky.

The frightened horses were making a noise. 'Best get them out and on to the enclosed pasture, Daniel,' said Jeremy. 'You can take them through the garden.'

Just then one of the constable's men came from the garden dragging a half-conscious and bleeding Dowdy. 'Beg your pardon Mr Goodway for comin' through your garden. Couldn't seem to get down the lane. Caught this cove stumblin' across your pasture land, tryin' to find a gap in the hedge. Thought you'd like to know we got him.' He looped Dowdy's manacles over a hook high on the stable wall so his feet barely touched the ground. 'Best hang about here for a bit to keep folks at a safe distance.'

Indeed a trickle of people from the village had started to arrive, having left their beds to see the fire. It was just after three o'clock. Constable Scott arrived on his horse. 'Is this the one?' he asked his man. The deputy assented. He pulled Dowdy's sagging head up by his hair. 'Your name is Jonathan Bentley, I believe?'

'How did you know that?' gasped Dowdy.

'I know a lot of things,' replied Scott. 'But somebody with a grudge reckons that's not you're real name. Says you're Obadiah Dowdy. Now that's before my time, but perhaps there are some here will recognise you if put to it.' He turned to the deputy. 'Fetch me water and a rag.'

Daniel handed a pitcher of water from out the stable. Constable Scott washed blood and other substances from Dowdy's face. 'Mr Goodway. Is this him?'

Jeremy came close. 'As far as I can see in this light, it might be. But what a change!'

'Never mind. It'll keep until daylight. I'll just take and lock him up. Back shortly.'

'I best take Bess and the children to our cottage and come back,' said Jeremy. 'We've nothing but night clothes. I shall have to break in. The key's in there.' He pointed to the blazing Grange.

Having got his family into the cottage, Jeremy wrapped a spare blanket round himself and went back to the fire. Mrs Bloom met him on the way back. 'Mercy me,' she cried. 'Are they all right?'

'Yes in the cottage, but we've no clothes.'

Back at the Grange, the flames had started to subside but it would be many hours before the fire went out. There would be nothing left. He waited until daybreak, by which time the crowd had drifted away.

'Just come back with me,' said Constable Scott. 'I'll lend you a suit of clothes. You're about my size. We can stop by the bridewell and you can take a better look at the prisoner.'

Back at the lock-up, the constable dragged the prisoner from his cell to the door and the gathering light. 'Yes. That's Obadiah Dowdy,' said Jeremy. 'Aged somewhat.'

Scott put Dowdy back in his cell and locked the door. 'Come over to my house for the clothes I promised.'

Jeremy changed in the constable's house. The clothes fitted. 'This is very kind of you, Constable Scott,' he said after he came down stairs. 'How did you guess about Dowdy and his false name?'

'A few days ago, that Merton woman came and volunteered information that there was a man called Jonathan Bentley messing about round the area, but his real name was Obadiah Dowdy and I should know because he might mean mischief in Brentham.

'Coming from her, I found it difficult to believe. Thought she was trying to curry favour because of her immoral activities. Nothing to do with me because she's just outside Brentham anyway.

'However, today–or perhaps I must say yesterday now–I was at the constable's office in Sudbury and they told me there was a man called Jonathan Bentley staying in the town a few days ago asking a lot of questions about Brentham.

'Now separately those two pieces don't mean much, but together quite a lot. So I called out extra deputies and had them take in turns patrolling the village day and night. I'm surprised he managed to set fire to the Grange.

'According to my records he's supposed to have three-hundred lashes just for breaking his bond to stay away from Brentham. Do you think it's worth having his skin off now? The chief constable is bound to want him sent to the assizes for arson and attempted murder. For certain he'll hang.'

'It's up to you Mr Scott,' said Jeremy. 'But it doesn't seem worth while in the circumstances. Now I must thank you again and make my way home.'

The first day after the fire was hectic for Jeremy and Bessie, both now in borrowed clothes until others could be made. Their two maids came along early asking what they were to do now that the Grange was burnt down. 'Tell them they can work here until we have the Grange rebuilt,' said Jeremy. 'But as there won't be enough work for both, get one, the eldest, to take on the cooking. Daniel Peters sought an opportunity after all the confusion during the night to tell me she could cook.'

It was business affairs which presented the greatest problem, because although the amount of cash lost in the blaze was luckily fairly small, all the books had been destroyed. Jeremy had to write up new records as best he could from memory insofar as they affected current business. It was a task that took many days of hard work and thought to accomplish. All the past records of transactions by the Pearson family, virtually the history of Brentham itself, was lost forever.

Jeremy was so preoccupied that the news that the constable and his men had found Dowdy's residual materials in the summer-house and his horse tethered in woods less than a mile away, almost passed over his head. He almost forgot to tell Bessie that Dowdy was to be tried at the next Bury St Edmunds assizes. There would be several weeks to wait.

It was during the intervening period that Bessie brought up with Jeremy a matter that she had been turning over in her mind. 'Scripture says we should love our enemies and forgive those that do bad things to us.'

'Indeed it does Bess. Were you thinking of Obadiah Dowdy after what he tried to do to you and the children? If so, it would stretch my faith to the limit.'

'It is a lot to forgive I know. Yet I am still troubled that I prayed for Eve's death and it happened. A wicked thing I did and must answer for. It would help make amends if I forgave this enemy.'

'I've many more sins than you to atone for Bess, and if I should forgive him it might help with those. But where would that leave him? We can't halt the charges now standing against him. It's not up to us. The law demands that he stands trial. Neither can we refuse to give evidence against him at the assizes. Whether we forgive him or not, he's still bound to hang.'

'Could we not plead for mercy from the judge?'

'I don't know if there's a procedure for that Bess. I'll ask our own lawyer to advise me, though he's not involved in the case. But what sort of mercy would he be likely to get? A prison cell for the rest of his life? Transportation to the New World? He's already sixty-nine. Whatever we do, his hold on life will be tenuous.'

'Yet we must try, Jeremy dear. If we are to forgive, we must try.'

The trial was very short and the guilty verdict predictable. Through the efforts of his own lawyer, the agreement of the judge and the lawyers involved had been secured for Jeremy to make a plea for mercy on the grounds of the Christian doctrine of forgiveness.

The judge listened to what he had to say, then seemed to hesitate for several moments while he wrote on papers in front of him. At length he addressed the prisoner. 'Obadiah Dowdy. You have been found guilty of arson and attempted murder for which the law prescribes death. However, I am allowed to exercise mercy in exceptional circumstances. I have listened to what Mr Goodway said on behalf of himself and his family, and have decided to exercise my prerogative and pass a lesser sentence.

'All your worldly goods except the clothes you wear today are to be confiscated, just as they would be if you were going to the gallows. You will be taken back to Brentham, where you committed these heinous crimes. There you will be tied to a cart tail and beaten with the cat o' nine tails once every tenth step for a distance of two miles. If after a period of seven days from that punishment you are ever again found within the western half of Suffolk, formerly known as the Liberty of St Edmund, you will be transported to the plantations of the New World for the term of your natural life.'

There were some gasps in court at the severity of this sentence. Several were heard to say as the crowd dispersed that it was a death sentence anyway.

'Is that supposed to be mercy?' Bessie asked Jeremy as soon as they were alone on the way home. 'How many lashes is that he'll get; every ten paces for two miles?'

'Don't know, Bess. Bound to be over four-hundred. At sixty-nine he's unlikely to survive. Even if he did, he'd be unfit for any work and would starve.'

'Oh Jeremy. We did more harm than good, interfering.'

'Looks that way, Bess.'

'Is there nothing we can do?'

'About all I can do for him now is to ask the constable and Reverend Jones to let me give him a Christian burial.'

'What if he didn't die? Could we have him home and tend his wounds?'

'You surprise me at the lengths you will go with forgiveness. Yes, I'd be willing to have him home and get Doctor Mills attend his wounds. But none of this is going to happen, Bess. The judge intended him to die one way or the other.'

On the day of Dowdy's punishment, Jeremy waited with a small covered cart at the two-mile marker that had been set up by Constable Scott. Many from Brentham lined the route to watch the grisly spectacle. The yelling of the crowd and the cracking of the whips could be heard long before they reached him. When they came in sight, Jeremy could tell that Dowdy was no longer on his feet, but being dragged along unconscious or dead as the punishment continued.

At the marker, Dowdy was cut loose and dragged from where he fell to the verge, there to die if not already dead. His torso was a mass of blood; his back a pulp through which bones could be seen. Several spectators came to spit on him until restrained by Jeremy and Constable Scott.

The constable pulled up Dowdy's head by his hair. 'It seems amazing, but I believe he still lives–just.'

'Then since I have permission to give him a Christian burial, I presume it's in order for me to take him to my home to die?'

'I can't stop you doing that,' said Constable Scott, 'but remember; if he still clings to life, he must be away and out of the county within the week. Otherwise I shall be forced to arrest him for transportation whatever his condition.'

With the aid of the man he had brought to help pick up a dead body, Jeremy lifted Dowdy into his cart and laid him face down. On his way back to the cottage, he called on the physician, Doctor Mills, and asked him to come along.

'The best I can do is ease his way to death,' said Doctor Mills after they had cleaned Dowdy up. 'He'll not live. Give him some of this. It'll ease the pain when he comes round and send him back to sleep. It's a mild poison; too much at a time will kill him.'

When Dowdy started to regain consciousness, he cried out at the soreness of his mutilated flesh. Bessie spooned broth into his mouth to which Jeremy had added some of the liquid made up by Doctor Mills. They did that for three days and as the soreness lessened, Dowdy started to ask 'Why do you . . .?' but would drift back to unconsciousness before he could finish his question or get an answer.

On the fourth day Doctor Mills called again. 'Stop giving the potion now. More would be dangerous,' he said. 'What will you do? In little more than two days he must be gone, and he'll still not be fit enough to walk away and face the world on his own. He needs at least another week from then to recuperate sufficiently for that. In fact he may yet die.'

'I'll try and find him a room in a tavern across the nearest point of the county boundary,' said Jeremy.

Dowdy was allowed to recover consciousness fully on the fifth day. At first he alternated between anger at the punishment he had suffered and curiosity as to why they, of all people, should be helping him.

'We sought to save your life because scripture tells us we are to forgive our enemies if we are ourselves to obtain pardon,' said Jeremy. 'By the same doctrine we must help you fully recover.'

'Yet I would be better dead, for I have ever served the Lord,' said Dowdy. 'At this age with these grievous wounds and all my possessions confiscated, nothing faces me but starvation, when you turn me out, as you must.'

'You say you have ever served the Lord, yet you sought revenge for imagined wrongs and to kill the innocent, both of which are against His word. As for your confiscated goods, we will see what can be done about those. You'll not be allowed to starve.'

Over the next two days when time permitted, Jeremy discoursed with Obadiah Dowdy. At last it seemed that the kindness was having effect. Yet when he had to go out he would not leave Bessie and the children in the cottage alone with him, but insisted they visited her mother. 'I don't rightly understand wot you two are doin',' Mrs Bloom said. 'He never had no pity on nobody else. Still thass your business.'

Bessie told her mother that the idea of forgiveness was hers because she had sinned by praying for Eve's death.

'You was sorely provoked into that gal, an' I'm sure the Lord understood. No need to help that there ole sinner what richly deserved wot the law did to him.'

After the sixth day Jeremy took Obadiah Dowdy to a room he had found in a tavern no more than a mile across the county boundary at its nearest point. In all it was no more than six miles from Brentham. He was still not fit to ride a horse so had to travel in the cart.

'Doctor Mills has promised to come with me in three days' time to check on your progress,' said Jeremy as he installed him in the room. 'He estimates that you need another week of rest before you make your way. I have spoken to Constable Scott about your confiscated goods. There was about twenty-five pounds in money. That I'll make good to you. Your goods and horse I am being allowed to purchase and will give you on the day you leave.'

'You make me miserable with shame, after what I did to you and your family,' said Dowdy. There was unusual emotion in his voice as he spoke.

'I'm well able to afford it, thanks to the kindness and generosity of Mr Nathaniel Pearson, who you once tried to destroy. A man who offered nothing but good to all he came in contact with. Do you realise he even helped Tobias Winscombe get back on his feet?

'If my actions make you miserable with shame, then use this week to reflect on how you have spoiled your own life and the lives of several others, first with greed and envy, then with an excessive belief in your own rectitude. But for all this you might still have been a prosperous merchant of Brentham. A respected member of the community.

'Reflect on poor Rebecca Brown who suffered a cruel death because you provoked a riot. I know she would have died anyway because she confessed. But it would have been an easier death. Reflect on Constable Stark who was murdered in the riot you provoked. Reflect on all those you denounced as witches.'

'But in that last I was doing the Lord's work,' protested Dowdy.

'Have you not yet learned, after losing your second ill-gotten fortune over the same nonsense!' exclaimed Jeremy. 'Witches do not exist except in the spiteful imagination of the ignorant against their neighbours. Nonsense from pre-Christian times. Learned men, some of them judges, now protest that such folly can still be part of our law.

'When you leave here, take my advice. Move far from the East Anglia where many will not forgive you, and live in peace with your neighbours.'

Jeremy left Obadiah Dowdy deep in thought.

Three days later, Jeremy came back to the tavern with Doctor Mills to check on Dowdy's progress. They were met by the landlord at the door.

'Look like your man must hev died in the night,' he said. 'Looked right still an' di'n't answer at all when wife took him his breakfast.'

They went to the room. 'He's dead alright,' said the physician. 'The wonder is that he survived the punishment so long at his age. No doubt his internal organs were damaged.'

'I'll get him back and see to his funeral then,' said Jeremy.

'He left this here letter for yer by his bed,' said the landlord, handing a piece of paper to Jeremy. 'Reckon he knew he was gooner die.'

Reverend Jones performed the funeral rites the next day. Only Constable Scott and Jeremy attended. Afterwards Bessie asked, 'Do you still think we did right interfering, Jeremy? I mean, he died anyway.'

'I think we did, Bess. We bought him time to repent.' He showed her the letter Dowdy had left.

'Will you really have that put on his grave-marker, Jeremy?'

'Yes. It's what he asked for, and I think It'll be good for some in Brentham who are still bigots in spite of all.'

✷✷✷

The next Sunday, Reverend Jones preached a strong sermon about forgiveness and understanding each others' failings. He even ridiculed those who would denounce their neighbours as witches, though he said there were no doubt some who might seek to have him displaced as a "scandalous priest" for such sentiments. He counselled those who doubted, to read the marker on Obadiah Dowdy's grave when it was placed.

'I never thought I'd live to see the day when ole Jones had the nerve to speak out come what may,' declared Samuel Bloom.

✷✷✷

252

The people did come to read Dowdy's grave-marker and think upon it.

OBADIAH DOWDY

FORMER MASTER TAILOR & MASTER SINNER OF BRENTHAM

Died 21st DECEMBER 1654

Aged 69

I WAS WRONG

LORD HAVE MERCY